The Adventures Of Harry Marline

Or, Notes From An American Midshipman'S Lucky Bag

David D. Porter

Alpha Editions

This Edition Published in 2020

ISBN: 9789354360398

Design and Setting By
Alpha Editions
www.alphaedis.com
Email – info@alphaedis.com

As per information held with us this book is in Public Domain.
This book is a reproduction of an important historical work. Alpha Editions uses the best technology to reproduce historical work in the same manner it was first published to preserve its original nature. Any marks or number seen are left intentionally to preserve its true form.

PREFACE.

THE following "adventures" were written thirty years ago for the amusement of my boys.

They were loaned about in the navy, in manuscript, with accompanying illustrations, which latter were very well executed, and I am sorry they are lost.

The manuscript disappeared for some twenty years, and, about ten years ago, was returned to me in a bundle, minus the illustrations. I don't know how many cruises they have made in the mean time.

One day Mr. D. R. Hamersly, editor of the "United Service Magazine," asked me to write something for his monthly, and I told him he might have the bundle of manuscript, hardly recollecting what it was all about.

Mr. Hamersly published it, people were amused over Harry Marline's adventures, and, as I think it better for people to laugh than to cry, I thought I would have the adventures published in book-form. They will amuse the middies of the present day, as showing the life of midshipmen in the olden times.

As the book was written for young people, I shall not be disappointed if elderly ones fail to be amused.

THE AUTHOR.

CONTENTS.

CHAPTER	PAGE
I.—IN WHICH THE HERO IS INTRODUCED TO THE READER AS A VERY BAD BOY	7
II.—IN WHICH MARLINE IS INTRODUCED TO NAVAL LIFE, AND PROVES TO BE A HARD BARGAIN	16
III.—MARLINE REPORTS FOR DUTY, AND IS MUCH ASTONISHED AT THE PROCEEDINGS OF A MAN WITH A WART ON HIS NOSE	25
IV.—AN IRISH SCHOOL-MASTER, AND HIS DIFFICULTIES ON FIRST ENTERING SERVICE—A MIDSHIPMEN'S SUPPER AND A GOOSE WITHOUT LEGS OR WINGS—A CATERER'S APPEAL TO THE MESS, AND THE DISCOMFITURE OF A SCHOOL-MASTER	41
V.—VERY SNAKY	51
VI.—SCENES IN A BREAD-LOCKER; AND HOW TAILORS SOMETIMES GET PAID OFF	58
VII.—AWAY, AWAY, WE BOUND O'ER THE SEA	70
VIII.—A MERMAN HUNTSMAN	73
IX.—THE CAPTAIN MAKES AN ADDRESS, AND ALL HANDS ARE CALLED TO WITNESS PUNISHMENT. WITNESSES GET INTO TROUBLE	79
X.—ARRIVAL IN PORT. A NEW METHOD OF BENDING A BUOY-ROPE. PRACTICAL HINTS TO SAILING-MASTERS	94
XI.—VERY STRANGE AND WONDERFUL, IF TRUE	102
XII.—MARLINE VISITS THE SHORE, MAKES A NEW ACQUAINTANCE, FINDS ALL IS NOT GOLD THAT GLITTERS—A DUEL—AN EXQUISITE—BROTHER JONATHAN AND JOHN BULL TOWING A DISABLED FRENCHMAN INTO PORT	153
XIII.—ARRIVAL OF THE GINGERBREAD—INTRODUCTION TO THE COMMODORE AND HIS COOK, TO SAY NOTHING OF A LITTLE BLACK PIG—DISMAY AND CONFUSION ON BOARD	172
XIV.—INVITED OUT TO DINNER—SIXTEEN KINDS OF DISHES MADE OUT OF A LITTLE BLACK PIG	179
XV.—A DESCRIPTION OF SOME OF MARLINE'S SHIPMATES, AND A VERY LONG SONG FROM OLD SHACKLEBAGS	185

CONTENTS.

CHAPTER		PAGE
XVI.—Very Snaky indeed, and sharp Practice with Shells—The Devil on the Horse-Block, and Ship going Ten Knots under Bolt-Ropes—Strange if True		197
XVII.—Codfish and Onions bad for Sea-Serpents—Sea-Serpent in Cable-Tier—Patent Anchor and Cable—Death of Old Crab, etc.		211
XVIII.—Much geographical Knowledge displayed, and a long Tail		219
XIX.—Very Fishy and Stupid—The Story of a Whale-Ship		235
XX.—Sail for Naples—First Gale—Nothing in Particular—Familiar Poetry		239
XXI.—A Call on the King of Naples—Mr. Bluff's Adventure with a Countess		252
XXII.—The Commodore visits King Bomba—A Wig Adventure—The Commodore's extraordinary Address to the King—Cat and Dog Salutes—What befell us at the Banquet to the King		271
XXIII.—A Demand for the abducted Cats and Dogs—A Court of Inquiry—A Transformation—A Duel between Teaser and Bluff		290
XXIV.—About Matters and Things in General—An Irruption of Termites—Mr. Shacklebags gets Something in his Eyes and a Blowing Up—Can't go on Shore till the Mainmast goes—The Captain gets Outwitted by twenty-four Midshipmen		306
XXV.—Which contains an Account of a wonderful Miracle, and describes a very imposing Ceremony		317
XXVI.—A tedious Dog-Watch, and a tough Yarn from a Quartermaster		322
XXVII.—And Last		359

THE ADVENTURES OF HARRY MARLINE.

CHAPTER I.

IN WHICH THE HERO IS INTRODUCED TO THE READER AS A VERY BAD BOY.

I WAS a very small boy when I first made acquaintance with the sea in the year 18— as a midshipman, and could easily have been stowed away in the pocket of a pea-jacket without any one's knowing I was there. But I was acknowledged by every one to be knowing far beyond my years, and my friends always guaranteed my growth, as we had never known a runt on either side of the family. There were various surmises about my future end; some old fogies about and in the old town of Babel, Pennsylvania, where I was born, shook their heads sorrowfully as they passed me in the street, and predicted that I would end my days on a gallows, while the more charitable said that I would sow my wild oats, and turn out in the long run a clever fellow.

I remember that I was the terror of all the inhabitants of Babel, each of whom in turn had suffered from the effects of my mischievous pranks. No mischief was committed in or out of the town but I was sure to be named as the author of it, and I often had the credit of doing things of which I was entirely innocent. Be that as it may, the elders of the town came to the conclusion that I was a perfect nuisance, and must be got rid of by some means or other. The worst offense I committed was tying the queues of Deacon

Kirk and Farmer Brown together while they were asleep in the church, and sticking a pin in the calf of the deacon's leg, for which I was banished from the church. I had a kind old grandfather who took care of me in childhood, and spoilt me with his indulgence as I grew up. Now all the old fellows determined to wait upon him in turn with a list of their grievances and demand my immediate banishment. They insisted that I should be sent away to some strict school, or else placed before the mast under the charge of a tyrannical captain, who would never permit me to say my soul was my own. My old guardian looked sad when he heard in detail the accounts of my follies, and though he knew I was full of mischief, and sometimes indeed played off my practical jokes on him, his kind heart would not permit him to believe that I was guilty of half the pranks laid to my charge. He was a good and amiable old man, and remembered that he was once a boy himself, though I am sure that the boys of his day were not half so bad as the boys of the present time, for now Young America takes the wind out of Old America's sails altogether.

He was urged very hard, particularly by old Ephraim Shaker, to send me to sea. "For," said he, "Friend Job, if thee does not get the urchin out of these parts, he will verily go to the Evil One, and thy conscience will smite thee if he does not turn out well." A tear stood in the good man's eye as he promised to think over the matter, and he arranged to meet them all that night at the Quaker's house and give his final answer over an oyster supper.

My grandfather could never resist an oyster supper, and I felt that in accepting the invitation he had sealed my fate, for I knew that the enemy would carry the day. Consequently I determined in my own mind to have my revenge that night out of those who were plotting my downfall. I had overheard all that was said through a window looking out on to the back porch, where I was busily engaged shaving our Thomas cat's tail with one of grandfather's best razors. I formed my plans even while the conversation was going on, and I looked forward impatiently for the night to come that I might serve up the trimmings for that oyster supper.

It was a cold November evening with a light drizzly rain; just such a night as a thief would select to rob a hen-roost, or a mischievous fellow prefer to play his pranks in. I looked into the back parlor window of old Shaker's house, and there sat the solemn conclave assembled around a warm fire, and urging my grandfather with all their eloquence to get rid of me. Said I to myself, "My old fellows, I will make that room too hot to hold you before I have done with you." And I went to work to make my preparations for attack.

I heard my grandfather say in a quavering tone of voice, "Only convince me, friends, that he is guilty of any one act laid to his charge, and I shall hesitate no longer to send him to sea."

The idea of going to sea was not distasteful to me, and, although I knew the pain I was going to inflict on my grandfather, I determined to put an end at once to all his doubts, and at the same time have a fine lark before I was banished from the delights of Babel.

But I will not relate this adventure, not wishing to revive reminiscences that might call forth the criticisms of the Babel newspapers, which are still run by the descendants of the ancient proprietors, with ideas as limited as those of their illustrious predecessors.

Suffice it to say I committed a very reprehensible action toward my presumed enemies, serving them out to my satisfaction, if not to their own, and I am willing to say that I would not do it again under like circumstances.

My mischief led to a *dénouement* of which I little dreamed, and never intended. I went in for a lark, and was the cause of a great fire, which created immense confusion in that quiet town.

I little anticipated such an adventure when I set out so gleefully from home. The town was badly supplied with water, and the fire department not having been called out for some years, everything went wrong. The hose got a dozen "cable-tier pinches" in it, and, in the anxiety of the firemen to put on the water, it burst in several places. There were no fire-buckets to be had at the moment, and the result was the entire destruction of a carpenter-shop with all its contents.

I was on the point of making my escape, to go I cared not whither, for the matter was looking much more serious than I had intended it should, and I had already turned up the main street leading out to the country, determined to rid the town of my presence, and escape the punishment I felt I most justly deserved, when I was suddenly seized from behind by a nervous grasp, while the tremulous tones of my grandfather addressed me for the first time in his life with ill-concealed anger.

"You young villain!" he exclaimed, "see what mischief you have done with your foolish mad prank! Home, home with you, sir, at once, before you are detected by others; and I promise you

you will never see the town of Babel again while I live. Go get your clothes ready to start for Washington in half an hour!" And grasping me roughly by the collar, he strode along at a rate I could with difficulty follow, and which I had not the least idea his age was capable of. He never spoke a word until we reached the house, and, flinging me inside the door as if I was an old meal-bag, said, "Get up-stairs at once, sir, and pack your trunk; and mind, I give you but twenty minutes to do it in."

I ascended the stairs rapidly, and in less than the required time was ready. On going down, I found my grandfather sitting on the sofa, pale as death, with his hands clasped tightly over his eyes, and tears of anguish streaming through his fingers. My heart severely reproached me for the unhappiness I knew he was suffering. I burst into tears myself, and, throwing my arms about his neck, besought his forgiveness, and promised that I would never during my whole life do an act of mischief again.

Taking his hands from his face and looking at me sorrowfully, "Ah, Harry, Harry!" he said, "you will bring my gray hairs in sorrow to the grave by your misconduct; but it is my own fault, my child, for not doing my duty more strictly toward you, and I have no one to blame but myself. Who can tell what the consequences of this night may bring forth? Be your future career ever so bright, you will always feel that you left your native town with your name scorned by all who knew you, and there will always remain this blot on your escutcheon, which you will find it difficult to wipe out."

"At all events, grandpapa, you shall never have cause to blush for me again," I said; "and, believe me, I feel deep, deep sorrow for the pain I have inflicted on you to-night. Do forgive me, dear grandpapa, for dear mother's sake, who is dead and gone, for I shall never be happy until you call me your own Harry once more."

It was not in the old man's nature to remain angry for any length of time with me, no matter what I might do, and his heart, I truly believe, was more pained at parting with me, perhaps forever, than by the cruel trick I had practiced on his friends. He took me by the hand, kindly saying, "I shall forget to-night, my boy; only promise me that the predictions made by your enemies shall not be fulfilled. Disappoint them all, and I shall be satisfied."

The clock was just striking nine when the sound of the stage-horn was faintly heard in the distance, and, bidding me to hurry

I AM SENT AWAY.

down with my trunk, he called to old Abram to come and take it to the stage-office.

"Why, whar you gwoin, Massa Harry, wid you eyes a-lookin' as if you jus' done a-crying? I trus' de Lord you ain't been a-wexin' old massa; 'cause if you have, honey, you won't come to no good nohow. I hope, child, you ain't been a-spilin' massa's bes' raser, 'cause I seed you wid it mysef shaving dat foolish tomcat's tail."

"No, Abram," I replied, "I have not spoilt grandpa's razor, but I have done worse than that. I have made him ashamed of me, and he is going to send me away because I tied fire-crackers to the tomcat's tail and shoved him into Mr. Shaker's window. He jumped on to his shoulders, scorched his hair and eyebrows off, and burnt his best shad-belly coat off his back."

"Pshaw!" said Abram, "he ain't gwoin to sen' you 'way for dat, sure. Bress de Lord! I thought you been spilin' old massa's raser, and dat I know wexes him for sartin. Why, old Shaker's nuffin. He ain't nobody, for sure; an' no matter if dat dare cat done eat him up, dare's better men lef' in de town. What's I gwoin to do for backer when you'se gone 'way? I wonder if old massa tink of dat circumstance? Whar you gwoin to, Massa Harry, and what massa done gwoin to do wid you?"

"I am going to sea, Abram," I said, "and may never return; but I shan't forget you, you may be sure. I will send you your tobacco every chance I get."

"Well, dat's some constollation anyhow; but who gwoin to gin my quarter dollar ebery Saturday aternoon? I wonder if old Shaker's gwoin to suply de necesties ob natur in dem ar premises? May de Lord drat him for a good-for-nuffin feller! I never like him much no how, no fashen. He once tell me he done sell me long time ago if I was his nigger, which I tank de Lord I ain't. I only wish him one ting, and dat is I had him on a strait line wid a skunk, and I could shute at de skunk wid massa's duck-gun, dat's enuff for me."

"Don't make yourself unhappy, Abe, about the quarter every Saturday afternoon. I will make grandpa promise to give it to you regular as long as he lives."

"Well, den, dat's what I calls talkin' to de pint, Massa Harry, and I doesn't know but's bes' for you to go to sea, and, bress de Lor'! I shall be proud when you comes back a kurnel. Won't dis here nigger crow den? He will for sarten; 'cause I know you're gwoin to be a great man, prowiden you awoids splittin' on de rocks of temtashun, and don't run de wessel on de quicksan's ob 'niquity."

The stage had arrived, and my trunk was getting lashed on while old Abe was holding forth so learnedly; and bidding the old negro good-by, I followed my grandfather inside and took my seat. No one had seen us get in, or knew that I was going to give the town the benefit of my absence. Crack went the whip, away went the horses at the rate of ten knots an hour, and the town and lights soon disappeared from view.

My heart rejoiced when I felt that I was well clear of the town of Babel, and my grandfather looked more at his ease also. A crowd of people were gathered about the porch of the old inn, and were animadverting in most unmeasured terms on the conduct of the perpetrator of the fire, for as yet no one knew who the culprit was. One said that the old Quaker would surely die, and that his wife had gone crazy; another said whoever did the deed would be tried for murder and arson; while a third recommended lynching as the course most likely to meet the public approbation.

I almost felt that the officers of justice were on my track like a pack of bloodhounds. My fears on that score were soon dissipated, however, when I reflected that the town of Babel could only boast of one police officer, or constable, a decrepit old fellow, seventy years of age, who held his sinecure office owing to his good luck in being wounded at the battle of Brandywine. I knew that the old fellow was confined to his bed with rheumatism, and there was no danger of his being stowed away anywhere in the stage. Besides, there were no witnesses against me except my grandfather, who was hurrying me away from the place as fast as four post-horses could travel. Those were not the days of railroads, and our journey was slow in comparison to what it would be now, and it was not until forty-eight hours after we started from home that we brought up at a good hotel in Washington City.

Next day my grandfather called with me on the Secretary of the Navy, the Honorable Mr. Pinebranch, of North Carolina, a remarkable old gentleman who held the destiny of the service in his hands. I knew very little about the navy then, although I have learned a good deal since, and the number of funny stories that I have heard of this old fellow have hardly indicated the wisdom of taking a gentleman farmer from the old Tar State to put at the head of the Department.

Fortunately, the navy was virtually governed by three old com-

THE NAVY AT THAT TIME.   13

modores, constituting the Board of Navy Commissioners, who had spent many years at sea and understood the wants of the service, and the Secretary was the financial and political head of the Department, paying all the bills, and recommending all appointments to the President.

This seemed on the whole to be a good organization, and at that time the United States navy had no superior in proportion to its size. Our vessels were few in number, but they were looked upon as models by foreign officers, and our guns were the heaviest and best in the world.

The funds then appropriated, about six million dollars annually, were expended with scrupulous care, and nothing was wasted to help elect members to Congress. Indeed, the people of those days were ignorant of our modern improvements in the way of buying votes, and candidates depended for election upon their own individual merits.

Still, there were defects in the system, for the professional heads of the Department frequently had their opinions overruled by the civilian Secretary. For instance, Mr. Pinebranch, at the solicitation of his friends, directed that the naval ships should call at old Topsail Inlet, near Cape Lookout, and lay in their sea-stores. The Honorable Secretary was from Morehead City, and wanted his native town to derive all possible advantage from his appointment. He was quite astonished when told that the ships could not enter old Topsail Inlet for want of water, and accordingly applied to Congress in his next report to have the place dredged out, expatiating on the many advantages to be derived from such an undertaking.

On another occasion Mr. Pinebranch directed the commissioners to send a load of North Carolina lumber, tar, pitch, and turpentine to the Mediterranean, as he noticed in the squadron account some bills for Norway pine which he thought should not be purchased. Most of the midshipmen and all the pursers and doctors were appointed from the "Old North State," and the Honorable Secretary made arrangements for constructing a dry-dock off Cape Hatteras, with a breakwater around it to make a harbor for ships to drop into, when informed that our vessels could not enter Pamlico Sound.

The old navy commissioners were sometimes astonished at the extent of the Honorable Secretary's geographical knowledge. On one occasion he directed a ship to sail for the Bight of Benin, and thence directly along the coast to the Cape of Good Hope, not having any idea of the existence of trade-winds.

Mr. Pinebranch had been two years at the head of the navy before he discovered that a ship was hollow, and once he kicked up "hob" because he found that petty officers were being appointed without their names going to the Senate for confirmation.

But, after all, these were comparatively trifles, for the Secretary was a jolly old gentleman, who let everybody do pretty much as they pleased. If an officer disliked going to sea, he let him stay on shore as long as he wished, unless the commissioners interfered on the ground that the efficiency of the service was being impaired, when the Secretary would reluctantly yield to their opinion.

On one occasion Mr. Pinebranch took passage in a frigate from Norfolk to New York, and when, at sunset on a mild summer's evening, all hands were called to reef topsails, the Honorable Secretary was appalled with the perils to which the men were exposed in going aloft. He said that in future he should always think of the dangers of the sea when he signed an officer's orders.

This old gentleman was very kind to me. He regretted exceedingly that I was not from North Carolina, but took into consideration the fact that I was unfit for anything but a midshipman, and that he had appointed twenty-four boys from his native State that very week.

So after two or three days' sojourn in the capital city my grandfather obtained for me the desired appointment as midshipman, and the Secretary promised to give me orders to the frigate Thunderbum, then lying at Norfolk, ready to sail for the Mediterranean. The orders came; my grandfather bade me adieu at the steamboat landing, having liberally supplied me with money to purchase my outfit, and I found myself afloat the first time in my life, my own master, to do (I thought) just as I pleased.

I shall never forget the feeling of pride with which I stepped up to the clerk's office to pay my passage. "Harry Marline, midshipman in the United States navy," I replied (as I hauled out my pocket-book) in answer to the clerk's question demanding my name, and I was quite surprised that the crowd did not fall back in awe at the announcement of my rank, of which I had formed a very exaggerated idea. Some one in the crowd cried out, "Does your mother know you're out?" and another fellow asked me very politely if I had lost my "cheese-toaster," and I recollect, at the time,

I AM APPOINTED MIDSHIPMAN.

feeling very grateful for the interest they seemed to take in my affairs.

I was up at early dawn of day, determined to have the first glimpse of my future home. The vessels of war loomed up in the distance like great castles as we neared Hampton Roads, and my heart beat with pleasure when some one, in answer to my inquiries, pointed out the frigate Thunderbum lying among them, "all ataunto," and ready to sail at a moment's notice.

I could scarcely resist my desire to ask the captain to stop alongside and put me out, but then I recollected that I had not yet obtained my uniform, and I was determined to make an impression when I did go on board. So I bottled up my impatience for a day or two, and took up my lodgings at Glen's Hotel, which was the rendezvous of all navy officers.

I found here, crowded together, all classes of officers in their gay uniforms, and was somewhat pleased (though not astonished) at the respect paid me by the book-keeper, who immediately gave me Room No. 1, and also ordered the best supper in the house to be got ready for me. I found Room No. 1 at the top of the house, with ten beds in it, and the best supper consisted of oysters and sausages, which only had the effect of reminding me of old Shaker's feast, and the ill effects of it.

"At last I am in the navy," I said to myself as I sat down to my tea, "and all these fine fellows are to be my companions. What a glorious career you have before you, Harry Marline! and don't forget old Abram's advice, and 'avoid the quicksands of temptation';" for I had seen enough during the short time I had been in the town to know that a young gentleman of my yielding disposition could easily be led astray. I made some terrible resolutions, however, about my future course of conduct, and determined to do my best to verify old Abe's prediction "that I would return a kurnel."

I found my way to Room No. 1, which I supposed I was to have all to myself, seeing none of the beds occupied, and no baggage being in the room (I did not know at that time that midshipmen were never troubled with baggage). Being tired out with the fatigues of the day, I was soon fast asleep, dreaming that old Shaker was turned into a great cat, and old Abram was riding him to death, with a large plug of tobacco sticking out of his jaw.

You now know, good readers, who have had the patience to follow me thus far, how it was that Uncle Sam became possessed of so valuable an acquisition to the navy as myself, and if you think it worth while to follow me through my naval career, I promise you some tough yarns from my "Lucky Bag." I shall not draw upon my imagination for anything I shall herein describe. "Nought extenuate, or aught set down in malice," shall be my motto, and if the history of my cruise shall but enliven one fireside, I shall think myself amply repaid for my trouble.

Kind readers may exclaim, "Can it be possible such events happen on board our naval ships, and do we send such captains abroad as representatives of our country?" They must not forget the oft-quoted axiom, "Truth is stranger than fiction."

CHAPTER II.

IN WHICH MARLINE IS INTRODUCED TO NAVAL LIFE, AND PROVES TO BE A HARD BARGAIN.

I SPENT a most restless night in Room No. 1, and began to think the house was haunted. My bedclothes were taken off me more than a dozen times during the night, and I had to grope about in the dark to find them. The candle had disappeared, and so had the bell-rope, which hung over my bed when I turned in. The room seemed full of rats, for I heard them scampering over the floor, making a noise like the feet of a dog, and jumping on to the beds like the weight of a good-sized boy, and I got so many wipes with their ugly tails across my legs that I determined at last not to get out of bed any more.

After a while I was beset with a new persecution. My eyes, nose, and ears were bitten by some disagreeable insect, which tickled me so that I could not sleep, and whenever I attempted to cover my head the rats pulled the cover away. Once I was awakened by something heavy falling on me, and I heard a deep groan in the farther end of the room, but I never was afraid of ghosts, so I determined to get a light and see what the matter was. Much to my surprise, I found the door locked, and the key taken out, so I was obliged once more to seek my bed, without obtaining any redress. I soon sank again into a sound slumber, and was left unmolested for the rest of the night.

PRACTICAL JOKES.

What was my surprise when I awoke in the morning to find every bed occupied with youngsters about my own age, snoring away at a tremendous rate, and laying in sleep enough to last them a week. There was the bell-pull hanging in the right place, and there was the door with the key in it, while the candle stood in the same place I had left it, burnt down to the socket. "It was a dream after all," I exclaimed, "and owing to those greasy sausages, which never do agree with me anyhow," and, seeing the sunlight streaming into the room, I arose with the determination to dress myself.

The first thing I laid my hands on was my shirt, with the sleeves tied into hard knots I found impossible to cast loose. The middle of my coat-sleeves and the legs of my pantaloons were sewed up so tight that a tailor could not have cut them adrift in an hour; and, worse than all, when I took up my boots, I found them half full of water.

I thought to myself that it was rather a dangerous thing for any one to play such practical jokes on me, for my abilities for retaliating were of no ordinary character. I began now to remember all the annoyances I was subjected to during the night, and knew that some of the present party had been amusing themselves at my expense. I looked up, involuntarily thinking which of the eight sleepers it might be, when my eyes encountered those of an older-looking boy than myself watching my movements, but he turned over as soon as he saw me watching him in return, and tried to make me believe he was asleep. I slipped quietly to his bedside, and, placing my wet boots there, appropriated his to my own use, and found that they fitted me admirably. I slipped my clothes into my trunk, and, taking out others, made my toilet.

Before I got through dressing my watchful friend seemed to awake, and, sitting up in bed, he cried out, "Halloo, sleepers! wake up. All hands ahoy! Turn out, idlers, or you will get cold sausages for breakfast." Up popped the little heads in a minute, and the officious young gentleman jumped out of bed, saying, "Mint-juleps for all by the fellow who is last dressed."

There was a great scrambling to get out of bed, and such shouts of laughter at the poor fellows who could not get their legs through their trousers and untie the knots in their shirt-sleeves. The older midshipman of all seemed to be enjoying the fun amazingly; he had got his pantaloons on without any trouble, and seized hold of the boots at his bedside in a hurry to save his juleps. Squash went the water as his foot slipped in, and in an instant he was wet away up his legs. "Sold, by the great Lama!" he exclaimed. "May I swell up and sneeze if I would not like to know who played me this trick," and looking at me very inquisitively, he said, "Are your boots wet, sir?"

"Very wet," I replied, "and feel very uncomfortable."

The middies fairly shouted with fun when they found Mr. Edward Reckless (as he was called) in a worse plight than themselves, and they redoubled their efforts to win the juleps, while that gentleman was vainly endeavoring to get on my boots. The result was, Mr. Reckless had to treat to the beverage. He took it good-naturedly, however, and asked me to join them, but it was evident that he strongly suspected me.

"May I ask your name, sir," he said, "and I will introduce you to your future messmates?"

"Harry Marline," I said, "at your service."

"Mr. Marline, let me introduce you to Mr. Bibb and Mr. Tucker," he said, bringing up two little fellows about twelve years of age. "Bibb and Tucker—you have heard of them before, I'll bet, in the nursery. Mr. Hare and Mr. Ketchum, two good fellows you will find in the 'long run.' Mr. Neat and Mr. Tareall; and this chubby-faced-looking youngster here is little Jimmy Block, a sailor every inch of him. The only fault he has is being nephew to our captain, who is the meanest white man in the navy. He would steal the cents from off a dead marine's eyes if he thought that no one was looking at him, and rob a beggar of his cold victuals. He is a bigger liar than Tom Pepper, who was kicked out of a certain unmentionable place for lying, and he is as cruel and tyrannical as a butcher's bird. Jemmy, relate to Mr. Marline how your uncle used to tell about that Arabian horse he bought in Asia."

"Why, he told about it so often," said Mr. Block, "that at last he began to believe it himself, so one day he went out and bought a saddle and bridle for him, but we have never seen the Arabian steed yet." This story caused great fun, and I was soon at home with my future companions.

Breakfast being over, I began to think of getting myself fitted out with a uniform, and applied to Mr. Reckless, who seemed to know all about Norfolk. "Give yourself no trouble, my good fellow," he said. "I will go down to old Camphor's, the navy tailor, and fit you out in no time; and you need give yourself no trouble about paying, for he will trust you till the day of judgment,

I AM GIVEN SOME ADVICE.

and then you will have hard work to get your account from him."

"Oh, as to that," I replied, "I don't want him to trust me; I have plenty of money, and will pay him cash."

"Well, that's good, now! Pay old Camphor cash! Why, sir," said Reckless, "he never heard of such a thing; and, speaking seriously, Mr. Marline, you would compromise your character. Midshipmen never pay cash, my dear boy; it is not expected of them. Why, even the lieutenants don't do it."

"But the last promise I made my grandfather was never to run in debt, nor get anything if I had not the money to pay for it."

"Now, that is better than the last. These dear, good, amiable, verdant old grandfathers! What in the name of sea-gulls do they know about naval customs? Nothing, my dear fellow; that advice of your grandfather would do very well in the army, but it would never pass muster in the navy. Now, Harry, my boy, listen to the advice of a young man who has sailed some, who has been in three different ships in the navy, and who should by this time know all the ins and outs of the service, and who always stands by when he sees a friend drifting on to a lee shore, to jump into the life-boat to save him. Now, my good fellow, with your notions you will soon get into the breakers, and I think it a duty I owe your grandfather to pilot you out of them.

"Cash, sir, is an article that is not to be lightly trifled with. It is a sacred article, and should command our highest respect; it is an article that should not be thrown away on tailors, shoemakers, and hatters; but it is to be kept for the sunny shores of Italy, for the San Carlos Theatre, where you can't get in without it; for cameos, conchillas, and mosaics, which can't be bought without cash; for Johnny Cacho's supper in Port Mahon, rides on horseback, ice-creams, chocolate and milk-punches in Naples, and a host of other things too numerous to mention which are only to be obtained with cash, cash, cash!

"Moreover, my boy, you would be setting a bad precedent, and every tailor in the United States would be quoting Harry Marline as an example. You would be looked upon as a kind of Miss Nancy, and all good fellows would steer clear of you. There is too much good stuff in you to let you go to ruin that way, and I mean to be your friend whether you will or no, and give you my best advice. I took a fancy to you from the first, Marline, and my heart warmed toward you from the fact of your having played that clever trick upon me with your boots this morning. I knew it was you, but did not like the youngsters to know that there was a smarter fellow than myself present."

"I don't like to break a promise I made my grandfather," I replied; "he is always so kind and indulgent to me."

"Why, who ever thinks of keeping promises made to grandfathers or grandmothers? For my part, I am always making promises to my old grandame, and, sensible old woman as she is, she always forgets them herself. And the only thing she ever bothered me about was a rat-tail cactus I promised to bring her from Port Mahon, where there are plenty of them. That is too good a story to keep to myself, so I must tell it to you.

"You must know that my venerable grandmother is very fond of flowers, and will spend any amount of money to obtain a rare plant. She had heard me speak of the 'rat-tail cactus,' which produces a beautiful yellow and red flower, and I described it to her as so much resembling the tail of a rat that you could not tell it from one if you saw it growing in a flower-pot. The old lady was in ecstasies at my description of the flower growing right out of the end of the tail, and was determined to have one if she was to charter a ship to get it.

"'Now, Ned,' she said to me, 'you must bring me a rat-tail cactus the next time you come home, and you forget so many things you promise that I am going to buy you a ring for your little finger, so that you shall not forget this; and mind, Ned, if you do not remember it, I will cut you off with a shilling.'

"That was a very severe penalty, I thought, for forgetting so small a thing, so I determined to remember it. The ship sailed for the Mediterranean, where I spent a year, and then came home in another ship, to which I was exchanged. Like Aladdin, I always looked at my ring every morning, and thought of the rat-tail cactus. I saw thousands of them, but they were so plenty, and, as I did not wish to have the trouble of taking care of one the whole cruise, I put it off until I was about to return home.

"As ill luck would have it, we put into Gibraltar and found the sloop-of-war Kite there, whose captain was short of midshipmen, so I was ordered to that ship to make up some of the deficiencies before I had seen half of the Mediterranean.

"I thought of my grandmother's disappointment when I should return without the rat-tail cactus, for I had written her word that I had procured one that would delight her beyond measure; but I

THE STORY OF A RAT'S TAIL.

could not make that an excuse for not wishing to join the other ship, so I had to go. I was not at all afraid of her cutting me off with a shilling, mind you, but I wanted my purse well filled when I got home, and I knew the rat-tail cactus would open the old lady's heart.

"We made a quick passage home, and three or four days before we got in I saw one of the wardroom waiters going on deck with a live rat in a trap for the purpose of throwing him overboard. An idea struck me, and I seized upon the rat and put him in a wire bird-cage so that he could not escape. Everybody wanted to know what in the name of sea-gulls I intended to do with such an ugly pet. I looked very knowing, and told them that Barnum had written to me to get this very kind of rat for him. He was a tremendous fellow, and had a tail a foot long, and as thick round as a good-sized marline-spike.

"The captain, who was a queer kind of fellow, tried to get him away from me. You must know (though it's hard to believe) that he was very fond of rats to eat, and when he was a lieutenant he would sit all night at the wardroom door (through the bottom of which he had made a hole) with a two-pronged fork in one hand and a piece of cheese in the other, waiting for the rats to come in from off the berth-deck. They had become too cunning to be caught in traps, so he used to catch one every night for his breakfast in the morning. Besides rats, he would eat every other kind of queer animal, and I heard him say once that he liked everything but turkey buzzard, and that he had tried it boiled, roasted, and fricasseed, but he always found it turkey buzzard. After he became captain he did not fare so well, and often wished himself a lieutenant again. Rats seldom or ever get into the captain's cabin in our navy, for they find rather poor fare there.

"But to return to my grandmother's affair. I fattened up my rat, and carried him on shore with me, where I procured a large and handsome flower-pot, and the night before I went on board the steamboat I gave the rat a dose of arsenic, which soon put an end to his wicked career. I planted him in the flower-pot head down, and then stuck a nice stick in the pot and tied his tail (which I stiffened with a couple of coats of varnish) to the stick, and a neat label with 'Cactus Rattailium' printed on it completed the best imitation of the 'Simon Pure' flower that was ever seen. My heart really leaped with joy when I saw the result of my experiment, for visions of full purses were flitting before my eyes all night long, and I knew that I should get all I wanted before the cheat was discovered.

"I can not describe to you the pleasure with which my grandmother greeted me when I entered the house with the long-coveted flower under my arm in the flower-pot. She kissed me a hundred times oftener than she had ever done before, and it seemed as if she could never tire of feasting her eyes on the plant. 'Ned,' she said, 'you are one in a thousand, and no grandmother ever had a more thoughtful grandson. Now just give me some idea how this curious affair is to be tended, for I would not lose it through any carelessness of mine for the world. La me! I never saw anything look more like a rat's tail in my life.'

"'Well, grandmother,' I said, 'all you have to do is to put it in the window and water it regularly every day, and it will take care of itself pretty much.' So the 'Cactus Rattailium' was placed in the window, the admiration of my grandmother and the wonder of all the visitors. The day after my return I went to my grandmother's room and found her old tabby cat in a high state of excitement, trying to jump up to the window-sill, where the flower-pot was standing.

"'Did you ever see anything like it, Ned?' said the old lady. 'Even the cat is deceived, and takes it for a Simon Pure rat's tail, and all this morning she has been going about the room with her back up and her tail as stiff as a poker. I am only afraid that she will fly at it and upset the whole concern.' 'The best thing is to turn her out of the room,' I said. So Tabby, who had always had the monopoly of that room, was ignominiously expelled from it.

"I had been home just a week, when one morning I went into grandmother's room, and was almost knocked down with the stench that issued forth as I entered. I found the old lady in a great state of excitement about something. She declared there was a dead rat in the room somewhere, and two waiting-girls were turning everything upside down to find out what the nuisance might be. I 'smelt a rat' at once, and knew that an exposure must soon take place, but it was brought about much sooner than I expected. In the confusion the old cat had mounted the window, and was scratching away with all her might at the earth in the flower-pot, and was throwing it with the rapidity of a steam-engine all over the window-sill and floor. My grandmother got sight of her, and almost screamed with agony when she saw her favorite 'Cactus Rattailium' undergoing such dreadful treatment. 'The cat, Ned! the cat!' she screamed. 'Knock her away or she will ruin my flower.'

"I jumped to do as the old lady requested; but it was too late—puss had dragged it up by the roots, and, seizing it in her mouth, disappeared through the door in an instant. The old lady nearly fainted at the idea of losing her favorite flower, but in the end was consoled by my promising to get another for her when I went to Port Mahon again. I felt great relief when I saw that the cat had done me such a service. My grandmother never for a moment suspected anything, for, being very short-sighted, she mistook the body of the rat for the roots of the cactus. Eventually it became a favorite story with her, and she would entertain her visitors by the hour with an account of the curious plant and its strong resemblance to a *real rat's tail*. A few days afterward I stumbled over the body of the dead rat, with his stick and label still fast to him, and I soon hid away these evidences against me. As to the old cat, she was never heard of again, having either run away to escape the vengeance of her once fond mistress, or else had died a victim to the poison she imbibed from the rat's body."

By the time Reckless had got through with his story we reached the shop of Mr. Camphor, the naval tailor of Norfolk. I was formally introduced to him by Reckless, and particularly recommended to his favor.

"Happy to serve you, Mr. Marline, and can fit you to a notch; you have just the kind of figure I like to measure—just the figure;" and with two flourishes of his tape-string I was measured from top to toe.

"Now, Mr. Camphor," said Reckless, "let me have something to say about Mr. Marline's outfit. He is a growing boy, and, although he is small now, you can tell by the size of his foot that he will be a whopper. He must have clothes for present use made easy. He will want another set for the end of the year, when he will be just my height and size; so for that part of the outfit you had better *take my* measure."

"What!" I said, "grow four inches in one year? Impossible! the clothes will be too large for me."

"Nonsense, Marline! I should not be surprised if you were to grow a foot in that time; besides, you will grow into them some time or other."

"True," I said, wondering at myself for opposing so far-seeing a person as Reckless; and the arrangements were all carried out to suit himself. It ended in my getting three full-dress coats for the size of thirteen years, fifteen, and sixteen, three jackets, and indeed three of every kind, the largest being made on Mr. Reckless's measure.

After a short consultation with Mr. Reckless, Mr. Camphor told me that my clothes would be ready in the morning, and to give myself no kind of uneasiness about paying, as he would give me an unlimited credit. I endeavored to oppose this arrangement, but to no purpose; the kind-hearted man would not listen to cash payment. It was not his way of doing business; he only wanted my promissory note and ten per cent interest, and *that was enough for him.*

"I might die, sir," I said.

"No fear, no fear of that; midshipmen never die, my dear sir; but if you have any fear of that kind, you can quiet your conscience by leaving an unfilled order on your guardian, which I will use only in case such a misfortune as you speak of should fall upon the navy. But keep your cash, young gentleman, Mr. Reckless will show you what to do with it. He is a discreet person, and you can rely on his advice."

What could I do but follow the advice of two such disinterested persons? It was contrary to my instructions, but I submitted at last with the best grace to all the arrangements made here and elsewhere for me by Reckless, and in the course of the day got through with my outfitting.

I have often thought since how much better it would have been for me if my grandfather had accompanied me to the place where I was about to embark, had superintended my outfit, and introduced me personally to the commander under whom I was to sail. As it was, I was thrown into the hands of strangers, who plucked me as if I was a blackberry-bush, and, as is very often the case in the navy with youths of thirteen, I was thrown upon the world without a friend to guide and direct me. It did not strike me then with the same force it does now, for I was not aware of the danger I escaped, but I have, since that time, seen many a youth join a ship whose future career was often marred by the associations he made on his first entrance into the navy.

The day prior to my joining the ship was spent in roaming about with my disinterested friend Reckless, and that kind-hearted fellow endeavored, as far as lay in his power, to initiate me into the necessities of cash. He had left his own purse on board, and I placed mine at his disposal. Having drank a couple of mint-juleps, I remember becoming very belligerent, and threatening to knock down a huge cart-driver who was standing in my way on the pavement. And I shall never forget the indignation I felt when he quietly picked me up and seated me across his horse, a huge animal seventeen hands high, all the people in the street laughing heartily at my situation.

CHAPTER III.

MARLINE REPORTS FOR DUTY, AND IS MUCH ASTONISHED AT THE PROCEEDINGS OF A MAN WITH A WART ON HIS NOSE.

It was a bright morning in the month of December when I started to report myself on board the frigate, lying about two miles off. I was pulled alongside by two darkies, who fairly made the little wherry skim over the water.

I had dressed myself in full uniform, and thought, after surveying myself in the glass with great complacency, that I would at least make an impression. I had found out from Reckless that I should be a very subordinate person on board ship (inferior even to the boatswain and carpenter), and I was somewhat surprised as I came alongside to be received by two little sailors, who, dressed in white shirts and trousers and tarpaulin hats, all looking as neat as wax-work, came running down the sides of the ship to hold out the ropes to me as I ascended. When I got on deck, a young midshipman (younger than myself) stood by to receive me and give me a military salute. I was somebody after all, I thought to myself.

At first I was so bewildered by the sight of the huge guns, the innumerable ropes, the crowds of men running to and fro, the boatswain's mates whistling through their pipes, and the officers going about giving orders, that I stood still perfectly amazed, until the middy who received me informed me, in a voice about as loud as a kitten's, that I must report to Mr. Barnacle, the first lieutenant; and he pointed to a short, fat man standing at the capstan, with a very forbidding countenance, and a very red nose with a very large wart on it.

Mr. Barnacle was evidently very much out of humor with a person he was blowing up sky-high, and who it appears was the boatswain; and I heard him say as I came up, "Mr. Bight, I could make a better sailor than you out of a piece of putty. Do you call that mizzen rigging a job, sir, for a man who has been to sea thirty-two years, and been brought up on selvagee steaks and tarpaulin sauce? Why, sir, two of those end seizings are not blacked yet, and you reported the job finished."

"I beg your pardon, sir," said Mr. Bight; "I don't think I said as how the job was finished; I thinks as how I said the mizzen riggin' was sot up. I don't think I said the job itself was done, sir, 'cause as why I knows jobs is never finished exactly in the navy, 'cause we allers has to alter 'em; we allers did so in the last ship I was in."

"Don't tell me, sir, what you did in the last ship; all you have to do is to do exactly as you are told in this ship, and never report the mizzen rigging set up until the end sizings are blacked. I knew that forward officers would not be worth half so much when they took to wearing claw-hammer jackets and got their pay increased," he grumbled. "What do you want?" he said, turning round on me, looking at me at the same time as if he had never seen anything of the kind before.

"I came to report myself for duty, sir," I said, handing him at the same time my official document, which I presumed for the moment would quite overcome him.

"Did you bring your nurse along with you, Mr. Marline, and did you provide yourself with a cradle?"

"No, sir," I said, imagining that I had made some sad mistake in my outfit; "I did not know that the regulations of the navy required it."

"Require it? Why, of course they do, sir. Do you think I have nothing else to do but play wet-nurse to twenty babies and dry-nurse to the captain besides? Here, Mr. Teaser," he said, speaking to the officer of the deck, "here is infant number fifteen for us to bring up. I wonder, in the name of bilge-water, what on earth the Secretary of the Navy can be thinking of sending us all these small fry. The whole of them put together would not make a good mouthful for a catfish. It is a crying shame to send these children away from their mothers when they are scarcely out of their swaddling-clothes. I have but two midshipmen on board who are fit to take charge of the lower decks and spirit-room, and I can't send the launch away because I have no one to send in her who can keep the men from deserting."

What a dreadful let-down was this to me! I once had fondly

imagined that the ship could not sail without me, but here I heard myself called a child scarcely out of my swaddling-clothes, and was asked if I had brought my nurse and cradle with me. My cheek fairly scorched when I heard these remarks, and thinking that perhaps some apology was due on my part to the first lieutenant, I timidly said, "I have done my best to comply with the regulations, sir, and am older than I look to be; I was fifteen last May, sir," drawing myself up to my full height.

"Ah! you don't tell me so?" said Mr. Barnacle. "You are like the nigger's pig, then—little but devilish old; or perhaps you are like valuable goods, which are always stowed in small packages. But with all that, sir, you don't know the main brace from the tiller-rope, and it will be some time before you do. Take him in your watch for the present, Mr. Teaser, and break him in, sir; he will make a good playmate for the captain's son and three nephews, and will do for the old French master to practice French on. Go below, Mr. Marline, and take off all those gill guys, stow away that claw-hammer jacket, and put your air-chopper in your locker; be smart, sir, and see how soon you can stow away your dunnage." And, turning away to attend to something else, he left me half stupefied at the innumerable commands I had received.

What could he mean by "gill guys," "claw-hammer jacket," and "air-chopper?" I asked myself; and I certainly had no more idea of what dunnage meant than the man in the moon. I inquired my way to the middy's apartment from the young gentleman who had received me at the gangway, and a large chest was pointed out to me in the starboard mess as the place in which I was to stow away my clothes.

My ears were almost deafened by the noise of some dozen youngsters in the steerage who were skylarking in various ways, and each one seemed to be trying how much more noise he could make than his neighbor. One had an old violin, on which he was trying to play "Begone, Dull Care," and my friend Reckless was trying to blow his brains out through a badly cracked flute. He came over to me as soon as he saw me, and with his habitual kindness volunteered to assist me in packing away my clothes.

I had scarcely begun the operation before a small squeaking voice sang out down the hatch for Mr. Marline; it was the young middy who had been sent in pursuit of me, and he informed me that I must hurry up, as Mr. Teaser said that I had been absent two minutes longer than I should have been.

"Hurry up and never mind your dunnage," said Reckless; "don't let Teaser get a hitch on you, or he will never let you up as long as you are in the ship. Scantling, the mess-boy, will have everything snug for you when you come down; and I have only to recommend one thing to you before you do go on deck, and that is, if you have any money in your purse put it in my locker, for you will get your pockets picked to a certainty by some of the side-boys, who are the veriest little pickpockets in the world."

I complied with this advice, and hurried up the ladder as fast as my legs could carry me, though not quite fast enough to suit the notions of the officer of the deck. "This will never do, Mr. Spunyarn," said Mr. Teaser; "two minutes and a half behind time, sir; quite long enough to hoist out a mainmast, run a ship on shore in the breakers, and cast loose and fire a whole battery. Why, sir, I can't carry on the ship's duty waiting for you. Time, Mr. Ropeyarn, is time, sir, and nowhere of so much consequence as in a ship of war. In the last ship in which I sailed, sir, we could furl sails from a bowline in ten seconds, and strip the ship to a girtline in one minute and fifty-two seconds, all of which time, Mr. Houseline, all of which time you have taken to get up the ladder."

Mr. Teaser had certainly given me names enough, but I found out afterward that this was one of his idiosyncrasies, and he never called anything properly, not even the ropes.

I commenced making an apology for my tardiness, but he interrupted me by saying, "Don't talk back, sir; we have no time to talk on board a man-of-war; it is a useless thing to waste words; indeed, in the last ship I sailed we abolished talking altogether and did everything by signals, which was an invention of Captain Botherall, and I only hope the captain of this ship will adopt the same rule. Midshipmen are so fond of 'talking back.' Let me see, sir, what did I want you for? Something of importance I am sure, but I forget what it was. You see the effects of talking back, Mr. Marline (though I had never opened my mouth); you have made me forget altogether what I wanted you for. Quartermaster, what did I want Mr. Ratline for?"

"I don't know, sir," said a short, fat old fellow, with a spyglass under his arm; "but I sees that the sun is just over the foreyard, sir, and this is about relief-time, sir."

"Ah! yes. Mr. What's-his-name, ask the second lieutenant, Mr. Bluff, to relieve me for a few moments, and be a little smarter than usual, sir."

I EXECUTE AN ORDER.

"Yes, sir," I replied, and had got half-way down the ladder in my hurry to be smart.

"Stop, young gentleman; never say 'yes, sir.' 'Ay, ay, sir,' is the proper way to answer a superior officer; none but landsmen and soldiers say 'yes, sir.'"

"Ay, ay, sir," I said, and had got to the foot of the ladder, when I was called on deck again.

"Look here, young gentleman, do you know the respect due to a superior officer? Touch your hat when you address me or I address you, and don't let me see you with your hands in your pockets or I will sew them up. Now hurry, sir, and don't keep me waiting."

I thought to myself that Mr. Teaser had a very appropriate name, and I was quite surprised at not being called back a third time before getting to the bottom of the ladder, but being anxious for his lunch, I presumed he would keep his annoyances for another occasion.

Where to find Mr. Bluff was now the difficulty, and when I got on the other deck I stopped to think what course to pursue. The only one I saw who was likely to give me information was an old midshipman who had charge (as I afterward learned) of the main deck; he was a good-natured, quizzical-looking fellow, and touching my hat to him, I inquired, "Can you tell me where I can find Mr. Bluff, sir? Mr. Teaser wants him to come on deck, as the sun is over the fore-yard."

"What does he want? A glass of molasses and water? For I am sure that Mr. Teaser never had soul enough to drink a glass of grog. Yes, my boy, I can find him for you. Do you see that old fellow with a silver whistle in his hand? that is the boatswain's mate, and it is his duty to find any one who is wanted. Order him to sing out for Mr. Bluff, and inform him the sun is over the fore-yard. Don't forget to give him the order in a loud voice, or he won't respect you."

I had heard enough orders given since I came on board to know how to make myself respected, so, walking up to the old boatswain's mate, I ordered him to sing out for Mr. Bluff, and inform him that the sun was over the fore-yard and that Mr. Teaser wanted him on deck.

"Ay, ay, sir!" he replied in tones that almost shook the ship, and the next moment I heard his thundering voice passing the order. At first there was perfect order and silence; but after the word was passed once or twice there was a titter along the decks and finally a loud laugh, in which every one joined. The first thing I saw was Mr. Teaser hurrying down to see what on earth was the matter, and he rushed forward to prevent the boatswain's mate from passing the order any farther.

"Silence, sir! silence!" he cried, crushing his cap almost to atoms in his anger. "Who told you to pass that order?"

"That young gentleman there, sir," said the boatswain's mate, looking at me.

"You, Mr. Marline! Ah! I thought how it would be when I sent you down. In the name of heaven what ship did you get brought up in? What do you mean by such conduct?"

"I was told that was the way to find Mr. Bluff, sir, and I did not know any better, as I never saw a ship before."

"Ah, Mr. Spunyarn, it is a great misfortune to be green, and I am sorry to say that you are greener than grass; you will always be green, sir, and my advice to you is to go home and join some other profession. Thank heavens, *I never was* green. Now go down that ladder and you will find Mr. Bluff in the wardroom, and don't make any more blunders. Shocking green," he muttered, as he ascended to the deck.

I at length found the wardroom, and almost instinctively walked up to Mr. Bluff, who was sitting at table with half a dozen officers, all of them laughing at something most heartily, and informed him that Mr. Teaser wanted him on deck at once.

"What does he want, my young sprat?" said this bluff, jolly-looking fellow, who fitted the name of Bluff admirably, and who was just in the act of tossing off something that looked very much like brandy and water.

"I don't know exactly what is the matter, sir, but Mr. Teaser seemed to be in a great hurry, and the quartermaster said that the sun had done something to the fore-yard."

There was a loud burst of merriment from all the lieutenants, and I thought Mr. Bluff would split his sides with laughter. He was obliged to call for another toddy before he could recover his gravity.

"Ah, Mr. Smoothface, you will know what the sun over the fore-yard is before many months go over your head unless, like Mr. Teaser, you adopt the molasses system. Steward, mix a glass of Switchell for Mr. Teaser, and don't forget to put a fly in it. I will be on deck directly, sir, and tell Mr. Teaser to keep cool and hold his wig on his head."

"Ay, ay, sir," I said, touching my hat, and hurrying on deck.

"Mr. Bluff says, sir, he will be on deck in one minute, and wants you to keep cool and hold your wig on your head," I said, approaching Mr. Teaser in the most respectful manner.

He looked at me for a moment in perfect astonishment, then turning to the first lieutenant, with whom he was talking when I delivered Mr. Bluff's message, "Here is a gentleman, Mr. Barnacle, who will throw this whole ship into confusion with his blunders before three days go over his head." And turning to me, he said, "Don't you know better than to bring me such a message, Mr. Ropeyarn ? Your conduct is inexcusable."

"I only obeyed orders, sir, which I thought I was always to do."

"Perfectly correct, young gentleman," said Mr. Barnacle ; "only carry that out and you will reach the top of the ladder sooner than those who use their own discretion. The difficulty I have with the midshipmen, Mr. Teaser, is to get them to do exactly as they are told, and I am glad to see that we have one young gentleman on board who has the spirit of discipline in him. Let Mr. Marline be one of the six midshipmen who are to go in the boat for the captain, and, as he is the largest of them all, give him charge of the boat. The captain is so fond of boys under twelve that he shall have a full benefit this time. I calculate it will take six of these youngsters to make a full-grown reefer. Give him orders to lie off the long wharf distant one hundred yards, and not approach the shore until the captain hails the boat."

"Go below, sir," said Mr. Teaser, in a freezing tone, "and get ready for duty, and don't forget the value of time, sir. When I was a midshipman I never kept the officer of the deck waiting for me ; it only took me one minute to dress from top to toe, and I always looked as neat as a clipper."

"Before she was painted or had her rigging over her mastheads," said Mr. Bluff, who was very leisurely coming up the hatch and heard the last of Mr. Teaser's speech. "Why, to my knowledge, Teaser, you were the greatest roughally in the navy, and, as to doing things quick, you forget that you were once my relief, and I swear that you never turned out at night under half an hour. How can you stuff Mr. Marline with such yarns ?" Mr. Teaser seemed quite vexed with Mr. Bluff, and I went down to obey the instructions I had received.

For the first time during the day I felt pleased that I was to have some confidence placed in me; I was to go on shore in charge of the captain's barge. I dressed quickly, and getting some information from Reckless about what I was to do, I hurried on deck, where I found Mr. Bluff in charge, rolling (like a true sailor as he was) up and down the deck, and squirting tobacco-juice with unerring aim into every spit-box he met in his way. A jolly smile lit up his hard old phiz, and he seemed mightily tickled at something that had pleased him.

"Well done, Mr. Marline; I swear Mr. Teaser never dressed in half that time. Now, where are the rest of the young gentlemen who are to act as captain's aides? Ah! here they come, like the little end of nothing whittled down to a point. Jump in, gentlemen, and don't keep the boat waiting. There, take command of them, Mr. Marline, and mind the orders you received from the first lieutenant; if you don't he will eat you, when you come back, without pepper or salt. Slew your air-choppers fore and aft, or you will never get on shore with this head-wind."

I accordingly shoved off, and took my station off the long wharf to await Captain Marvellous's arrival. Many were the applications of the sailors to go on the wharf, if only for a minute or two. One wanted to buy a pair of shoes; another had promised to leave a letter on the top of the post near the end of the dock for the post-boy, who was to take it to his wife. Another said he recognized his wife on the pier, who proved to be an old woman of sixty, and Jack was well laughed at by the rest of the crew when they got a view of the old lady's wrinkles; and one fellow recognized his brother on the dock, whom he had not seen for ten years. The old coxswain gave me a knowing look, as much as to say, "Remember, Mr. Barnacle will eat you without pepper or salt," so I turned a deaf ear to all Jack's entreaties, and told the coxswain to move farther off from the wharf for fear some one might jump overboard.

Hours passed away in this useless waiting; both myself and the crew were tired out and half famished, for we had eaten nothing since breakfast, and it was now past five o'clock in the afternoon. The little middies, tired of skylarking, had spread themselves out on the cushions and were taking their comfort in sleep, while like a trusty sentinel I was keeping guard and listening to the wonderful stories of mermaids, pirates, and shipwrecks told by the sailors to pass away time.

At last there was a bustle among the crew, and the coxswain informed me that the captain was coming with two other gentle-

A REMARKABLE DOG.

men—Mr. Tape, the purser, and Monsieur Bonbon, the French teacher.

"What does all this mean?" said the captain as he approached the boat. "What are you all doing in my boat, young gentlemen? Do you take her for a ferry-boat?"

"These is the officers in charge of the boat, sir," said the coxswain, touching his hat.

"And much use they are," said Captain Marvellous. "Make room there, gentlemen, and stow away in a small compass; some of Mr. Barnacle's doings without doubt. Make room for my dog, coxswain;" and in jumped a beautiful pointer that took up half the stern-sheets. "Shove off, coxswain, and give way with a will." The oars were let fall, the boat's head pointed toward the ship, and, to the delight of our empty stomachs, we went flying toward the Thunderbum.

"That is a famous-looking dog of yours, Captain Marvellous," said Mr. Tape, the purser. "Where did you get him?"

"Why, sir, that dog I raised, and he is the best blood in the country. I think I was telling you about that dog's father the other day; he was the most wonderful animal I ever saw, and no one would believe half that he could do unless they saw it with their own eyes. He was presented to me by the Grand Duke of Tuscany when I commanded the sloop-of-war Gripe. He was but three months old when I first took him into the field, but, sir, he hunted with as much precision as a well-broken dog, and stood at a covey of quails the first time I ever took him out."

"A remarkable dog that," said Mr. Tape, dryly.

"Diable! Mais c'est un chien merveilleux!" said the French teacher, shaking his head.

"Wait until I tell you more about him," said the captain, "and you will say, gentlemen, that the world never produced anything like him." And as near as I can remember the words, the captain commenced telling the following story:

"It was in the year 18—, while I was farming in Virginia, and raising one hundred bushels of wheat to the acre (which I flatter myself has never been beaten); growing corn eight feet high with ten ears on each stalk; gathering in strawberries that would make one's mouth water to look at them (for each one would fill a large wine-glass); and digging up sweet potatoes, twenty only to the bushel. It was at that time, I say, I had just procured a first-rate double-barreled Joe Manton, and started off one fine morning to give my dog Snap a little exercise and try my gun on some pheasants that had spent the winter about my farm-yard. I had not long been in the field before he smelt the birds, and there he was crawling up, his nose high in air, his eyes glistening with delight, and his quivering tail standing out as straight as a poker. I followed close behind, with my gun cocked, ready to shoot when the birds rose, and anticipating the luxury of a fine pheasant for supper. Snap had come to a full point with one foot raised straight out before him, and his head turned round toward me, as much as to say, 'Here they are, come and shoot them.'

"'There is many a slip between the cup and the lip,' and so I found in this case. For while admiring the noble animal and wishing that I was a painter that I might sketch him as he stood, I heard my name called loudly by some one, and, turning round, beheld my negro boy Ben rushing toward me as if he had lost his senses, and, knowing that he was not apt to over-exercise himself on ordinary occasions, I took it for granted that something very much out of the way had happened, and feared that some dreadful calamity had befallen some one of my family. I turned round and hastened to meet him, wishing to know the worst at once.

"'In the name of heavens, Ben, what is the matter?' I said, almost overcome with apprehension. 'Tell me at once, sir, and don't keep me waiting. Is your mistress ill? or are any of the children sick? Tell me quick, sir.'

"'Jis wait one minit, massa, till dis heea nigga get his bref; dis runnin' done tak' de wind out of his carcass in de mos' onaccountable manner; and I 'spec now I done buss a blood-wessel.'

"'Is anything the matter at home, sir?' I said. 'Speak quick, you black 'possum!'

"'Yes, massa,' he said, 'nuff's de matter at home; missus says dar's onexpected 'telligence in dis heea communication, and she 'spects you to hurry to de house wid all de haste it possible to expedite. Says she to me, "Ben," says she, "I knows you'se fustrate at runnin', and if you don't fin' your massa in fifteen minit I'll make him give you a tickler when he do come in." It was jis twelve, massa, when I lef' hum, and I wish you look at your watch jis to see if I'se up to time.'

"'What is it all about, Ben?' I said, my mind quite relieved for the moment.

"'Why, massa, it's all about dis ya yaller letter, which dun cum jis now from de navy offis at de District ob Columby, and missus says you must got it 'fore de 'teamboat go back ; she go in haf an hour. Missus dun read de letter, and say she hab your trunk packed by de time you got to de house.'

"I seized hold of the letter, and, setting my gun up against a tree, proceeded to read its contents, which were important. I was ordered to proceed to Washington with all dispatch, and to go by the first steamer. In the excitement of the moment I forgot my dog, and in less than half an hour was on my journey. On my arrival in Washington I called on the Secretary immediately, and felt much flattered at the reception he gave me. 'Just what I expected of you, captain,' he said ; 'in selecting you the Department picked out a man on whose promptness they could depend, and I only regret, sir, that it is not in my power to place so gallant an officer as yourself in command of a squadron, but the duty I am about to offer you is of the most important kind, and you, of all the officers of the navy, have been selected to carry out the views of the Government.

"'We have just received intelligence, sir, from the missionaries of Smyrna that the moral condition of our ships on that station is much to be deplored, and officers of one ship in particular had yielded to the seductive influences of the Mohammedan religion, and had all turned Mussulmans ; that it was necessary to send out an officer to command the ship on the Smyrna station whose moral and religious character was beyond reproach, and who could bring the officers to a sense of their own degradation. Now, Captain Marvellous,' said the Secretary to me, 'you are known to the Department as a strict member of the church, a man of great truthfulness, and we are convinced that you will not allow any Mohammedan demonstrations on board your ship. We have accordingly paid you the compliment to select you for the duty, and, although for a time it will take you away from your family unexpectedly, we know that you will make this sacrifice for the good of the service. You have but a few hours to make yourself ready in, for a ship sails from New York in two days for Smyrna, and you must depart in her.'

"What could I do, Mr. Tape, after all the Secretary had said, but obey the order cheerfully ? These are sacrifices of feeling a good officer must always be ready to make, and I flatter myself that no officer in the navy has submitted to more than myself.

"To make a long story short, I arrived off the harbor of Smyrna after a pleasant voyage of thirty-six days, and on entering the port passed close under the stern of the ship which I had come out to command. And there she lay at anchor with the vile symbols of Mohammedanism stuck all about her, and, but for the glorious stars and stripes floating at her peak, you could never have told that she was an American vessel of war.

"At each of her mast-heads or trucks she carried large gilt stars; at her dolphin-striker there hung suspended a star and crescent; she carried a star at her flying jib-boom end, and her catheads even were adorned with the execrable crescent. And what a sight did her officers present assembled on the poop, dressed in wide, loose pantaloons (*à la Turque*, Monsieur Bonbon), with hideous mustachios covering their mouths, and long beards hanging down to their waists! Each one smoked a long Turkish pipe. Their long beards were enough to condemn them if they had done nothing else, for it has been truly remarked by one of the oldest and ablest officers in the navy that no man could possess a good moral character who ever wore his whiskers below the tip of his ear. So important did he consider it to the discipline of the service that he has devoted his whole life to getting the present regulations adopted about wearing beards. Many officers have complained of it, and look upon it as a small-potato business, but you may depend upon it that no service can be efficient where whiskers and mustachios are allowed to flourish."

"Ah, Monsieur Capitaine Merveilleux," interposed Monsieur Bonbon, with some earnestness, "I do not sink dat you av seen ze offisairs of ze marine Française; zey ware ze whiskair and ze moustache toujours always, an' I av hear ze people zay dat ze French navie vas reckoned not even inferieur to ze marine of ze Great Bretagne."

"That will do to tell to the marines, Monsieur Bonbon; but, independent of beards, no navy can be efficient where they use ten words to put the 'helm a-lee' in tacking ship, and fourteen at least when they say 'mainsail haul.' You forget also, sir, that we licked the British, and the British always licked the French. These are matters, Mr. Bonbon, only understood by professional men."

This was a stopper on Mr. Bonbon, so he kept silent, and was quite subdued; it was evident, however, that the "Grande Nation" had been deeply insulted by the captain's remark, and, though he had to suppress his feelings, he evidently would have liked to have eaten him without sauce.

"For my part," continued the captain, "I never wore a whisker,

THE CAPTAIN CONTINUES HIS STORY.

and I don't think any officer ever went through harder service than I did."

"Why, captain," said Mr. Tape, laughing, "I have known you many years, and I don't think you could ever raise a pair of whiskers."

"Oh, my dear sir, you are very much mistaken; before the great hurricane in 1802 I could raise as fine a pair of whiskers as ever you saw, but on the 15th of August of that year they were actually blown out by the roots while I was trying to hold my hair on my head, and I have never been troubled with beard since that time."

"Ce fut un hurricain merveilleux," said the French teacher, dryly. "I zink, sair, dat you av loss some of ze air too in zat hurricain."

"It is probable that I did," replied the captain, "for I never saw it blow harder in my life; but that has nothing to do with my story. As soon as the brig anchored I went on shore, and was warmly received by the missionaries, who were really delighted to see me, and hailed my arrival as a new era dawning on them. I heard most unfavorable reports of the ship, and found that the captain had actually been making war upon the poor Greeks, who were accused of committing piracies on our commerce, and this he did at the time when the people of the United States were giving them all their sympathies and fitting them out with clothes.

"It is true one or two vessels were boarded by some Greek prows, and the men helped themselves to the clothes and the provisions, but, as they were sent out for their use, what great harm was there in that? Yet some people were foolish enough to say that this vessel had done more to put down piracy than all the English and French squadrons together, but that was all *bosh*. There were no pirates at all, and this persecution of the poor Greeks was carried on merely to gratify the Mohammedan propensities of the officers.

"When I went on board to take command of my ship, I can not describe to you my horror at what I saw. Two men with beards as long as any Turk's, and mustachios curling up to their eyebrows, acted as side-boys, and held out the man-ropes to me. When I descended the gangway-ladder leading to the quarter-deck you will scarcely imagine the group upon which my eyes rested. All the officers had assembled to receive me dressed up in full Turkish costume. The first lieutenant had his head shaved close to the skin, the second and third had theirs cropped like penitentiary felons, and some of the others had consulted their fancies by wearing those long topknots by which the Turks suppose that Mohammed will take them to heaven. One fat little lieutenant even had the audacity to hand me a pipe, making me a salam in true Oriental style. I took on board a pointer dog given me by the captain of the brig (I always keep a dog), and he was received by an angry-looking Angora cat with back up and ready to pounce upon him. I reckon we were both unwelcome visitors, though, to judge from my reception, the officers were delighted to see me; however, I soon pulled down the Turkish symbols that were stuck all over the ship, and a new order of things took place.

"Instead of chasing unoffending Greeks about the islands, I put my vessel at the disposal of the missionaries in Smyrna, who made our souls feel comfortable with good and pious discourse, and in a month such a change took place in the ship that you would never have known that heathen rites had once been practiced on board. I never lifted my anchor to go anywhere until I was ordered to return to the United States, and I stayed in Smyrna so long that the ship was aground on the beef-bones that had been thrown overboard. I had some trouble to get her off.

"After two or three days' experience in her at sea I did not regret having to protect the American interest so long in Smyrna. She was an awful old tub, and it was a happy day when I anchored her in American waters. She was one of the vessels built by the joint talent of the navy commissioners, and this one in particular was modeled after one of the old commodores. It was considered a good joke at the time, but rather a practical one on the navy, when asked by the constructor how he wanted her lines to be, he answered, 'Look at my lines, sir, and build her after my model; full round stern, sir, and bluff bow; plenty of beam and not too long; then she will carry her battery and stand up well under sail.' And according to these directions she was built, and remains a lasting monument of his capacity for ship-building. She had one great peculiarity: we never lost anything that fell overboard that would float; no matter what it was, we were sure to get it the first time the main-topsail was laid to the mast. I hove-to a week after leaving port to board a ship, when up popped from under the stern a lot of tarpaulin hats, caps, shoes, pea-jackets, bags, potato-peelings, and I don't know what besides. They had been thrown overboard at sea, and had followed us close under the stern, drawn along by the backwater caused by the full counter of this clipper. This is all true, I assure you, Mr. Tape; no doubt you have heard of it in the navy?"

"No, really, sir, I never did," said Mr. Tape, laughing; "but you have been so much interested in the ship that you have forgotten to tell us about the pointer dog; I am quite anxious to hear about him."

"Oh, I am coming to him now," said Captain Marvellous. "I had almost forgotten him; the story of that ship always runs away with me.

"I had been home a whole day," he continued, "and had so much to talk about, and so many visitors were constantly coming in, that I never thought of Snap, though I missed something, I could not tell what it was; but I remembered him at night, and asked my wife where he was.

"'Why, my dear,' she said, 'I have not seen him since the day you left home, and I thought that you had taken your dog and gun with you.'

"'Did not Ben bring the gun home?' I said, 'for I left it leaning against a tree.'

"'No,' she said; 'I have never seen it.'

"I rang the bell for Ben, who came in, quite glad to see me, and I said, 'Ben, you scoundrel, where are my dog and gun?'

"'What dog and gun, massa, you mean? I ain't done seen any dog and gun 'mong de baggige.'

"'I mean, sir, my dog Snap and my Joe Manton.'

"'I ain't done seen de dog, massa, since dat day when you gwoin to de seat ob gobernment; and as to Joe Manton, I ain't done know him, sar, mos' onaccountable as it may 'pear.'

"'Didn't the dog come home after me, sir, when I left?'

"'I dun know, massa; if he did, he gwoin off agin, an' I ain't done seen him since, dat's sartain.'

"Very queer, I thought to myself, and in the morning I determined to investigate the matter thoroughly. I suspected Ben knew something about it from his saying, 'Prehaps de gun gone off and shoot de dog, and dats de reson he no come home.'

"I could not sleep all night thinking of my lost dog, and was up at early dawn, and in company with Ben started for the spot where I had last seen him, and where I had left the gun.

"It was not yet quite light when we approached the spot, but I could see something white in the distance, and my heart almost leaped out of my mouth when I thought it might be Snap, until I recollected that a year had passed away, and the poor dog must have long since been gathered to his fathers. Ben crept behind me, somewhat alarmed. 'Bress de Lor', massa,' he said, 'if dat ain't Snap's ghos' den dis heea nigger dun know what a ghos' is; it's mos' onaccountable, an' dat's a fac'.'

"Now, Mr. Tape and Mr. Bonbon, you will scarcely credit what I am going to tell you; I would not believe it myself unless I had seen it with my own eyes. When I got up to the white object, what should I see but my poor Snap standing just where I had left him a year before, his fore-paw still straight out before him, his head turned round toward me as I last saw him, and his tail standing straight out as ever. But, gentlemen, life had passed away; the intelligent eye had shrunk in its socket, the worms had eaten the flesh, and nothing but the bones remained to tell the sad story. He had died, gentlemen, at his post, true to his duty, and the conduct of that dog offers a moral that I shall remember as long as I live; when through weariness or sickness I have faltered in my duty, I have thought of Snap and gained fresh vigor."

"I wonder he did not go home when the bird flew up," said Mr. Tape.

"Mais certainement!" said Mr. Bonbon.

"That's the thing, gentlemen; that bird never flew up; his bones were whitening in the sun about three yards from the dog, and Snap died rather than flush it."

"Mais c'est un chien remarkable," said Mr. Bonbon; "and ze Joe Manton, sair, ver was his bone?"

"Oh, I found my gun against the tree where I had left it, so rusty that I could never use it any more."

"And pray what did you do with the bones of that wonderful dog, captain?" said Mr. Tape.

"I sent them to Mr. Barnum, who has them on exhibition in his museum. If ever you go to New York I advise you to go and see them."

"Ah, I av had zat plaisir, sair," said Mr. Bonbon; "mais it is one leetel defferent now. Monsieur Barnum do rub ze bones wis ze hair-oil of Monsieur Granjean, and ze dog av now one goot skin on ze bone. Mais c'était un chien miraculeux!"

I don't know what the captain would have said to this clincher of Mr. Bonbon had not the coxswain sung out "In bow," "Way enough," and put us alongside the ship. The captain jumped on board and we all followed; the boatswain piped the side, the marines presented arms, and once more Captain Marvellous reigned "the monarch of her peopled deck."

"Walk into the cabin, Mr. Barnacle," he said, stiffly, and the first lieutenant followed him in.

In ten minutes Mr. Barnacle came out again, his face much flushed and the wart on his nose twice as large as usual. He looked as if he could have bitten the cascabel off of one of the quarter-deck guns.

"What's the matter, first luff?" said Mr. Bluff, who was officer of the deck; "is anything wrong with Tom Pepper to-day? I hope he is not troubled with rats."

"Umph!" he growled, "the skipper has undertaken to curry me down for sending so many babies in his boat, and told me next time I wanted to send the young gentlemen an airing to send them in my own boat. He has taken all these youngsters on board to please their papas, who are political men, and I am determined that he shall have the full benefit of them."

"Poor middies!" I thought, "you get more kicks than coppers, and because you are frequently sent to sea against your inclination, and have to commence somewhere to learn your profession, you are looked upon as perfect nuisances." I almost wished myself back in Babel helping old Abe to ride the horses to water, but I thought of the captain's dog, and resolved to do my duty or die in my tracks."

I went down to the steerage, where I found my messmates troubled with no melancholy reflections, and, joining in the fun, I soon forgot that middies were ever oppressed.

CHAPTER IV.

AN IRISH SCHOOL-MASTER, AND HIS DIFFICULTIES ON FIRST ENTERING SERVICE—A MIDSHIPMEN'S SUPPER AND A GOOSE WITHOUT LEGS OR WINGS—A CATERER'S APPEAL TO THE MESS, AND THE DISCOMFITURE OF A SCHOOL-MASTER.

THE object of these pages is not so much to tell of my own adventures as to relate the curious scenes I have witnessed and the wonderful stories I have heard in the navy. But I can not omit telling about the remarkable supper I sat down to on the first day

I joined a ship of war. I have partaken of many since, but do not remember one that afforded me more amusement.

Our mess was composed of eight midshipmen, all youngsters, the captain's clerk, and a most curious-looking individual, who ranked as school-master. Poor Mr. O'Classics! (for such was his name), I shall never forget the persecutions he underwent from the midshipmen, and I think that to his dying day he must have shuddered whenever he heard the name mentioned. He was an Irishman by birth, had only been in the country three years, and had a strong touch of that "beautiful rich brogue" so feelingly alluded to by one of our great men. He had joined the ship this day, and had never in his life before set foot on board a man-of-war. He had already got into innumerable difficulties, and just before supper was announced had opened his battery on the mess-boy for not showing him where his chamber was!

"An' is this the place, my man, where I am to pack away me beautiful clothes in, sure? An' faith is it a closet ye offer a gintilman, when he expicted a good mahogany bureau? Be the powers of Saint Patrick, who killed all the snakes in Ireland, if ye don't trate me better than that, may I bother my grandmother but ye'll get small book-learning out av me!"

"There is where the midshipmen keep their clothes, sir, and we don't keep no bureaus on board ship, sir," said the mess-boy.

"An' is it a midshipmate ye take me for, ye thundering gosshawk? An' is it to a gintilman, the author of three beautiful books of poethry, an' the writer of 'The Plume of the Classics,' that ye offer such an indignity? May the hills of Killarney bury me but I'll thump ye into an agy if ye don't show me a comfortable room, an' not mix me up with a set of spalpeens who don't know what good manners is!" And no doubt Mr. O'Classics would have given poor "Scantling" a touch of his shillalah if Reckless had not come to his rescue.

"What would you like to have, Mr. O'Classics? Can I do anything for you?" he asked.

"Faith an' ye can. Tell me only what divil's dam ever induced me to embark in such an interprise, an' I will give ye a shilling, me lad, an' a volume of 'The Plume of the Classics,' when I finish it. Och! but wouldn't me ould mother stare if she could only see me packing me duds in an ould miss-chist? Me, too, by the powers, who was tauld that I should be the President of the States in liss than no time, or, leastwise, the head of the national univarsity.

A REMARKABLE SUPPER.

First and foremost, me boy, can ye get me a good chamber? Secondly, I want to know where the bar-keeper is; and, thirdly, I want to know when and where I can git me supper, for divil a bit 'av I 'aten since breakfast."

"There is no difficulty, my good sir, in getting all you want, 'only be aisy,' as they say in ould Ireland."

"Is it aisy, ye mane? An' if ye'd said onaisy, ye'd have hit the mark sure. An' isn't it onaisy and aisy, too, for that, I've been since eight the clock this mornin'? An' 'aven't I been turned and tumbled about this auld ark since that time? An' faith, didn't I ask a filler up-stairs, wid a gold bunch on his lift shoulder, where the divil of a bar-keeper was, an' didn't the ill-favored baste till me to git off wid me on toder side of the dick? Didn't I ask quite a dacent-looking young man where me chamber was, an' didn't he tell me, 'In the starboard horse-hole'? An' is it in any horse-holes that ye would be for putting a rispictable gintilman? An' whin I asked a midshipmate where I was to sind me trunk, and who was to lift it down, didn't he tell me, 'Take it down yerself, Pat, an' ask the cook for the kay of the galley; ye'll find the chamber there'? Is that the word to spake to a gintilman? An' is it a galley-slave ye would make of a man? Och! but Barney O'Classics is not the man or boy to stan' it."

"All your difficulties have arisen, Mr. O'Classics, from not knowing the customs of the navy, but you'll find it all as smooth as cock-fighting in a day or two if you'll only follow my advice," said Reckless; "and now permit me to ask you to join us at tea, and I have no doubt you have a good appetite."

"Sure an' I kin ate a donkey and a hamper of greens, if I had 'em; an' I only hope, my kind friend, that yer cook has laid in a good supply, for Barney O'Classics is no baby at knife-an'-fork work."

Mr. O'Classics was placed at the head of the table, and we all took our seats, Reckless acting as caterer. As yet nothing had been brought in but the plates, cups, and saucers, and I presumed we were kept waiting so that we might get it all hot. We all sat perfectly still, being novices, waiting to see what was to be done, and had waited patiently for fifteen minutes without saying a word, when at last Mr. O'Classics spoke up:

"I say, Mr. Rickless, what may we be waiting for? Is it the tae-things we are to ate? For, by the powers of flesh, one can't kape aisy at this rate."

"One moment, sir; the drum will beat in a minute, and we will fall to as soon as the chaplain comes down to say grace. He is just getting through with the crew's mess."

"Och, murther! but it will be a long grace he will 'av' to say over those sax hundred men. I hope, me boy, that he has not had his supper, that's all the ill-luck I wish him."

Just at this moment the drum ruffled three times for sunset.

"Och! thir ye ar', me good music. Sind up an' till them to play 'Roast Beef of Ould England.' Faith, now fitch on the supper. Niver mind the grace; the Lord will forgive us this onst considering the sarcumstances."

"Bring in the supper, Scantling," said Reckless to the mess-boy; "but I am very much afraid, Mr. O'Classics, that the chaplain will feel hurt."

"Divil a bit, divil a bit will he mind it. Don't fash yer brains about that. No Christian chaplin would keep tin gintilmen waiting; an', if he gets hurt, let him take a mouthful of coald water, an' sit on the fire till it boils; 'twill make him as agreeable, faith, as a sucking turtle."

In walked Scantling with the supper, and placed it on the table with an air as much as to say, "There's a supper for you, beat that who can!" It consisted of one plate of cheese cut up into small pieces, one plate of hard biscuit, and a soup-tureen full of tea, the leaves of which were floating about on the top as big as splatterdocks.

"Supper is ready, gentlemen," said Reckless; "help yourselves."

"An' is this what ye call supper, me man?" said the schoolmaster, looking as much astonished as if a bomb-shell had exploded under his nose. "Is it a Welshman ye tak' me for, that ye want to fill me up with chaase? Faith, Mr. Rickless, I hope yer promises don't all correspond with yer supper."

"Scantling," said Reckless, with an offended air, "where is the rest of the supper? Bring it on, you scoundrel!"

"It's all on the table, sir, except the mustard and pepper, and the plate of hickory-nuts left from dinner."

"Where are the canvas-back ducks I bought in the market this morning, villain?"

"Why, the sail-maker took them to mend the first reef in the mainsail, sir."

"May the divil fly away wid him for an ill-mannered fellow, as he is!" ejaculated O'Classics. "All the ill-luck I wish him is, that he may live on chaase the rest of his born days."

"And where is that large turkey I bought at the same time?"

"He swam on shore, sir, and has been put in the pound for getting into a gentleman's corn-field."

"Ill-luck to the gintilman, an' worse luck to web-footed turkeys. Ain't you lyin' now, sure, Mr. Scantlin'?"

"What has become of that large piece of steak, sir, I ordered to be cooked for supper?" said Reckless.

"It would not obey the order, sir, and the cook said it positively refused to be placed upon the fire."

"Murther an' 'ouns!" exclaimed O'Classics, "an' was it a beefsteak that wouldn't obey orders on board an American ship of war? Faith, in the Irish navy it would have been cooked an' 'aten without saying a single word. That's discipline for you."

"And now, you wretch!" cried Reckless, apparently waxing wrathy, "what have you done with the woodcocks that were sent on board yesterday?"

"They were too ripe to be eaten, sir, and I swapped them for the goose we had for dinner to-day. Part of that's left yet."

"Och, mother of sin! an' is it a goose that's all ye've got? But, faith, goose is not bad for a hungry man, so bring it along, me lad," said the teacher.

At least ten minutes passed before Scantling entered with the goose. It was carefully covered up with a bright tin cover, and Scantling placed it on the table with an air of reluctance, and looked as if he thought the mess too exorbitant in their demands. At a sign from the caterer he removed the cover, and there appeared the goose, sans legs, sans wings, sans breast, sans stuffing, sans everything.

"Och! tunder an' Paddy O'Rafferty! but the legs have flown away an' the wings have run off," cried the teacher. "Och! Mr. Rickless, Mr. Rickless! ax the boy what's begone of the rest of the baste. May me old black mare run away wid me if ever I seen the likes of this! Ax him, Mr. Rickless, for the best parts of the goose."

"Look here, Scantling," said Reckless, rising with an air of offended dignity, "mind what I have to say to you. You are on the eve of losing the confidence of the gentlemen of this mess, which will be a loss you will deplore as long as you live. You will be deprived of all the perquisites of the office, such as cast-off boots, caps, shirts, pantaloons, and jackets, which would probably fall to your lot if you conducted yourself with propriety" (Scantling was six feet two and stout in proportion); "and now, instead of returning home at the end of the cruise with a well-filled trunk of fashionable clothes, you will get a good cobbing unless you account satisfactorily for these legs and wings, to say nothing of the breast and stuffing. Come, speak out boldly."

"Well, sir," Scantling replied, "all I have to say is this. Them kind of geese ain't got no legs nor wings, leastwise, I ain't seen none on 'em this season. Them's what they call the summer goose, and it's always preferable to buy them, because there ain't so much carving to be done. In two years the legs and wings will grow out, and then the goose is too old to be eaten. That accounts for the legs and wings, sir; and as to the breast and stuffin', that was served out at dinner, sir, and what the young gentlemen didn't eat was eaten by the other mess-boy, the cook, and myself, to say nothing of your hammock-boy, sir, who ate up all the stuffin'."

"I think, gentlemen," said the caterer, "that Scantling has explained the thing in the most satisfactory manner, and we should not hesitate to take him into our full confidence again. For my part, Scantling, I regret that I doubted you for a moment, but this was a serious-looking affair, and I am glad that you have explained it so clearly, for to me it is as clear as mud." And Mr. Reckless sat down amidst the applause of all the midshipmen, who took the joke and enjoyed the fun.

Not so the school-master. The cravings of hunger were too strong to allow him to look on this transaction in any other light than as a complete swindle. He seized the goose by the middle, and, holding it high in air, he exclaimed, "Is this a goose I see before me? No, gintilmen, this is only a liebill on a goose; it niver was a goose, an' it niver will be a goose. Mr. Rickless has exprissed himself intirely satisfied wid the ixplanation of Mr. Scantlin', an' says that we should tak' him into our confidence agin. May ould Ireland disown me if ever I do anything of the kind! for I am well agreed wid me own mind that (bad luck till him!) the whole thing is a willful misrepresentation. No gintilman here present can 'av' failed to 'av' read the history of Rome, when she was fightin' aginst all mankind an' was misthress of half the world. The great historian Gibbon tills us that Rome was once saved by a goose, which intitles it to be classed among the most intelligent of the brute creashun, an' brings it under the head of public benefactors. For what nobler act could a goose do than save a whole nation from the hands of a set of savages, who would have scalped all the women an' 'aten all the poor little children? Faith an' honestly, but ony man who would utter so foul a slander on a goose as to say he was born widout legs, widout which he couldn't fly, an' widout wings, wantin' which he couldn't run, he desarves such a bally-whackin' as would make his limbs ache for three centuries to come. That's all I 'av' to say on the subject, Mr. Rickless, and may the divil fly away wid Mr. Scantlin' an' his galley-bandering!"

Mr. O'Classics met with such loud applause from the middies that some time elapsed before Reckless could gain the floor. Shouts of "Go it, Reckless!" "Go it, Mr. O'Classics!" brought all the members of the other mess to witness the controversy.

"Gentlemen," began Reckless, "I find myself placed in a most trying situation. I had fondly hoped that I should have presided over this mess until the end of our cruise, or till death perhaps might put an end to my mortal career. But, gentlemen, I live to witness the presence of a total stranger in our mess, whose superior eloquence has wrested from me the applause which I fondly considered once all my own. He has deeply wounded me in the tenderest part by his insinuations about the goose and our faithful servant Scantling. Where, gentlemen, where shall we find such another? Can the ship produce him? I dare unhesitatingly to say no, and I defy the world to deny what I say."

"Och, honey, I agray wid you parfectly! The world can't produce him, but may the divil fly away wid him for all that!" said O'Classics.

Reckless looked daggers at this interruption, but continued: "Who, gentlemen, can keep our hen-coops filled long after we have eaten our supply of chickens and ducks? Who can elude the vigilance of the sentry and stick pins into the heads of the cabin and wardroom chickens, and then save them for our table? Who so adroitly could exchange our slapjacks fried in slush for the captain's fritters fried in fresh butter? Who is it that can dip out from the coppers the wardroom duff filled with raisins and made with eggs, and substitute ours made with slush and without raisins? Who was it, gentlemen, that cut off the heads of the captain's woodcocks last week and pinned them on to squabs so nicely that the captain's cook never suspected it, while we were quietly enjoying the woodcocks? Who was it last week that took the captain's twelve-pound turkey, after it was cooked with oyster-sauce, and substituted our six-pound bird in the place of it? And who is it, gentlemen, who borrows the best wine from the wardroom and replaces it with common stuff they can not drink? Why, it is Scantling, gentlemen, and he does it so quietly that no one besides myself knows it. He is a man without his equal, and saves each of us five dollars a month in mess-bill. To your caterer, gentlemen, you are partly indebted for the various accomplishments of our faithful mess-boy, though he has talents of his own of no ordinary character, but I have drilled him by the hour since the day I took charge of this mess, and now I meet my reward by having a gentleman (who never ate anything better than potatoes and buttermilk in his own country) come into the mess endeavoring to ruin Scantling's popularity."

"Is it me, Mr. Rickless, that ye talk buthermilk an' pretaties to? Faith, an' I'd 'av' ye to know that ye niver seen one nor the other of those articles; they won't grow in a counthry filled with snakes an' creeping riptiles; an', as to buthermilk, you don't know what ye're talking about; they are the staple commodities of ould Ireland, an' may ony one 'av' his tongue blistered who spakes disrespectfully of them, bad luck to ye!"

"I regret to say," said Reckless, without noticing the teacher's last remark, "that a *goose*"—emphasizing the word—"has been the cause of an unpleasant controversy in the mess, and as long as I am caterer no more goose comes on this table. If I am to remain as caterer I must be supported by my messmates, and I now ask the wishes of the mess. Am I to be caterer or not?"

A thundering "aye" was the response to this part of Reckless's speech.

"Take that goose off the table, Scantling," said the caterer; "for my part, I will sup on cheese; this discussion has taken away my appetite. Away with that goose, sir, and never let me see a goose again."

"Och! but that will niver do, Mr. Rickless; ye can't send that goose away yit. Ye may take a horse to water, but faith ye can't make him drink unless he wants to, an' divil a bit of your cheese do ye stuff down my throat. I'll tak' the side's bones out av him afore he does travel, Mr. Scantlin', an' may ye never know the taste of buthermilk if iver ye buy anither summer goose! Lit's 'av' him this way, sir, for divil the bit else do I ixpict to see between this an' sunrise; an' if yer brakefast's no bether than yer dinner, may the cat fly away wid it!"

"The caterer has ordered it to be taken away, sir, and I can't give it to you unless he permits," said Scantling.

"Och! is it there ye are, Mr. Scantlin'?" said the school-master, jumping up in a rage; "an' it's starving me ye are going to be at, me fine fellow? We'll see till that. Now put it down, I say, or I'll give ye sich a slavering that your own mother's child won't know himself in the looking-glass to-morrow mornin'."

"Can't do it, sir, without orders," coolly replied the boy, looking at Reckless for directions, while that gentleman, apparently satisfied with the applause of the mess, had recovered his equanimity and was enjoying the fun considerably.

"Thin here's at ye, an' may the divil pay the piper!" And jumping at the goose, which the mess-boy held in his left hand, he endeavored to snatch it from the dish. By some accident (no doubt) the gravy, of which there was an abundance, went all over the teacher's head and eyes, and, as Scantling stepped back to avoid his blows, Mr. O'Classics unfortunately tripped over his leg, went head foremost into the cock-pit, and split his nose against the after-stancheon.

"Now, fellows," said Reckless, "let's hustle him as he comes up. We might as well tame this wild Irishman at once; follow my example." And with that he took up the soup-tureen full of tea and soused it in Mr. O'Classics' face as he endeavored in his rage to get up the ladder. "Hustle him!" cried all the midshipmen in chorus, and before you could count ten the poor man was attacked with all kinds of missiles in the shape of old shoes, wet swabs, brooms, and plates, against which he endeavored in vain to make headway. He was forced at last to take shelter in the assistant surgeon's room in the cockpit, having been knocked down by the very goose for which he was contending, and having at the same time received the full contents of the slop-bucket in his bosom.

To describe the rage of O'Classics would be impossible. He roared like a mad bull, and gave some blessings in pure, unadulterated Irish. No doubt he would have renewed the combat if Mr. Barnacle had not opportunely appeared at the wardroom-door, and asked in a very rough and angry voice what was the matter.

"It is the mad Irish school-master, sir," said Reckless, "who has kicked up this row. He ran off with a goose, sir, we had for supper, upset all our tea, and then dove down head foremost into the cockpit, after attempting the life of the mess-boy and kicking over the slop-bucket. He is as mad as a March hare, sir, and I don't think our lives are safe if he is permitted to go at large."

"Is not this one of your mad pranks, Mr. Reckless?" asked the first luff, "for you are the head and front of all the deviltry on board this ship; and if I find you in fault, make up your mind to spend a week at the mast-head. Where is this mad school-master, sir?"

"An' is it me ye call the mad school-maester, Mr. Redface, wid a wart on yer nose as big as an Irish pretaty?" said the indignant O'Classics, who had heard the last words of the first lieutenant, as he stood in the cockpit with a cutlass in his hand. "Divil a bit there's mad ye'll find in me, ye ould catamaran; an' if ye mak' any more insinuations 'bout me, I'll knock that pretaty off yer nose in the twinkling of a sledge-hammer. May the cat fly away wid ye all, but yer a set of devil's imps altogithir! Arrah! but ain't this thratement for an Irish gintleman in the American navy?"

"Come out of that, sir, and go up on the quarter-deck instantly!" said the first luff, the wart actually presenting an alarming appearance as his ire increased. "I'll teach you to treat your superiors with disrespect. On deck at once, sir!"

"An' is it me ye're spaking of taching, Mr. Wartnose? Is it me ye're orthering about as if I was a nager? An' is it me ye're spaking to 'bout supariors? I'd 'av' ye to know that I came here to tache, an' not to be taught, ye auld bag of wind; an' may the pigs root me up whin I'm dead if I stir an inch for any of ye!"

"Send the sergeant of marines here!" said Mr. Barnacle, in a voice of thunder. "Go down, sergeant, with a file of marines, and bring that man on deck." And before Mr. O'Classics knew what he was about four stout marines had seized him and carried him to the upper deck, notwithstanding all his kicking and swearing. There he was kept between two gun-slides until the affair was reported to the captain. Finding that matters were growing rather serious, he became more gentle, and when the captain sent for him was quite a reasonable creature.

I don't know what the result of the interview was, but the captain intended to investigate the difficulty in the morning. The school-master was ordered to mess in the cockpit, and thus ended the first supper I sat down to on board a ship of war. Of course, none of us were any better for the meal, for the cheese was the only thing left, and no one cared about supping on that. Mr. Barnacle was down on the school-master, right or wrong, for he said he had no doubt he had commenced the difficulty, as he had been so insolent to him. His wart was always a great source of annoyance to him, and he never forgave any one who made an allusion to it.

CHAPTER V.

VERY SNAKY.

THE next morning after all the row we were ordered to prepare for general quarters, and I was stationed as one of the captain's aides, a position I felt quite proud of. I anticipated great delight in seeing the big guns manœuvred, and watched all the preparations with great interest. Every one seemed to be in a hurry, for it was the first time the guns had been exercised since the ship was put in commission, and it was not likely that everything would go right the first time.

At nine o'clock the drum beat to quarters, the officers and men hurried to their guns as quickly as if an enemy was actually in sight, and before the drum had stopped beating every one was at his post, and the ship throughout was as quiet as death. Then commenced the mustering of the men and the reporting of the divisions by the officers. When the last officer reported, the first luff in turn reported to the captain, who was standing on the poop with his sword buckled on, surrounded by four little aides, all smaller than myself.

When Mr. Barnacle made his report the captain ordered him to go on with the exercise. The guns were accordingly cast loose, and for one hour the men were drilled in all the evolutions likely to occur in a naval combat. We had a splendid crew as far as their physical appearance could be judged of, and they handled those large guns as if they were merely toys. I thought sometimes that they would injure the ship's sides by running them out so hard, but she was a strong-built old bark, and had stood worse hammering than that in her time.

After the exercise was over the lieutenants reported their divisions secure, and the first luff reported again to the captain, who ordered the retreat to be beaten and the men to leave their quarters.

"These men will require a great deal of drilling, Mr. Barnacle," said the captain, "to bring them up to high-water mark. They don't handle their guns as they ought to do, and they are very green at boarding."

"I was going to remark, sir, that I thought the men had done very well for the first time. I don't remember ever to have seen guns worked so well by a new crew. I should not be afraid to go into action with them to-morrow," said Mr. Barnacle.

"Afraid, sir; of course not. Who said anything about fear? It's a feeling I don't know anything about, but a man can wish to have his crew in discipline without being afraid, Mr. Barnacle."

"Certainly, sir; but the world was not made in a day, and no one can expect a new crew to work better than ours have this morning. In my experience in the navy I have never seen anything better."

"That may be, Mr. Barnacle, but you must not forget that my experience is greater than yours, and that I have seen many things which you have not seen. I have been attached to the service thirty-seven years, and, of course, sir, I must pretend to know more about it than a gentleman who has been in but twenty-four years."

"Granted, sir, granted," said Mr. Barnacle, the wart beginning to swell up with anger; "but recollect, Captain Marvellous, that nineteen years out of my twenty-four have been spent at sea, two on shore duty, and three years waiting orders, while, if I am not mistaken, you have only seen eight years' service at sea, twelve on shore duty and special service, and seventeen on leave of absence. This is the first frigate you ever sailed in, and you have never been first lieutenant of anything larger than a ten-gun brig. Excuse me, Captain Marvellous, for alluding to these things, but you are so continually speaking to me about my want of experience that I took the pains to overhaul the 'Navy Register' to see how we compare together."

"Pooh! my dear sir," said the captain, "that has nothing to do with experience. Experience ain't learnt by going to sea all the time. Why, Mr. Barnacle, the best sailor I ever met with in my life was never at sea, and never had his foot on board a ship of any kind. I don't mean to say that you have not seen sea service, but what I do mean to say is this, that you have not arrived at that age when a man can judge and act perfectly right in all matters relating to our profession. It is not so much being at sea that is required as a mature judgment which will allow you to jump to right conclusions at once. Now that kind of maturity can only be

AN OPINION ABOUT HISTORY.   53

found on shore, and for that reason I have not endeavored to swell up my list of sea service."

The wart grew pale once more, and Mr. Barnacle could not resist laughing outright. "Why, really, captain," he said, "I thought when a man arrived at the age of forty (which is my age) that he was in the prime of life, mentally and physically, and my own observation leads me to believe that if a man's judgment is not mature at thirty it never will be."

"All a mistake, Mr. Barnacle. Man's judgment is like wine—the older it gets the better it grows; and even at a hundred a man's judgment is better than at thirty, provided he don't go to sea too much."

"How is it, then, Captain Marvellous, that professional men on shore retire to the shades of private life at the age of sixty, and assign as a reason that they are too old to attend properly to public affairs, and you are now within three years of that age yourself? Not that I mean to say in your case that you are not fully capable of attending faithfully to your duties, but I merely say what I have said to convince you that experience of a profession is not always consequent on age. Now, sir, there was Napoleon, who commanded the army of Italy when he was a mere youth. Julius Cæsar was not thirty when he conquered half the world, and Alexander the Great was so young that he sat down and cried because he had no more kingdoms to conquer."

"I never read anything about Napoleon Bonyparte, Mr. Barnacle. He was a man whose character I despised. I believe he did win some few battles, but they were the result of good luck more than good management. He was entirely too young to have any judgment. As to Julius Cæsar, he was nothing but a savage, and Alexander the Great was not fit to be intrusted with the charge of a schooner's deck. But we are getting on to history, Mr. Barnacle, which I consider the worst thing an officer can overload his mind with. For my part I pride myself on never reading anything but the 'National Intelligencer,' which contains all the information an officer ought to know. Reading so much makes sea-lawyers of you all, and I hope to heaven they will never establish a naval school. If they do, it will be the ruin of the navy. But to return to the subject of the crew. Mr. Barnacle, were you on the lakes in the last war?"

"No, sir; I was cruising in the President frigate most of the time, and was only an acting midshipman."

"But I was on the lakes in Perry's squadron, sir, and there's where I gained my experience. Ah! you would have seen work if you had been there, sir; such sailors the world never saw. I was in the commodore's ship, and the smallest man we had on board was six feet two, and stout in proportion; many of them were four feet across the shoulders and one foot between the eyes. Why, sir, I have seen those men take hold of the long thirty-twos, throw off the side-tackles, and take off the tracks, and run the guns out with such force that they would recoil, run out and in again, and then jump up and strike the beams. And then after the fight, sir, it would have done your heart good to see them. There was no skulking on the doctor's list by the wounded; they scorned such a thing, and would not acknowledge even that they were hurt. You will scarcely credit it, sir, and I would not believe it if I had not seen it, but after the action the wounded only requested half an hour to prepare themselves for duty, and I saw them myself sitting on the gun-slides picking the grape-shot out of their bodies with marline-spikes; and the captain of the maintop, who lost his own arm, which was knocked overboard, actually spliced an arm of one of his messmates on to his stump, and was at the weather-earing reefing topsails the next morning."

"They must have been a wonderful crew, Captain Marvellous. I never heard that mentioned in the history of the war. Such deeds should be made public."

"Oh, we never thought much of such things in those days. It was taken as a matter of course," said the captain.

"I am afraid, Captain Marvellous, we will never bring our present crew to the same state of perfection."

"Oh, that I don't expect. If I can get them to do half as well, it is as much as I can hope for. Why, sir, I have seen the men on the lakes load and fire the thirty-two pounders four times in a minute, and firing at a hogshead six hundred yards off, nine shots out of ten struck it. That Lake Erie fleet," he continued, "was a remarkable fleet altogether, Mr. Barnacle. I remember the first axe that was put into the trees. When we had to cut the timber to build the ships the trees tumbled down so fast under the blows that it was like a game of nine-pins. Sometimes thirty or forty would fall at one time, and the ground was actually covered with dead squirrels which were killed by the fall. That squirrel business was a godsend to us, for we had no provisions on the lakes. So while one party were felling the trees another party were picking

BUILDING SHIPS OF GREEN TIMBER.

up the squirrels and salting them down in barrels. The men enjoyed the food very much, and I do believe that it affected their physical condition. They were the most active fellows aloft I ever saw, and I have seen them run in and out on the yards without touching anything with their hands in the heaviest weather; they were, if anything, more active than squirrels."

"I wonder the Government has never introduced it into the navy, Captain Marvellous; the Western country abounds with the little animals, and you can buy them there at three cents apiece."

"Wait, Mr. Barnacle, until I am navy commissioner, and you will see a contract made to introduce the squirrel-meat into the navy. I want all the credit of it myself, and, therefore, don't want the thing mentioned.

"But I was telling you about cutting that timber. You know that we were only fifty days from the time the first axe echoed in the forest until all the ships were ataunto and the sails bent. Quick work, Mr. Barnacle; but we had a devil of a time in getting the paints to stick on the sides. The timber was so green that the sap ran out like rain, and all the carpenters in the squadron were kept at work dubbing down the outside planking, for the wood sprouted so fast that there was some danger of the ships being covered with bushes; one tree actually sprouted off from the rudder-head, and was such a beautiful ornament to the quarter-deck that we allowed it to grow. The commodore used to take his afternoon nap under the shade of the branches; unfortunately, it was shot away during the action, and was cut off so clean that it looked as if it had been smoothed off with a carpenter's adze."

"You must have had some hard service and seen some very ticklish times on the lakes, and while you were cutting down those trees," said the first luff, whose wart had got quite pale once more, and who seemed amused at the captain's stories and was endeavoring to draw him out.

"You may well say so, Mr. Barnacle; no set of men ever went through more severe trials. Independent of the hardship of the forest life, which but few of us were accustomed to, we had to be on the lookout for the wild beasts and the innumerable venomous reptiles which almost covered the ground. I was once very near loosing my life by a hoop-snake. Did you ever see a hoop-snake, Mr. Barnacle?"

"No, sir; I never heard of one."

"Well, thank your stars you never met one, for they are the

most venomous serpents in the world. I was out in the woods one day with my gun in my hand looking for bear, when my attention was attracted by a little bee that was buzzing around a tree, and every now and then knocking his head slightly against the bark. At last I saw a little door open in the tree about the size of my button, a little bee popped out his head, and the fellow who had been buzzing about outside instantly popped in. The door was closed after him, and I could see nothing but the smooth bark. Four or five little bees came at intervals of one or two minutes, and always one at a time; they knocked three times with their heads against the tree, the little door flew open, the watchman inside looked out, and the little fellows popped in as before. I was so struck with the intelligence of these little insects that I stood watching them for nearly an hour. I knocked gently three times with a small piece of stick, wishing to see if they would obey my summons, but no answer came to my call for admittance. Presently I tried it again, when the little door was opened just sufficient to allow the watchman inside to peep forth, but it was shut to again so suddenly that I scarcely got a sight of his head. The garrison inside seemed in an instant to be on the alert, for they kept up such a humming that it sounded like a band of music. Suddenly I heard a noise behind me like the hissing of a goose, and, looking around, I discovered a huge black snake as thick as my thigh, and fifteen or sixteen feet long. He was within twenty feet of me, his head raised a foot from the ground, his eyes shining like diamonds, and his tail shaking with anger. It was such a beautiful animal that I was almost fascinated by him, and, having heard that these snakes had the power sometimes to charm smaller animals, I determined to get out of his way. I recollected that our good Mother Eve was once ill advised by the serpent, and it was through him that we were all doing penance on earth. How, indeed, did I know but what this was the same serpent? he looked so wicked and intelligent. I determined, however, to bruise his head with my heel before I had done with him, so that the predictions of the Bible might be fulfilled to the letter. Raising my gun, I took aim right at his ugly mouth, which he kept wide open, with his ugly fangs shaking as if they were hung on springs.

"Never in my life did I see such a sardonic-looking countenance as I pointed my gun down his throat; his eyes seemed to twinkle with merriment at the bare idea of my confronting him, and he looked at me as much as to say, Fire away; powder and

A PURSUIT.

ball can't hurt me. I felt nervous for a moment, but I said to myself, It will never do for one of Perry's men to be afraid of the devil even, so here's at your snakeship, and with that I fired a load of buckshot right into his throat. Lord bless you, Mr. Barnacle, he did not mind it any more than if it had been so much sugar put into his mouth. He shook his head at me, while his mouth actually had a hideous smile of contempt about it. His head gradually rose up three or four feet, while his tail commenced turning up in the air likewise, and, forming half a circle with his body, he came toward me, his wicked eyes looking at me with an intensity that almost made my blood run cold. Human nature could stand it no longer, Mr. Barnacle. I really thought it was the devil, and, must I own it? one of Perry's men turned and fled! Excitement, only excitement, Mr. Barnacle, lent wings to my speed, and I really do believe I was running at the rate of forty miles an hour. I had thrown away my gun, kicked off my shoes, and parted with my hat to make me as light as possible, but it was no use. On looking around to see where my pursuer was, I saw a large black hoop rolling along after me with the speed of a locomotive. He had taken his tail in his mouth and made a perfect circle of himself. How he was propelled along I could not tell; all I know is he moved as smoothly as an engine and was making a perfect whirlwind behind him, and gaining on me all the time. I had nothing else to do but put on more steam, but steam could not save me, for I could hear the snake close behind me, and knew there was no hope for me unless I could reach the wood-cutters, who were just heaving in sight. Just at that moment I heard something snap like a pistol, and, looking around, I found that the varmint had fastened his teeth in my coat-tail.

"This circumstance only added to my speed, and I fairly flew over the ground until the critter stood out straight behind me. If anything, Mr. Barnacle, his tail was a leetle topped up. I was obliged to slip off my coat and leave it in the animal's possession as the only means of getting rid of him. That was the last I saw of the hoop-snake."

"A most remarkable snake," said the first lieutenant. "No wonder, Captain Marvellous, that you never grew any after that adventure."

CHAPTER VI.

SCENES IN A BREAD-LOCKER; AND HOW TAILORS SOMETIMES GET PAID OFF.

I HAD been on board ship about ten days when orders came for us to proceed to sea. There was animation in every eye at this good news, for all hands were anxious to get to the Mediterranean and away from N——, where we were bored to death by tailors, shoemakers, hatters, and washerwomen. The middies had spent all their advance, and bid fair to pay off their bills with a flying topsail, a method of satisfying one's creditors very common in the navy at that time.

The day before the ship was to sail, the steerage was so crowded with tradesmen with anxious faces that it was impossible to move about with any comfort; and there were numberless inquiries for Mr. Reckless, who it appears had become indebted to the above-mentioned tradesmen to a large amount. That worthy gentleman had gone on the sick list, and had stowed himself away in a small empty bread-room in the cockpit, where, having rigged a table, he was amusing himself playing checkers with a midshipman by the name of Brace, who was also desirous of eluding his creditors. But it is astonishing what noses N—— tailors have for smelling out a midshipman who owes them anything, and Mr. Camphor, in searching about, found himself in the cockpit, where Mr. O'Classics was busily employed writing up "The Plume of the Classics."

"Have you seen Mr. Reckless down here lately, sir?" said the tailor to Mr. O'Classics, in a very polite and fascinating manner.

"To the divil wid Mr. Rickless an' all his crew! No, I niver seen him, an' may the cat fly away wid me but I nivir want to lay me two papers on him agin, onless it be to see him hung, which I'm sure he will be onless he minds his manners. Don't boder me 'bout Mr. Rickless; I 'av'n't time to be wasting on either Mr. Rickless or his friends."

"I only asked you a civil question, sir, and meant no harm. I am looking for Mr. Reckless to get some money which he owes me; I am afraid he is trying to give me the slip."

"Oh! is it there ye are? an' it's money he's after owin' you? Faith, an' I don't think he has a haporth worth of anything but

A TAILOR ON BOARD.

impertinence; but I can soon ferret him out," said the teacher, "an' it will give me a deal of pleasure to make him fork over. Och, Mr. Rickless, an' is it the poor tailors ye'd be after chating, bad manners to ye? Come this way, my good Tailorman, an' I'll show you the way to his private room, where no doubt you'll find a dozen of them hatching their diviltry thegather."

I had but a short time before gone into the bread-room to apprise Reckless that he was wanted, and that the hawks were about, and, as soon as we heard the conversation of the teacher and the tailor, the light was blown out and the door fastened on the inside.

Knock, knock, knock from the cockpit, but no answer from within. "Divil tak' me but he's here, Mr. Tailorman, an' faith we'll have him out, for it's a blessed shame to see a poor thradesman chated clane out of his money in this manner, an' this a free counthry, too; I wonder in what part of the blessed Constitution he finds the authority for his bad manners, bad luck till him. He calls me the mad school-maester, Mr. Tailorman; faith an' I'll show ye how much mad there is about Barney O'Classics in the twinkling of a bed-post. Come out here, I say, you mad divil, Rickless; come out, I say, an' pay yer honest debts, an' don't be for shaming the good name of yer farder and moderer if ye 'av' any. Come out, ye divil's brat, and face yer tailor."

No answer came to this appeal, and Mr. O'Classics proceeded to shake the door, in hopes of breaking it in, but it was too strong for him, and he at length reluctantly gave it up.

"An' is it a poor pine door that ye think will keep Mr. Madtacher from gettin' at ye? Oh, but ye's mistaken; I am not the man to give up that road. Just wait a minit, my good Tailorman, an' I'll nail him up so that he can't get out for a week."

"But that would not do me any good, sir; I want him to get out so that I can get my money from him," said the tailor.

"Don't you know, my good man, that in ould Ireland when we want to catch a fox we always stop up the hole he goes into, an' then he's always sure to come out?"

"But then, sir, you can take your time watching him, but here time is precious, and I can do more by seeing Mr. Reckless than I can by keeping him locked up."

"Faith, an' may the bats put the candle out, but I never thought av that; that is quite a different affair. So I must go to work and unearth the fox, but first and foremost I must nail fast the door, so that the divil can't escape. Whin I was in ould Ireland I was a bit of a carpintir, an' 'av' always taken my tools wid me whiriver I go; at least I'm cock sure I've a hammer an' nails, an' a small saw for boring square holes."

While Mr. O'Classics went in search of his tools, Mr. Camphor was left to look out for the prisoners, and as soon as the Irishman was out of sight the bread-room door was softly opened and Reckless put forth his head.

"Ah, my dear Camphor, how are you?" he exclaimed, "and what do you mean by joining league with that wild Irishman? He'll get you into all kinds of difficulties if you follow his advice, and I assure you I have not the least idea of not paying you. I intend to pay off every cent I owe you this very morning."

"I am really delighted to hear it, Mr. Reckless," said the tailor, who was all bows and smiles. "I thought the gentleman was rather queer when he talked of nailing up the door and fastening a set of gentlemen inside."

"Just get that light, Mr. Camphor, and walk in here and we will settle up in no time; our light has gone out." So handing the light to Reckless from off the cockpit table, Mr. Camphor walked into the bread-room, the door was hauled to behind him, and, before he had time to think, a large bread-bag was hauled over his head, his heels were tripped up, and he found himself treated like a prisoner.

"Don't be uneasy, my good fellow," said Brace (who was holding the tailor down while Reckless and myself were tying his legs); "we don't mean to hurt you, but have a desire to take you to the Mediterranean just for the benefit of your health. It is no use to holler down here, for no one can hear you but the mad Irishman, and the first word you utter in the way of complaint you will get your mouth and eyes full of bread-dust."

Poor Mr. Camphor was frightened almost out of his senses, and the idea of going to the Mediterranean for the benefit of his health, shut up in a dark bread-room, was more than the nerves of a ninth part of a man could bear.

"O gentlemen! gentlemen!" he piteously exclaimed, "you can't be in earnest surely, even to keep me here one night, much less play me so foul a trick as to let the ship sail with me fastened up in a bread-locker? What have I done to merit this unkindness at your hands? I only came on board to get my money, and I think this is very shabby treatment after all the credit I have given you; and you, Mr. Reckless, in particular, who have been on our books three years."

"All of which time, sir, I have been paying you ten per cent interest," said Reckless, interrupting him.

I don't know what the reply of the tailor would have been, but he was interrupted by the voice of the school-master calling for him.

"May the cat ate her kittins but the tailor's flown up the chimbly! an', divil take him, he's carried off the light. I say, my Tailorman, where are ye? Is this one of the divil midshipmate's tricks? Faith, an' I shouldn't wonder if they roast an' ate him afore they're done wid 'im, if they 'av' 'im. May I nivir wear a nightcap but I'll fasten 'em all up, anyhow!" And with that he proceeded to nail up the door, which he did most effectually.

"Now, Mr. Camphor," said Reckless, "you see we are all innocent of this business; it has all been done by the very person with whom you were plotting against us, and if you do go the cruise, it will be through the agency of that madman; for our parts, we have bread enough to live a month on, though we will be rather short of water. We, of course, will divide the biscuit with you, but I am sorry to say you must not count on any of the water in the pitcher, for there is not more than enough for us three."

"But, my good friend, Mr. Reckless, what is the necessity for our staying here prisoners when all you have to do is to cry out and we will soon be relieved?"

"And do you think, Mr. Camphor, that any of this party would cry out for the sake of being let out of prison, after being nailed up by a fellow who has not an idea above a pig and potato? No, sir!" said Reckless, in a decided tone of voice; "and I answer for the whole party, I would stay here and starve to death before I would make one sign of submission to that Paddy. There is but one way I know of, Mr. Camphor, to make me change our resolution, and I don't know exactly about that."

"In the name of heaven, gentlemen, what way is there to get out of this? I am sure I will do anything to assist you."

"Well, that is getting to be reasonable, Mr. Camphor; but you must swear to agree to all we ask, and to assist us in all our endeavors to get out."

"Oh, anything, anything! I swear to do anything rather than stay here all night and run the risk of sailing with the ship to-morrow."

"Well, then, sir, *our* proposition is this : you are first to sign a paper releasing me from payment for three years to come, and to accept a draft from me on the Sandy Hook Sand Bank in full of all demands. I don't intend that you shall lose anything by me; I only desire to defer payment, allowing you to charge your ten per cent as usual. Are you agreed to that, Mr. Camphor?"

"I suppose I must, Mr. Reckless, though the times are rather hard; but never mind so that I get out of this."

"Hold on, my good friend, you have not heard all the terms: we expect you to advance us enough to pay for a good oyster supper to-night, provided we can get on shore; and now write down on the back of the bill the acquittance you have agreed to."

Camphor fairly groaned at such terms, but it was no use to object, so he signified his assent.

"And now, Mr. Camphor, we will get you out of this, provided you assist us in punishing the mad school-master, for we must serve him out for all this nailing up."

"I will do anything, Mr. Reckless, only let me out; and if ever you catch me chasing midshipmen into the bread-locker again, may I forfeit my character—"

"As the ninth part of a man," added Brace.

Everything being settled according to agreement, Mr. Camphor was let out of the bag and the papers signed.

"And now," said the fertile Reckless, "let us think what is to be done; we must first get out and manage somehow to get the Irishman in, and I promise him he shall have less for supper for two days than he got the first night he came on board. Now, gentlemen, follow my motions."

Reckless commenced pounding and kicking at the door, in which all of us joined, and no one more heartily than the tailor.

"Ah! are ye ther', me spalpeens? Faith an' I thought ye'd all flown up the chimbly. Kick away, my horses, but little oats will ye get from me."

"Let us out, Mr. O'Classics, we are suffocating; one of us has fainted already."

"Och! divil a bit onything could sufficate one av ye; ye could brathe brimstone an' it would not hurt ye," he replied; "the divil always takes care av his own."

"I assure you, Mr. O'Classics, that Mr. Marline has fainted, and the poor tailor is at his last gasp."

"Och! are ye there, my poor Tailorman? An' 'av' the divils

got you in their clutches? Faith, but I pity ye. I'll give ye fresh air, my boys, but a very small portion, I assure you."

We heard something at length boring into the door, and presently a boring-bit came through on our side; then it was withdrawn and came through at another point, until finally he bored a complete circle about the size of a man's head, and then proceeded to cut it out with a circular saw.

"That's capital," said Reckless. "We must get him to look through the hole by some cajolery, and then, Brace, you and I must seize him by the hair of his head and hold him there, and the first thing we must do is to commence groaning in a feeble voice, and make believe we are dying. Brace and myself will stand on each side of the hole and seize him when he puts his head through, which I am sure he will do the moment he finds we are silent."

The saw had gone nearly round the circle, when the teacher knocked it in with his fist. "There's a brathing-hole for ye, me fine fellows. Faith an' ye'd be glad to see the carcass of that summer goose coming through, wouldn't ye? Arrah! an' it's but little goose ye'll get from Barney O'Classics. Yer silent, ar' ye? an' will ye may be, ye ill-favored loons, after all yer cantankerin', but ye'll spake fast enough afore I draw a nail for ye's. I say, me good tailor, how do ye fare in that divil's den? You'll be lucky if ye are not atin an' roasted afore ye get out; an' but for you, may I nivir hear the piper agin if I'd give them a mouthful of fresh air. Oh, ye ar' all a-gruntin', ar' ye, like pigs as ye are? an' maybe ye ar' sick, an' I'll take a look in and see how yer doin'." And with that he commenced working his head through the hole, which was not any too large for it. His chin had no sooner crossed the lower part of the hole than he was seized on both sides by the two midshipmen, and held as firmly as if he had been in a vise.

"Let me go, ye tundering villains!" he screamed. "An' is it me that's caught in me own trap? May yer teeth drap out, ye villain Rickless, yer pulling my hair out by the roots! Och! but I'll murther every mother's son av ye when I get my ten fingers on ye. An' it is ye, my fine tailor, that was prethending ye were dead? But may the cat fly away wid me an' I'll make ye swallow yer own goose hot, an' shave yer eyebrows off wid yer own shears! I will, I will!"

"A good idea, Mr. Camphor," shouted Reckless. "Get out your shears and be beforehand with him. Hold him tight, Brace, while he does it *secundum artem*. There's Latin for you, Mr.

School-master. *Multum in parvo,* which means a big head in a small hole, Mr. O'Classics. And now we are going to give you a *quid pro quo,* which means a good lathering with this paint-brush, and cut off your hair *seriatim,* which means after we have shaved off your eyebrows; and, moreover, *cæteris paribus,* which means when we have clipped you into something like ship-shape; *quantum sufficit,* which means until you look a little decent; *ne plus ultra,* which means when we can do nothing more to you we will place you in *statu quo,* which means let your head out of that hole; *penxit,* which means beautifully illustrated, *pro bono publico,* for the admiration of the whole ship's company. Now, Mr. O'Classics, there's Latin for you to chew, and take the advice of a friend and submit to your fate like a good Paddy. Marline, give him a potato to keep his courage up."

"Do it if ye dar, ye ill-born imp! I scorn yer Latin as I scorn ye all. An' ye vile tailor, for every hair ye clip from me I'll make yer life *tedium vitæ* to you, which, according to younder villain's translation, manes to break ivery bone in yer body."

"Do your duty, Mr. Camphor, *tempus fugit,* which means we have no time to lose." And the timid tailor marched up, and with one clip took off the starboard eyebrow.

"Well done, old Camphor! Off with the other one, and get him on an even keel; he has a heavy list to port." And off went the other, amid the shouts of the party—except the tailor, who was too frightened to laugh.

"An' there's a broken leg for ivry eyebraw ye cut off, ye robbers; an' while yer at it ye might as will cut off the rist av them. Och! ye scoundrils, ye'll rue the day whin I get hauld av ye. Cut away! cut away! Barney O'Classics can live widout hair."

"You hear what he says, Mr. Camphor?" said Brace. "Now let's trim him like they do the fellows in the penitentiary. Go to work and shave the starboard side of his head, and his beard is not cut according to the regulations anyhow. Don't be frightened, Pat, we won't hurt you; we are only going to treat you as you would treat us, if you could. Go ahead, Camphor, or you will never get out of this." And with that the tailor went to work with his shears and soon cut away the starboard side of the school-master's hair, and then made an attack on his whiskers. While performing this delicate operation, Mr. Camphor approached his hand rather too near the Irishman's mouth, and before he knew what was coming he found his forefinger suddenly seized in Mr. O'Classic's teeth, and

MR. O'CLASSICS IS RELEASED.

held there as if it was in a vise. The pain was so great that he dropped the shears in a minute, and sung out "Murder!" "Fire!" "Thieves!" and then fell to awful cursing and swearing, which astonished us all very much, knowing him to be a strict member of the Church.

Reckless and Brace pulled away at the teacher's hair in hopes of releasing the tailor, but it was no use, for the more they pulled the harder he bit, and the tailor was near fainting with pain when he was rescued by a party we little desired to see.

It appeared afterward that the captain had appointed the day before the ship sailed for the commodore of the station to inspect her. They had gone their rounds, and were about going on deck again when the smothered cry of murder met their ears. In a moment the whole party descended into the cockpit, when they were astonished at the sight of some one with his head through the door of the bread-room, and his arms and legs flying about like a jumping-Jack's, for just at that moment I was painting his face with some red lead which had been left in the bread-room, and he was making violent struggles to get away. The cries of murder still went on, and even the school-master began to bellow like a bull.

I could hear the captain's voice amid all the din singing out, "What in the name of heaven is all this, Barnacle? Here's a murder committed! Bless my soul, if Mr. O'Classics has not committed suicide! Poor fellow, poor fellow! such an elegant scholar as he was."

"He is not dead, sir, that's very certain, as his arms and legs testify. He is as mad as a March hare, and is always running his head into difficulty, and I should not be surprised if he has run it through the door."

"Och, but thir murthering me outright!" yelled the teacher in agonized tones. "May the cat fly away wid 'em for a sit of divil's midshipmates!"

"Have him got out somehow or other, Mr. Barnacle; we may save him yet," said the captain. And Mr. Barnacle, who did not seem to care whether he was dead or alive, coolly proceeded to call some men to release the teacher from his perilous position. Four sailors came down, and, seizing him by the body, they went to work to haul him out "by main strength and nonsense," as they say in the navy, and at last succeeded in landing him on the deck more dead than alive. Such a spectacle as he presented, with his face painted red, his eyebrows cut off, his hair shaved close to his head, and his whiskers horribly mutilated, no one ever saw. The doctor was sent for immediately, and everything was done to restore the poor fellow to his senses. In the mean time the most piteous moans came from the bread-room—the poor tailor still suffering perfect agony from his finger, which had nearly been bitten off.

"There is something wrong inside the bread-room, Mr. Barnacle," said the captain. "Have the door opened and see what it is. Make haste, sir, some one may be dying." But the door being nailed, it was found necessary to send for the carpenter to open it.

"This is the most inexplicable circumstance I have ever met with," said the captain. "Here I am showing the commodore around the ship, my ears are startled by the cry of murder. I rush down into the cockpit, find the school-master has run his head through a plank in the bread-room door, and has died in an attempt to commit suicide; I have him hauled out, find him stone dead, his head clean shaved, his eyebrows pulled out by the roots, and body covered with blood. Why, sir, the Newgate calendar never contained anything to compare to it. It's worse than arson or breach of promise, both of which I look upon as horrible. Are there any deep gashes about him, doctor? I expect you will find the cuts in the region of the heart."

"He is not dead, sir," said the surgeon; "only a little faint. Neither is this blood, sir; it is only red lead which some one has been smearing his face with. Don't be uneasy, sir, he is coming to now. Some one has been playing him rather a practical joke, and judging from the nails in this door and those implements (pointing to the hammer and saw), some one is locked up inside who, by their moaning, may require more assistance than this gentleman."

By this time the carpenter had arrived and proceeded to break open the door, and there stood revealed the persons of the inside party looking as innocent as white mice; the tailor did not wait to be questioned, but, to the astonishment of every one, bolted up the hatch and over the ship's side before any one could stop him, and that was the last we ever saw of Camphor, the tailor. I am told that he has never put his foot on board a ship of war since that time.

"What in the name of heaven does all this mean, gentlemen?" said the captain. "Come out of that, sirs, and explain the mystery at once. Oh, you're there, Mr. Reckless! well, that accounts for half of it at once. Speak out, sir, immediately, and explain this mystery."

"No, Captain Marvellous," said Reckless, who pretended to have his feelings much hurt, "I must leave Mr. Brace to explain, for you always consider me in the wrong; and in this instance you will find me a much wronged and injured individual."

"Well, then, Mr. Brace, give us your version of the affair, and remember, sir, to tell the truth and nothing but the truth, for there is nothing I so much dislike as prevarication of any kind."

"The facts are these, Captain Marvellous," said Brace: "being rather a cool day, Mr. Reckless and myself thought we would try and warm ourselves in the bread-room, as we both had chills this morning. Mr. Camphor, the tailor, came on board to take our measure for a vest apiece, and invite us to an oyster-supper this evening, so we sent for him to come down in the bread-room. He had no sooner entered the room than the door was closed behind him, and some one on the outside commenced nailing it up, and, as we were almost suffocated for want of fresh air, we commenced begging the party, whoever it was, on the outside to let us out. In answer to our appeal we heard Mr. O'Classics in the cockpit laughing at us, and he threatened to suffocate us all, and called us the most horrible names in Irish you can possibly conceive. After a while he condescended to cut that hole in the door, and then put his head through to laugh at us, and there he stayed talking nothing but Latin to us for twenty minutes or more, and finally told us in his brogue that officers in the navy were all ignoramuses, because we did not comprehend his Irish Latin. He had a great deal of trouble to get his head in the hole, and after being there so long his head must have swollen, for he could not get it out again. He called on us to help him, but fearing he wanted to play some tricks upon us we refused to go near him. Mr. Camphor, who is a good-hearted man, feeling a pity for him, undertook to help him get his head out, but the ungrateful wretch seized him by the finger while he was doing him an act of kindness, and held him there as if he had been in a vise; that is exactly what he wished to do with one of us, for what reason I do not know, for we have always treated him with the most profound respect! Finding that Mr. Camphor was nearly fainting with the pain, we endeavored to pry Mr. O'Classics' mouth open with the only thing we could find, which was a red paint-brush, but without effect, and Mr. Camphor, out of revenge, cut off his eyebrows, hair, and whiskers, in hopes that would make him let go his hold. I am perfectly satisfied, sir, that he intended to murder us all, and I am as well convinced as I ever was of anything in my life that he is crazy."

"I knew it was one of that mad school-master's pranks, Captain Marvellous," said the first luff, "and it will end in his doing them some injury yet; for a man who could shut up three persons in a bread-room for the purpose of suffocating them would be guilty of any act."

"*Suav-i-ter in Modo, For-ti-ter in Re,* an' that's what I am," said the school-master, slowly settling himself on end; "but if ye say I'm mad, or crazy, ye *Lu-sus Natu-ræ*, wid dat tundering wart on yer nose, yer guilty of a *Lap-sus Lin-guæ*, which manes, accordin' to the translation of that divil's imp, Rickless, that yer telling now a most tunderin' lie."

"Mr. O'Classics! Mr. O'Classics! do my ears deceive me?" said Captain Marvellous. "Can it be possible that it can be you talking in that way to the first lieutenant of my ship? Silence, sir, immediately, and don't let me hear you speak another word of that kind, or I will prefer charges against you, and have you dismissed the service."

"Oh! to the divil wid your sarvice! May old Satan himself take me av this is the kind of sarvice you do a man! May my bagpipes burst but I want none av it! Faith, doctor, yer the only gintilman prisint, for ye did go flotherin' about me when ye thought me was dyin'; but divil a bit is Barney going to die till he gets his rivenge out av the United States navy. And, look here, Captain Marvellous, they may will call ye Tom Pipper, who was kicked out av hell for lying, for av yer not lying yersel', yer aidin' an' abettin' others to lie, an' I don't care a snap of a copper for ony av ye. As to your fast lieutenant, wid a wart on his nose, the divil will only get his own when he haves his net over him, for he's a bigger scoundrel than that divil's son, Rickless, who I 'av' promised to brak ivry bone in his body whiniver I git my tin fingers ontill him."

"The Lord have mercy on the poor man's soul," said the captain; "he is crazy as a March hare. What do you think it is best to do with him, Mr. Barnacle? He may get over this in a few days, and I don't want to lose him, for he is an elegant scholar. Didn't you hear him quoting Latin just now?"

"Yes, sir," said Mr. Barnacle (whose wart was as large about this time as a good-sized strawberry), "I heard him speaking Latin, and I think the best thing to be done with the gentleman until he comes to his senses is to put him in the bread-locker, and see if he won't cool off. He can quote Latin there to his heart's content and learn what is due to his superiors. I do not think it safe at present to let him go at large."

"If yer goin' to lock me up on the ground av being *non compos mentis*, yer much mistaken, auld blanderbuss. I'd like to see the man that'll touch me." And with that he seized the saw which lay near the door, and, jumping to his feet, put himself in an attitude of defense. Mr. Barnacle made some sign to the four sailors who were standing in the cockpit waiting orders, and in the twinkling of a tea-pot—to use one of Mr. O'Classics' metaphors—he was down on the deck again and tied hand and foot, the bread-room door was opened to receive him, and then, by orders of Mr. Barnacle, nailed up so securely that he could not open it from the inside.

"Poor man!" said the captain; "what a pity it is to see so brilliant an intellect clouded with insanity! I am afraid we will have to part with him, Mr. Barnacle, for he is really dangerous. And now, gentlemen," he said, turning to the midshipmen, "see the evil effects of going into the bread-room instead of keeping to your own apartments. If you had not gone there this would not have happened; but at the same time I am glad that none of you were in the wrong, and I hope you never may be." And turning round, he proceeded up the cockpit ladder.

Just at this moment the school-master, who had got his legs loose, put his head to the hole in the door, and a most ludicrous-looking object he was. "One ward wid ye, Captain Marvellous, 'fore ye go," he said, and the captain stopped half-way on the ladder. "All I 'av' to say to ye is this: I belave what the warld say av ye—that ye tould so many lies about a harse ye said ye bought (a full-blood Arab), that ye actally belaved it yerself, and bought a saddle an' bridle for the baste. An' that's as near the truth as ye can come. For shame on ye, ye wizen-faced divil; and that's what I call *utile cum dulce*, which means spaking the truth to ye, so that ye may mind yer manners."

"Poor man, what an intellect is there ruined!" said the captain. "Treat him kindly, Mr. Barnacle. Give him nothing but bread and water for a few days, and put him in a strait-jacket and double irons if he gets the least outrageous." So the school-master was left to his own reflections, and the midshipmen had such a laugh over the frolic that the first lieutenant had to threaten to send them all to the mast-head if they did not make less noise.

CHAPTER VII.

AWAY, AWAY, WE BOUND O'ER THE SEA.

At daylight next morning all hands were called to "up anchor," and the whole ship seemed to be alive with excitement, every one was so happy at the idea of getting to sea and on our way to the Mediterranean. The capstan-bars were shipped, the messenger brought to, and in five minutes from the time we left our hammocks the capstan was flying round to the tune of "Such a Getting Up-Stairs," played by a full band of music. Then came the order from the quarter-deck, "Paul the capstan," and the boatswain and his mates, piping through their shrill whistles, called "All hands to make sail." Again the decks were alive with bustle, each seaman trying his best to get to his post first, and before one could well look about him the gun-deck was clear and the men were all on the spar-deck ready to mount aloft. "Now, boys," said Mr. Barnacle, in his clear voice, "let us have some smart work, and you men at the sheets and halyards don't let the topmen complain of your not sheeting home quick enough, and hoist the yards as if you hadn't a sand-bag tied to your legs."

"Aloft, sail-loosers." And away flew the seamen up the rigging like so many monkeys.

"Trice up, lay out, and loose." "All ready on the top-sail yards, all ready with the lower yards, sir," came from aloft, and then the order was given to "let fall" and "sheet home." The sails fell in graceful folds from their gaskets, and as quick as lightning were hauled out to the ends of the yards, everything going "home" together. "Hoist away the top-sails," said the first lieutenant, through the speaking trumpet, and his ringing tones seemed to inspire every man in the ship and make him jump to his work. Then the fiddles struck up "First upon the Heel-tap, then upon the Toe," and the top-sail yards flew aloft as if they were propelled by steam; the topgallant-sails and royals were set with like celerity, and in as short a time as I have taken to tell of it the ship was a cloud of canvas from her deck to her trucks.

Then came the order to counter-brace the yards ready for casting, the capstan-bars were manned once more, and the anchor hove up to the bow, while the ship was gracefully turning her head to seaward.

"Hook the cat and walk away with it." And the anchor was soon at the cathead, fished, and before the ship was before the wind everything was secure.

The yards were squared as we got before the wind, the lifts and trusses hauled taut, and everything looked as trim as if it had been set for a month; the good ship seemed to be as glad to be in motion as ourselves, and, with a nice breeze after her, was soon "walking the water like a thing of life."

This was the first evolution I had ever seen performed at sea, and, though a very common one, it made a deep impression on my mind. I have seen it done in later years, but not with the same precision as on that occasion. There is sure to be some bungling in later times: one yard goes up a minute after the other, a topsail sheet gets foul of a boom-iron, one royal is set before a top-sail is fairly aloft, and the men go to work as if they were performing a penance instead of doing their duty. How is it? this will be asked; and I give the following reason, which, to the best of my belief, is the true one:

In 1820 the navy was the true home of the sailor. No one would enter the merchant service who could get employment in the Government ships, and because they were better paid and better fed than in any other marine. Then, too, every man *had* to do his duty, and skulks could not shirk their work and make the good men do double what they shipped for. We had better men because there were inducements held out to them to ship, and though that useful little animal, the "cat," sometimes scratched the back of some good-for-nothing fellow, it was always popular among the good sailors, and held in great reverence by all. Now the times are different: the pay in the merchant service is nearly double and often treble that in the navy, an unwise legislation broke up the discipline of the service, and our ships are roaming the ocean perfectly at the mercy of a set of reckless fellows who hold the places that were formerly filled by seamen. The quarter-deck is now crowded with a set of gray-headed lieutenants and unambitious passed mids, most of whom are grandfathers, and the dear little midshipmen, who used to be the admiration of all young ladies, and were sent by dozens into every ship going to sea, have no longer an existence.

Notwithstanding Mr. Barnacle's grumbling and growling about having on board "so many babies in swaddling-clothes," I can't help thinking that the service would be brisker if more of such little fellows were sent to sea in ships instead of the overgrown passed mids, who by rights ought to be elbowing the grandfather lieutenants off the quarter-deck into good sloops of war as commanders. And must I speak my regrets when that dear little "cat" fell overboard? Oh, what a loss was there, my countrymen! She was the life of the whole ship's company, so playful and so active! The very sight of her was enough to inspire the men and make the yards fly round with the braces; and then to see the boatswain's mates, how affectionately they passed their fingers through her fur, and then the kind inquiries made after her by the crew when she stayed in her bag, as sometimes happened for months. Ah! it is painful to think of her falling overboard; and if she had only left a little kitten behind, why, we might have some consolation still; but there is none: the "cat" and the little midshipmen have both disappeared from the service, and the navy will never be again what it has been in quick work.

I felt a little sad as the pilot took his leave of us after piloting us fairly outside. I remember looking at his tiny little boat, as it danced upon the waves, until it was lost sight of alongside the schooner to which it belonged. Then the officer of the deck made all sail, the ship began to move about in an uneasy manner, and I was feeling the top of my head to see if my cap was not too tight. I know I looked pale, for I felt so; and old Ben Binnacle, the quartermaster, came up to me and said, "Shall I get you a piece of fat pork, Mr. Marline?" That settled me. "Oh, horrible! fat pork!" when the sight of salt water made me sick. "Oh, take me down, quartermaster, I'm dying! Oh, Abe, why didn't I stay at home? Hurry, quartermaster, get me a bucket. Oh, grandfather, what did you send me to sea for? Forgive me, Mr. Shaker, for whitewashing your horse and tying crackers to the cat's tail; I'll do it no more. Farewell, quartermaster, I leave you my hammock in remembrance of your kindness; don't let them throw me overboard, oh, ah!" And that's all I remember that day.

CHAPTER VIII.

A MERMAN HUNTSMAN.

It was not until we had been on the ocean two days that I was able to hold up my head at all, I had been so sea-sick, and at the same time sick of the sea; but there was no retreat for me, and I had to go through with it, whether I liked it or not. I had some consolation in knowing that all the little middies were more sick even than myself, and I was the first to get on deck to my watch. Sea-sickness is an ordeal almost every one has to go through with on his first initiation in the navy, and it is so common an occurrence that no one thinks anything of it. You get little or no sympathy while you are almost throwing up your boots, and some kind-hearted person will likely offer you a piece of fat pork with a string tied to it, and assure you it is a sovereign remedy against this dreadful sickness.

Mr. Teaser was quite astonished when I told him that sea-sickness alone had kept me below. He said he thought I had more grit in me, and assured me that he had never been sea-sick in his life. Nevertheless he was kind enough not to call on me for duty, and told me I might go up on the poop and lie down on the boat's cushions, which were spread out to dry. Old Binnacle, the quartermaster, threw a flag over me, and I began to revive the moment I felt the effects of the pure fresh air.

It was a beautiful evening in the month of December, though rather cool. The sun had just sunk to rest in the western horizon, and the new moon was rising up out of the great ocean, shedding a mellow light on all below her. Our gallant frigate was slowly wending her way through the pathless deep, with scarce wind enough to fill her sails, and the little waves were running along after us like pleasant companions of our voyage. They seemed to be chasing each other in very sport on the broad breast of their ocean mother. How little did they resemble the huge and angry waves I have since seen chasing and leaping after each other in their envy and strife, and ingulfing ships and human beings in their hungry maws! I thought then that the sea was always smooth and pleasant, and I began to anticipate the delight I should feel when my sea-sickness left me, and I could go about the vessel and ascend the tall masts, which almost appeared to touch the skies.

The officers were lounging about the decks, listening to the band playing "Home, Sweet Home," and the whole ship seemed so quiet that it soon made my eyelids to droop.

I was fast forgetting my troubles in slumber, when I heard the captain's voice, and saw him coming up on the poop in company with Mr. Spicy, the chaplain, a gentleman who had the reputation of being fonder of his wine than he was of writing a sermon, and who quoted Scripture by the yard for the purpose of making himself pass for a saint. I was on the point of getting up and running away, but the fear of getting some angry reproof kept me rolled up in my flag, and, much to my inconvenience, the two came and took a seat on the taffrail close beside me.

"I think your idea is a very good one, Mr. Spicy," said the captain; "and I have no doubt but that a speech from me to the sailors every Sunday morning would have a very good effect on both the officers and crew. Jack likes a speech from the captain now and then, and it is setting a good example to the officers, and showing them the importance of sometimes holding familiar intercourse with the sailors. By the way, chaplain, how do you think it would do for me to read a chapter in the Bible every Sunday, and make a few remarks at the same time by addressing myself to the understanding of the men?"

"I think it would have a good effect, sir," said Mr. Spicy, "a capital effect; officers generally are opposed to religious services on shipboard, but when the captain sets so good an example in his person, I think it would help to remove many of the prejudices they have against chaplains. Your remarks, Captain Marvellous, would no doubt be very interesting, for you have such a delightful way of narrating facts, and, besides, you are very happy in your illustrations. I like the plan very much, sir, and, instead of objecting to it (as some chaplains might do on the ground of its interfering with their duties), I applaud your zeal, sir, and have no fear that any religious subject you may undertake to handle will suffer for the want of eloquence on your part."

"Oh, I flatter myself, Mr. Spicy, that few men can beat me at eloquence. If I had not joined the navy I should at this time have been a lawyer of no trifling repute, and I don't know but that it would have been better than going to sea. You will not feel ashamed of the manner in which I shall handle any subject I may take hold of. You've seen me handle this ship, Mr. Spicy, haven't you?"

"Why, no, not exactly, sir. I have only seen those evolutions that have been performed by Mr. Barnacle, who seems to be a thorough sailor."

"Well, but Mr. Spicy, when Mr. Barnacle performs an evolution it is the same as if I performed it myself, unless he makes a bungle of it, when, of course, he must take all the blame. But to return to what we were talking about. I shall commence to-morrow (which is Sunday) and give a chapter in the Bible, and, as we are to be absent three years, it will become a pleasant pastime. I shall commence at Genesis and go through to Revelations, and I flatter myself that my crew, when they are paid off, will know the Bible by heart. They shall not say at home that we were no better than Mohammedans, as they said of a certain ship I could mention in the navy."

"Well then, sir, it is all settled," said Mr. Spicy, "and I will have everything prepared for you to-morrow, and may your pious endeavors receive their full reward. Did you ever see a more lovely evening, Captain Marvellous?" said the chaplain, changing the subject. "This is just such a time as one might imagine the mermaids would take for their gambols on the smooth, quiet sea, though, if I mistake not, they are always to be found in the neighborhood of some solitary rock, where they sit combing their hair. That idea of a mermaid is a very poetical one, captain, don't you think so?"

"There may be a great deal of poetry about it, Mr. Spicy, but nevertheless it is true that mermaids do exist, as numerous persons can testify; and I know from my own experience that such things have been seen."

"Why, you don't mean to say, Captain Marvellous, that you have seen a mermaid with your own eyes? for, though I have often read of them, I have always considered them fabulous."

"I have not only seen a mermaid, Mr. Spicy, but a merman also, which is the most remarkable sight I ever saw; and I believe that I am the only person living who ever saw anything of the kind. *Mermaids*, you know, sir, are often spoken of, but I don't think you ever heard of a *merman*, Mr. Spicy."

"Never indeed, sir," said the chaplain. "And, pray, where did you see this wonderful creature, and under what circumstances?"

"I saw the merman after crossing the banks of Newfoundland on my return to the United States from Europe in a national vessel.

76 THE ADVENTURES OF HARRY MARLINE.

It was some years ago, in the year 1809, on the 16th of March, exactly at seven bells; we had been running to make Sable Island, but a thick fog set in and shut out everything from sight. You could not see the mainmast of the ship while standing on the poop, and the pea-jackets of the men were covered with globules of water as large as a pigeon's egg; it might as well have been night, it was so thick. We were slipping along through the water as quietly as we are now, and going rather faster than was desirable in such a fog. The captain, imagining that he heard the sound of breakers, determined to heave-to and send out a boat to reconnoitre, and, being a lieutenant at the time, I was ordered to go in charge of her. I pulled in according to the instructions I had received from the captain, and in about an hour, sure enough, I made the breakers ahead. The captain was right, after all; he *had* heard breakers, and the ship was running right into them. I pulled back immediately, directed by the sound of the bell, which I heard faintly tolling in the distance.

"While looking out anxiously ahead, I heard something like a sneeze close to the boat, or, more properly speaking, it was between a sneeze and the blow of a porpoise. I at first thought it was one of the men sneezing, as I could see nothing whatever near to. The sneezing continued, and appeared to be on our starboard quarter, and I at last made up my mind that it was a porpoise that had a very bad cold. It seemed to keep up with us, whatever it was, and I had got quite accustomed to the sound, when suddenly I was startled by a flying-fish falling into the boat, transfixed with a curious-shaped arrow, and the sneeze sounded close to my ear. Just at this moment the fog lifted, and there stood the queerest-looking thing I ever beheld. In appearance he was half man, half fish, and seemed to balance himself on his tail as a man would on his feet; his face was a deep scarlet, and he had one fierce-looking eye right in the center of his forehead; his ugly mug was covered with a long beard resembling sea-weed, and the hair of his head hung down low on his shoulders; the scales on his tail shone like burnished gold, and the end of it seemed to be covered with large barnacles. In his hand he carried a small bow, and at his back a quiver full of arrows. Just as he showed himself through the fog he was taking aim at a flying-fish which was skimming along near the surface of the water, and, letting fly the arrow, the fish was struck, and fell quivering into the sea. He made one bound toward it, and, before you could say Jack Robinson, he had seized it and transferred it to a bag hanging at his side. Here, then, I saw a merman sportsman shooting the flying-fish for dinner, and it was witnessed by the whole boat's crew; we saw him shoot five fish without missing one, when he suddenly turned round toward us, fixed an arrow in his bow, and pointed it at the forward part of our boat; we all dove our heads down under the thwarts, not wishing so unerring a marksman to show his dexterity on us. I could hear the twang of his bow as the arrow left it, and directly afterward heard something hit the bow. When we lifted our heads up he was nowhere in sight, no doubt having dived under water; but there was his arrow sticking right in the center of a gilt star, which we carried on all our boats, and he left it there as a fair sample of what a merman could do. We were rather glad to get rid of such a disagreeable customer, and pulled as hard as we could to regain the ship. It was a pleasant sight to us to see her looming up in the fog, and I did not feel sure that I should not get an arrow in me until I was standing safe on the deck."

"A very curious incident indeed," said Mr. Spicy; "and coming from such an unquestionable source is not to be doubted. One thing I like about your stories, captain, is the exactness with which you remember the dates, even to the day and hour."

"That I always make a point of doing, Mr. Spicy; it affords an opportunity to persons who have any doubts on such matters to refer back to the chronicles of the times. Now, by looking at the ship's log-book in the year 1809, on the 16th of March, at seven bells, you will see mention made of lowering a boat in a fog and sending a lieutenant to look out for breakers. But no mention is made of seeing the merman, because such matters are never inserted in the ship's log-book, any more than you would mention a booby alighting on one of the yards, or if you were to see the sea-serpent."

I remember once after this hearing the captain tell of various mermen and mermaids he had seen. He was a firm believer in the existence of these famous denizens of the ocean, and, although a devout student of the Scriptures, was convinced that our first parents came out of the sea.

"Why not?" he inquired. "Is there anything more beautiful than the ideas embraced in the heathen mythology? Could our first mother have done any better than to spring from the sea, as Venus is said to have done?"

Now, the captain instanced so many cases where the habits of the mermen and mermaids were analogous to the human race, that he may be forgiven for not strictly following the sacred book on which he pinned his faith.

For instance, his witnessing the actions of a mermaid brushing away the flies which settled on her infant's face when basking on the sunny side of an iceberg, or watching an affectionate mother of this species washing her baby's face from a clam-shell basin and then drying it with her luxuriant hair.

One of the most remarkable incidents that the captain witnessed was a mermaid picking the sharp fragments of a sea-egg from the tail of one of her progeny, and then giving the youngster a sound spanking, while the indulgent father merman stood by remonstrating against his wife's barbarity, and offering to scoop up all the shells in that vicinity so that the children could play undisturbed.

Among the multitude of incidents related by the captain I remember one where a pair of these denizens of the sea had laid out a garden upon a cake of floating ice, upon which they had undertaken to force early vegetables by using dried jelly-fish as a substitute for glass, which was placed in frames formed of the shell of the sea-horseshoe.

However, the captain never carried his theory beyond mermen and mermaids, and he was perhaps justified by what he had seen of the beautiful sirens of the sea in thinking that our first parents were produced from that quarter. Love influences the inhabitants of the ocean as it does those of the land, and, according to Captain Marvellous, it is not an uncommon circumstance to see a lover sitting on a lonely rock with one arm around a mermaid's waist, singing plaintive ditties, while she gazes lovingly into his eyes, drinking in all he utters.

It seems that these people are subject to emotions of terror, like those of the human race. When frightened they turn pale, their hair stands on end, and they dive under water to seek safety in the caves of ocean.

Like ourselves, they are suspicious, and under no circumstances will they permit an old whaleman to come near them, although they often allow young sailors to sit by them while combing their long tresses and surveying themselves in their polished mirrors. So spoke the captain.

CHAPTER IX.

THE CAPTAIN MAKES AN ADDRESS, AND ALL HANDS ARE CALLED TO WITNESS PUNISHMENT. WITNESSES GET INTO TROUBLE.

SUNDAY morning was ushered in with beautiful weather; it was almost a dead calm, and the sails were flapping lazily against the masts. The decks had been nicely holy-stoned, and looked clean enough to eat off them, and, from the unusual bustle, it was evident that we were about to have a general muster of all the officers and crew, which is always the custom on board ships of war on Sundays, when the weather will permit. Sea-sickness had almost disappeared, though the greenhorns still carried pale faces, and spoke in rather subdued tones as they delivered the orders of their superiors. The ship, however, was all life and animation, the men were dressing themselves out in their best bib and tucker, and the officers were going up and down the ladders in handsome undress and gold epaulets, while the fussy old quartermasters were running about getting their signals to dress the capstan with, and grumbling at everything under the sun. Grumbling is one of the long-allowed privileges of this class of petty officers, and no quartermaster is supposed to know his duty unless he is a thoroughbred grumbler.

At six bells all hands were called to muster: the crew assembled aft on the quarter-deck, the lieutenants ranging themselves on the starboard side and the midshipmen on the larboard side, while the marines were drawn up in the gangway. It was an imposing sight to see so many persons assembled together, preserving such perfect silence, and all looking so clean and nice that you could not detect a tape-string out of the way. How different was the appearance of the crew to what they were when they first came on board in charge of their landlord, who took the greatest interest in their welfare, and never lost sight of them until he received a receipt for them from the proper officer! He then considered he had complied with his obligations to the Government, drew the poor sailor's advance (out of which Jack receives about ten per cent), and then made arrangements to steal him away the first favorable opportunity and ship him in the merchant service.

When the sailor is delivered over to the Government he is always half drunk, or at least not sober enough to know his nationality, and generally begins by cursing the Yankee flag and swearing allegiance to good John Bull, who resorts to a less mild means of obtaining crews for his ships.

Jack's first appearance is not very prepossessing as he balances himself with some difficulty on his feet, and peers about with his swollen, bloodshot eyes, which have been bunged up by some of his messmates; and he stands hitching up his pantaloons, spitting tobacco-juice all around him, and damning all creation at the same time. Poor wretch! he soon gets himself put in double irons, and only awakens to a consciousness of his folly next morning, when he finds himself handcuffed, and hears that he has sold himself to Uncle Sam.

It is true that we don't resort to the system of impressment in the United States navy, but the Government encourages a system ten times more pernicious, for they encourage the landlord system, by which the very life-blood of a sailor is sucked out of him before he goes on board ship. He is kept drunk for a week before he enlists, so that he can not get away, and, instead of an able-bodied seaman, the Government receipts for a drunken, disgusting-looking beast, who looks unlike anything human. A week after they are on board they present quite a different appearance; their shabby old clothes give way to the trim uniform of the navy, the black eyes disappear, and, with the regular duties of the ship, their ruddy, healthy appearance returns. They then look every inch the sailor.

Our crew had had ample time to get over the effects of the landlord system, and stood on the quarter-deck as fine a looking body of men as any one would wish to see, and though, to the eye of the experienced officer, their dress might not be as trim as the regulations required, yet to me they looked as if they had just come out of a tailor's shop. I felt while looking at them that the stars and stripes were safe while under their charge. The superior officers looked like men who would never fail in their duty, and our commander, from his own account of himself, was not afraid of anything excepting hoop-snakes.

Ten minutes elapsed before the captain emerged from his cabin in company with the first lieutenant, who had gone in to report everything ready for muster. He stood for a moment looking around upon the crew, and a smile of satisfaction lit up his countenance, as much as to say, "You're all right"; then walking straight up to the capstan (which was dressed out for service), he hauled from his pocket a paper, which he laid out before him. After clearing his voice two or three times, and looking sternly at the crew, as if he was going to annihilate them, he commenced speaking, and, as near as I can recollect, delivered himself of the following address:

"OFFICERS, PETTY OFFICERS, SEAMEN, AND MARINES:

"Who would not brave the battle fire, the wreck,
To reign the Monarch of this peopled deck?

"I feel proud, men, when I look upon you, and see myself supported by such stalwart-looking sailors, and in less than a month I hope to drill you in such a manner that you will beat everything hitherto heard of, except the Lake Erie fleet, which I hold can never be beaten. All I have to say to you is this, men, so long as you behave yourselves, don't get drunk, don't disobey orders, don't fight or quarrel, keep yourselves clean, and conform yourselves to the rules and regulations of the ship, you will find me an indulgent captain, and not disposed to punish you; but just let me catch you tripping, and you will find me as hard as steel. I would not forgive my father if he was brought to the gangway, and no man need ever expect to escape punishment who is brought up before me. You will find me like a sucking dove as long as you go straight, but like a roaring lion going about seeking whom he can destroy when my orders are trifled with and my dander is up.

"If occasion offers to go into battle, depend upon it that I will place you yard-arm and yard-arm alongside the enemy, and will never surrender as long as there is a shot in the locker or a charge of powder in the priming-horns. That glorious flag which floats above us will never come down so long as I live, and if we go into action I will make the records of it more famous than the battle of Thermopylæ was in ancient times. I shall not even hesitate to engage a ship of the line after I get you all in good discipline, and I shall feel as certain of taking her as if she was only our equal.

"But you must remember one thing: I expect you to be able to fire four shots in a minute, and every shot to hit its mark. You must every one of you be able to whip a Frenchman at broadsword exercise (have two pairs of single-sticks made for each mess, Mr. Barnacle," he said, turning to the first lieutenant), "and I expect you to work the guns without trucks and side-tackles better than any other ship in the navy can work with them. Do this, men, and you will be invincible. I don't intend that this shall be a prison-ship. No, men, you must look upon her as your home, and

I promise you now liberty on shore once a year and five dollars of your pay to spend, so that you may have no excuse for selling your clothes. The black-listers, let me tell you, are not included in this liberal arrangement, for no man sees the outside of this ship (unless it is to scrub the copper) who breaks one of my rules. That's all I have to say, men; I hope you will remember it."

Thus ended the captain's speech, and it was received with silent applause. The sailors looked glum enough at the prospect before them, and I doubt if they would have gone into action at that moment with a hearty good will.

It was expected by all that the chaplain would now step up and perform divine service, but the captain still kept his place, and, laying the Bible before him, he turned around to the officers, much to their astonishment, and addressed them:

"It is my intention," he said, "to read a chapter in this good book every Sunday, and make a few remarks thereon. The rules and regulations enjoin a commander to show in himself a good example, and I trust that all will benefit by my remarks."

He now commenced reading, and, forgetting that he had promised to read only one chapter, he had got as far as the ninth verse in the third before he stopped.

The chaplain now went through with the service, and after that the crew were mustered by their names, about one in every ten being stopped at the mainmast on account of some irregularity in their dress. After muster I saw the quartermasters and boatswain's mates assembled at the gangway, and they were busily engaged rigging the gratings and hauling some little instruments out of their bags, which little instruments, I was informed, were called "cats," used in former times to preserve discipline among the crew.

I was told that the captain was about "clearing the brig," which in plain English means wiping off old scores with delinquents, and I went to the mainmast to witness the ceremony.

The captain came out with the prisoner-list in his hand, and looked stern and unforgiving as he approached the gangway. I thought to myself these poor sailors are now going to be whipped to death, for how can the captain forgive any of them after his warning at the capstan? There were about twenty men at the mast waiting to receive their doom, and a more doleful-looking set of faces it is scarcely possible to imagine. As the commanding officer approached they dropped their eyes upon the deck and waited in silence to hear their sentence.

The first man was John Smith the seventh. He was accused of getting drunk the day he was brought on board by his landlord and cursing the American flag, striking the master-at-arms, and throwing a quid of tobacco fresh from his mouth into the midshipmen's soup.

"Well, Mr. John Smith the seventh, what have you to say to that? A pretty list of crimes this to be committed in one day! Why, sir, the Newgate calendar contains nothing like it. If you were in New York you would be sent to Sing Sing for six months, and in some countries they would try you by court-martial and likely shoot you. Who ever heard of a true-born American cursing the stripes and stars?—that glorious flag which bled and died in defense of free trade and sailor's rights. Now listen, sir, to what the laws of 1800 for the better regulation of the navy and preservation of discipline says." And the captain commenced turning over the leaves of this dreaded little book in search of the article relating to cursing the American flag. He appeared to have some difficulty in finding the exact thing he wanted, but eventually hit on something which he thought would suit the present case.

"I find here," he said, "that 'any one guilty of mutinous conduct shall suffer death, or such other punishment as a court-martial shall adjudge.' What more mutinous conduct can you be guilty of than cursing those glorious stripes and stars, which have befriended you and defended you when you were oppressed by a cruel nation, and now you eat Uncle Sam's duff and curse his bunting? You are a disgrace, you rascal, to the name you bear, for I know one or two very respectable families of the name of Smith, and I am confident they would blush for you if you are anyways related to them.

"For getting drunk, as a matter of course, you expect a dozen; for striking the master-at-arms, another dozen; and thank your stars it was only the midshipmen's soup you threw your quid of tobacco into, for if it had been mine I should have given you three dozen at least under the article where it says, 'You shall not draw or offer to draw on your superior officer, under penalty of death, or such other punishment as a court-martial shall adjudge.' Now, as I do not consider that midshipmen have a right to eat soup more than twice a week, I will remit that part of your punishment, and only give you three dozen altogether. If the midshipmen's soup had not been there your quid would not have gone into it, so I forgive you on that score. Now, step out, sir, and let me hear what you have to say for yourself, and cut your yarn as short as possible."

John Smith seventh was a fine-looking fellow, about twenty-four years of age. He looked as if no battery could stop him if ever he made up his mind to storm it, and one could tell at a glance by the manner in which his rigging fitted over his mast-heads that he was every inch a sailor. The captain's speech had unmanned him more than the fear of the cat, and there he stood playing nervously with the ribbon on his hat, and trying to muster up something to say in reply to the captain in extenuation of his fault.

At last, after settling first on one leg and then on the other, hitching up his trousers, and drawing his right arm across his nose, he commenced:

"Captain Marvellous, please your honor, I have been in the service, man and boy, going on eighteen years, and this is the first time in my life that I was ever brought to the gangway. No, sir; since the time I was messenger-boy in the Lake Erie fleet up to this time, I have never been flogged, and I hope your honor will forgive my first offense."

"Ah! you were on Lake Erie, were you?" said the captain, his face somewhat relaxing; "and pray what was your name then?"

"John Smith the fourteenth, sir. I was in the commodore's flag-ship, and powder-monkey to gun No. 6, sir."

"John Smith the fourteenth!" said the captain, pondering to himself, and looking down as if to refresh his memory. "I think I remember the name; it seems very familiar to me, and I won't doubt your story. Well, John Smith, it is lucky for you you were on Lake Erie; you have saved yourself a flogging, and I will let you off this time, and give you twice as much as I intended if you are ever brought up to me again. Stand back, sir." And John Smith, much to his astonishment, found himself a free man.

"Step out, the next man," said the captain. "What is your name?"

"John Smith the ninth, sir," said the sailor humbly.

"Well, Mr. John Smith the ninth, you stand charged with pretty much the same offenses. You heard what I said to John Smith the seventh, what have you got to say for yourself, sir?"

"Why, you sees as how, Captain Marvellous, this is the first time I ever been brung up to the gangway since I was on Lake Erie."

"The devil! were you on Lake Erie also? Well, that is some recommendation; stand aside, I will examine your case."

"Step up, next man. What is your name, my man?"

"Brown Smith, sir, and if you will allow me to spake, yer honor, I will soon shew ye that I'm as innocent as a sucking tartle. Says John Smith the ninth to me, 'Brown Smith, lits ship,' sis he, 'in the frigate with good Captain Marvellous,' and sis I to him, sis I, 'I don't care if I do, being as how I sailed with his honor on Lake Erie.'"

"Thunder and blood," said the captain, "you are all Lake Erie men!"

"Faith! an' ye may well say that, yer honor; we are all Lake Erie boys and full-blood Americans, as my own fader and moder can sweare to, if they were alive, yer honor. It was drinking yer honor's health at a small 'ating-house, where we had hired a bit of a room, that we got boosy, an' unfortunately fell into the landlord's hands, who insisted on taking us on board in that condition, bad manners to him! That's the whole truth, yer honor, and it's the first time Brown Smith's iver had his hands in the darbies."

"Well, now," said the captain, "if that don't beat everything I ever came across! I should not be surprised if they were all named Smith. What's your name, my lad?" he said, addressing a short, thick-set, fair-looking sailor.

"Mine name is John Schmit, sir; I'm an aple-bodied semen, an' fight on te chipes in te Lake Erie fleet; mine moter and mine fater all born in tis countrie, an' lifes in New York, and mine wife's lifes ther' too. Tis is te fus time I'n get trunk, an' I hopes youse forgiv' me tis once."

"As you are all Lake Erie men, I will forgive you, and take it for granted that you got boosy accidentally; but remember this is the last time I will ever let any of you escape. Go along with you." So all the John Smiths escaped, and after that time almost every man in the ship had served on Lake Erie, according to his own account.

There was one batch more to be examined, and the captain commenced by calling up William Brown the fourth.

"William Brown," he said, "you are charged with quarreling and fighting; now, I will have no fighting done on board my ship, unless it is when we go to quarters to fight the enemy. What have you got to say to this, sir?"

"Why, captain," he said, "the case is this, sir. I was a-sittin' on the fore'ard bitts, makin' on a duff, and Jim Green was a-making on a duff on t'other end the bitts. Says he to me, 'Bill, jist hold on to my duff while I gets some water from the butt;' and says I, 'I will, Jim,' and he goes for the water. So while he's gone, you know, I kept a-making of my duff, and was just a-mixin' in the slush when he returned, and I giv' him the pan. Says he to me, 'Bill, you been a-stealing of my raisins;' and says I to him, 'I ain't no such thing, and if you don't look out,' says I, 'your mother's monkey will get a lick in your nob.' 'I'd like to see it done,' says he, 'and I'd make you wish you never seed a duff-bag. It ain't the first time,' says he, 'that you've stolen plums from my duff.' Says I, 'That remark of your'n is worthy of an after-guard, thou' you ain't fit to be one, and if you say much more I'll march you up to the mast.' Says he to me, 'You're a lickspittle and a tell-tale, and I'll take a licking any time so that I can serve you out,' and with that he gave me a wipe over the face with his duff-bag, and knocked me off the bitts into the cook's tub. As I rose up he pitched into me right and left, and knocked me down the forehatch. He threw my duff after me and pocketed all the plums I left in the pan on the bitts. That's all I did, captain, as I can prove by witnesses."

"A very pretty kettle of fish, indeed," said the captain; "and pray, Mr. Jim Green, let us hear your side of the story."

"I was a-sittin' on the bitts, you know, sir," commenced Jim, "and Bill Brown, you know, sir, was a-sittin' on the t'other end. I axed him, you know, sir, to hold on to my duff until I got some water to mix it with, and when I came back, you know, more nor half my raisins was gone, you know; so I civilly axed him, you know, sir, what had gone with my plums. He flared up at onst, you know, sir, and called me a molly cod, axing me at the same time if I took him for a thief. I told him I called no one a thief, you know, only his duff looked as if it had double allowance of plums, you know, sir, and no doubt if I examined his fingers that I would find fish-hooks on the end of them, you know, sir. He told me I was a Doncaster thief, you know, sir, and stole my own plums, you know, and then tried to stick it on to him. I told him he daren't tell me that on shore, you know, sir, and he said he'd tell it to me at the Tombs in New York, you know, sir, the first time he saw me taken up for chicken-stealing, you know, sir. With that he hit me a backhander in the mug, you know, sir, and in fending it off with the duff-bag he fell over the bitts, you know.

GUMBO CHAFF'S TESTIMONY.

He jumped at me then with the cook's fork, you know, and to save my bacon I tripped up his heels, and he rolled down the forehatch, you know, sir. That's all I knows about it, sir, and I can prove it by the ship's cook, you know, Gumbo Chaff."

"A very contradictory story, indeed," said the captain, "and no doubt both of you are in the right, though I should be doing perfectly right if I flogged the pair of you. Where are the witnesses to this fray? Where is the ship's cook, Gumbo Chaff?"

"Hyar I is, sar," replied a son of Africa, about sixty years of age, whose black, shining face bespoke anything but hardships at the galley, and whose white teeth shone out through his red lips like pure ivory. He stood pulling his top-knot and bowing to the captain as if he was awaiting orders for a dinner.

"Well, Mr. Gumbo Chaff, what do you know about this quarrel? Give your account of it in as few words as possible, and recollect, old nigger, the whole truth, and nothing but the truth."

"Why, Massa Captain, I dun know nuffin' at all 'bout dis har circumstance. I han't seen none ob de salt and battery, dough I is heard werry aggrawatin' language and unobjectionable conbersation, dat's a fac', and it all turn out jis' as I 'spected, and de two men get fetched up to de mast, which I suppose day desarve to be. All I knows dey was a monstrous sight ob talkin', and dey boff call each oder a mizzable sight of names. Den I 'gin to be afeard like they was a-gwine to be a muss, an' I gwine rite to work den to collect my cooking 'tensils. Fac' is, Massa Capen, dey was talkin' jis like two b'ar, and arter all dey turn out jis' for all de worl' like two sheep. I tought dey was boff wrong in de ways of usin' aggrawatin' spressions, specially the one dat stole the plums, and also de one who hab loss 'em.

"If you'l jis' excuse me, Massa Capen," continued old Gumbo, "I'll jis' explain a few carcumstance dat will trow some light on dese matter. You mus' scuse dis old nigga, Massa Capen, for speak so freely in de peresence of a gempleum, but I want to say dis har onexpected carcumstance hab quite discombibolated de kitchen 'tensils. It was de mose unaccountable thing I eber seen. De cook's fork ain't nowhar to be seen, two hoops is dun knocked off de mess-tub, and all dis happen from dose two men a-foolin' togeder on de bitts, sar. Dat's all I knows about dis muss, sar, so help me Bob!"

"And that's what you call throwing a light on the subject, is it? Stand on one side for the present; I have not done with you yet."

"Yes sar," said old Gumbo, pulling his top-knot and ducking his head with the politeness of a French dancing-master, and looking as consequential as if his evidence had settled the whole matter.

"Who is the next witness? Step up, my man," said the captain to a tall, gawky, slab-sided-looking Yankee, who looked as if he had been fed on pumpkin-pies all his life and drank nothing but vinegar and water.

"What's your name, my lad?"

"Zedekiah Longshank Whitler," replied the fellow, with a strong nasal twang, keeping his hat on his head and his hands stuck into his pockets up to the elbows.

"And where the devil did you come from?" said the captain, "and what part of the ship are you stationed in?"

"Wal, I didn't com' at all, I reckon, and I rather guess I was fetched down on a raft from Skunk River, down in Maine; and I mout as well say I'm fixed at the pump, whar I'm kept a-pumpin' the tarnal live-long day; and I reckon it's a leetle the hardest work I ever done since I seed salt water."

"Take your hat off, you mutinous rascal, and make none of your mutinous remarks here, or I'll have your back scratched with the cat before you know where you are," said the captain, quite indignant at the greenhorn's careless manner. "Tell me what you know about this fight, and don't go out of your way to tell me about your Skunk Creek and being fetched down on a raft."

"Wal, now, did you ever?" said the Yankee. "Wal, the folks down yonder they did larf at me, to be sure, when I talked of sailoring in the navy-ships, and I kinder think they was harf right in the ind; but if this ain't a leetle of the hardest doin's and fixin's I ever seed, my name ain't Zedekiah Whitler. Wal, I rather guess, capting, that you'll have to cross-question me, for that's the way we do it up down East, and I ain't obleeged to answer no questions that will go for to criminate myself."

"Well," said the captain, who seemed to be rather amused at the odd fish before him, "where were you when this quarrel took place?"

"Wal, I reckon I was at that tarnal pump, almost a-burstin' my biler and jerkin' my arms out of the sockets every clip I took at it, while a darned soldier is doin' nothin' all day long but stand thar and larfin' at me. When I think he's got a leetle of the easiest work on the boat, I rather think the member of Congress from my

THE YANKEE'S TESTIMONY.

county will make a small muss about it, or else Zedekiah Whitler can't write."

"Silence, you scoundrel!" said the captain; "and don't let me hear you talk again about writing, or I will tie you up and flog you to a jelly."

"Wal, I'll silence if you like, but I guess you'll find it a leetle of the hardest thing to cross-question me, if I silence, you ever undertook."

"Who commenced the quarrel?" continued the captain; "tell me that."

"Wal, how should I know," said Zedekiah, "when I was a-pumpin' all the time, and tarnation mad myself at the soldier for larfin' at me?"

"Didn't you hear the controversy about the duff, and did you see Bill Brown and Jim Green strike each other?"

"Wal, what if I did? You don't come for to go to think that I'm goin' to answer such cross-questions as them? No, no, capting, I rather guess I won't. All I knows is, that the capting of the waist told me to keep to that ar pump, and he says I'm a leetle of the best pumper he ever seen; but I rather think I ain't so easy pumped."

"Well, then," said the captain, "tell us in your own way what you do know about this matter, for I want to know the truth."

"Wal, now, that's getting to be like a reasonable critter; and if you hadn't been so pesky cantankerous at first you'd a-hearn it all by this time. Wal, you want to know who first began the quarrel?"

"Yes, I do," said the captain.

"Then you want to know, I guess, who hit first?"

"Yes, I do. Go on, you fool."

"And then, I reckon, you want to know who got the worst of it?"

"Yes," said the captain, "I want to know all about it."

"Wal, it was a leetle of the darndest fight I ever seen in my born days. I was a-pumpin', and the soldier was a-larfin' at me, as he allers does, when I hearn a-talkin' and a-cussin' loud enough to split thunder. Then I stopped a-pumpin' and the soldier stopped a-larfin'. Then, Jehu! but I saw such a-taring and a-squealin', gougin' and a-scratchin', that I was entirely flambergasted. One man war on top and the t'other war underneath, then the t'other war on top and the top war underneath; they gin dreadful b'ar hugs, and both looked as flat as pancakes. Then agin they would swell up and sneeze, and stretch out as long as an eel. Thar arms kept a-flyin' like the wings of a granddaddy's wind-mill, and when they put in the licks it was like a horse kickin' you with all four shoes on one foot. I thought all along that one of them would a-busted his biler, because he kept a-kinder wheezing like a steam-engine. Then I hearn a-belloring, an' a-squealin' and a-thumpin', till I thort all creation war a-rattlin' a pieces. Then I see one feller knock t'other feller through a squar' hole in the for'ard ind of the boat. I says, There's a dead Ingian anyhow, 'cause I thort he went clean through the boat's bottom down that tarnal hole. Then I 'gan the pumpin' an' the soldier he 'gan sorter to laff at me agin, and so I been a-pumpin' and he a-larfin' at me ever since. I rather think, capting, you'l have to git another chap to stop in these diggin's, 'cause I'm a sorter minded to leave an' go to hum the first land we come to. Skunk Creek's good enough for me anyhow you can fix it, and no mistake. Now, you got the hull grit of the matter out on me, an' if it ain't all truth, slap up and strai't down, may I never eat a pumken-pie or whittle a stick agin."

Zedekiah's evidence set almost every one to laughing, and the captain could scarcely keep his countenance himself; he ordered Zedekiah to stand on one side, and informed him he would settle with him directly. The next witness was then called up, and he answered to the name of "François Jean Julien Pettit Pois." He was wardroom cook, and a Frenchman by birth, though, I presume, from being in an American ship of war, that he had become a naturalized citizen; at all events, he had escaped the vigilance of the Know-Nothing Committee, and held this important office under the Republican flag.

François Jean Julien Pettit Pois was a very small specimen of a man—so thin he would scarcely cast a shadow, and so short he must have had some difficulty in overlooking the cook's table; but he looked every inch a cook, and one could almost see the *paté foie gras* beaming from out his intelligent countenance.

"Come, François, let's have your evidence; what are you on board ship?"

"Oui, Monsieur le Capitaine, I av ze honor to be ze *chef de cuisine* to ze war room *officier*, and I av zeen wiz my two eyes ze battaile between zese two '*matelot*.' Alzo my attention is much engage wiz ze bisness of my science I av look at de battaile wiz one eye, an av stuff de roas pig wiz de oder."

"Are you a good French cook, François?" said the captain, "and what can you cook?"

"I can cook every zing, sar, every zing. I av been *chef de cuisine* for the Duke de Reinfort, segond *chef de cuisine* for the Prince of Salerno, an general taster of ze wine of ze Bishop of Pisa. You mus axcus me, sair, I no speki ze English language too mosh."

"Go on, then, and tell me what particular dishes you can make," said the captain.

"Well, sair, I can tak ze pig and make one turkey ov him; I can tak ze turkey an mak one pig of him; wiz ze chickaine I shall mak every zing: soup, pie, pigeon, *perdrix*, phaisan, woodcock, and ozer small bird; wiz ze maccaroni I shall mak seventeen deffirant zing—beautiful zing, fit for ze monarck; wiz ze bone of ze pig I shall make ze mos beautiful jellee, and wiz ze bad egg ze most splendeed glaci. I can mak ze marong, ze caramelli, ze bonbon, and every zing for ze ladie, and, sair, I shall cook ze bullfrog in one manner vera remarkable. I can cook *à l'Anglais* rost bœuf, befstek, muttang-shop, muttang-roti, and muttang boulli, muttang avec olive, muttang avec pomme de terre. When, sair, you av nosing, I can mak you one good dinaire wiz one ole boot for ze foote; I shall mak ze good soup and beautiful frigasce wiz ze ole hat for ze head; I can mak ze maccaroni paté and ze beautiful mushroom; wiz one old stocking I shall make one beautiful frigasce and ze good jellee; and wiz one bone of ze hammon I can make seven, eight soup, and fourteen, twenty ozer zing. I speak vraiment, Monsieur le Capitaine, and av one vera good recommend from ze *chef de cuisine* in ze Hôtel Havre at Genoa."

"Very well, François, I will try you. Mr. Barnacle," he said, turning to the first lieutenant, "have François rated as captain's cook, and let my present cook take his place; he knows no more about cooking than a horse."

"But, Captain Marvellous," remonstrated Mr. Barnacle, "we took a great deal of trouble to obtain this cook and pay him something besides his pay; it is an act of injustice to deprive us of him, and I doubt if he wishes to change."

"Mr. Barnacle," he replied, "when you want to change the captain of the foretop into the maintop, do you ask him if he will like it? We will discuss this matter in the cabin, sir," he said, drawing himself up with much dignity, and turning round to François, he ordered him to tell what he knew about the fight.

"Well, sair, as I av tole you, I av seen ze battaile wiz one eye an av stuff ze roas pig wiz ze ozer; I av look Monsieur Brown and Monsieur Green mak ze fight wiz ze duff-bag; Monsieur Brown hit Monsieur Green in ze mous wiz ze duff-bag; zen Monsieur Green cashe Monsieur Brown by ze hair, and Monsieur Green cashe him by ze nose; zen Monsieur Brown pule Monsieur Green hair, and zen Monsieur Green blow Monsieur Brown's nose; zen Monsieur Brown holler all same like one bule, and zen Monsieur Green squeale all same like one pig; zen I put my two eye on ze stuffing ov ze roas pig, and when I put ze tozer eye on ze battaile, ze two monsieurs boss fall down ze fore-hash, and I look no more."

"Well, then, all I can make of this, you two rascals," said the captain, addressing the two culprits, "is that you have knocked up a precious row on the gun-deck, and are both in the wrong, and I am going to make an example of you. Not a word," he said, seeing they were going to reply. "Rig your gratings, quartermaster, and, boatswain's mate, get you out your cats.

"And now, Mr. Gumbo Chaff, stand up there."

"Me! Massa Capen?" said Gumbo, his eyes dilating to the size of saucers and his red lips turning the color of ashes. "Me! Massa Capen? I ain't done nuffin', sar, bress de Lor'; I'se nuffin' but a witness, sar, and I'se dun tell truff, so help me Bob! Massa Capen, dis har ole nigga neber git a-lickin' at de gangway, and I tink, Massa Capen, dat it is a mos' unaccountable ting if dis har nigga is whipped just 'cause he's nuffin' but a witness. Pray de Lor', Massa Capen, sar, but don't whip dis har old nigga; it dun kill him for sure."

"This is one of the witnesses, sir," interposed Mr. Barnacle, who began to think the captain had taken leave of his senses; "there must be some mistake, sir."

"No mistake whatever, sir," he replied, haughtily; "I am going to lick witnesses and all, and then I will be sure to punish the right one. Better that one hundred innocent persons should suffer than that one guilty person should escape, so my Bible teaches me, and I always carry out the principles of the Christian religion."

"I rather think, sir, your Bible contains a misprint, and I would respectfully suggest the propriety of looking at it again before you punish these men. I think you would regret flogging Gumbo Chaff; he stands high in the estimation of the officers, and has never been flogged since I have known him, and this is the third ship in which we have sailed together. I think you are too humane, Captain Marvellous, to commit an act of injustice."

This little compliment to the captain's justice carried the day, and the flogging was postponed for the present until that misprint could be looked into. He asked Mr. Barnacle to walk into the cabin, and in a few moments an order came out to unrig the gratings and put up the cats; but the first lieutenant informed the belligerents that the captain had sentenced them to fight out their difficulty in the presence of the crew, each armed with a duff-bag filled with duff, and the conquered man was to be put on the black list for the rest of the cruise. This decision, worthy of Solomon himself, seemed to meet the approbation of the crew, who flattered themselves they were going to see rare sport. It was a pleasant Sunday afternoon's amusement to discuss the matter, and many were the jokes cracked at the expense of Brown and Green by their messmates and acquaintances.

Next morning the following lines were found fastened to the captain's door, and created some little merriment. The author was never known, though Gumbo Chaff's name was signed to it:

1.

Brown and Green, as has been seen,
  Were very fond of duff;
But Green and Brown both got knocked down
  Before they had enough.

2.

When Green got blue, I swear 'tis true,
  His tongue could scarcely wag;
And Brown turned black, while on his back
  He slung round his old duff-bag.

3.

So fierce they fought, the captain thought
  They both had got enough;
The wisdom he'd shown was all his own,
  So the sailors they christened him Duff.

4.

Away with the cat, we'll no more of that,
  The duff-bag shall settle disputes;
While Green and Brown shall be knocked down,
  And treated as if they were brutes.

CHAPTER X.

ARRIVAL IN PORT. A NEW METHOD OF BENDING A BUOY-ROPE. PRACTICAL HINTS TO SAILING-MASTERS.

FAVORING gales carried us rapidly along on our voyage, and on the nineteenth day after leaving the United States the joyful sound came from aloft of "Land O!" In an hour after the shores of Africa and Spain began to loom up in the distance, and the white sails of the corsair-looking craft were seen in bold relief against the background. Every one was on deck, looking at the long-wished-for land, and many were the enjoyments they promised themselves when they should put their feet on shore at Gibraltar, whither we were bound. I could scarcely convince myself that the cloud-like-looking thing before me was terra firma, it presented so wide a contrast to the narrow streak of sand we had last seen when we left the United States; but we rapidly came up with it, and there was land without a doubt. We passed the Straits with a spanking breeze, and had to keep a bright lookout to avoid running over the innumerable small craft that were seeking their way to the Atlantic, some bound to Portugal, some to the coast of Africa, many to France and England, and many that bore tidings of us to our own cherished homes. My heart beat with longings for home whenever we passed an American ship, and I wished myself on board of her as she flew past us on her homeward-bound voyage; but the feeling was only transient. I thought of the captain's dog "Snap," and determined to stick to my duty, and bear my load with cheerfulness and resignation. Could I have looked into the future, and seen all the annoyances and privations I have since undergone, I think I should have been tempted to jump overboard and ask some American skipper to throw me the end of a rope.

We were fairly flying along the land, impelled by wind and current, and bid fair to reach our anchorage long before it was dark. The pillars of Hercules, like mighty giants, seemed to be upholding the heavy clouds that we might pass safely under them, and sent from their gorges as we passed brisk squalls that made us stand by our top-sail halliards. Soon after the rock hove in sight, its high top capped with snow-white clouds, and its base lined with unapproachable fortifications, over which the British flag was proudly floating. The harbor was crowded with vessels of all nations (many

COMING TO ANCHOR.

of them ships of war), from a three-decker down to a felucca. Proud as we were of our saucy-looking frigate, we could not but acknowledge that she sank into insignificance alongside of the three-deckers of Great Britain, but Captain Marvellous felt sure he could sink the largest of them after being three months in active service: that was some consolation.

All hands were called to "bring ship to anchor," and every one repaired to their stations. Mr. Barnacle took the trumpet, and kept the little middies flying about carrying orders to all parts of the ship. This being the first time we had entered port since leaving home, great anxiety was felt about making a handsome "come to," though we all felt sure that if any one could do the thing to perfection it was our old first lieutenant, Mr. Barnacle. The harbor seemed to be crowded with vessels, and I did not think it possible to get by them without a collision of some kind; but threading our way through the French, English, and Dutch men-of-war, the gallant frigate approached her anchorage in beautiful style, and picked up a good berth between two English ships of the line. The Englishmen complimented us afterward on the handsome manner in which the ship was handled, and I presume they ought to be very good judges. Our captain was the only one who did not seem to appreciate the evolution, for though he said nothing while we were working in among the shipping, nor gave a single order to the first lieutenant, yet he became as brave as a lion when the anchor was down, and seemed determined to show that he was captain, if any one had a doubt on the subject before.

"Mr. Barnacle," he said, "I don't see the buoy watching; it must have gone down with the anchor."

"No, sir," replied the first luff; "there was no buoy-rope bent, and, expecting to come to with the other anchor, we had no time to bend it."

"Who ever heard of an anchor being let go without a buoy-rope bent to it? Very unseaman-like, sir; very unseaman-like," he grumbled.

"Just as you please about that, sir; but I shall never apply to you, Captain Marvellous, for credentials for my seamanship," replied Mr. Barnacle (and the wart grew to an alarming size). "I will defy any one to tell which anchor he is coming to with in a crowd of ships like this, and you informed me yourself that we would come to with the starboard anchor without assigning any reason."

"Commodore Truxton always came to with the starboard anchor, sir," he replied, "and that is sufficient reason for my doing it. I presume you won't question his being a sailor, sir?"

"No more than I would question the captain of the foretop being a sailor; but it don't follow from that," he continued, "that he knew more than any one else. I should be sorry to think that Commodore Truxton was the only sailor, or rather seaman, we have had in our navy. The fact is, sir, officers knew so little in his time that it became the fashion to acknowledge his superiority, and look up to his decision in all points of seamanship."

Strange as this conversation may appear between captain and first lieutenant, it was an every-day occurrence. Old Barnacle *would* talk back, and the captain, though always the first to begin the controversy, and say something to enlarge the first luff's wart, was very careful not to go too far for fear of losing the services of so good an officer. He knew his own deficiencies, and also knew that "Old Wart-nose" was a prime seaman, and that the ship could not do without him. A good first lieutenant is a rare thing in the navy, and when a captain gets one he should make the most of him.

"I don't know, Mr. Barnacle," said the captain, "whether you intend to reflect on me or not by your remarks; perhaps you think you know more than I do about a ship?" and, putting his arms akimbo, he looked at Mr. Barnacle in an egotistical manner, as much as to say, Can you have the impudence to entertain such an absurd idea for a moment?

The first luff was a very plain-spoken man, and would have told a king what he thought of him if he had been asked to do so, so he quietly replied, "I not only think, Captain Marvellous, that I know my profession better than you do, but I am sure of it; and I say it without in the least intending any disrespect to you, sir."

Mount Vesuvius in an eruption could not have looked more angry than did our captain at this announcement, and he sarcastically replied, "Perhaps you consider letting go an anchor without a buoy attached to it a sample of your seamanship, when you have had the whole day before you to do it in?"

"I still reply that we had no time to bend the buoy-rope, Captain Marvellous."

"Time, sir!" he replied; "it requires no time to bend the buoy-rope; I will give you a proof of it, Mr. Barnacle, and then perhaps you will admit I do know something about such matters.

BENDING A BUOY-ROPE.

When I was acting-master of the frigate Horsefly we were standing into Callao Bay, where the ships were crowded together twice as close as they are here; our anchor had been 'cock-billed,' and they were about to give the order from the quarter-deck to let it go, when I sang out to hold on, that the buoy-rope was not bent. 'Never mind the buoy-rope,' said the first lieutenant; but I considered it of so much importance that I took the end of the rope in my hand, put a dozen yarns in my mouth, and jumped down on the anchor. I had no sooner got seated on the arm of the anchor than the first lieutenant thundered through the trumpet to 'let go,' and let go they did, and down I went with it to the bottom, in nine fathoms water; but I held on, sir, like grim death, and never once thought of letting go. After the anchor had settled, I went quietly to work and bent the buoy-rope with as much care as if the anchor had been hanging to the bow; and not only that, sir, but I stopped the end back with a neat seizing, notwithstanding a large shark was attacking me all the time I was at work, and I had to keep him off with my right foot. When I got through I arose to the top of the water, and found that the ship had veered out fifty fathoms of chain, and the men were aloft furling sails. I looked at my watch, and found that I had been down under water exactly three minutes and ten seconds."

"I wonder the shark did not keep company with you," said Mr. Barnacle; "they are rather dangerous customers under water."

"He would have done so, Mr. Barnacle, but I threw him my boots, and one of them stuck in his throat, and while he was trying to get it down I stuck my pen-knife in his left eye, and he went off in another direction."

"Sharp practice that, sir; and I must confess the idea never struck me before to send some one down with the anchor to bend the buoy-rope; the next time I will think of it, and give our master a chance to distinguish himself."

The idea of sending our master down after an anchor, and to bend the buoy-rope, struck the captain as so absurd that he burst out laughing, and fortunately regained his good humor just as an English officer came alongside from the admiral's ship to inquire where we came from, and to offer us the courtesies of the harbor.

The gentleman who came to perform this piece of service was by grade a lieutenant, and the most perfect exquisite I ever laid my eyes on. Our lieutenants looked like rusty old hulks alongside of him, and then when he began to talk and flirt about his white hemstitched pocket-handkerchief, the veriest dandy we had on board (our second master) could not hold a candle to him. When he ascended the side and saluted the officer who received him, he turned round toward the bow, and, taking out a peculiar-looking eye-glass, made a minute survey of the ship, below and aloft, and then paid the quarter-deck the same patronizing attention.

"Twemendous ship, 'pon my 'onor," he exclaimed, "one of your first-wates; I suppose scantling of a three-decker, eh? and all that. Bless my soul! vewy remarkable size frigate. No doubt one of those, aw! you used in the last scratch with the English?" he said, turning toward Mr. Bluff, who, with his thumbs stuck in his waistcoat pockets, and his right eye half closed, was eying the individual to see what genus he belonged to. The last question rather woke him up, and he answered, rather quickly, "No, sir; she is one of the frigates we captured from you last war."

"Aw! 'pon my soul!" said the Englishman, nothing disconcerted, "I was not haware that you 'ad that 'onor before. I was thinking, aw! that the Chesapeake and His Britannic Majesty's ship Shannon, Captain Brooke, was the honly time you hever ventured to hengage one of hour frigates; perhaps she was taken by a squadron?"

"I will take the liberty to refresh your memory, sir," said Mr. Bluff (looking fierce), "and send you a list of the vessels we captured, if you will favor me with the name of your ship."

"Aw! don't trouble yourself, sir; shall be 'appy to see you on board, and all that; foine frigate, no doubt; do me the 'onor to present me to the captain," and Mr. Bluff trotted the exquisite up to Captain Marvellous, who was standing on the poop to receive him.

"Hadmiral Blazer's compliments, and all that, sir, and would be 'appy to be of hany service to you; wishes to know if you 'ave met hany of His Majesty's cruisers, and if you 'ave any news."

"No, sir," replied the captain; "we have not met any English ships; the news we bring from the United States is rather stirring; the election returns have not all got in, but fourteen counties were sure for Jones, member from Annapolis, and no doubt he would be elected by the largest majority ever given in the United States; Colonel Hawbuck has been elected mayor of Norfolk by a majority of ten, being the closest election between the Whigs and Democrats we have ever had.

"There has also been a large fire in New York," continued the captain, "and over twenty houses burned, and the President has vetoed the bill for planting a row of poplars along the avenues."

"Aw! the Governor, I presume, you hallude to; very intewesting, 'pon 'onor! The hadmiral will de delighted to hear it all, and 'appy to see you on board the flag; foine ship, and all that, sir. Sails well, eh?"

"Yes," said the captain; "seventeen knots an hour off the wind, and fifteen knots close hauled."

"'Pon my soul! quoite good for a fwigate. The hadmiral sails well—one of Boodle's models, you know—nineteen knots large, seventeen close 'awled."

"I hope the admiral is well, and enjoys good health," replied the captain, rather outdone by the Britisher.

"Aw! yes, quoite well; that is to say, no. He don't henjoy very hexcellent 'ealth; he's one of the hold fogeys, you know, and 'as water hin 'is legs. Sawbones, the surgeon, taps him hevery day, takes hout six gallons of water; he's to be hinvalided in May, sir. Vice-Admiral Ginblock takes his place, you know. Aw, good morning; 'appy to see you on board." And so the *petit maître* took his departure, leaving behind him a strong smell of cologne.

I wondered if this kind of officers composed the British navy. Certainly I thought such a looking chap as that would not be worth much on hard boat service, but when I came to know more of the English navy I found (like ourselves) that they had a certain set of dandies fit for nothing but to dance attendance on admirals, while men without influence worked hard during their whole lives without scarcely advancing a step.

We were visited by officers from the French and Dutch fleets also, and in a short time after the American consul came on board, bringing us news that the commodore of our squadron was in these waters, and was waiting our arrival to make a flag-ship of us, as he had nothing larger than a sloop of war in the squadron. The captain did not seem at all pleased with this piece of intelligence, though the lieutenants seemed to rejoice at it. They had great hopes of seeing the whole of the Mediterranean, as the commodore was very fond of going about, while it was well known that our captain had no taste for sight-seeing, and would rather live in some cheap port to save his money. He adored a sixpence more than a Feejee Islander loves human flesh, and a dollar always looked to him the size of a cart-wheel. Even François Jean Julien Pettit Pois, after his promotion to the high office of captain's cook, was heard to exclaim, "Mais il est impossible to mak' so many differen' zing from one bone of ze ham when you 'av' cook him over one, four, ten time; and 'ze soup de grille'" (which is made by holding a chicken over a bucket of water and let him crow) "may be ver' goot for ze captaine ov ze fregat Americaine, mais it won't do nevaire pour un captaine Français wizout ze vermacelli."

Much to the regret of every one, an order was issued that all the midshipmen should be on board the ship by sunset, and the curses in the steerage were loud and deep among the oldsters against such an arbitrary curtailment of their liberties; but they were not wanting in fertility of invention among that crowd, and half a dozen plans were already proposed to evade the captain's orders.

Every one was for getting on shore whose duty did not keep them on board, and the day after our arrival the streets of Gibraltar were crowded with American officers, some dashing along on hired horses seeking the country, or bound to Algesiras, others scrambling up the sides of the rock, and bound to the great cave said to communicate with the Hill of Apes on the opposite coast of Africa, and a majority of them whiling away time in the cafés and at the billiard-tables.

It is not my intention to write a description of the Rock of Gibraltar. Mr. Spicy has written a book, and I am told has described every stone and piece of mortar in the fortress. Mr. Spicy was something of an antiquary in his way, and could always be seen running about with his basket and hammer, procuring specimens of everything interesting with which to enrich his cabinet at home. There is very little chance for an officer to distinguish himself in a literary way, as nearly every ship that goes to sea carries one or more learned gentlemen, either as chaplain or commodore's secretary; and, as the object of these voyagers is to benefit their health and travel, they are always to be found in the most out-of-the-way places, carrying away all the knowledge to be obtained, and leaving none for those who come after them; they are perfect cormorants in the way of picking up information, and often steal that which has been picked up by some one else; as Mr. Bluff sarcastically remarked of them, "They always stand by to paint the expression of a dead fish's eye after a navy officer have cotched him." While such a score of scribblers invade the navy, it would be useless for any one to attempt writing a book of travels—they would soon get possession of the pages and transfer them to their own lucky bag.

MR. SPICY'S JOURNAL.

I must refer my friends to a perusal of Mr. Spicy's journal, entitled "Notes of Travels through Europe, Asia, and Africa, with Descriptions of the Manners and Customs of the Inhabitants thereof; also a Geological Description of those Countries, including an Interesting and Startling Encounter with Fleas near Jerusalem."

Some persons might think I was disposed to be malicious if I informed them that the only part of Africa ever seen by Mr. Spicy was Apes' Hill as we came through the Straits, and that he never saw Asia at all. He writes very fluently about his researches in Africa, speaks of his friends, the Tibboos and Sacatoos, and hints something about having eaten a stuffed elephant in company with the Emperor at Timbuctoo. I myself often heard him talk of his trials while traveling over the unexplored parts of Africa, and the risks he ran from the horrible animals with which the country was filled, and so curious was I to get a peep at a journal so full of wonderful incidents, that I must confess to having used rather disreputable means to gratify my curiosity. One day, when I was requested by the chaplain to take a trunk and bundle on shore for him, a small roll of papers fell out into the bottom of the boat and got soaked with water. I was quite annoyed for fear that he would think it carelessness on my part, and took them up with the intention of drying them. How natural it is, when you pick up a sheet of paper with writing on it, to cast your eyes over the leaves; at least, I have always had a weakness that way, and I have noticed the same failing in others, particularly in women. On this occasion I could not resist the curiosity (that was almost devouring me) to read the manuscript I held in my hands. I felt convinced that I should be sick if I did not gratify myself, and rather than be sick and thereby annoy the doctor, I determined to remain well and enjoy myself reading the chaplain's journal. I have never regretted the circumstance, for I derived information from those pages not to be found in any work of travels or in any encyclopædia. I took out my watch-bill and copied the whole thing carefully, intending that no one should be any the wiser of the theft, and drying the manuscript, I returned it to the bundle. I have taken a good deal of pains to inquire if Mr. Spicy ever published that particular manuscript among any of his journals, but I found that the article in question remained unpublished, and but for me would likely have remained buried in obscurity. I feel convinced that Mr. Spicy will ever remain indebted to me, if he reads these pages, for the pains I have taken to make his adventures known to the world, and the world will be much indebted to me for bringing to light so much valuable information about a country that has always been a sealed book.

CHAPTER XI.
VERY STRANGE AND WONDERFUL, IF TRUE.

It appears that Mr. Spicy was sent abroad by a certain society, called the "Warming-Pans," or "The Society for the Diffusion of that Comfortable Article, the Warming-Pan," among the tribes of negroes in the interior of Africa. A very important part of his mission was also to collect information on the history of the banjo, supposed to have been brought originally from Africa, and now attracting much attention in our large cities. At the Negro Minstrel's Academy, etc., it has always been a mooted point whether the musical instrument in dispute was indigenous or exotic, and that fact, I am told, has been discussed and settled by Mr. Spicy in a pamphlet of six hundred pages. In the following journal no mention, however, is made of the banjo, and only a passing allusion to the success he met with in the diffusion of warming-pans among men, but there are some matters equally as interesting, if not more so; and, if the reader has the time to spare, he could not do better than look over the journal; he will add to his stock of geographical knowledge, and learn the history of a people heretofore unknown to him.

The pages in question are entitled:

"Adventures in Africa, by the Rev. Eli Spicy, LL. D., A. S. S., P. P. C., and Vice-President of the Warming-Pan Society for the Diffusion of the Warming-Pan among the tribes of our Colored Brethren in the Interior of Africa, with a treatise on the Manners and Customs of the Natives thereof. Together with an outline of a Treaty concluded between the United States and a Princess of Africa, etc."

MR. SPICY'S NARRATIVE.

In the year 1818 I was a young man, and had just graduated from a divinity school. Having no influential friends to help me along, I was obliged to make my way in the world as best I could.

MR. SPICY'S NARRATIVE.

Shortly after graduating I was introduced to a Mr. Smiler, who was president of a society recently formed for the purpose of rescuing the nations of Africa from their state of bondage. His official title was "President of the Society for the Diffusion of Warming-Pans among our Colored Brethren," and the society was at that moment fitting out an expedition to the coast of Africa, to sail from Baltimore in the brig Creole.

When President Smiler found that I was a graduate in divinity he shook me warmly by the hand and said, in a most emphatic manner, "Young man, Providence has thrown you in my way at an opportune moment, not only for your own good, but also for the benefit of the great cause which I have so much at heart. You have your way to make in the world, and the door is open for you to enter upon the path that will lead you to fame and happiness; for what greater happiness can there be than to contribute to the welfare of the millions of our fellow-men who are held in mental and physical bondage in the benighted regions of unhappy Africa?"

"Pray, sir," said I, "explain to me the objects of the expedition which is soon to sail from Baltimore."

"Well," he replied, "we are fitting out a fine brig of four hundred tons, commanded by an experienced old seaman, Captain Cringle, who is well acquainted with the African coast, and, although he has realized a large fortune in diamonds, gold-dust, and ivory by his many voyages, yet the captain is anxious to make another voyage in the cause of philanthropy. The vessel is fitted with every comfort and convenience for passengers and for trading with the natives. We have put on board six hundred warming-pans, which will be found very useful in those regions where the climate is so changeable, forty bales of blankets, fifty boxes of glass beads, forty saddles, two fire-engines, sixty coal-scuttles, two hundred boxes of dried codfish, twenty barrels of peanuts, four tons of pumpkins, four tons of dried apples, sixty Argand lamps, ten tons of bricks, eight bales of flannel drawers, eight bales of flannel shirts, sixty suits of oil-cloth coats and trousers, sixty nor'westers, one box of tracts, ten boxes of Bibles, six dozen shovels and tongs, six dozen pokers, twenty cooking-stoves of the latest pattern, and a large quantity of Shaker-made carpeting, very thick and warm. This is the list of the cargo going out in the Creole, and a more judicious assortment, considering the climate, was never selected.

"We can not," continued Mr. Smiler, "offer you a large salary, for we hope that those who engage in this great work will look for compensation by Divine Providence hereafter, but I will tell you what we can do. Captain Cringle is an old whaleman, and will take out with him a whaleboat fitted with harpoons and other appliances. He will probably fill up a large part of his vessel with oil before he returns, and I will guarantee you one sixth of the profits in case you conclude to accompany the expedition."

I did not hesitate to accept Mr. Smiler's offer, for, thought I, what better chance could a young man ask than this? Besides, I can write a book of travels, and publish it when I return.

"We must not lose any time in securing your berth," said Mr. Smiler, "for fear some one else may get ahead of us." So down we went to the pier where the Creole was lying, and repaired on board.

Captain Cringle was sitting on a hatch, rebottoming an ancient pair of trousers, while a lady, who was introduced to me as Mrs. Captain Cringle, was washing dirty linen (very dirty at that) on the quarter-deck.

In response to my introduction to the captain, that worthy said, "All right! Ever strike a whale?"

"No, sir," I replied; "I never had the pleasure of seeing one."

"Old lady," said the captain, "blow, and let him hear what it is when they sing out, 'There she blows!'" Whereupon Mrs. Cringle sent forth from her such a sound, between a sneeze and a whistle, as would no doubt have made any old whaler feel happy.

"Ever eat buzzard?" inquired the captain.

"No, thank God!" I replied. "I never did, and hope I never shall."

"Fine buzzards, though, on the coast," said the captain. "After you boil 'em eight hours, roast 'em six, then put 'em in a stewpan over the fire for twenty-four hours, then mix 'em with codfish and potatoes and plenty of mustard, you never eat nothin' better, provided you don't eat nothin' for twelve hours."

"Very likely, sir," said I; "but I don't think I'll try it."

"Can you take a trick at the wheel?"

"No, sir; I don't play cards; I never made a trick in my life."

"Wife," said the captain, "greenhorn."

"Yes, sir," I said; "truly I am a greenhorn at sea; but as I am going passenger, I shall not require the accomplishments you speak of."

"You kin wash, I hope?" said Mrs. Cringle, "for darn my kittens if I don't get enough to do to wash my old man's clothes."

I was about to back out and give up the cruise when the captain remarked, "Plenty gold-dust and diamonds where I'm goin'; plenty ivory."

That settled me. Gold-dust and diamonds could not, of course, be procured without hardships, so I said, "Will you show me the cabin?"

"Well," said the captain, "it's full of pervisions just now, but by the time you come aboard it will all be cleared out and be ship-shape and Bristol fashion. Ever shoot an albatross?" he inquired, changing the subject.

"No, sir; I never saw one."

"Wife, show him how an albatross hollers in a gale," whereupon the old woman gave the most unearthly shriek to which I ever listened.

Well, thought I, this is an interesting party, but perhaps they are better than they look to be at first sight.

I inquired of Mr. Smiler how they fared on board the vessel, when the captain spoke up, "Oh, everything you want in the world; got Admiral Coffin's cook—sailed with me six years."

I could ask no more than that, and we bade the captain and his lady good-morning.

"Fond of singing?" said the captain as we moved over the side; "bring a copy of Dibdin's songs, and a needle-case to mend your clothes—voyage pass like winkin'."

"A queer fish that," I remarked to Mr. Smiler after we had quitted the vessel.

"Yes, sir," said Mr. Smiler; "but just as good as gold. He is a sincere Christian; but I was not aware that he sung secular songs; I must inquire into that. But you will have several missionaries and their wives on board, so you will not want for company, and we will supply you liberally with books."

My arrangements for the voyage were soon made—one trunk carried my worldly goods—and I went on board the Creole on the morning of the day appointed for sailing.

I was shown into my cabin by the steward, the captain and Mrs. Cringle being just then engaged in bending the mainsail; but, heavens, what a place in which to make a voyage! There were but four berths, and not an air-port to be seen. A smell of onions, codfish, and tobacco pervaded the apartment powerful enough to knock one down. However, I was in for it; there was no retreat, and I sat down and waited for the captain to show me my bunk, till I was driven on deck to get a breath of fresh air.

When I reached the deck I saw the mate coming on board with six sailors, all pretty drunk; these, I learned, constituted the crew; but the thoughts of the diamonds and gold-dust reconciled me to the situation, although I could not help wondering how it was, if Captain Cringle had all the wealth for which Mr. Smiler had given him credit, that he should go to sea in such a vessel and with such a crew.

At about noon Captain and Mrs. Cringle commenced to make sail on the brig, the pilot came on board, and all was ready to cast off from the wharf. I wondered what had become of the missionaries who were to be my fellow-passengers; but they did not appear, and I supposed we would pick them up at some point in the bay. At length I asked the captain if he should wait for them.

"Never wait—sail at twelve," was the answer. "Did you ever eat sturgeon? got some for dinner," and he gave the order to cast off. Mrs. Cringle was doing all the hauling on the braces, the captain and mate were aloft making sail, and the pilot took the wheel.

The captain sang out to me from aloft, "Ever pull ropes? no haul, no sturgeon," which I did not understand then, but did at dinner-time. So we sailed for Baltimore, and I found myself the only passenger.

We anchored for the night off the mouth of the Potomac to let the crew get sober, for the captain, Mrs. Cringle, mate, and the pilot had worked the vessel down to that point.

Next morning the crew succeeded in getting up the anchor, and we sailed for Cape Henry with a fair wind. Next day, after discharging our pilot, we steered to the southward and eastward to strike Cape Blanco, on the African coast somewhere about the latitude of twenty-one north. In half an hour I was so sick that I offered the captain every cent I had in the world if he would put me on shore, but his answer was, "Never put ashore," and I supposed myself left to die, for not a soul came near me for five days, when I recovered sufficiently to crawl on deck, where the sea-air revived me.

I found Captain Cringle sewing in the seat of a pair of trousers, for it seems it was his custom to burst them out every time he went aloft, while his wife was engaged in strapping a block, having just finished putting a width into the spanker, which was lying beside her.

"Alive?" queried the captain, glancing up at me.

"Yes," said I; "and feel as if I would like to peck a bit."

"Never peck," said he. "Lobscouse ready in half an hour, gull-pie second course, peanuts for dessert." It seems that one day, while it was nearly calm, the captain had managed to kill a dozen gulls, on which he was now about to regale the ship's company.

I was glad to hear dinner announced, and sure enough we had lobscouse with a vengeance. I could not even "peck a bit" at the scouse or the gull-pie, but I thought the latter delicacy must be very much like buzzard.

For four successive days we feasted on lobscouse, when I began to think I should prefer a change. So one day I ventured to remark, "Captain, it strikes me your cook does not make much of a variety. I thought you said he had been cook to Admiral Coffin."

"So he was," answered the captain, "off and on for six years—that is, he was one year on and five years off; but the admiral never ate anything but lobscouse for breakfast, dinner, and supper. That's the reason this cook makes it so well. He is like the man who was so perfect on the hand-organ, having played it for twenty-seven years."

We got nothing but lobscouse while I sailed in that brig, and I learned to detest the very name of Admiral Coffin.

We had a prosperous voyage across the Atlantic, its monotony being varied by Mrs. Cringle strapping blocks, taking the wheel, mending sails, holy-stoning decks—in fact, doing everything except what a woman should do, while her husband spent much of his time in repairing his trousers.

One day we had a heavy squall, and it blew quite briskly for several hours, during which time it became necessary to reef down the sails. Mrs. Cringle led the way aloft, and jumped to the weather-earing, while the captain took the lee one. The old woman said she always made it a rule to keep dead to the windward of Cringle on all occasions.

It was the custom of Captain Cringle, whenever he went aloft with his wife, to sing out, "Wife, let's hear yer blow," when she would give a shriek like a steam-whistle.

On the twenty-fifth day out the captain's calculations made us in the longitude of the Canary Islands, and he began to look sharp for the land, as several canary-birds had been seen on the yards.

To my knowledge the captain had never taken an observation since leaving port. Once a day he would go forward and throw a shingle into the sea, and then walk aft, keeping as near abreast of it as he could, sometimes running, sometimes going slowly. This gave him his latitude, longitude, azimuth, and distance. "And," said he, "what does a man want more than that?" He said that he wouldn't be bothered with a quadrant, for he could always tell when he was within two hundred miles of his destination, and then he began to look out.

So on the twenty-fifth day out Mrs. Cringle took her lookout on the cross-trees and stayed there till night. She gave several unearthly blows while she was aloft, singing out, "There she spouts!" but it turned out to be only blackfish, so we kept on our course till the twenty-seventh, when the captain concluded we had passed the Canaries "and couldn't see 'em on account of misty weather."

That night when the old woman came down from aloft the sea was rolling in heavily from the westward. The captain, in anticipation of reefing top-sails, had put an extra patch on his trousers, and the mate took the lookout forward.

At about ten o'clock, while Mrs. Cringle was at the helm and the captain asleep on the "hen-coops" (though why they should be so called when they never had any chickens in them I couldn't understand), the mate bawled out, "Breakers ahead!" By this time it had fallen calm, and the brig had no steerage-way.

I heard the appalling cry, and rushed on deck in my shirt and drawers. "Captain," said I, "for God's sake, what is the matter?"

"Ever see breakers?" said Cringle; "there's plenty of 'em; wife, go forward, get up range of chain; mate, heave lead overboard." The mate reported no bottom in twenty-five fathoms. It was evident that we were tending fast into the breakers, which could now be seen frothing white on both bows, when the mate sang out, "Ten fathoms!"

"Stand by the anchor, wife!" yelled old Cringle, "and give us one of your blows: it may be the last one, old gal, and I want to hear the sound of that familiar voice in my ears as I go off the ways."

Mrs. Cringle gave a blow like a hippopotamus coming out of the water, and let go the stopper. Down went the anchor, the

MR. SPICY'S NARRATIVE.

brig thumped heavily, swung round to the anchor, and commenced driving toward the beach, carried in by the rollers. At length the chain snapped, the vessel drifted broadside on, and finally stuck fast on the bottom, the sea making a breach over her.

For some time the captain and his wife had not uttered a word; they and the crew worked like beavers, cutting away the masts, which were secured alongside to make a raft.

The captain walked aft and said, coolly, "This is the last of the warming-pans, Mr. Spicy. Wife, give a blow like old times; 'taint no use trying to save the boat."

The captain said he thought the place where we had struck must be near the mouth of the Gambia, or off Mogador, these two places being only fourteen degrees in difference in latitude, which I think was about as near as the captain generally came in his reckoning; his shingles had evidently put him much at fault this time.

We held on to the wreck to prevent being washed overboard, and when morning dawned we found ourselves close to a long line of sandy beach, extending up and down the coast for miles. Not a sign of a living thing nor even a blade of grass, and I at once comprehended that we had struck upon the most desolate part of the coast, bordering on the great Desert of Sahara. However, the captain thought otherwise, and maintained that we were on the coast of Tripoli. "Wife, blow your loudest," said he, "and you'll see some of those Arabs coming down on their camels."

I had taken the precaution to go below and pack my valise, putting in two revolvers, a well-filled powder-horn, three or four cases of cartridges, some percussion-caps, and a dozen boxes of lucifer-matches, all of which I managed to keep perfectly dry by wrapping them in oiled silk.

By this time the sea was setting in very heavily, and the constant thumping soon began to break up the vessel, and the crew were washed off one after another until only the captain, Mrs. Cringle, and myself remained on board. As the poor fellows were washed overboard they struck out for the shore, and as they neared the edge of the breakers we could see the huge African sharks seize them and take them under water, dyeing the waves with their blood. It was a horrible sight, and this was what we might expect when it came our turn to be driven from the vessel.

I said to the captain, "What is the use of our attempting to reach the shore? Better lash ourselves to the wreck and die where we are."

"Not a bit of it," said the captain; "sharks won't touch my wife; she has only to blow and they will be frightened off. Wife, put on the life-preservers, and stand by to tow us on shore."

Mrs. Cringle went below, and soon appeared with three life-preservers, the only ones on board, strapped around her. I suggested that it would be better to divide them between us, but the captain said, "Let my wife alone; she has helped me take care of this brig eleven years and never got out of her reckoning. If it hadn't been for these breakers and pitching up in here we'd 'a' been all right; or even if we'd been in the daytime things'd 'a' been different; or if we'd stood more to the norrud or suthard; or if we'd 'a' sailed a little slower and hadn't overrun the reck'nin'. But it's all the same. Wife'll tow us ashore, and we'll get our cargo out when the sea goes down, and them warming-pans'll be a good speculation yet."

I agreed with the captain in everything except in regard to the warming-pans. The sun was now high in the heavens, and its rays were scorching. I could not for the life of me see the utility of warming-pans in such a climate; but I had no opportunity to argue the question, for just then a heavy sea split the vessel open and pitched the captain and myself overboard and into the breakers, I keeping fast hold of my valise, to which I was resolved to stick to the last.

As soon as the captain came to the top of the water he sang out to his wife, "Come on, old lady, shriek one blow for the United States of America and take me in tow!"

Mrs. Cringle, who was standing on the gunwale with a harpoon in her hand and a coil of whale-line on her left arm, gave the most unearthly shriek, jumped into the water, and was soon alongside of us. Giving to each the end of a tow-rope, she struck out for the shore.

The sharks were pretty thick, and, having tasted blood, they rushed at us furiously, but as soon as they got a good look at Mrs. Cringle the monsters sheered off. There was something about her they didn't like, and if one came anywhere near her she struck him on the nose with her harpoon. We hadn't much trouble with the sharks, and as soon as we got inside their limit (the outer breaker) we were quite safe.

"Blow a screamer now, wife," said the captain, "for Yankee Doodle," and the old lady gratified him to his heart's content.

We reached the land in safety, though much exhausted, Mrs.

Cringle not being able to blow, although the captain was extremely anxious she should give one shriek for the Warming-Pan Society, and we sat down in the broiling sun without the slightest shelter.

The brig was fast going to pieces, and the boxes of warming-pans and other articles of the cargo were all the time coming ashore. "Good speculation yet," said the captain; "worth twice what they were yesterday." But I was still unable to appreciate the value of the warming-pans.

We had been on shore about four hours, and were sorrowfully watching the portion of the brig's hull that still held together, and Mrs. Cringle was overhauling the boxes to see if she could find any biscuits and codfish, when suddenly our ears were saluted by a savage shout, and, looking up, we beheld a party of about sixty negroes on camels approaching at full speed and brandishing their spears in not the most friendly manner.

"Hurrah!" sang out the captain, waving his bandana handkerchief; "here's the very Arabs I've been expecting! Wife, give 'em one of your loudest blows, to let them know we belong to the Warming-Pans." The old lady fairly snorted, and the negroes immediately wheeled around and retreated about half a mile, where they seemed to hold a consultation.

For my part I was not pleased with the appearance of the captain's "Arabs," and being much alarmed for my safety, I stole away down the beach, seeing an object at a distance of a few hundred yards which I thought would afford me a shelter. I dug out the sand and got under my shelter in double-quick time, my companions being so occupied in watching the strangers that they did not notice my desertion. From my hiding-place I could see all that was going on.

In a few moments the negroes moved toward Captain Cringle and his wife, and when within two hundred yards made a charge and surrounded them so that there was no chance for an escape.

The negroes now dismounted from their camels, and a dozen of them rushed to seize Mrs. Cringle, but she planted some heavy blows with her fist between the eyes of those nearest her, and they kept their distance, while the captain kept shouting, "Give' em an unearthly shriek, wife, and they'll keep off; it's a good speculation yet, don't spoil it." But just at this moment the unfortunate captain was transfixed by a spear hurled by one of the savages, and he fell weltering in his blood. Then the savages overpowered Mrs. Cringle and tied her hand and foot.

As soon as the old lady recovered her senses she began to shriek like mad, much to the astonishment of these unsophisticated children of the desert, who evidently didn't know what to make of it.

As for the captain, they probably thought he was dead, and bothered themselves no more about him, except to strip him naked and pull the spear out of his body.

After Mrs. Cringle had become somewhat quiet, the negroes began to break open the boxes that had come on shore from the wreck.

The first thing they came across were the articles which had given the name to the philanthropic society which had fitted out this unfortunate expedition.

I never saw such delight as was evinced by these savages when the bright copper warming-pans were brought to view. Each man put a warming-pan on his head, the lid hanging down behind. Then they proceeded to ransack other boxes.

The red-flannel shirts and drawers seemed to afford much pleasure, and were fastened to their spears and held aloft as banners. In fact, I am happy to say, for the satisfaction of the Warming-Pan Society, that their selection of articles was perfectly satisfactory to the interesting natives of Africa, and, could the latter have had an opportunity of thanking their benefactors, they would undoubtedly have done so.

The savages spent the day in hauling the things out of the water and piling them up near the beach. They then loaded the camels with all they could carry, tied Mrs. Cringle across the back of one of the animals, and, leaving one of their number to guard the pile of boxes, started off to the southeastward as fast as they could travel, no doubt in search of assistance to remove the rest of the goods.

The sentinel who remained behind now made his camel kneel, and passing a strap across one of his knees so that he could not rise, went to work to plunder a little on his own account. He collected a large pile around the camel, and as the sun went down he commenced chanting a plaintive air, which finally subsided, and all was quiet. The negro had evidently gone to sleep.

After waiting an hour or more I ventured to crawl from my hiding-place, and could see the outline of the sleeping savage, by the light of the moon, lying close alongside his camel, and could hear him snoring loudly.

Much to my surprise, I found that I owed my shelter to a huge crab-shell, about ten feet in diameter, with all the claws still attached to it. I suppose the proprietor of this covering had come out of the ocean to shed his shell. I saw numerous other remains of crab-shells, but had no time to speculate in regard to them, being too intent on more serious matters.

I crawled on my hands and knees to the poor captain, who, I found, still held in his hand the rope with which his wife towed him on shore, and, on trying to disengage it from his fingers, what was my surprise to find that life was not extinct. In my selfish regard for No. 1, I did not linger long by the captain, but crawled on my way toward the sleeping negro, the rope I had taken from the captain in my hand, and the revolvers which I had brought ashore in my valise buckled to my side.

I was young and powerful, yet my heart beat as I looked at this savage, wondering if those small arms and legs and that pot-belly contained sinews superior to mine. But I "cast my life on the hazard of the die," and jumping suddenly upon the negro's breast with my whole weight, and clutching him around the throat, I proceeded to secure him with the rope.

I found this an easy task, for I had so completely knocked the breath out of the African's body that he was entirely helpless, and in a few minutes he was tied so fast that I had no further fear of him.

In about ten minutes my savage came to, and, on realizing his condition, began to chatter like a monkey, which animal he closely resembled. I tried to make him understand that I would not hurt him, but the more I talked the faster he chattered.

I now went to see what was the condition of Captain Cringle, whom I found with his mouth open, asking for water, but none was to be had. He raised himself on his arm and said, in a feeble voice,

"Mr. Spicy, I shall never throw nary a harpoon again. I am dying; but if I could only hear wife give one blow, I should die contented! But where is she?"

"She is alive," I replied.

"Thank God!" he said. "Carried her off with them? I knew it. Would never lose a chance of getting a woman like that. Never was another like her. Ever married?"

"No," I said.

"Well, if you ever get a gal like that, who can reef a top-sail,

mend a sail, strap a block, or turn in a dead-eye, you are made."
Here his voice began to fail him.

"Tell the President," he said, "that I died at my post, with a warming-pan nailed to the mast. Tell him it was a good speculation if I hadn't overrun reck'nin', or got in breakers, or got too far south or too far north. Tell him how wife blowed to the last. The Arabs got a fine woman when they got her. Not much at sewin' buttons on, but dead-eyes! reefing! hear her blow! there she spouts! Let 'em hear you, wife," and he fell over and died.

I had no time to spare, so picking up one of the shovels that had been thrown on the beach in the boxes, I dug a hole and buried the poor captain, covering the spot with sea-weed in such a manner that the negroes would not detect it on their return.

I had tied a flannel shirt over my prisoner's face during these operations, so that he could not see what I was about, and having given the ropes which confined him a dozen extra turns, so that he could not possibly release himself, I prepared to depart, trusting to Providence to take me safely through my trials.

I found a gourd of water and a bag of dates on the camel, which satisfied me that the negroes had come from some oasis in the desert.

When they left the scene of the wreck they went off in a southeasterly direction, and not being at all anxious to follow them, I mounted my camel, and, heading him northeast as near as I could judge by the stars, started on my lonely journey.

I never drew rein till noon of the following day, when the sun's rays seemed to be consuming me. My camel carried his head bowed almost to the ground, and he tottered at every step. I had constantly to goad him with the sharp spear I had taken from the native to make him continue his course. At sunset he came to a full stop, and all my efforts to make him continue were unavailing. Even camels must have rest or they will fall down in their tracks. I slipped off the animal, which immediately lay down and sought the repose so necessary to a camel's constitution.

I, too, needed repose, for I estimated that I had been traveling eighteen hours at the rate of twelves miles an hour, and without much to eat or drink. Being quite worn out, I soon sank to slumber.

At daylight I was again on the way, but my half-famished camel could not make more than four or five miles an hour. I rested at noon, and continued my journey as the sun went down. So I proceeded for five days, when my camel broke down completely and could not stir a step farther.

During all this time I had not seen a blade of grass nor a living thing. I was fainting for want of food, and began to think that Providence had deserted me. I had traveled at least four hundred miles since leaving the scene of the wreck, and now I was left alone in the desert, with the prospect of losing the camel, my last hope.

What an unhappy situation! Here I was, as I supposed, in the center of the great unexplored desert regions of northern Africa, night coming on, and my camel dying before my eyes. Poor fellow! he had done his duty faithfully, although under no obligations to me; but a stronger friendship had grown up between us during the last few days than would have been cemented in many months under other circumstances.

Large tears of sympathy for me stood in poor Saadi's eyes (for so I called him), and he seemed to say, "Poor master! how much more enviable is my lot than yours!" and then, with such a long-drawn sigh as only a camel can express, he departed to the undiscovered country from whose bourne no camel returns. I felt as if I had lost my best friend when he died; and what grieved me most of all, I was so overcome with hunger that I was obliged to cut off the faithful animal's tail and make my supper from it. Though nearly worn out with hunger and fatigue, I could scarcely close my eyes, but I lay down under the lee of my poor camel, endeavoring to seek some repose. It was a beautiful starlight night, and the heavy dew was falling like rain. It was a great relief to me after the scorching heat of the day, and when my clothes became saturated with dew I wrung them out and filled my bottle for the next day's journey.

In a short time after lying down my eyelids began to droop, and I was almost in a sound slumber when a noise in the distance like the trampling of horses awoke me. I started up to see from whence came the noise, and after a while beheld the faint outlines of a large body of animals moving toward me. Onward they came, almost shaking the ground with their weight; and I at once gave myself up for lost, thinking it could be nothing else but a troop of hungry wolves, attracted, doubtless, by the smell of my dead companion, or the negroes in pursuit of me. My first impulse was to fly, but fly I could not, for on looking in all directions I found myself surrounded by the moving mass, and I could see no means of escape. Recommending myself to that divine Providence which had always guarded me in more trying circumstances even than this, I quietly awaited the approach of the invaders of my repose, expecting every moment to find myself torn to pieces by the jaws of ferocious beasts or killed by savage negroes.

On, on they came, as numerous as the host of Attila when he overran Europe, and when they approached within twenty yards of me they stopped, all drawn up in regular order. One of them approached the spot where I stood without in the least noticing me, and, rather sidling out of my way, what was my astonishment at beholding a large crab six feet high and as large in other respects as a Conestoga-wagon horse! I was struck dumb with astonishment at the sight of this hideous-looking animal, but much relieved in mind when I found it was only a crab, although his crabship was as large as a horse. It was very evident that he was much more afraid of me than I was of him, for he kept his large, glassy eyes fixed upon me while he took a survey of the dead animal before him. After the space of a minute or two he backed out toward his companions, and after an apparent consultation ten of the hideous-looking things came toward the camel. I moved aside to give them room, for they exhibited as much respect toward me as the first one did. They looked eagerly at the camel and then at me, as much as to say, "Can we take a piece?" I nodded my head in assent, and in an instant they dove into the carcass, and with their sharp, heavy claws took out three or four pounds at a clip. After this performance ten more came forward, and the first ten retired in good order with their prize clutched in their claws, and so on they manœuvred until the entire flesh and bones had almost disappeared. By this time they had evidently begun to regard me as a friendly creature, and carried on their work within a foot of me without heeding my presence at all.

Wishing to discover what degree of intimacy was permitted by their crabships, I placed my hand on one of their backs without the least inconvenience to him. I then moved closer up and took some liberties with their claws, though in a friendly way, but they did not seem to mind me, so intent were they in stripping the camel. Not one twentieth part of the main army had moved at all, and only about two hundred of the crabs had approached and carried off their portions, showing that a perfect system or organization existed among them. Very little of the camel now remained, and the last ten were preparing to join their comrades when an idea struck me, and I determined to put it into execution.

"Why," I asked myself, "can not I make use of these creatures to take me out of this desert? And what objection is there to my mounting one of them, and make him take me to some settled part of the country?" And with the thought I put my hand on the back of the one nearest to me, and placing my foot into one of the hinges of his claw, I mounted him without difficulty and with seemingly no objection on his part. He wheeled round at once, and in a brisk trot, though a rough one, he carried me right toward the army of crabs, which opened right and left to let me pass, and then closed up behind me. The animal I bestrode seemed quite proud of his burden, for he carried me safely through the whole army, composed of many thousands, and stopped about twenty yards outside of them. Then they all wheeled round facing toward us, and, knocking their two fore claws together, which sounded like a clap of thunder, they put themselves in motion, my crab taking the lead.

Here, then, by universal acclaim, and without any electioneering on my part, I was evidently elected general of this large army, and I had the satisfaction of knowing that my position was a perfect sinecure, for all the duties of the army seemed to be carried on by some great instinct known only to the brute creation. Most generals travel in the rear or center, out of the way of danger; but here I found myself in the very front of danger, if any was to be encountered, and my curiosity was very much excited to see where this would end. One reads the fictions of "Sinbad the Sailor," "Jack and the Bean-Stalk," and the "Seven Knights of Christendom" with surprise at their wonderful adventures, but they all sink into insignificance alongside of my being elected generalissimo of a large army of crabs, and there are persons now living who will likely imagine this a tale of fiction, and it would cause them to discredit my story. If they discredit this, I am sure I don't know what they will do when they come to parts of my history almost too wonderful to relate—so wonderful, indeed, that I am almost tempted not to make them public; but I must leave it to posterity to do me justice, and perhaps when I am dead and gone some enterprising traveler may succeed in reaching these inaccessible regions, and will find my name handed down by tradition among the natives, by whom I was worshiped with nearly the same veneration as one of their gods. But to resume my story. The army of crabs traveled to the north at a most rapid rate, keeping all the time the most perfect order, and now and then throwing out scouts far in advance of us, which scouts were relieved every half-hour by others, and then joined the main army. On their return they always struck their fore claws together as a signal that all was safe.

I presume we had traveled at the rate of twelve or fourteen miles an hour; daylight began to streak the eastern horizon, and I could perceive by the dim twilight that we were not entirely in the desert, for we had passed one or two palm- or date-trees, and I had noticed several patches of grass. At last the sun began to appear in the horizon, rising up, as it were, from out the depths of some great ocean, for the desert looked like an ocean of liquid fire. I was almost blinded looking at the scorching luminary, and it was some minutes before I could get the cobwebs out of my eyes. What was my astonishment and delight to behold, at a distance of only two miles, a broad and expansive lake, its margin surrounded with clusters of beautiful trees, and numerous white dwellings peeping forth from among the undergrowth. I thought for a moment that I could see human beings running to and fro, but my hopes were disappointed, for on a closer examination I could see nothing of the kind.

At this moment my army (without any orders from me) came to a dead halt; part of the main body wheeled to the right, and the other part to the left, and then started off in a brisk canter, each taking a road leading around the lake and leaving me with an escort of thirty crabs, which proceeded slowly toward the village. So much deference had been paid me by these truly amiable creatures that I supposed myself about to be introduced into their own domiciles, as I took it for granted that they were the only inhabitants of these deserts, when my attention was suddenly arrested by the appearance of a body of cavalry coming right toward me. I could plainly see the mounted men, with their spears brandishing in the air, and as they approached nearer I could see that they were negroes mounted, like myself, on crabs. My escort stopped, awaiting their approach, and I did not know whether I should felicitate myself on encountering human beings or not. I had seen enough of the inhabitants of the desert to know that to exhibit fear with them would be losing caste at once, so I determined to put on a bold face and treat them as my inferiors.

I accordingly rose on my feet, stood on one leg, and stretched out both arms toward the east and west, bowing my head slowly toward them as they approached. When they got within twenty yards of me they drew up in line, poised their spears, as if in the act of throwing them, instead of which they stuck them in the ground, and, throwing a somersault backward, landed on the sand face downward. This I knew to be a sign of friendship, if not of adoration, and my mind felt perfectly relieved on the score of hostilities. After a moment they arose from their position and commenced crawling toward me in the most abject manner, throwing sand over their heads, and crying out, "*Sfisa Rotan, Sa, Sa, Fame,*" which, in the language of the country, means, "Spare us, good Lord," as I afterward learned.

I saw at once that I was looked upon as a divinity, and, leaping from my animal, I walked toward them, holding a red silk pocket-handkerchief in my hand, and whistling "Yankee Doodle," a tune the natives I had hitherto read of had shown a great liking for.

I approached so close to them that I could hear their hard breathing, and see their bodies trembling with fear as they heard my footsteps near them; but wishing at once to relieve their minds, I exclaimed, in a loud voice, "*Sawi mito aras vaga,*" which means, "Fear not, children, I come in peace." This I learned at college. In an instant they all turned another somersault forward and stood upon their feet, shouting, "*Gori Anisa Larpai Radif!*" which means, "Our chief is here; he comes from the sun!"

Everything was now joy and excitement, and they danced around me, throwing sand over their bodies all the time. Much to my astonishment, I discovered that they all had long tails like monkeys, covered with red hair, and the end of the tail was finished off with three long prongs, made of horn, which they frequently stuck into the ground to assist them in turning rapidly and in preventing them from falling. After dancing about me for five minutes, they formed in a circle, stuck their tails in the ground, and, forming a spiral spring with them, they sat down on what appeared to be a very comfortable seat. They then put their arms akimbo and looked full at me, their countenances beaming with the most intense delight.

Among all the Africans I had heard of in the desert, these certainly were the most peculiar, and no better opportunity than the present occurs for describing them.

They were all as black as the ten of spades, which is acknowledged by every one to be nine times blacker than the ace, and their faces, being rubbed over with cocoanut-oil, shone as bright as if they had been polished with copal varnish. Their heads went up to a sharp point, on the apex of which they carried a small tuft of hair dyed red, out of the top of which peeped forth a small red berry. In their noses was a large hole, through which was inserted a long, thin shell of the same kind; through each ear holes were also cut out, leaving scarcely anything but the rim and the lobe, the latter hanging away down on their shoulders. Some of them had their lobes buttoned together under their chins. One who seemed to be their chief carried two large pendants, made of crabs'-claws, hung in his ears, with a metal band going over the top of his head to take off the strain of so great a weight, for I calculated that his ear-rings each weighed ten pounds. They wore no clothing with the exception of a waist-cloth hanging down to their knees; their entire body was painted with round spots of deep red, the size of a dollar, resembling very much a pattern of the same kind I have seen in mousselaine de laine, and generally called the devil's mourning. A bracelet on the left arm, made of polished crabs'-eyes, completed their costume, and a more picturesque-looking party I never looked upon in my life.

I had learned to speak three different languages during my intercourse with the collegiates, and determined to see which of these was best understood by my present friends; and as there was very little difference in the three languages, I presumed that we would comprehend each other after a fashion; so, putting on all my dignity, I took up a handful of sand and threw it into the chief's eyes, saying in a loud voice, at the same time, "*Timis Noimo lene zordel brefa oziv chesit oarof gomfara polliwog.*" A mixture of the three languages of the Watoos, the Snotoos, and the Bombaras, meaning, "Don't be afraid of me, boys; I will take you under my immediate protection."

A shout of joy burst forth at once on my saying these words, and the whole party, taking hold of each other's tails, turned six somersaults around the circle, and resumed their places again; when the chief, having turned three somersaults backward, and filling his mouth with sand, which he blew in the faces of his right- and left-hand man, thus addressed me: "*Dot elli stherea nythin ggre enin oure ye, do ezyo urmo therkno wyouro ut.*"

The language, though new to me, sounded not unlike what I had heard at college, and the chief in those few words made over to me all he possessed in the world, consisting of his palaces, ten wives, sixty children, three thousand crabs, four hundred boats, three thousand date-trees, twenty trained apes, four alligators, and six hundred "Scratchymaus," or idols. I accepted them all in the

"Do ezyo urmo therkno wyouro ut."

MR. SPICY'S NARRATIVE.

name of "Che Che" (the sun), and then again they all yelled with delight, and wound up with the following song, which is untranslatable :

> "Ohgetalon goldd antucke
> Ryo uto olatetocom etos uppe
> Roldd antucke reigh tynin
> Ehis hairti edu pwi thabun.
>   Choft winé, ya, ya, ya, etc.,
>   Choft winé, ya, ya, ya, etc."

And then they wound up by turning three somersaults and flourishing their long tails. They picked me up gently and placed me on a superbly caparisoned crab belonging to the chief; two negroes jumped up behind me and shaded my respected head from the sun by holding over me a "jawtank" (umbrella) made of the thin shell of small crabs.

Thus honored, I proceeded toward the village or city, whichever it might be, whistling "Yankee Doodle" all the way, and with my red silk handkerchief hoisted on a spear. I found that the "Chawtees" (such was the name of my friends) had manifold uses for their tails besides using them as a spiral spring and chairs to sit upon. My right-hand man in particular used his very dexterously by turning it under my crab's belly and tickling him under and above the short ribs ; it answered, in fact, all the purposes of a spur at one moment, while at another my umbrella-holder used it for scratching his top-knot, and then, by tying a bush to the end of it, he played the very devil (I beg pardon) with the flies that were swarming about us.

I had read of many specimens of African negroes, but these beat anything I had hitherto heard of. I had read of the Nianis, a race with an elongation of the spine—spoken of by Herodotus—the Bombaras with three separate rows of teeth like the shark, and the Watoos with a false pocket in their sides (something like the kangaroo) in which they carried their young, but the Chawtees, in my opinion, excelled them all, not only in personal appearance but in their intelligence, and as regards civilization they were far ahead of all the tribes of Africa.

As we entered the outskirts of the town called "Chawteewarrawarra" we were met by the entire population, who came out in great excitement to receive me, approaching me tail foremost, so that they might not be dazzled by the appearance of "Che Che Radif" (the offspring of the sun) ; four negroes now came toward me carrying something made of wicker-work, and in shape of a dice-box, and while I was regarding the prostrate people before me and felicitating myself on being made so great a personage of, I was suddenly put out like the snuff of a candle by having the wicker-basket put over my head.

I supposed this to be the custom they adopted toward their idols for fear that the first sight of them would be too overpowering for the people, who were considered sufficiently honored by being permitted to look on the basket, and therefore I felt no alarm when I found myself so suddenly extinguished. But I felt disappointed in not being taken direct to the town, for nature began to yearn for something to eat, and I longed to get hold of the flesh-pots of Chawteewarrawarra.

There was no prospect at present of my wishes being gratified, for my animal was put in motion, and the cavalcade, if so it may be called, moved off toward the lake, as I could plainly see through the wicker-work of my extinguisher. When we arrived there, I was gently lifted off my crab and as gently carried to a splendid barge made of an inverted crab-shell of a great size, and lined inside with the skin of the boa-constrictor. I rested on pillows made of birds' down, covered with feathers of the most beautiful colors and worked together in the most ingenious manner. Fifty young girls with timbrels in their hands accompanied me in the journey, and kept time with the oars as we paddled down the lake. I could not see their faces, as they were entirely concealed with masks. They were virgins of the temple of the Sun, and their faces were never seen by any one but the high-priest himself.

After pulling about two miles my barge stopped, and I could perceive through the interstices of the basket that we had "come to" among a number of vessels much larger than the one I was on. I learned afterward that it was the war-fleet of "Chawteewarrawarra," and in appearance the vessels resembled somewhat the old Chinese junks, being much smaller it is true. Each vessel was formed of four large crab-shells, with turret growing from the center of each, and spanned together by bridges thrown from one turret to the other. These were crowded with soldiers, who turned their tails toward me like all the others.

My barge had remained stationary about ten minutes, and the most perfect silence prevailed. I observed a crab-shell shove off from the shore, in which sat a very old negro. He was entirely naked, and the only ornament on his person was a string of red

beads around his neck. It was with great difficulty he could be
lifted into my barge, and he was held up while he dragged his
worn-out limbs toward my cage. The basket was raised gently,
and, inserting his long tail, he commenced stirring me up with it
in a manner I thought anything but pleasant, and I felt disposed
to think the Chawtees were not treating me with as much respect
as my high position entitled me to; however, I supposed it was
part of the ceremony I was to go through, and I afterward learned
that the high-priest was trying to see if "Che Che Radif" was
capable of feeling pain. He was not gratified, however, in his curiosity, for my long, thick boots protected my legs; otherwise they
would have been streaming with blood. This operation was repeated three different times. I began to feel now that it was too
much of a good thing, and determined to put a stop to it in such a
manner that they would have a high opinion of the powers of "Che
Che Radif." I had landed with my powder-horn in my pocket
and my Colt's revolver slung to my side. While the boat was gone
for another persecutor I mixed up some powder in the palm of my
hand with spittle, and, tearing off a piece of my cotton shirt, I
made a fire-cracker with it, and drew out some threads to make it
fast with; then I smeared my face with the rest of the powder,
and looked as black as any negro of them all. Taking out a lucifer-
match and preparing my revolver, I waited for the next high-priest,
who was not long in coming. When he got in my barge he had
the basket lifted, and the tail was poked in as usual, and commenced poking up my legs with a vengeance. I stooped down
gently and took hold of it, taking care not to hurt myself with the
three prongs. The moment I touched it it stopped poking me and
lay perfectly quiet in my hand, when I immediately tied on my
cracker; the lucifer-match was then applied, and phiz it went in a
minute. Sticking my penknife into the high-priest's tail, I gave
one yell and fired the six barrels of the revolver right through the
top of my extinguisher, which, being made of a peculiar kind of
wood, light and dry, was soon in a blaze. I waited a minute until
it was fairly lighted and burning briskly, when I threw it off, and
there stood their great idol, "Che Che Radif," his face as black as
thunder and his countenance inflamed with anger. Never in my
life did I witness such a scene as now presented itself to my sight.
There was the high-priest with the fire-cracker tied to his tail (and
still phizzing away at a great rate), lying down in the bottom of the
barge, yelling out, "Che Che Radif Makarra Makarra!" while the

water was fairly alive with the poor wretches, who had jumped overboard in their fright, for they considered that "Che Che Radif" had brought fire from heaven and was going to destroy them all with it in his anger.

Now is the time, I thought, to make an impression, so I took the high-priest by the tail and sang out in a loud voice, "Garo-pangé!" (get up, sinner), when in an instant he turned a somersault and stood trembling before me. He had not yet dared to raise his eyes, when I took him by the chin, and made him look me full in the face; but the sight was too much for him; he was so dazzled by the appearance of the great idol that he gave one unearthly yell, and, turning a somersault into the water, he sank to the bottom like a stone, and rose no more. Poor fellow! I did not intend to kill him, but they could well afford to lose a high-priest, they had so many of them, and I was glad to make an example. Many of the people declared that they had seen him melted up, consumed by a flash of lightning from heaven, while some said the fire came from the mouth of "Che Che Radif," who slew him in his anger.

Unfortunately, this was not the end of the catastrophe; in throwing off the basket I used great force; it fell on board one of the war-ships close alongside of me, and in an instant the whole fabric was in a blaze; this communicated the flames to the rest, and before one could well think the entire marine of the Chawtees was destroyed. The inhabitants were so frightened that they never stopped to put out the flames, but hurried to the woods and desert in hopes of escaping divine vengeance.

Finding after three or four hours that no one returned, and being almost starved, I began to look about for something to eat. I could not reach the shore through the burning mass of vessels, as the wind blew directly toward me; so I took up the mat from the bottom of my boat, bent it on to an oar, and made a sail of it; my light, flat-bottomed crab-shell fairly skimmed the water with a fair wind, and this little circumstance added very much to my importance in the estimation of the natives, who had never yet known the use of sails; they attributed it all to the magic power of "Che Che Radif." In a very few moments I reached the opposite shore, and sailed my bark into a beautiful little haven, where I landed and hauled her up after me. I then sat down and carefully reloaded my revolver again, for though I had no apprehension of being harmed by any one, yet I thought it best to be prepared for any contingency. I found that my little knapsack had been placed in the boat with scrupulous care when I was taken off from the back of the crab, and not having changed my clothes for some days, I determined to take this opportunity to make my toilet. I selected from my wardrobe a new red flannel shirt and a pair of drawers of the same color, and I dressed myself up in these only, determined to astonish the natives; I hauled my long boots on, and tucked the drawers inside of them, tied a long green comforter around my straw hat, and, when dressed in full costume, considered myself fit to be presented to any monarch in the world, at least in the African world.

After getting through my toilet I took out of my knapsack any little things I thought I might require, and carried them in the breast of my shirt, and I then dug a hole and hid away my other clothes until I should want them.

I had scarcely got through with my toilet when I heard the sound of music not far off, and, climbing up the side of the bank, I found that I had landed close to a little grove of trees, through which I could see a number of picturesque-looking houses, whence came the sound of the music I had just heard. I then saw a procession of females coming out, headed by a man whom I recognized to be the chief who had first encountered me, and carrying before them a female in something resembling a sedan-chair open at the sides.

Finding that they were coming toward me with some hesitation, I stood perfectly still with my arms outstretched and standing on one foot to show them I was a friend. This reassured them, as I could see by the chief's turning two somersaults and blowing sand into the eyes of his right- and left-hand man, and the procession moved on briskly toward me. I now noticed that the only covering the females had was a mask over the face; in every other respect they were perfectly naked. Their tails also, I observed, were nearly twice as long as the men's, and each tail was carried by a beautiful little boy or page, such as ladies have to carry their trains at European courts.

The chief, whose name I afterward found out was Manave, now came toward me in the humblest manner, crying out, "Che Che Radif Makkarra Makkarra"; to which I replied in a mild voice, "Garopangé" (get up, sinner), and, turning a somersault, he stood before me. It would be useless to attempt giving our conversation in the Chawtee language, for it would not be understood; but I asked the chief what was the meaning of this procession, to which he replied,

"It is our good queen, Che Che Radif, whose charms have conquered the hearts of all the neighboring chiefs, and who now comes in person to see if she can appease your wrath. She is as beautiful as the moon and as chaste as the limpid lake you see before you; she offers you all she has in the world if you will not destroy her people."

"Present me to the queen," I replied, haughtily; "and after I look upon her beauty I will make up my mind what to do."

Manave now led me toward the queen, turning a somersault now and then by way of testifying his joy, and throwing sand over his head as he alighted on his feet.

Her ebony-colored majesty was so overcome with my appearance that she crouched down in the bottom of the palanquin, and I thought she would never undo herself again, having taken five or six turns with her tail around her legs and body, and made the whole fast with an overhand knot; the best sailor in the American navy could not have done the thing better.

After waiting for some time to see if the lady would come to, I ordered the chief to inform her that I was a friend, and would do her no harm; that I came from the country of twenty-four stars, and that I longed to see her beautiful countenance.

Then her majesty uncoiled herself, and, stepping out of the palanquin, she stood timidly before me, the most beautiful form I ever beheld. I approached and knelt down before her, and, taking hold of the end of her tail, I respectfully pressed it to my lips. "Thus, great queen," I said, "do I honor beauty and worth, and I hope to be a blessing to yourself and people."

To describe the scene of joy that ensued would be impossible; the whole procession turned somersaults simultaneously, and embraced one another with their tails, while the chief amused himself blowing sand into the eyes of every one within his reach.

I then arose, and, stepping up to the queen, removed her mask, and beheld before me a young girl of sixteen, with the most beautiful features it is possible to imagine. Had she been cut from a piece of marble by Canova himself her features could not have been formed more regularly. She smiled graciously upon me, and, throwing her tail around my body, she drew me toward her, and kindly sprinkled my head with sand. I then led her majesty to the palanquin, in which she insisted I should take a seat, but, the

MR. SPICY'S NARRATIVE.

chair being too small for two to sit side by side, I was obliged to take her on my lap, which seemed to please her very much, and she testified her pleasure by taking four turns with her tail around my neck, by which I was nearly choked.

The palanquin was now raised on the shoulders of four negroes, and the procession moved on toward the grove from whence they had come. All was now joy and excitement; the men turned somersaults, and the women chanted in plaintive voices some of their native songs.

At length we stopped in front of the queen's palace, where we were to alight; but her majesty did not seem to be disposed to slacken her embraces; she kept her tail coiled around my throat in the most affectionate manner, and by various little attentions while we were carried along, such as sticking her fingers in my ears, and rubbing her nose against mine, I could see that she was deeply in love with me. I may say I was carried a captive into the palace, for I walked alongside of her with my arm around her waist and her tail firmly fastened around my neck; I was, in fact, getting rather red in the face.

I was led to the throne by her majesty, and placed upon her right hand, the post of honor generally reserved for the queen herself, and then she condescended to relax her embrace. Turning to her court, she exclaimed, "Che Che Radif Gorrele Buckra," meaning, "The child of the sun sits on the throne."

I must not omit to describe this throne, which was the most curious I ever saw. It was a large stuffed alligator, twenty-five or thirty feet long; its upper jaw had been forced back so as to stand perfectly upright, and the lower jaw was used as a platform on which to sit; a canopy made of a large crab-shell, inverted, and fringed round with small claws, was supported by four date-trees, and from the center of it hung a large egg-of-ostrich chandelier, which was used at night. Now, just imagine me sitting in an alligator's mouth, with my sable beauty at my side, quite as happy as Victoria and Albert on their gilded throne at Windsor.

My queen's name was "Raka," which means "love's delight"; and I began to feel, while sitting so close, very queer about the heart but much queerer about the belly. If I had fasted much longer I should have bitten off a piece of her majesty's tail, and dined off of it; but I recollected that the last meal I had tasted was my poor camel's tail, and I was almost ashamed to look a tail in the face, so, squeezing her majesty's hand gently, I said, "Raka,

Che Che Radif Gombera," that is, "Love's Delight, the child of the sun is hungry."

In an instant twenty of the courtiers disappeared, and everybody commenced turning somersaults, crying out all the time, "Che Che Radif Gombera." I waited, I suppose, about an hour for the eatables, and began to think they would never make their appearance; the gracious Raka was too happy twisting her fingers in my curls, and every now and then tickling me with the end of her tail, to think of eating, and the absence of the good things of life did not give her the least unhappiness.

At length my doubts about there being nothing to eat in the city were dispelled, for the courtiers returned bringing in a huge crab, whose back fairly bent under the weight of the provisions. He was unloaded in our presence, a mat was spread out on the floor, and Raka, giving me her hand and a sly kiss (I ought not to publish that) at the same time, led me to the feast, which was served up in different kind of dishes; the first that was offered me was crabs' eyes served up in honey, but not liking the looks of the dish I refused it. I saw at once that I had made a mistake, for Raka commenced to weep; so, seizing hold of the mixture, I pitched into it as if I had never eaten anything before. I offered some of it to the queen, but she, dear creature, was too much interested on my account, and amused herself picking up the choice bits (the eyes) and presenting them to me on the end of a long stick. I feasted very heartily on them, and afterward learned to look upon crabs' eyes in honey as a great delicacy.

The next dish brought upon the carpet was crocodile-eggs and ant sauce. The eggs I managed to dispose of very well, but I rather avoided the ant sauce, until I saw the tears starting in the fond eyes of my queen, and I bolted them down as if they were shrimps; indeed, they were in no way inferior to that delicious little fish, and I soon became very fond of them. When I got through with the eggs and ant sauce all the ladies commenced tickling me under the ribs with their fans, which set me to laughing heartily, and I was told it was done to promote digestion, for the Chawtees consider no meal wholesome if the person eating is not made to laugh.

The third dish was now brought on, and in this her majesty deigned to join. It was tree-frogs stewed in rice, and a more delicious dish I never tasted. Her majesty made them disappear like rice before chopsticks, and while I was eating one she managed to stow away a dozen; she very innocently asked me why, like her,

I did not use my tail in picking out the choicest pieces, and large tears stood in her eyes when I informed her that the children of the sun were born without that useful appendage; but the dear creature consoled me by telling me that I should never suffer for the want of one while I stayed with her, for she would always feed me herself at meals.

After the third course the chief stepped up and laid me gently on my back, which I quietly submitted to, wishing to conform to all the etiquette for fear of bringing tears into the eyes of the amiable Raka; while I was in this position I was gently rubbed from my head to my feet and then placed upright again.

Now came the fourth course, consisting of dried grasshoppers and curds sprinkled with Cayenne pepper, and it required some determination to attack this formidable-looking mixture. I hesitated for a moment, but I thought of Raka's tears and bolted it down. Good heavens! how my throat was burnt by the pepper! and to make matters worse one of the grasshoppers went down the wrong way. I was near being choked by this unlooked-for accident, but my kind Raka came to my assistance, and, putting her long finger down my throat, she soon relieved me of the grasshopper; tears stood in her eyes when she saw how much I suffered, and she kissed me affectionately; when she had relieved me she immediately passed an edict that no more grasshoppers should be allowed in her dominions.

We now wound up the entertainment by taking sour crab's-milk and dates, after which we took coffee made of a peculiar kind of bean; then cigars three feet long were put in each person's mouth, and in less than ten minutes you could scarcely see any one for the smoke. The odor emitted from the cigars was not quite so pleasant as that produced by the genuine Havana, but that will not be wondered at when the reader is informed they were made of the poke-weed; the effect was wonderfully soporific, and in a few moments I lost my senses in a deep sleep.

When I again opened my eyes I was lying on a stuffed snake's-skin, with soft feather pillows under my head, while the gentle Raka was sitting beside me keeping off the flies with her tail, to the end of which she had fastened the feathers from an ostrich; four of her maidens were kneeling around me and rubbing me with date-oil, while a dozen musicians in the next room were discoursing sweet (!) music on some covered gourds. Raka, for fear I should run away, in my sleep had taken two half-hitches with her tail around one of my legs. The remainder of the day I devoted myself to this amiable queen, ate everything she put before me, and drank everything her maidens offered me. I was so infatuated that I would have taken poison for her sake.

"Come, Raka," I said, "tell me something about yourself. I long to know who you are, and what extent of country you own; who you are descended from, and what number of people claim you as sovereign."

She complied immediately with my request, and informed me that she had been queen only for two years, and had succeeded to the throne owing to the death of her father, whose skin she kept stuffed, and promised to show it to me whenever I felt disposed to see it. She claimed dominion over the whole of Africa, but many of the neighboring kings had declared their independence and refused to pay her the usual taxes, or to show her that respect which was paid to her father. Her army, she informed me, consisted of three thousand well-drilled crabs, four hundred trained apes, which did the duty of light infantry, and three hundred "Bangwangs" (birds or slingers), which I will describe presently.

She informed me that the large crabs did all the service generally performed by camels, but that they were stronger, more hardy, and could go any length of time without eating; they were drilled to go out every evening after food, and to return by sunrise; and hers were so well disciplined that they gave her generals very little trouble. It was part of her army that I encountered in the desert, and to which I was indebted for introducing me to so much happiness. At my request she ordered a review on the morrow, and I looked forward with much pleasure to witness their curious proceedings.

The population of her dominions, she thought, consisted of about twenty millions, though she could only command at present three thousand fighting men, owing to the secession of so many chiefs, who had misled a large portion of her people.

I promised her to settle that matter in a very short time, and made up my mind to use up the disobedient chiefs as soon as I could muster her army together and see of what ingredients it was composed. "But, my sweet Raka," I said to her, "before I take any steps in the matter a treaty must be drawn up between the kingdom of Chawtee and the great republic of twenty-four stars, a treaty of alliance and friendship; and after you have ceded certain privileges to the stars you shall receive in return my assistance to put down your enemies, and your subjects will be allowed the same privileges in the great republic as an American is allowed in Chawtee."

Raka was quite delighted at the proposition of making a treaty with so great a nation, and, as I liked to do business briskly, I proposed to her to send for her ministers of state, and let us go at it at once. To please me she complied, though I could evidently perceive that she was too well pleased with my society to wish to have our intercourse interrupted by the dull matters of state.

She sent immediately for her prime minister, who soon presented himself, and made known to him my wishes and her own. Old "Chaffyman" (such was his name) looked as wise as an owl —about as wise as all prime ministers look when their sovereigns propose anything to them; but he had seen such evidences of my power in drawing down fire from heaven that he wisely concluded to hold his peace and conform to his mistress's desires. He bowed his head in token of obedience, and endeavored to turn a somersault in token of his pleasure, but I regret to say that in doing so the old man fell on his nose, and was laid out senseless for nearly half an hour.

Much discussion ensued between Chaffyman and myself in relation to certain articles of the treaty, and on one occasion we were very near coming to an open rupture, he was so stubborn and would not yield a point; fortunately, I recollected that I had some lucifer-matches in my pocket, and taking one of them out, I ignited it by rubbing it against the heel of my boot, and held it toward him, looking him steadily meanwhile in the face; the sight of the fire produced in so magical a manner, with the smell of the brimstone, brought the old owl to his senses, and he appeared anxious to seal, sign, and deliver as soon as I pleased to have it done.

The following articles of agreement were accordingly drawn up, and I flatter myself that never was more ability displayed than on this my first attempt at treaty-making. If the United States do not take advantage of the liberal concessions made by her majesty of Chawtee, it will be their own fault; and if I am not voted the freedom of the cities with a gold snuff-box, it is because my countrymen have more to do with their money than they used to have:

"ARTICLES

Of Agreement between the chaste and lovely Queen Raka of the Sandy Kingdom of Chawtee, Sovereign of all Africa, from the rising of the sun to the setting of the same, and owner of all the stars that shine by night on her dominions, with the Country of Twenty-four Stars, the smartest country in all creation, whose boundary extends from the North Pole to the Equator, who has annexed the Aurora Borealis and Magnetic Pole, and who can whip all Everlasting if they want to.

"ARTICLE 1. Each nation binds itself to assist the other in its wars against their enemies, and bind themselves not to make peace without the consent of each other.

"ART. 2. Persons belonging to each nation shall enjoy equal privileges in the separate countries of each other, with the exception that the Chawtees must not wear their tails out in public in the country of twenty-four stars, and the children of the stars must not squirt their tobacco-juice in presence of her majesty of Chawtee.

"ART. 3. In case her majesty of Chawtee should think proper to send a minister plenipotentiary to the country of twenty-four stars, said minister is not to be accompanied with more than fifteen wives, as the governor of one of the stars has but sixteen, and it would be a mark of disrespect to him for any one to have more than that number.

"ART. 4. The citizens of Chawtee shall have the privilege of settling in any part of the country of twenty-four stars with the exception of four of the southern stars, where they will have to submit to incarceration, owing to the dissolute character of the negro population, who would lead them astray, and likely cut off those beautiful ornaments, their tails.

"ART. 5. The Chawtee government cede to the country of twenty-four stars the right of way through their dominions, with the privilege of constructing a railroad; they also cede three leagues on each side of the road for the benefit of contractors, giving them full privilege to use as much sand as they like.

"ART. 6. Her majesty of Chawtee also gives to the government of stars the privilege of using three ports in the Lake of Chawtee for coal depots for steamers, or for any other vessels in distress. Pilots shall be established at each of these ports, whose sole business it shall be to look out for American vessels and take them to a secure anchorage; and for performing this service their compensation shall be one pound of salt pork, two quarts of dried apples, and one quart of peanuts.

"Art. 7. It is expressly stipulated between the high contracting parties that the minister plenipotentiary from Chawtee is not to use his tail in picking out the choice pieces in case he should dine with any of the high functionaries of the twenty-four stars, as it would give the said minister a decided advantage over the high functionaries in question, who use nothing but forks and knives.

"Her majesty of Chawtee binds herself by her High Minister Chaffyman to see the conditions of this treaty faithfully carried out; and Che Che Radif, on the part of the nation of twenty-four stars, promises to do likewise, provided that the said treaty is accepted. (Signed) CHE CHE RADIF.
CHAFFYMAN."

Now, I thought to myself, after I had signed, sealed, and delivered, this is what I call a treaty. It gives the United States everything she possibly could ask for under the circumstances, and leaves her at liberty to do pretty much as she pleases, provided she does not want to comply with the stipulations. I thought of the excitement there would be when I returned with this treaty in my pocket, and already began to figure out the amount of money I should receive for diplomatic services. My face bespoke so plainly what I felt, and I looked so happy, that her majesty could not refrain from throwing her arms around my neck and giving me a kiss, at which old Chaffyman, as in duty bound, endeavored to turn a somersault, but as usual fell on his nose and knocked himself senseless. He was carried from the presence covered with blood, and did not leave his couch for many weeks.

The government of Chawtee sustained no great loss by his absence, for I administered the affairs of state myself, and brought about a system of reform very beneficial to her majesty.

In the evening Raka proposed that I should join her in a review of a favorite body of her troops, called "Bangwangs," or Sharpshooters, and accordingly we sallied forth, accompanied by her court, to the parade-ground.

The reader will be very much astonished when I inform him that the Bangwangs were not men, but birds of a large size and perfectly drilled in every evolution necessary to be performed in battle; in form they very much resembled the large white crane, only they were larger and stood more erect; they were nearly seven feet high, had a long bill elastic as India-rubber, and on the end of the bill they carried something resembling an egg, which, when opened, presented the appearance of two bowls of spoons; their eyes were as sharp as those of an eagle, and their feet were so large it seemed impossible to trip them up.

They are the only living thing that can come within the influence of the upas-tree without meeting death; but in that poisonous tree they make their nests and breed in great numbers; that is the reason, I suppose, they have never been met with. They are taken when quite young, their tongues cut out, and then trained as I shall presently describe.

They were drawn up in companies of twenty, each company commanded by a Chawtee captain, one lieutenant, one sergeant, and two corporals, whose business it was to direct their movements and supply them with ammunition. The ammunition consisted of small stones about the size of a pigeon's egg, and these were carried in bags around the necks of the officers.

A target was set up at the distance of fifty yards, and at this I was told the bangwangs were to shoot. The target was a large crab-shell about the size of a horse, the said crab-shell being stuffed and set up to look like a living one. The invasions in this desert were always made on the backs of crabs, which was the only animal the chiefs possessed for transporting soldiers.

At the word of command, "Marrá," the birds all stood in line; at the second, "Chawtee," they opened their mouths and allowed the officers to deposit a stone in the spoon part of their bill; and at the third, "Chuck," they commenced turning with great velocity on one foot, and, after making ten rapid revolutions, let fly the stones from their bills, which rattled like hail against the body and legs of the target. They went through this performance ten times, when the target began to totter and look very shaky. I was just stepping up to see what effect the stones had upon it, when I was interrupted by a shout behind me, and, looking round, I saw a Chawtee coming in from the desert full speed on a crab, shouting, "Rawacker, Rawacker!" This was the name of a dreaded chief, an enemy of Raka, and so frightened was she at the sound of his name that she flew to my side.

The Chawtee courier (if so he may be called) informed us that Rawaker was advancing on Queen Raka with twelve hundred camels, four hundred elephants, and ten thousand foot-soldiers, and that the advance-guard was only ten miles distant.

Raka shuddered when she heard this news, because I had already informed her that although her trained crabs and bangwangs might serve very well in time of peace to amuse her with their drillings, they could never stand against heavy troops, elephants, and trained dromedaries.

The army of Raka was, in fact, about as serviceable as the navy of the United States. There were great numbers of *useless crabs* in both, and her bangwangs were pretty much on a par with our *naval bangwangs*, which may serve to frighten the Chinese, but would never drive off a Rawaker.

I smiled at Raka's perturbation. "Have you," said I, "no confidence in Che Che Radif? Now, Raka," said I, "give me, without delay, two of your swiftest camels; for although your people seem to prefer Conestoga crabs, and what few camels you have are unaccustomed to long journeys, yet they are swift, and that is all I desire."

Raka answered, "I have but six camels, but they are swifter than the wind, and are employed by the priests of the temple of the Sun to bring the holy fire from the cave to the altar. It is half a moon's travel for a man, yet those camels can go and return in one day and one night. The two swiftest are named 'Ayshia' and 'Cepha.' You can take them all, if you will."

Ayshia and Cepha were ordered out immediately, and I acknowledged that I had never seen two such beautiful camels before. I at once mounted Ayshia, and made an athletic young wanin (who was famous for his skill in throwing the lance) mount the other.

"Now, Raka," said I, "I am going to victory or death, but I feel certain of victory. Therefore stay where you are, with your bangwangs drawn up in close order, to look as much like soldiers as possible. Get your crabs to the rear, also in close order, and pile dried plantain-leaves over them, to try and make the enemy think they are elephants; then watch the result."

In twenty minutes my advice had been strictly carried out, and I prepared to advance with the two camels and encounter the celebrated Rawaker.

I waved an adieu, and started with my guide in the direction of the enemy.

I asked my companion what sort of a person this Rawaker was, and was informed that he was a large man, weighing as much as any other three, and so fat that it took six men to lift him on to his elephant; that he was a cruel monster, who traveled with one hundred wives and a corresponding number of children; that he formerly paid tribute to the queen's father, but since the latter's death had forsworn his allegiance, and had undertaken to subjugate all the tribes within half a moon of him, and reduce them to slavery.

When we reached a large plain about a mile distant, I could see the vanguard of the enemy emerging from a narrow gorge in the sand-hills, and at first thought I would make the attack there, but finally concluded that Ayshia's speed on the plain would be of more service to me.

As the head of the column came out upon the plain, the enemy perceived us, and ten negroes mounted on camels made toward us, and two mounted on elephants followed hard after them. I let the first ten get pretty close, and then commenced circling around them, whereupon they made a rush at me and my companion, who was following my movements with the utmost confidence. "Now," thought I, "is my time," and, drawing a revolver, I deliberately emptied all the barrels, and six camels were riderless, their owners having fallen dead, under their feet.

Their companions seemed paralyzed with astonishment for a moment, and then fled pell-mell; the riderless camels following; but it was no use. Ayshia was soon on one side of them, and Cepha on the other, while in less than a minute I had emptied the barrels of my other revolver into the backs of the six mounted men, all of whom fell to the ground, while my native was spearing and hamstringing the camels, that were trying to reach Rawaker's army.

I loaded up my revolvers again and prepared for further hostilities. The army set up a shout, and a fresh party came charging down upon me. This consisted of twenty-four elephants, each with a tower on his back containing two soldiers. I laughed at the idea, and so did my companion, who at once comprehended how useless it would be for such a party to attack us.

When the elephants were within a hundred yards of us, the native called out to me, "That is Rawaker on the white elephant." And, sure enough, there was an enormous negro, with his eyes glistening like live coals, holding in his right hand a spear at least thirty feet long, while a huge club hung at his elephant's side, filled with sharp spikes, all of which did not trouble me in the least.

I said to my native, "I'll take that fellow alive and present him prisoner to the queen." "Bombaree !" said the native—which, translated, meant "Bully for you !"

MR. SPICY'S NARRATIVE.

When the elephants were close aboard, I commenced circling around them and picking off the occupants of the turrets. Twelve had fallen, and my native was busy hamstringing the animals, which stood perfectly quiet after their riders had fallen.

After retiring a short distance to reload, I again advanced to the attack.

Rawaker rushed to meet me, although his elephant, more intelligent than himself, did not seem disposed to hurry his movements, notwithstanding two negroes on his back were goading him with spears.

"Now," cried I, "for Rawaker!" and, riding as close to him as I desired, I planted a bullet in his majesty's left thigh, which broke the bone and caused excruciating pain. The king squirmed like an eel, and at length fell to the ground, uttering the most unearthly shrieks.

As soon as Rawaker fell, his surviving retainers took to flight; but it was no use. Ayshia and Cepha could travel ten miles to their one, and I had only to ride close to the elephants and shoot the poor wretches at my leisure.

I had now put forty of the negroes to death, and the few remaining my native knocked from their elephants with the butt end of his lance, and then by my direction tied them hand and foot.

The elephants rushed back to the main army, and so frightened were these unwieldy animals that they trampled down everything with which they came in contact, killing some twenty of the king's wives and forty of his children.

The negroes were so frightened at the sight of the elephants rushing back covered with blood that they were seized with a panic, and the whole army took to flight, and never stopped until sunset.

I then untied the three captive soldiers, and directed my native to tell them to return to their army and say that the Great Being had sent a general against them who could not be defeated; that he only spared the army because he had killed as many as he desired to eat for the present; that he had taken their king and great white elephant prisoners, and that he was going to present them to Queen Raka and make a bonfire of the king in her majesty's presence; that they must immediately send the queen two hundred camels, five hundred elephants, and all the king's sons, as hostages for his subjects' future good behavior.

After these people had been impressed with a suitable notion of our power, I discharged my revolver right over their heads, and they started off at full speed to join their rapidly retreating army.

The king still lay upon the ground, with his white elephant standing mournfully beside him, when my native and myself approached him. I stood over his majesty with a revolver, while the native tied his hands and feet, and then, making the white elephant kneel close to him, we endeavored to lift Rawaker on to his back; but we found the task beyond our strength, until a happy thought struck me.

I remembered having seen Mrs. Cringle get a barrel of pork out of the hold on a certain occasion by a process called *parbuckling*, and, taking some of the grass ropes that formed a portion of the elephant's equipment, I finally succeeded in getting the king on the animal's back and making him secure in that position.

Rawaker bled like a bullock, and the white elephant was fast becoming crimson. The king did not utter a word, and, the native taking the elephant in lead, we started back to our queen.

Raka was just where I had left her, having witnessed at a distance the result of the battle; but when she saw the white elephant with the king lashed to his back her joy was unbounded.

Raka was too humane to put Rawaker to death; so, at her request, I cured him, and sent him back to his tribe, with injunctions to behave himself better in future; but he was killed by some of his own people before he could join the main army, on account of the sufferings he had caused them, and the fear of Che Che Radif.

Rawaker's people complied with all my demands, and sent the requisite number of elephants and camels, and also all the king's sons, who were reduced to the station of domestics and appointed to wait upon the queen and myself.

Raka was never again troubled by any of the tribes on her borders, but, on the contrary, she received every attention and kindness from them, and from that time forward they paid her double the tribute that had been exacted by the king her father, and no queen in Africa was ever more loved and respected.

A whole year passed away in Raka's delightful society. I had done much toward introducing reforms in her system of government, although I did not think it advisable to make radical changes in the manner of ruling this simple people.

I found old Chaffyman, the prime minister, to be a great scamp, and he was accordingly banished to a place some three hundred miles from court, where he died in extreme poverty, being only allowed sufficient to keep body and soul together.

I introduced a better system of building houses to protect the natives during the rainy season, and showed them how to lay out their gardens and irrigate their grounds.

At the end of the year, however, I began to get homesick, and thought it high time to return and give Mr. Smiler some account of his warming-pans, about which he no doubt felt uneasy. He must, however, I thought, have given up by this time all hope of ever again seeing Captain and Mrs. Cringle and the brig Creole.

So, one day when the queen was in her happiest mood, I said, "Raka, it is time I began to think of my friends at home, and I must prepare to return to them."

"You shall never leave me," said the queen, weeping. "If you did, I should die. Why do you want to go away and leave me broken-hearted, or to be destroyed by the surrounding tribes, who will attack me as soon as they find you have gone."

I hadn't thought of that, but said, "Raka, let us discuss this matter calmly.

"Raka," said I, "why can't you go with me? I will take you to my country, the most favored land upon which the sun ever shone." Her face beamed with joy, and, clapping her hands, she said, "I will leave everything to go with you and be queen in your country. We will take all my valuables, and I will leave some one in charge here until you are ready to return." So it was arranged that we should go to the United States as soon as we could make the necessary arrangements.

It took us a month to mature our plans. Ten elephants were selected to carry our baggage, tents, provisions, etc., fifty camels for our mounted escort, and two palanquins for the queen and myself to travel in.

I did not know exactly what course to steer for a seaport whence I could embark for home. As near as I could judge, our brig went ashore somewhere near Cape Blanco, and the negroes who surprised us at the wreck must have come from the south and east of the cape, near Senegambia. So I determined to steer to the southward, hoping to strike some portion of Senegambia.

Raka had packed up a large quantity of useless articles, among them the stuffed crocodile which composed her throne; but to this I made no objections, knowing that ladies must always find many articles absolutely necessary to their comfort for which man can not appreciate the necessity. I have seen one of my cousins start out for a summer trip with a dozen large Saratoga trunks crammed full of flimsies; and a queen should certainly be allowed at least as great a quantity of rubbish.

Everything being in readiness, we prepared to start on the first of the moon, so as to have bright nights. The people were all assembled, and a kind farewell was taken. They were exhorted to be faithful to the person the queen left in charge, and to always be prepared for the inroads of enemies; and, after saying all that could be said on such an occasion, we departed, followed for several miles by a vast crowd of people, weeping as if their hearts would break.

During the day Raka and myself traveled in the same palanquin, carried by six men, and she amused herself by asking me questions in regard to the manners and customs of the people of my country.

We made about thirty miles the first day, and encamped for the night on the edge of a small lake surrounded by date-trees. We had been traveling along a belt of soil about fifty miles in width apparently, and with a few hills of moderate height, sparsely covered with verdure, in the distance.

Next morning we started before the dawn of day, and traveled until the rays of the sun were so overpowering that we pitched our tents in the coolest place we could find, and waited until evening.

We thus proceeded for twelve days, making about fifty miles per day, and traveling mostly by night. This was easy work for elephants and camels, who can, if necessary, travel twice as fast as we did. Raka was in good spirits, and the days passed very agreeably to me; in fact, I feared that I should be sorry when we reached our journey's end.

At length the herbage got very sparse, and the animals began to suffer for the want of the short, crisp grass, which was all they had to subsist on, except now and then when we came to a grove of date-trees. Our men were working hard to collect a sufficient quantity of grass to last us across the desert we were evidently approaching.

In four more days we reached the limit of vegetation, and filled up our water-jugs, and dug up all the grass we could get hold of by the roots, not knowing how far we would have to travel to get across the waste of sand. We now moved altogether by night, the

MR. SPICY'S NARRATIVE.

stars being our only guide. All around was nothing but a dreary plain of sand, with no trail to guide us, and the heat by day was almost stifling.

The elephants began to give out, and day by day they would drop out of line and refuse to go farther. When one of them fell by the way, we would divide his load among the remaining elephants and the camels. So far we had left eight of our poor elephants to perish in the desert, and their awful trumpetings as we left them behind showed that they realized the fate that awaited them. We had still kept up our fifty miles a day, but on the fifteenth day in the desert we had not a single elephant remaining, the fodder for the camels had given out, and the party had to be put on short allowance of water, every man carrying his own gourd.

On the eighteenth day in the desert we all felt dispirited. The camels continued their regular pace, but they were little more than skin and bones. Fortunately, a shower of rain that night enabled us to fill our gourds and give the camels a good drink all round.

Next morning, as we were about to halt for the day, there was a shout from the negroes in the advance, and one of them came riding back to inform us that an oasis was in sight, and that trees could be seen rising above the horizon. All shouted at the joyful news, and, pressing forward, in the course of an hour trees and green hills were in plain sight.

For some days past I had felt very uneasy, but now my mind was at rest, and I smiled all over. Raka, too, looked pleased, although she had felt no doubts, thinking me capable of accomplishing anything.

At sunset we were within a mile of this agreeable oasis, which we saw was of considerable magnitude, stretching as far as eye could reach, the low hills increasing in size as we advanced.

In a few moments we saw smoke in the distance, and soon after descried a large number of men, mounted on camels, advancing toward us. There were at least a hundred in the party; but I did not fear men as much as I did the danger of starvation in the desert.

As the party advanced rapidly and in rather an unfriendly manner, I mounted Ayshia and rode to the front. Circling about so as to draw their attention from the party, I led them away, and, when in full chase of me, I let them come close up, and emptied the six barrels of a revolver, which left six saddles vacant.

At this unexpected attack they seemed panic-struck, turned, and fled; but, as my camel was fleet as the wind, I was soon alongside of them, and emptied six saddles more, when I let them retreat wheresoever they wanted to go.

I thought it prudent to encamp for the night, and, having set a watch, lay down with my revolvers at my side and slept soundly. The queen, near whose palanquin I reposed, was evidently nervous after the events of the day, and did not feel comfortable unless she knew that I was near her.

Next morning at daylight our camp was in motion, and we proceeded in a southerly direction, and were following a well-beaten path through a grove of date-trees, when we encountered six negroes, each with a large calabash on the end of a pole, and kneeling right in the path. This, among the negroes, is a sign of submission, and so we received them.

It soon appeared that these six persons were none other than the cabinet of the Emperor "Bongolo"—viz., the minister of state, minister of war, minister of the marine, postmaster-general, and attorney-general—and they came to apologize for the conduct of the people who had molested our party, and whom we had slain by drawing fire from heaven. Their emperor deprecated our anger, and we were invited to enter his dominions and to partake of all he had.

"Tell your emperor," said I, "that in case of any treachery I will bring down fire and kill all his people." The poor frightened cabinet ministers thumped their heads against the ground in token of respect, and, lowering their gourds, retreated backward from our august presence.

We had no difficulty in conversing with these people; for the whole region of Senegambia, Soudan, and the borders of the Great Desert is inhabited by Jaloofs, Tanimaroos, Katobas, Woolis, Konkodos, Fooladoos, etc., who can all understand each others' dialects, while the Mandingo and Foullah languages are to the savages of Africa what the French is to the civilized nations of the world.

Our party now proceeded to the town, which contained some ten thousand people and was prettily located on a lake surrounded with palm-trees.

Here the emperor and his cabinet came out to meet us, accompanied by the nobility and principal inhabitants, and all bowed their heads to us in token of submission.

I saluted the emperor haughtily, who stooped down and picked up a handful of earth and offered it to me, which signified that all he owned was at my disposal.

MR. SPICY'S NARRATIVE. 143

I then briefly explained to him that this was the great and good Queen Raka, who was known as having conquered the celebrated King Rawaker, that she was bound on a visit to the sovereigns of Africa, that she had an immense army coming up, and that her elephants were behind in detached parties. The latter part of the statement was true enough, for the elephants certainly were very much detached.

All the people had heard of Raka and her illustrious general, and all threw themselves on the ground in token of submission.

It was all clear sailing now, and I ordered his sable majesty to arise, and, holding out my hand to him, he put it on his head.

This emperor was rather stout, weighing, as near as could be estimated, about four hundred pounds. He had to be supported by the minister of war on one side and the minister of the marine on the other, in order to maintain his perpendicular; although in this respect he did not differ materially from potentates the world over.

His imperial majesty then showed us the quarters he had provided for our accommodation, consisting of a commodious house in the center of a large *corral* and surrounded by some thirty smaller habitations.

These contained every comfort known to the country, and we proceeded to occupy them forthwith. Raka and her attendants kept closely veiled, and a guard was stationed around the palace while we transferred our effects to the different apartments allotted to us.

Meanwhile, the emperor had fallen asleep, supported by his two distinguished ministers, but, after I had everything arranged, I woke him up and proposed a visit to the empress, to whom I desired to pay my respects, and we started together toward the palace.

This we found similar to the one provided for Raka—a square house, with a thatched roof, inclosed by palisades; but what surprised me most of all was a harpoon of the real Yankee pattern hanging over the main entrance. The emperor informed me that no one could enter until the harpoon was taken down.

A message was now sent to the empress, and in a few moments a guard of four Amazons came and removed the instrument, and we passed into the presence of her majesty.

As I entered the imperial apartment, my ears were saluted with a terrific snort, like the blowing of a whale, and, looking up, I beheld a sight which struck me with astonishment. Unless my eyes deceived me, there sat my old shipmate, Mrs. Cringle; but how unlike the Mrs. Cringle of former days! She was clad in imperial robes, and looked every inch an empress.

On her head was a crown made of a calabash; a light mantle, drawn tight at the waist, enveloped her person, descending a little below the knee.

Her arms and neck were bare, and sandals were on her feet. As a symbol of her rank, she held in her right hand the identical harpoon which she had brought on shore from the wreck of the Creole.

Her throne was a huge stuffed crocodile, with his tail curved fiercely up, and bearing in his jaws a small pig. The empress had evidently not forgotten her ancient fondness for pork.

Her majesty evidently did not recognize her old shipmate, for a year's exposure to the African sun had made me nearly as black as a negro. My hair was long and sunburned, and my beard had grown to my waist. My dress, although better suited to a hot climate, was wholly unlike what I had been in the habit of wearing in Mrs. Cringle's presence.

The empress eyed me closely, but did not move, and, wishing, no doubt, to impress me with an idea of imperial power, she gave one of her old blows, which frightened the natives present half out of their wits.

I determined to surprise the old lady, and sang out, as loud as I could bawl, "There she spouts, Captain Cringle, three p'ints on the starboard bow."

The empress jumped from her throne as if she had been shot out of a gun. "Gracious mercy!" she exclaimed, "who are you? You can't be Cringle, 'cause he was a little fat man. Who are you, anyhow?"

"No, your imperial majesty," I replied, "I am not Captain Cringle, nor half so good a navigator; but I am your old friend and shipmate Spicy, who, after innumerable adventures, has arrived in your dominions with his beautiful queen Raka, on his way to America."

I had no sooner uttered these words than the empress dropped her harpoon, and, clasping me in her arms, almost smothered me with kisses. "The Lord be praised," she said, "for once more meeting an old white friend, for I hain't seen nothin' but niggers since I came to this place."

All this time the emperor stood transfixed with astonishment, not comprehending the extraordinary antics of his consort. He put his hand toward his club, but the empress said, "This is an old friend and countryman, and you must do all in your power to make him happy while he remains with us." The emperor bowed assent, and kissed her majesty's hand.

"Nothing," said I to the empress, "could astonish me more than to see your majesty occupying your present exalted position at the head of these realms; for his imperial majesty your husband, it seems, plays only a secondary part."

"Yes, Spicy, I am empress, and a happy one at that; but my happiest days were when I could follow the sea and go to the weather-earing. Here I do nothing but amuse myself and grow fat, and I am two hundred pounds heavier than when you saw me last."

"Yes," said I, "I perceive you are somewhat stouter than you used to be; but it becomes your majesty, and I can truly say I never saw such a noble-looking empress before."

"Oh, you flatterer!" said the empress, pinching my cheek. "Yes, I know I am handsome; and the Emperor of Wallawoo adores me." His majesty, however, seemed a little uneasy while the empress was taking these liberties with me; in fact, his emotion was so great that the Secretary of the Interior had to assist the war and navy departments in holding him up.

"But, Spicy," said the empress, "I must get home again and rejoin my old man Cringle, for I can't feel happy while I know he is grieving for me, and he can't sail a vessel without me."

"Why," said I, "is it possible that your majesty is not aware that poor Captain Cringle was killed?"

"No, he wasn't," said the empress; "he escaped, for the negro who was left as a guard over the goods told me that, after the rest of the party went away, Captain Cringle seized and tied him while asleep, and then rode off on his camel."

I then explained the whole affair to her majesty, who listened attentively to the recital of my adventures.

"Ah, well!" exclaimed the empress, with a sigh, "perhaps it's just as well. If the old man had lived, he'd been busting out his trousers all the time, and making me do his work. This emperor don't wear no trousers, and don't have no buttons to sew on; so I guess I'll stay and be empress, and, if you say so, you shall remain and be prime minister."

I reminded her majesty that I was already prime minister to

the most powerful sovereign in Africa, Queen Raka, and could not change, as my heart was also in that quarter.

"I don't know about her being the most powerful sovereign while I'm about," said the empress. "However, we won't quarrel over that, for I am too glad to see you, and I will call at once on Queen Raka. La! how old Captain Cringle would stare if he could see me ruling over these dominions!"

She then related to me how she was brought to this mighty empire of Wallawoo, and how the emperor at first sight fell desperately in love with her, and had given her the privilege of being named first in all matters of state; how she grieved three weeks for Cringle, and then dried her tears and married the emperor; how she made him put away all his other wives, some two thousand in number, and board out all his children, and now reigned sole mistress of his affections. Her majesty further stated that she intended to live and die Empress of Wallawoo, which, on the whole, was a better berth than sailing an old brig.

During all this time the emperor stood with an air of profound respect, supported by the distinguished members of his cabinet, even the secretary of state and the attorney-general lending their aid to hold him up.

At last, seeing that his majesty was getting much fatigued, I bade the empress good-morning, kissing her hand respectfully, when, seizing me around the neck, she exclaimed,

"Pshaw! Spicy, give me a good American hug," which I accordingly did, and returned to Queen Raka.

By this time the emperor was almost asleep, but as I went out her majesty gave an awful snort, which brought him at once to his senses.

Raka was delighted at the recital of my interview with the empress, for "now," she said, "everything will go smoothly."

Our palace was a very comfortable place, and we fared sumptuously. At noon of that day we sat down to lunch, consisting of young monkey-tails à la Serranoollis with curds and pepper, dogs' eyes in mustard à la Tanimaroo, grasshoppers en papillottes, dried squash in vinegar à la Toolado, poke-berries, and sour milk.

Raka relished these delicacies very much, for they reminded her of home; but they did not altogether accord with my simple republican tastes, so I managed to purchase a small pig for a brass button, which I roasted and devoured in my private apartments.

MR. SPICY'S NARRATIVE.   147

In the mean time I got Raka ready to receive the Empress Kringleoo, for so her majesty was now called, and, as the empress had not been informed that Queen Raka was possessed of that beautiful appendage, a tail, I advised Raka to coil it up spiral-spring fashion and secure it in that way while she remained in Kringleoo's dominions. She accordingly put on a richly dyed cotton mantle, and sat down to await her majesty's coming.

I had told Raka how to behave and what to say, for I knew Kringleoo was a shrewd woman, who would observe her narrowly.

At length the empress entered, harpoon in hand, attended by four Amazons. She shook hands with me, and offered to do the same with Raka; but the native dignity of the queen would not brook such familiarity; and, bowing courteously, she motioned the empress to the skin of an alligator, on which she requested her to be seated.

"Come here, Spicy," said Kringleoo, "and sit alongside of me; plenty room for two. You dear old fellow, it does me good to see you once more." With that the empress pinched my cheek and tweaked my nose in the most familiar manner.

This was a little more than Raka could bear: she didn't like my sitting quite so close to Kringleoo, but when it came to taking such liberties with me as I have narrated, finishing by the empress's laying her hand on mine, Raka jumped from her seat and rushed across the room to prevent it. She stood before the empress with nostrils distended, hands clinched, and eyes gleaming like coals of fire. Her blood was up, and she was evidently anxious for a set-to with the white woman, and looked to me to be her backer and bottle-holder.

This was the first time I had ever seen Raka exhibit anything like temper or jealousy; and I must confess that she looked like a Tartar. Human nature was evidently the same the world over: when the little god Cupid plants his arrows, they are sure to do their work thoroughly. When love is the absorbing passion, it makes no difference what may be the color of the skin; and in this case love for me reigned supreme in Raka's bosom.

She commenced scolding rapidly in the Chawtee language, using many uncomplimentary expressions, even going so far as to call her imperial majesty an old white elephant, a fish-woman, crocodile, hyena; all of which was lost on the empress, who did not understand a word of it. However, Kringleoo soon comprehended how matters stood, and said, "Ah, Spicy, you rascal! the gal's dead in love with you. Don't let me interfere." And she withdrew her hand from mine.

Raka was quieted, but she did not let go of me while the empress remained, and would never afterward let me go alone to see her.

An hour afterward, the emperor called, accompanied by his cabinet, who had their hands full to hold him up. He could not keep his eyes off Raka, with whom he was evidently smitten, and when he left he presented the queen with a magnificent bracelet made of a piece of iron hoop; but as soon as the door closed behind the emperor Raka spat after him, and threw his costly present to one of her maids of honor.

We remained with these good people a month, and then prepared to continue our journey. Everything that friendship could suggest was lavished upon us. Kringleoo cried heartily at our departure, exclaiming:

"Farewell, friends! Some day you will hear of my descendants populating these regions, and I hope to be the mother of a noble line of emperors." With that she waved us an adieu, and we never saw her again.

The emperor fell down in trying to kiss his hand to Raka, and the last we saw of him his whole cabinet were employed in trying to set him on his legs.

I have already delayed too long on this journey. Suffice to say that, after many adventures, and the receipt of much kindness from the various tribes through which we passed, we finally reached the coast at the mouth of the Senegal River, having traversed the countries of Yerra, Elimene, Bakel, Makarra, Warrenskio, Teoriko, and Gadana.

I can not describe Raka's astonishment or my own delight at getting sight of the great ocean. To add to my joy, several vessels were at anchor off the mouth of the river, one of which bore the American flag.

As soon as we got to Senegal, I secured good quarters for our party, and engaged passage on the first vessel that was to leave the port.

Then, without saying a word to Raka, I disposed of the valuables she had packed up and brought away from Chawteewarrawarra. These consisted of ten boxes of polished crabs' eyes, six boxes of birds-of-paradise, four boxes of stuffed monkeys, ten boxes of beautiful grass cloth, three boxes of feather flowers, two dozen stuffed alligators, ten jars of live snakes, forty jars of preserved tree-toads, ten boxes of ant-sauce, and many other articles, too numerous to mention.

I also disposed of Raka's stuffed alligator, which she used as a throne on state occasions. This circumstance would have caused her great uneasiness had she known anything about it.

These articles brought me over six thousand dollars, which was more than enough to pay our expenses across the Atlantic.

I now made arrangements for the return home of all our native escort, and, after rewarding them liberally, sent them on their way rejoicing.

In the mean while I had kept Raka in strict seclusion, not wishing her to be seen. She had now learned to dress in European fashion and stow away her caudal appendage so that it could not attract attention.

I engaged three state-rooms on board the American brig—one for Raka, one for her two maids, and one for myself.

The brig was bound to Baltimore, and I found there were to be three other passengers—a missionary, his wife, and their daughter, a beautiful girl only seventeen years old, who was returning home on account of her health. These persons were now on board, and seemed to promise pleasant acquaintanceship for the voyage.

The cabin of the Pigeon was very comfortable, and a great improvement on that of the Creole. The captain was also an agreeable person, and had an efficient crew under his command.

Two days after, I came on board with Raka and her attendants closely veiled, to take up our quarters. I had not explained to the captain that the ladies were not white, and did not know how he would take it.

He seemed startled at first at the idea of having colored persons in his cabin; but when I assured him that Raka was not only of a light complexion but a great queen in her own country, and offered to pay double passage-money, all the captain's scruples and prejudices vanished. It is astonishing how quickly Americans bow to royalty, no matter what the color; and I am satisfied that if the king of Dahomey were to visit the United States he would receive the greatest honors, and the young ladies would struggle for a lock of his sable majesty's hair.

Two days after we went on board, the brig got under way for the United States, running down the trades in about the latitude of eighteen degrees. Nothing could be more delightful than this kind of sailing. The steering-sails were set on the starboard side, which kept the vessel steady, and the sea was comparatively smooth. The nights were beautiful, the moon being in her first quarter, and the stars were brighter than I ever remembered seeing them before. Now and then we would make out a sail ahead, bound in the same direction with ourselves. These were generally colliers trading to the West Indies, returning with a load of molasses. The Pigeon did credit to her name, and passed all these vessels as if they had been at anchor.

Raka had become acquainted with her fellow-passengers, who tried to make themselves agreeable with the smattering of Mandingo which they possessed, but my poor queen never seemed happy unless she had me all to herself; but I could not be with her all the time, for I was obliged to do my share toward making the voyage pass pleasantly. Besides, it was so long since I had been in civilized society that I pined for the companionship of my fellows.

The Fowlers were an intelligent and respectable family, and the daughter, Miss Lucille, was not only very beautiful, but had a mind of that order which seems to grasp every subject intuitively.

She was none of your namby-pamby misses who have left school with a feeble smattering of everything, but she was one of Nature's choicest ornaments.

Her father had devoted much time and pains to his daughter's education, and her mind drank in the choicest literature as the earth absorbs the dews of evening. There was not a particle of guile about this young creature, and it was impossible to be long in her society without feeling her influence; and I must confess that I soon experienced the magnetism. Even Raka, who could not, of course, comprehend such a mind as Miss Fowler's, was struck with her great beauty, and was never tired of gazing at her, her eyes wandering from Miss Fowler to myself, and frequently filling with tears.

While I was in Chawtee and was alone with Raka most of the time, I could not help reciprocating her affection, for she was a noble creature, wonderfully superior to all around her. Then, like most men, I was willing to sail down the stream of pleasure without much thought of the shoals and quicksands concealed beneath the treacherous waters. Pleased with the queen's society, I never thought of the future.

I could not bear to leave Raka in the desert, for I knew I should never see her more, and dreaded lest some of those monster kings of Africa should sweep down upon her kingdom and reduce her and her people to slavery.

It was painful to think of any being left so helpless after having learned to put complete faith and trust in me, and I had, therefore, determined to take Raka with me, regardless of consequences.

From the first moment that Raka laid eyes on the beautiful Miss Fowler there was an evident change in her manner, and when I asked her what she thought of the young lady, she burst into tears and pressed my hand to her lips. Actions are more eloquent than words, and it needed nothing more to express her thoughts.

Before many days I felt that I had committed a great mistake in bringing Raka from her home, and realized that my happiness was now in the keeping of Miss Fowler, who was growing every day more beautiful in my eyes, although she seemed unconscious of my admiration.

It was my custom every evening to sit with Raka on the weather side of the quarter-deck aft, watching the sails as they bellied out with the breeze, or admiring the phosphorescence of the water, which sparkled as if the vessel was sailing through myriads of stars.

At such times the queen was always happy, and would sit with her hand in mine while I discoursed to her of the wonders of nature. She was an apt scholar, and, had she possessed the advantages of her fairer rival, would have been equally intelligent.

During the day, when Raka was not on deck, or was taking her *siesta* at noon, according to the custom of her country, I would enjoy the fascinating society of the young American.

When Raka had retired for the night, which she did at an early hour, I would again contrive to enjoy Miss Fowler's society, often until a late hour.

Raka always made me promise, when she withdrew for the night, that I would also retire to rest, and, possessing implicit confidence in me, she was generally asleep as soon as her head touched the pillow.

One night when she had as usual retired to her state-room and closed the door, I went on deck to seek the company of Lucille. We had been walking the deck for at least two hours, but time flew so pleasantly that neither of us noticed the number of bells that had been struck, nor did we observe a figure on the lee side watching us, although it was bright moonlight.

It was a beautiful night, the air so soft that it was scarce felt upon the cheek. Everything seemed propitious for me to speak of that which was nearest my heart.

This night I was more tender than usual, and Lucille more silent. Suddenly I took her hand, which she did not withdraw, and told her how fondly I loved her, and should love her until death.

At that moment I fancied I heard a stifled sob at the cabin-door, and said, "Lucille, stay a moment, until I see who is there."

I went toward the door, and was entering the cabin, while Lucille leaned over the low bulwarks, looking on the sea. Suddenly a white figure glided from behind the mizzenmast. I saw that it was Raka, but before I had time to think she had thrown her tail around the neck of the hapless Lucille and jumped with her into the sea. A fearful shriek, and the waters closed for ever over the unfortunate girls. I was struck with horror at the sight, and lost all consciousness.

Every effort was made by those on board the brig to save the victims. The quarter-boat was lowered as soon as possible, and pulled for a long time in the wake of the brig, but no trace of the unfortunates could be discovered, and the brig filled away on her course.

It was many days before I recovered my senses, and when I ame to myself I heard the cry of "Land!" and the pilot-boat was alongside.

But I would fain drop a veil over these mournful events. Would to God that I had never seen Raka, or that the other victim had never crossed my path! I was the cause of two deaths, and not the innocent cause. Peace to their *manes*.

I got away from the brig after her arrival in port without encountering anybody, and, obtaining quiet lodgings in Baltimore, I withdrew from the world to indulge my sorrow and remorse.

It was about six months after my return, when one day I was walking down Market Street, when whom should I see but President Smiler!

The philanthropist started when he met me, but seemed in doubt for some time as to my identity; but at last he left me, apparently satisfied with his scrutiny. Next day I was arrested on a complaint preferred by the noble-hearted president of the Warming-Pan Society, charging me with conspiring with one Captain Cringle to run off and make away with one brig, called the Creole, the same being the property of the said society; also of embezzling the cargo of the said brig, consisting of warming-pans and many other valuable articles, and making no return of the same, etc., etc., etc.

I soon satisfied the court of my innocence, and that the speculation was still considered a good one by Mrs. Cringle, who was now Empress of Wallawoo, in Africa, who would undoubtedly make a return of the proceeds to the Warming-Pan Society as soon as Congress appropriated the money to build a railroad to her dominions.

I brought the captain of the Pigeon as a witness to prove the wreck, and the Court dismissed the case, thus ending my connection with Mr. Smiler and the Warming-Pan Society.

CHAPTER XII.

MARLINE VISITS THE SHORE, MAKES A NEW ACQUAINTANCE, FINDS ALL IS NOT GOLD THAT GLITTERS—A DUEL—AN EXQUISITE—BROTHER JONATHAN AND JOHN BULL TOWING A DISABLED FRENCHMAN INTO PORT.

THE day after we arrived I went on shore with the captain in his barge to call on the Governor of Gibraltar—that is, I was to wait in the boat until he came down, and see that the men did not get drunk in his absence; but the captain did not return at the appointed time, and hours passed away, while myself and boat's crew were kicking our heels together on the pier; we could see nothing to pass off time but the grim-looking fortress frowning upon us from above our heads, and by way of variety the guard changing the sentinels every two hours at the gates.

Two or three boats came on shore loaded with wardroom officers and midshipmen bound in the pursuit of pleasure, and I longed to be among the latter—they looked happy. Reckless and Brace were in for a regular spree, I could see that, and told me, if I would come up to the hotel after a while, I should have a first-rate dinner. "Don't make yourself uneasy about the captain," said Reckless; "he is old enough and ugly enough to take care of himself; he has likely dropped anchor at the consul's; and if he once gets a bottle of *his* old Madeira under his nose, he will sit over it like a terrier over a rat-hole; he is temperance in his own cabin, but to oblige his acquaintances he leaves it all on board ship. Good-day,

Marline, don't make a tom-cod of yourself and stay by that boat all day; the coxswain will take care of her better than you can." But I was proof against temptation; I thought of the captain's dog "Snap," and determined to stand at my post. I would likely have carried out my intention if just at that moment a boat from the English squadron had not pulled in to the pier. A little midshipman, no bigger than myself, was officer of the boat, and, jumping out with a jaunty air, he said to the coxswain, "I say, Smith, look hout for the boat while I go up and get a glass of 'alf-and-'alf, you know;" and then turning to the crew, he said, "Mind, fellows now, you don't get groggy while I am gone; if you do, I'll just speak a word to the first luff about ye, ye know," and with that he bolted through the gate; the crew sat still waiting his return, and I thought to myself, Why won't my boat's crew do likewise? So I walked up to *my* coxswain and said, "Brown, look out for the boat while I go up and get a glass of lemonade;" and then turning to the crew I said, "Mind, men, that you don't get groggy, or I will speak a word to the first luff about you," and with that I bolted through the gate after the English middy.

I found out afterward that the English boat's crew, headed by Smith, the coxswain, bolted after the English middy left; and that my boat's crew, headed by Coxswain Brown, followed in my wake the moment I was out of sight.

After a search of half an hour I discovered my two friends, Reckless and Brace, at the American Hotel, such was the name of a man-trap for taking in and doing up brown poor unsuspecting Americans. American! forsooth, there was nothing American about it; it was neither English, French, nor Dutch, and was the filthiest hole I ever put my foot into; there I found my two shipmates, in company with a tall, slab-sided down-East Yankee, a supercargo of an American brig, said Yankee answering to the name of George Washington Thaddeus Kosciusko De Lacy, high-sounding names to be sure, and Mr. De Lacy turned out to be a high fellow.

"Bless my soul," he said, "how fortunate it was in you gentlemen to fall in with me! it does me good to meet my countrymen abroad. Now, gentlemen," he continued, "I know all the ropes here, and it is in my power to add very much to your pleasure. These scoundrels all know me, and are afraid of me as they are of the devil. All I have to do is to order, and the order is obeyed before you can snap your fingers. I cleared the whole room the other night, pitched the waiters out of the window, knocked the landlord up the chimney, and then pitched all the crockery into the street, merely because they did not cook my beefsteak quite enough. That is not the best of it, either: the fools ran off to fetch the guard, but I soon played hob-scotch with them; the English ruffians undertook to charge bayonets on me; but I seized a chair, and had the whole party on the floor before they knew what they were about. I would have cut the throats of all the scoundrels, but they begged so hard for their lives that I let them go, with a warning never to molest a De Lacy. I kept the muskets and the sergeant's sword, which latter is now in my room, dyed to the hilt in the best English blood."

"How did that happen?" we asked, in some astonishment. We were all taken aback at the abrupt manner in which our acquaintance boasted of his exploits, and in my verdancy I swallowed it all.

"Why, you must know, gentlemen, that the day after punishing these fellows the officer of the guard, a noted swordsman, six feet six inches, called on me to demand an explanation, and I kicked him down-stairs; that afternoon I received a challenge from him; went out to the neutral ground; found he had dug a grave already for me; drew the sergeant's sword; put myself on guard; the officer attacked me; killed him at the first pass, poor fellow! put him in the grave, covered him up; dined that day with the British officers in the guard-room; next day dined with the governor, and now every one steers clear of me; women all in love with me; room full of notes and bouquets; and now, just tell me what you would like to have, and it will come like magic."

"Well, let us have some fresh fish to begin with," said Reckless, "and then we will take a chance at roast beef."

"Oh, damn fish!" said De Lacy. "I can't bear fish; and the fact is, I have been living on it ever since I came here; and as to their beef, it tastes like cow, and is not fit for a Christian to eat."

We all thought Mr. De Lacy rather selfish, but, as he had been so kind as to offer to take care of our personal comfort, we thought it best to let him do it in his own way; and, moreover, none of us felt like disputing the orders of one who had used a six-feet-six guardsman up. So Brace, in a conciliatory way, said, "Well, Mr. De Lacy, let it be boiled mutton and caper-sauce, and finish off with a roast goose."

"Well, now," he said, "if that don't beat cock-fighting altogether! Why, gentlemen, what do you take me for? Do you think I would compromise myself by ordering boiled mutton and roast goose? That would be a good joke. Why, I should be the laughing-stock of the garrison before an hour went over my head, and should likely have to fight a dozen duels before I could wipe out the disgrace. Boiled mutton and roast goose, indeed! Ha! ha! ha! That's too good! and to a De Lacy, too! Ha! ha! ha!" And then his brow lowered and he assumed a dark frown.

I must confess that our small party rather cowered before this man, and we spoke not a word, until suddenly he turned round, and in rather a freezing tone said, "Well, gentlemen, what is to be done?"

It was now my turn to speak, and I scarcely knew what to say. I hemmed once or twice, and, observing that I was going to say something, he fixed his eyes keenly upon me, as much as to say, "Be careful how you speak, sir, and remember the dead guardsman!" Assuming all the confidence I could muster, I timidly proposed that we should have some stuffed veal, and wind up with apple-dumplings.

Down came his hand upon the table and startled us all nearly out of our propriety. "Well, that's d——d good!" he said. "Why, young man, remember where you are. You are not in Connecticut, where they live on cow's baby all the year through, and I doubt if they ever heard of apple-dumplings in this part of the world. Well, gentlemen, you are really unfortunate in your selections, and now I will tell you what I will do to get you out of this scrape: I will order the dinner myself, and you will confess that I know something about such matters when you see my list. Waiter," he cried out, "bring me pen, ink, and paper!" And when the articles were brought he wrote down the following elaborate dinner: Turtle soup *à la Française;* turbot, with prawn-sauce; woodcock; Barbary partridge; becaficoes on toast; mutton-chops *à la Maintenon;* sweetbreads; mountain oysters; date-fish; larded pheasants; turkey-wing *en salmi;* raw oysters in the shell; roast ditto; humming-bird pie; asparagus; green peas; egg-plant; spinach *à la Française;* potatoes and macaroni; then, for dessert, ice-cream, Charlotte russe, jelly, blanc-mange, meringue, Bohemian cheese; *finale,* all the fruits of the season.

We had to admit that De Lacy knew how to order a dinner, though it was one far beyond our means; we thought, considering that we had lived on pork and beans for a whole month, that we

AN EXTRAVAGANT DINNER.

could have dined luxuriously on any one of the dishes *we* had selected, though we were wise enough to keep our thoughts to ourselves. Here were three midshipmen, with only six dollars among the whole party, about to order a dinner that would cost a month's pay at least, and order it, also, against their will, but we were either too proud to acknowledge our poverty or felt a secret dread of the terrible man-killer who had so disinterestedly taken charge of us.

After gaining our acknowledgment that he knew how to cater for us, Mr. De Lacy asked Reckless to order the dinner, which was accordingly done, and the waiter, with many bows and smiles, promised that it should be forthcoming in no time.

"And now, gentlemen," said De Lacy, "what shall we order to drink?"

Of course we left it to him, fearing to make some sad mistake if we ventured to call for anything ourselves. I thought of asking for a lemonade, and the other two had not an idea beyond a winesangaree, but it was fortunate for us that we did not express our wishes openly, for we would have differed so widely from De Lacy.

"Well, then," he said, "I think we can get along by commencing with a bottle of old cognac, two of champagne, two of sparkling hock, a bottle of old Madeira, and a bottle of sherry—and that's as little as any four gentlemen should sit down to."

We naturally wondered where the man was going to stow it all, for surely we three could not make away with more than one bottle; but we kept very quiet on the subject, though we wished Mr. De Lacy to the devil all the time.

"*En fin*," the dinner was at length served up, and we fell to. Every mouthful I took I thought of the consequences when paying up came, and for the first time in their lives Reckless and Brace looked quite subdued, notwithstanding the efforts of our friend to amuse them by telling of the wonderful feats he had performed while in Gibraltar, the number of duels he had fought, and the number of *billets-doux* he had received from ladies who shall be nameless. While we were in the middle of the repast our jolly second lieutenant, Mr. Bluff, made his appearance. He came rolling in like a ship in a heavy sea-way, and took a seat at a table close to us. He had evidently been sacrificing at the shrine of Bacchus, for his jolly countenance had old Madeira impressed on every lineament of it, and a little more sail would have capsized him right off.

"Garçon," he sung out, in a voice that shook the building, "punci caldi per dui; do you hear, garçon?" The old fellow thought he was in Naples at the time, and flattered himself he was speaking pure Italian.

The waiter rushed in, at the unexpected order, inquiring, "What'll ye 'ave, sir?"

"Punci caldi per dui, and be d——d to you! And, garçon, let me have it quick: I am as dry as a powder-horn."

"I really don't think we 'ave hany hin the 'ouse, sir," said the garçon, apologetically.

"What! not got any punci caldi per dui? What have you got, you infernal lazzaroni?"

"Oh, we've got heverything helse, sir: roast beef, chicken-salad, mutton frigasse, and—"

"Hang your eatables, garçon! I want punci caldi per dui; and if you don't want your throat cut you had better go and get it."

"That's the way to talk to them, sir," said our friend De Lacy. "My plan is to cut their throats and then talk to them afterward." Mr. De Lacy had finished the bottle of brandy and emptied a bottle of champagne and sparkling hock; he was, in consequence, disposed to be very loquacious, and ready to talk to any one who would listen to him. "That's the way I like to hear Americans talk abroad; it shows 'em we're a free and independent country."

Mr. Bluff had not seen our party when he came in, and, turning round leisurely to take a look at us, his eyes rested for a moment on the speaker, who was just tossing off a glass of hock.

"And who the devil are you, sir?" he inquired. "What right have you to put your oar in when a gentleman asks for punci caldi per dui? I don't owe you nothin', do I, sir?"

De Lacy was taken quite aback at a shot from such an unexpected quarter, but placing his glass upon the table, and looking very fierce, "Do you know who you are talking to, sir?" he said. "Blood and thunder! blood will have to flow for this, sir!"

"Do I know who I am talking to?" said the lieutenant; "of course I do: you're a tin-peddler from east of sunrise; I can see wooden nutmegs and horn-flints in your face as plain as day. Garçon, hurry with that punci caldi per dui; and let me tell you, Mr. Down-East, if you put your spoon in my porridge you will get your mouth burnt!"

"My name is De Lacy, sir! George Washington Thaddeus

A DUEL THREATENED. 159

Kosciusko De Lacy, and I ain't afeard of anything living. You would not be the first man I have killed, by a long shot."

"No doubt you have choked many a poor fellow with your wooden hams, you skin-flint. Garçon, punci caldi per dui. You're just the fellow I have been looking for all my life. I want you for shark-bait, though I am afraid a shark would not bite at you."

Poor Mr. Bluff! I thought, you don't know what dreadful trouble you are bringing on yourself; and wishing to save the effusion of blood, I jumped up and whispered in the lieutenant's ear, "He is a great duelist, sir, and killed the best guardsman in the garrison only two days ago."

"What! that fellow?" said Mr. Bluff, laughing heartily. "Why, he hasn't got pluck enough to kill a kitten; and you, youngster, haven't allowed that queer-looking animal to gull you that way? that's too bad! Here, garçon, punci caldi per dui."

"Blood and Mars, sir!" exclaimed De Lacy, who had grown valorous as the liquor in him began to take effect, "I demand immediate satisfaction for this conduct, and I give you the privilege of having your own grave dug. I'll cut you into a thousand pieces to-morrow. Thunder and lightning! you don't know, perhaps, that I am death with a broadsword, and that I keep a private burying-ground?"

"Cutting up sausages, no doubt, you are; but look here, mister, you're just the kind of fellow I like to get hold of, and as you want satisfaction, I will give it to you on the spot. Punci caldi per dui, garçon. Mr. Marline, just step out, my boy, and hurry up my punci caldi while I settle with this nutmeg-maker;" and in a whisper he said, "Tell the landlord to get me a couple of muskets with fixed bayonets. I'll serve this blood-thirsty fellow out."

By this time De Lacy was to all appearances furious; he swore worse than they ever did in Flanders, and declared that he should never feel happy until he drank the heart's blood of his antagonist, who paid very little attention to his ravings, being busily engaged drinking his "punci caldi per dui," which I had managed to get brought in.

There were a number of persons in the room whose attention had been drawn to the altercation between the two, and they seemed very much amused at the prospect of having a little fun. The landlord, who came in, had got the muskets from some of his soldier friends, and was informing the lieutenant that they were all ready, just about the time he had finished his liquor, when he heard the familiar sound of "punci caldi per dui."

"All ready; coming, sir!" and in walked the garçon with two muskets with fixed bayonets laid out on a large tray.

"Ah, those are the beauties, my boy!" exultingly said Mr. Bluff; "and now, Mr. Nutmegs, if you have taken liquor enough to screw up your courage, step out with me into the yard, and I'll soon make daylight shine through you; and for fear of accidents, landlord, you had better get some powder and ball; I'd like to make him weigh an ounce heavier."

De Lacy, drunk as he was, looked rather pale at the prospect before him; but he had bragged so much that he could not well back out, so in a tremulous voice he said, "Come on, and make your will before you go out, for this is your last night on earth."

All hands proceeded to the yard, Mr. Brace being appointed as De Lacy's friend, and Reckless as the friend of Mr. Bluff.

By this time it was pitch dark, with a light drizzle of rain— so dark, indeed, that two people ten feet apart could not see each other; the lieutenant proposed that they should each tie a lantern to their breast-buttons, stand back to back at ten paces, wheel, and fire, and then charge bayonets, to which "Nutmegs" tremblingly assented. The affair now began to look very serious, and some of the bystanders, fearful of bloodshed, ran off to call the police. In the mean time the combatants were placed back to back, the word one, two, three was given; when at three the lieutenant turned round to fire, his antagonist was nowhere to be seen; he had quietly snuffed his light out, dropped his musket, and pushed for the nearest opening into the street. Mr. Bluff was indignant at such treatment, and he sung out, "Stop, George Washington Thaddeus Kosciusko De Lacy, you have disgraced five illustrious names." But the representative of the De Lacys never stopped, so the lieutenant consoled himself with a glass of "punci caldi per dui."

This was the first duel I ever witnessed. I thought it was going to end in a very blood-thirsty manner, but it had the good effect of relieving our party of a very disagreeable customer. Fortunately he had only finished two bottles of the wine, and we were saved so much expense in our supper, for we declined using what was left. We were always careful thereafter how we formed acquaintance with illustrious American people.

Mr. Bluff was quite put out because he could not have the pleasure of crossing bayonets with De Lacy, and it was the first time in my life that I ever saw him look displeased. He called for so many "punci caldis per dui" that he began to talk rather incoherently, threw his cap on the floor and imagined it was a spit-box, tried to cut up a bird with his fork, and snuffed the candle with a pair of sugar-tongs; he was half disposed to go to sleep in his chair, which would have looked very disreputable, when fortunately two new characters came upon the stage, and gave a new direction to his thoughts.

One of the persons in question was another Yankee, or rather, I should say, a Hoosier from one of the Western States. He was just the kind of individual I should suspect of jumping through a crab-apple-tree, or sliding down a rainbow, grinning a wild cat to death, or going over Niagara Falls in an iron pot.

The other was the exquisite who had come on board with Admiral Blazes' compliments when we first anchored, and showed so much ignorance with regard to the naval history of the United States. He entered with his eyeglass up, taking a familiar survey of everything in the room, and fixing his stare rather longer on Mr. Bluff than that gentleman thought desirable.

"I hope you have made out my number, sir," said the lieutenant. "If you haven't, that must be a d—d poor spy-glass of yourn, for I could have counted every gun in a three-decker by this time, and the blocks aloft, to boot."

"Ah! 'pon my soul, beg pardon, and all that; but I took ye for the *mate* on board His Britannic Majesty's three-decker Britannia. Beg pardon, on my 'onor; the hofficer I saw on the deck of the Yankee frigate, I presume."

At that time this was the style English officers sometimes adopted toward Americans until they were taught better manners; and although Mr. Bluff had not many ideas above a "punci caldi per dui," he could see that the Englishman was disposed to be facetious, and he determined to serve him out.

"I belong, sir," he said, "to the United States frigate Thunderbum, and remember, now, that I had to refresh your memory on some little matters relating to naval combats. I believe, at least, that you are the same person who came on board, judging from the smell of cologne about you."

"Ah! yes, cologne. Bless my soul, it's a capital thing, 'pon 'onor; destroys smell of tar and tobacco, and all that 'orrid practice you Americans 'ave of chewing, smoking, and spitting. You don't use cologne, eh? His Majesty's navy all use it, 'pon 'onor."

"Me use cologne?" said the indignant lieutenant. "No, sir; I always rub myself down with a dried codfish or old cheese, and sprinkle my pocket-handkerchief with old rye whisky. Those are the smells I like; and as to tar, I always carry a piece in my pocket to kill shore smells with."

"Bless my soul, 'ow very hodd! Well, really, you Yankees are a go-ahead people. I should not be surprised to see you quite a country some of these days after you 'ave paid your debts to the Henglish."

"Look here, my young perfumery-shop, I don't owe you nothin', I believe," said the lieutenant. "Pray, what's your name? and what ship do you hail from? and what's your number on the ship's books? and what's your captain's name? and who did you say the admiral was? and what'll ye take to drink?"

"Hale," said the Englishman, in answer to all these questions. "Ah! I'm Lord Telltail, haid to Hadmiral Blazes. Ah! that is to say, His Majesty's ship Britannia. Hadmiral's a bloody old 'umbug, you know, son of old Blazes; wears chafing-gear on his legs, you know, and all that, and 'as water in 'is legs."

"Punci caldi per dui," said the lieutenant.

"Ah! bless my soul; yes," said the Englishman. "Excellent, 'pon 'onor. Ah! waiter, be kind enough to get me a life-buoy and a tub for this gentleman to spit hin. Bless me soul, sir, you spit enough tobacco-juice," he exclaimed, "to float 'is Majesty's line-of-battle ships."

All this time the Pike County boy sat with his legs cocked up on the table, thumbs stuck in his vest-pockets, and his hat cocked back on the top of his head. He seemed very much interested in the conversation, and when the English officer made the remark about the spit-box, he pointed his mouth at the fireplace, about fifteen feet off, and threw out a jet of saliva with a force that would have done credit to a New York fire-engine. Having discharged his cargo, and cleared away a space in his mouth, he gave a whistle, and exclaimed, "Whew! darn my buttons, but you'll run 'foul of a snag presently, Mr. Britisher; an' I reckon if that ere remark of yourn were made out in Pike, scratch me if thar wouldn't be some tall gougin' goin' on. I reckon," he continued, "that 'Merican frigate out thar to anchor would knock them ar two old hay-ricks tew pieces in two minutes, although the darn'd things carry a hundred and twenty guns each."

"Ah! 'pon my soul," said the Englishman, coolly taking up his eye-glass; "ah, who's yer friend? one hof yer hofficers, I presume," addressing Mr. Bluff.

"No, darn it," said the Hoosier, "I ain't nary officer; but if I was, bus' my biler but I'd screech like thunder at that 'ere remark of yourn, and pitch into yer like a pile of bricks."

"I'd thank you, Mr. Punkin-pie," said Bluff, "jist to mind yer own affairs, and not talk about what don't concern you. I can attend to this gentleman (punci caldi per dui, garçon), and don't want any of (hiccough) your assistance."

"Well, darn me," said the Hoosier, "if I'd let a Britisher abuse one of the institutions of our country without a telling of him of it; and I reckon when I get to Congress the country 'ill hear tell on this, or else I can't talk none. At all events," he said, "Mr. Britisher, I hearn tell of one of our frigates a lickin' two of yourn at one pop, an' I reckon a true-born American can lick two Britishers at any time."

"Bless my soul," said John Bull, "what remarkable creatures you Hamericans har, really, 'pon 'onor'! Ah—waiter, bring me a glass of 'alf-and-'alf."

"With a fly in it, and a little saw-dust on the top of it," said Mr. Bluff.

"No, deuce thank you; I would positively not prefer the ah—fly, and the—ah—what-e-ma-callum. You've seen 'is Majesty's ship, the Rhumjungleballamsphoor," addressing Mr. Bluff again; "'ow long do you think it would requiah her to captu' the American frigate?"

"Why, about as long as it would take you to strap a block or turn in a dead-eye" (hiccough), said the lieutenant; "and d—n my timbers," he continued, "I don't believe you could do one or the other until (hiccough)—punci caldi per dui, garçon."

"Ah, 'pon me soul! we—ah—think different in 'is Majesty's service. I discussed the matta—ah—with Captain Softspot, of the Rhumjungleballamsphoor, and he decidedly coincides with me—ah—and, 'pon my soul, thinks 'e could captu' 'er in 'alf an 'our."

This was a little too much for the lieutenant, and as to Pike County, he was hitching up his breeches and getting ready to scream thunder. He squirted a jet of tobacco-juice all the way across the room, and knocked a pane of glass into a thousand pieces.

"Look here," said the lieutenant, "my box of cologne, if you ain't a little (hiccough) more particular in your—punci caldi per dui, garçon (hiccough)—observations, your mother's monkey will get into a muss. My real idea is (hiccough) that your d—d frigate Ramshacclebunglescum, or whatever you call her, would take as long to (hiccough) us as it would take you to scull up Niagara Falls in a (hiccough) pot, or roast a (hiccough) before a galley without fire."

"That's the way to giv' it 'em," said Pike. "Chaw 'em up like sassage-meat. Giv' 'em molasses."

"And what's more," continued the lieutenant, "I think you're a d—d impertinent (hiccough) and not worth the powder and shot that would shoot you (hiccough). Punci caldi per dui, garçon. If you are a specimen of His Majesty's (hiccough) I would volunteer to drive a thousand like you overboard with our afterguard; and I'll tell you one thing, if you don't look out one of these days (hiccough) somebody will plant a keg of gunpowder in the center of your miserable little island, and (hiccough) you English all to thunder; and now, Mr. Cologne, there's the door, and the sooner you get out of it the better."

At this moment Pike County crowed like a cock, and turned down his sleeves; he thought the lieutenant could take care of himself.

"Why, bless my soul," said the Britisher, "really, 'pon 'onor, you Americans are a go-ahead people, quite original, has I live. Waita, I say, bring my bill, one glass of hale!" and coolly rising up, His Majesty's lieutenant took a good look at Mr. Bluff through his quizzing-glass, and then one at Pike County, and quietly moved off to the door, humming "Rule Britannia!"

This was a little too much for our lieutenant to bear: his steam was up at least forty pounds to the square inch; and seizing a "punci caldi per dui" (which the waiter had just brought him), he threw it at the exquisite just as his hand touched the knob, and as he was about taking a last survey of the couple through the quizzing-glass. Crash went the glass against the panels, and covered the floor with the pieces.

This time the Englishman was really tantalizing. Looking down at the pieces on the floor, and then at the lieutenant, he said, "Ah, my good fellow, you've broke the glass. Waita! Waita! I say, come 'ere and pick hup the pieces before some of 'is Majesty's hofficers henter and cut their feet," and then taking a last deliberate look, he departed.

"Otro punci caldi per dui, garçon!" shouted Mr. Bluff, greatly incensed at John Bull's coolness. He knocked over two or three chairs, and went to the fireplace, out of which he seemed disposed to take his revenge by poking the fire out.

Pike reared and tore about like a catamount, squirted out two panes of glass at one pop, and, striding up to the lieutenant, he gave him a hearty slap on the back, hard enough to knock the breath out of his body, and seizing him by the hand, he almost shook his arm out of the socket.

"Well, now, capting," he said, "you done that 'ere up brown, and you served the tarnal critter jist as ye ought to 'a' served him, and darn me if he's any man to take it; you're a fust-rate un, and no mistake, and darn me if I don't cotton to you right off, slap up, straight down," and then came another slap on the shoulder which made Mr. Bluff wince.

The lieutenant did not feel disposed to appreciate the familiarity as warmly as it was given; he was as mad as a spring bull, and the great wonder was that he did not knock Pike County down on the spot. "Keep your hands off, sir, and your (hiccough) familiarity to yourself," he said, "or you and I will quarrel on the spot. I don't know you, sir, and I want to know by what right you dare to (hiccough) such a liberty with me?"

"Wall, now, capting, if yer ain't mad with one of your own countrymen, may I be blowed up, cut down, and sawed into pine plank. Why, I hope yer don't take me for a Britisher, 'cause I ain't, nowhow you can fix it; I ain't. My hand is tarnation heavy, I knows, and perhaps I mought a hurt you; but darn me if I thought you was a feller to get mad with a Pike County boy. Now, capting, here's my hand, and I axes yer pardon if I done anything to hurt your feelin's."

"I'm not a captain, my friend," said the lieutenant, getting smoothed down a little; "but I never take the liberty of slapping (hiccough) a person I don't know on the shoulder, and I never (hiccough) any man I don't know to take such a liberty with me, and all I have to say is (hiccough) do it again."

"A course not, capting, seeing you don't like it; but we hearn tell so much on you navy folks out in Ohio, and being intimate with an old feller out thar who licks all everlasting at tellin' stories, I thought I might take a liberty with you, 'cause you look mightily like him. He was a darned good feller, although he was all-fired ugly; but that, you know, runs in the family, and he's the best-lookin' of them as is living, after all."

The equivocal compliment paid him made the lieutenant smile, and brought back the good-humored look which was scarcely ever absent from his face. "Well, let us say no more about the matter, my friend," he replied. "You did hurt me (hiccough) with that sledge-hammer of yours pounding on to my shoulders. All I ask is not to do it (hiccough), and I accept your apology."

"That's something like reason, now, capting, and here's my hand on it." And they shook hands together, and were good friends; at least the lieutenant made it appear that he was satisfied, though it was evident he would have been gratified to get rid of his quondam acquaintance.

"Wall, now, capting," said Pike County, "you are just from Ole Virginny, and I sorter reckon you've got some of the best old weed that grows thar, and being as how we're sworn friends now, I'll take the liberty of asking you for a chaw of tobaccer."

Mr. Bluff evidently wanted to close the intimacy, and determined to get rid of Pike County at once; so, picking up his cap from off the floor, where for some time he had been using it for a spit-box, "I never chew tobacco, sir," he said, and then sung out to the waiter, "Garçon, punci caldi per dui."

But Pike County was not going to be put off in that fashion. He looked at the puddle of tobacco-spit upon the floor, then at the lieutenant's mouth, and then at the puddle again. "Darn me, capting," he said, "if you don't chaw tobaccer, you've got the greatest chaw-tobaccer mouth on yer face I ever seen, and that ere puddle looks very much like the tobaccer-juice I seen in old Ohio. I rather think, old feller, yer a stretchin' a leetle."

Mr. Bluff put down his punch, looked at Pike County in perfect astonishment, and buttoned up his coat. "What in the devil's name do you mean, sir, by (hiccough) addressing me in that way? Do you mean to insult me by doubting my word?" he said. "Did not I tell you, sir, that I did not (hiccough) chew tobacco, and, damn your familiarity, I don't want any more of it" (hiccough).

"Thar you go ag'in now, capting," said Pike. "Thar you go. Why, darn me if you would not set a powder magazine on fire. Why, who ever said anything about insulting you? It's more nor I'd dar' do to insult one of the military. No, sirree, horse; I'm none of them kind, *I tell you.* I only axed for a chaw of tobaccer, and said you had a chaw-tobaccer-lookin' mouth on you; and if that's any offense, why, I humbly axes your pardon, and thar's my hand on it ag'in; that's as much as any Christian orter expect."

Pike County looked so contrite that the good-hearted sailor could not help getting better pleased, and he thought he would get rid of his acquaintance the sooner by doing so. He took the proffered hand, accepted the apology, and called for the "garçon" to bring him his (hiccough) bill. "I believe I will go on board now," he said, "so, sir, I will bid you (hiccough) good-night."

"No, no, capting; yer can't do that yet," said Pike, "until yer take a drink with a feller. We've done had a sorter quarrel, and now you must make it up with Pike County over a rum tickler."

"I am very much obliged to you (hiccough), Mr. Pike County," said the lieutenant; "but I never drink anything, and I can't stop a moment (hiccough) longer." And Mr. Bluff put on a virtuous look, as if he had never tasted anything stronger than cider all his life.

Pike County could not stand this last clincher; he laughed so hard that the decanters absolutely danced upon the table. "Well!" he said, "that beats old Ohio all hollow. Now, capting, yer larfin' at me. Yer might fool me about that ere mouth, but darn my buttons if you can fool me about that ar nose; 'cause if that nose ain't ring-streaked and speckled, darn me if I know what ring-streaked and speckled is." And, putting his right forefinger to his nose, and pointing to the empty glasses on the table, he sat down and laughed heartily.

The joke was so good that Mr. Bluff had to join in the merriment, and consented to drink with Pike County after all. I got up to go and look after my boat's crew, and heard him call out for "punci caldi per dui," while Pike County called for old American rye whisky with a bee in it.

At this moment a jolly-looking red-faced Briton, with an epaulet on his right shoulder, came rolling into the room holding up a very seedy-looking French officer who had evidently been drinking something stronger than "vin ordinaire." He had on two epaulets and an immense aigulette on his right breast, the epaulets hanging quite clear of the straps and down on the breast, looking very much like two anchors a cock-bill at a merchantman's cat-head.

"May I never see salt water again," said the Briton, "but if this ain't the hardest-steering craft I ever see, tho' man and boy I been follerin' the sea these twenty-two years. Ship ahoy!" he said, catching a glimpse of old Bluff. "What ship is that?"

"The American ship (hiccough) Punci Caldi per Dui," answered the lieutenant, "bound on a (hiccough) cruise."

"Well, if so, you're not hordered to go with dispatches," said the Briton. "'Eave to and lend us a 'and with this 'ere Frenchy; he's all ahoo, like a midshipman's kit, and I found him going afore the wind with his yards braced sharp up, hall sail sot, and both on 'is anchors 'anging to the cat-'ead."

"It's werry certain he ain't (hiccough) water-logged," said Bluff; "and he looks to me as if he had 'odyvee' stowed in bulk and pumps choked."

"Mayhap he has," said the Briton, "but I know he tows reg'lar 'ard. Why, bless your soul, mister (yer from the American frigate, ain't ye?)"

"(Hiccough)—yes," said Bluff.

"Well, I was in the battle of Trafalgar, on board the Bullyruffin, and we 'ad to tow two French liners into port, an' one of 'em a three-decker at that; but, bless my heyes, this 'ere fellow tows a deal 'arder nor either of 'em, or both of 'em together."

"Prenez garde de tomber," said the Frenchman, talking very thick; "je ne puis pas bien m'exprimer en français, parce que je n'ai pas l'habitude de le parler, mais je parle l'américain. Ah, Monsieur Soufflet, si l'on savait abord le frégat ce que vous avez fait, Got d—n."

"He speaks Henglish like a book," said the Briton.

"Parley wous (hiccough) francy, Mossure?" said Bluff.

"Je ne sais que répondre," he replied. "Vive le roi! Je vais me sauver—je vous demande—mille tonnerres—mettez-vous à votre aise et apportez du vin—"

"We, mossure," said Bluff. "Garçon, punci (hiccough) caldi per (hiccough) dui."

"Non, non, non!" said Crapaud; "j'ai bien parler; vous ne m'écoute pas, pas, pas."

"Oh, thunder! I understand him now," said the Briton. "He says he wants his pa. Monsieur, wolly wou de boire, oh, wolly wou de mangay?"

"Ah, ma pauvre téte!" said the poor Frenchman. "Cet officier anglais n'a pas le courage de parler français—vive la France!

THE BOAT'S CREW ARE DRUNK.

Garçon, avez-vous encore du vin? Ah, ma pauvre tête! du vin, du vin."

"How thi-hic-hic he talks!" said Bluff. "He says something about the 'vang.' I guess he means the spanker vang. Comy wous porty wous, mossur; woolly wous de kickshoos?"

"Appuyez-vous sur moi, Monsieur l'Américain. Diantre, vous êtes un joli garçon, et vous parle le français très-bien. Je ne doute pas que vous ne soyez mon ami. Vive l'Amérique!"

"Poor devil!" said Mr. Bluff, "he's so far (hiccough) that he don't know his own (hiccough) language. I think, old feller," he said to the Briton, "we had better take him in tow, and (hiccough) him on board (hiccough) ship."

"Dom a Frenchy, anyhow!" said the Briton. "They're hawful 'ard to tow; but 'eave ahead, my 'earty, and we'll take him san'wich-fashion, like a piece of 'am between two slices of bread and butter." And each taking the Frenchman by the arm, they staggered out, the Crapaud incoherently muttering, "Est-ce que je ne vaux pas autant que mon capitaine? est-ce que je—je boirais du vin ordinaire—mille tonn—vive Napoléon! Sacre mille bombes, messieurs, il me fait d'argent!" And he went off singing,

"Lisette, est-ce vous, vous en riche toilette?
Non (hiccough), non (hiccough), non, vous n'êtes (hiccough) Lisette."

It was about nine o'clock when I arrived at the wharf, and what was my disappointment to find that Coxswain Brown had broken the trust confided in him. He was gloriously drunk, and so were the rest of the boat's crew. I was informed afterward that the English midshipman fared no better, for his boat's crew, Coxswain Smith included, were so drunk that they had to be towed off to the ship. I made up my mind never to place any confidence in persons of the name of Brown or Smith, for I had noticed more peccadilloes committed by persons of that name than any other.

Here was a go. What was I to do? Every moment I was expecting the captain to come down, and his crew drunk. I appealed to the crew, and they were in that state when they did not know their officer from a bale of goods. I sat down in despair, and wished that I had followed the example of the captain's dog Snap. How many trials midshipmen would save themselves if they would only remember the moral of that story!

Fortunately for me, a servant came down from the consul's and informed me that the captain was not going on board that night, and that I must return on board with the boat. This was a great relief to me, but how was I to return on board? There was the rub. I went back to the hotel and found my two messmates still enjoying themselves over their dinner. Pike County was leaning back fast asleep in his chair, with mouth wide open, holding on with his teeth to a sperm candle some one had stuck into the aperture, and the large "chaw tobaccer" he had got from somebody lying on the table alongside of him.

My messmates returned to the wharf with me, and after a great deal of trouble, by sousing the men with water, we managed to bring them to their senses. We were just on the point of shoving off when Mr. Bluff and the Briton appeared in sight, holding up the French officer, who had lost the use of his tongue altogether. The lieutenant's voice was very husky, and he wanted his rolling-tackles hooked very badly to keep him from surging from side to side, though he could generally carry sail through any squall, no matter how many "punci caldis per dui" he had taken, and the jolly Briton looked as if he had stopped somewhere besides the pump.

"There, dom him," said the latter. "Ye'll jest be kind enough to tow him alongside his ship, and leave him in the main chains. The Frenchies all bundles in at four bells and leaves the sentry to look hout, an' if you'll drap him in the chains, with a wet swab hunder his 'ead, he'll be as comfortable till mornin' as can be. Bon jour, mounseer," he said, addressing the Frenchman; "conny wous, porty wous, twosyour."

"Adieu, mon (hic, hic, hic) ami. Vive l'Angla (hic)—"

Mr. Bluff stepped in just as we were shoving off, tumbled the Frenchman in as if he had been a bundle of hay, and then ordered me to pull for the French frigate. The coxswain being half-tight, and not being able to tell one ship from the other, I directed the boat for what I took to be the French admiral's ship. The lights came over the side, and I commenced helping Mr. Bluff to get the Frenchman up, not noticing at the time anything remarkable about the frigate. After a good deal of trouble we succeeded in reaching the deck, the Frenchman singing snatches of the Marseillaise hymn, and the lieutenant trying to keep him quiet, for fear the French admiral would hear him, and likely arrest him.

When Mr. Bluff felt himself secure on his legs, he walked in rather an unsteady manner up to the officer of the deck, who was coolly looking on to see what it all meant. Taking off his cap and making a low bow to the officer, Mr. Bluff commenced the conversation.

"Parly vous francey (hiccough), musshure?"

"Oui, monsieur," responded the officer.

"Well, then, if you do (hiccough) parly vous francey, I wish to inform you that I found your first (hiccough) lieutenant on shore, without any (hiccough) chart or compass; he was scudding in a heavy sea-way (hiccough), and was on the (hiccough) point of broaching to, when (hiccough) I took the helm and steered him into (hiccough) port; his spars are badly sprung, and I think he is a little water- (hiccough) logged (bookoo de vang, I think you call it), and will require to go into dock for twenty- (hiccough) four hours."

The officer thus addressed burst out laughing. "Why, what in the name of heaven are you thinking of, Bluff? you don't take your own ship for a French frigate, do you?" he said. "This is a good joke, don't know your own ship, eh? Well, Bluff, I thought you would know your own barkey in any weather."

"Pshaw! you can't fool me," he replied, "parley vous francey, and be d—d to you (hiccough), and take your drunken (hiccough) lieutenant and stow him away. You can't fool me (hiccough) with your French frigate," and, making a low bow to the officer of the deck, he walked, or rather staggered, to the ward-room hatch, and tumbled down into his state-room.

The Frenchman was stowed away for the night, and was quite surprised the next morning to find himself on board an American frigate instead of his own. Mr. Bluff's messmates quizzed him awfully about the Frenchman, but he swore to the last that he had never seen him before that morning at breakfast, and that it was all a yarn. Thus ended my first visit to Gibraltar. I have often laughed when I thought of that day. I can't say that my morals were likely to derive much benefit from the exhibition of three inebriated lieutenants, but it finally did me no harm, and I can conscientiously say that I have never drank anything stronger than brandy from that day to this.

In those days a little lark was viewed more leniently than at the present time, when a man's value in the service is estimated by the quantity of cold water he can drink without getting the cramp in his stomach, or the number of times he goes to prayer on a Sunday afternoon. Men of "social habits" are no longer tolerated, and, instead of sitting cozily over a bottle of good old Madeira, officers devote themselves to lemonade, eau sucrée, orgeat, and soda, talk earnestly on scientific matters, write books in which they call lizards *Enemidophorus presignis;* a fish, *Tricomycterus maculatus;* and a crow-blackbird, *Psaracolins curacus;* they can tell you to a fraction how many ten-penny nails it will take to shingle an ant-hill, describe to you psychologically everything pertaining to *Terebratula subexcavata* (vulgarly known as clams), and can tell you how many of said *Terebratula subexcavata* a New York alderman can eat at his dinner; but will the present system get a ship off a lee shore, or fit the rigging neatly over the mast-head, or will our batteries be worked with that practical knowledge that insured us some advantages in the war of 1812 over a brave and powerful adversary? I remember the time when some of the old-fashioned fellows would go on deck and make the blocks talk, and the yards fly around like magic. Old Tom Hardface would detect in a moment a rope-yarn mousing on a hook, even were it ever so far aloft, and a spot on the paint-work caused more agony to his mind than a rent in his coat. Small as the matter is, it is a proof of knowledge in the profession, as the fine touches in a picture show the ability of the painter. There were lots of those old martinets in my time—men who did taste brandy, flogged a good deal (bad faults, to be sure), and always had ship ready for anything; but where are they now? Echo answers, Where? They have been gathered to their fathers, and it is only by tradition that we know of them; though they made our ships models in their lifetime, yet the present generation don't altogether copy after them. They carried their discipline, station-bills, recipe for mixing whitewash, blacking for guns, and all the little etceteras for making a ship look as she should, to their graves with them; at least we must believe so, for we see little or nothing of the kind now. Peace be to their ashes!

CHAPTER XIII.

ARRIVAL OF THE GINGERBREAD—INTRODUCTION TO THE COMMODORE AND HIS COOK, TO SAY NOTHING OF A LITTLE BLACK PIG—DISMAY AND CONFUSION ON BOARD.

On the morning following the scene I described as having occurred on shore, the United States sloop of war Gingerbread, bearing the broad pennon of Commodore Blowhard, came into port, and, much to our regret, we were informed that the commodore intended transferring his flag to our frigate. I say much to our regret, though I myself had no particular regret on the subject, being rather elated at the idea of serving in the flag-ship; and being full of youthful aspirations, I flattered myself that I might be promoted to the rank of commodore's aide.

Our little captain was in a great flutter at the idea of not being any longer "sole monarch of her peopled deck," and was overheard to say that it was "blasted bad luck," and he wished the commodore to the devil. Such an ebullition from an ordinary frail mortal might have passed without comment; but, coming from so renowned a pillar of the church, why—well, such things do happen.

The captain had fondly hoped that old Blowhard was cruising up the Archipelago in search of pirates, as it was rumored that the Greeks were making rather free with Uncle Sam's merchant ships, in return for the sympathy thrown away on their distressed nation by philanthropic Americans; and when the report was made to him that an American sloop of war was standing in to the Bay of Gibraltar, with the blue swallow-tail at the main, he popped off his chair as if a bomb-shell had burst under him—three hops, a skip, and a jump brought him up the ladder and landed him safe upon the poop with a formidable-looking telescope under his arm, and a face sour enough to spoil a whole dairy.

Reconnoitring the advancing vessel closely, he put down the glass, saying, "Tut, nonsense, Mr. Teazer; how can you make such foolish reports to me? That is no sloop of war, sir; it is only a merchant ship."

"I only know what Binnacle, the signal quartermaster, reported to me," replied Mr. Teazer (looking very fierce at the same time). "You have said yourself a dozen times, sir, that he had the best eyes in the ship."

"Do you say that is the broad pennon, you d—d old fool (the Lord forgive me), as I used to say, Binnacle?" exclaimed the captain. "Look again, you old loggerhead."

Old Binnacle took the glass, touched his hat with an air of injured innocence, and then made a long and faithful survey of the approaching ship.

"Well, pumpkin-head, what do you see?" said the captain.

"I sees, sir," he replied, "a Yankee cravat comin' inter port, and I knows her to be the Gingerbread, 'cause as how the Gingerbread is the only cravat in service as carries four Pisen guns in her waist. I sees," he continued, "a blue swallow-tailed flag at the main, and I sees as how she has got a list to windward, and by that sign I knows that Commodore Blowhard is on board, 'cause he allers has the lee guns run in, and the crew sittin' to wind'ard, each man with a thirty-two-pound shot in his fist to keep the ship from capsizing; moreover, I knows her by—"

"Silence, you infernal old fool!" cried out the captain, in a rage; "don't dare to talk such nonsense to me! Your eyes are no better than two burnt holes in a blanket. I have half a mind to break this glass over your head."

"Well, Captain Marvellous," said Ben, with the most imperturbable gravity, "if it will do you any good, sir, you can break my head with your glass, if you like; but if that ere ship a-comin' in ain't a 'Merican cravat, with four Pisen guns in her waist, then I ain't fit to be signal quartermaster."

"Another word out of your stupid mouth," said the captain, almost boiling over with passion, "and I'll break this glass over your old numskull."

"Well, Captain Marvellous, as I said before, you are at liberty to do as you please with that glass of yourn; but I honly has to say that that ere 'Merican cravat, with four Pisen guns in her waist, are a-hoistin' her number at the fore—and if these old peepers ain't mistaken, there goes a signal, 131, at the mizzen, which means, in the 'Merican navy, to send a boat to that ere 'Merican cravat."

There was no longer any cause for disputing about the matter, for there, sure enough, was the signal displayed, and the captain, in a most unhappy frame of mind, ordered the answering flag to be run up.

"It is well for your head, Mr. Binnacle, that she turned out to be what you said she was, though you guessed at it by mere accident," said the captain; "had she been anything else I would have broken my glass over your skull, as sure as you are signal quartermaster." And with that he descended into the cabin, giving the messenger-boy a kick as he passed along.

Old Ben turned around and winked at the midshipmen on the poop, as much as to say, "I knows a 'Merican cravat, and can see four Pisen guns in her waist as well as any one."

"Ben," said one of the middies, "I wonder you were not afraid of 'bullyragging' the captain so; I expected every minute to see him smash his glass over your head."

Ben gave a hearty chuckle at so absurd an idea. "Why, Lord bless you, young gentleman," he replied, "don't you suppose old Binnacle knows a buzzard from a hand-saw, or a cross-cut saw from a sausage-knife? You may reckon he does. Why, didn't you see that the captain had his own best glass in his hand? and it would not look well in the expenditure-book to have it said that the captain broke the best glass in the ship over the signal quartermaster's head, just because he happened to see a 'Merican cravat with four Pisen guns in her waist. Had it been the quartermaster's *old* glass, I should have been more particular-like, you know. This are the third cruise," he continued, "that I have sailed with Captain Marvellous, and he's allers a-threatening to break that ere dientical glass over my head; but, mind you, he ain't done it yet." And Ben marched off with an air as if he was a great judge of human nature. Without doubt he had sailed long enough with the captain to understand him.

The Gingerbread came rattling into port; the boat was sent in answer to the signal, and who should descend the side of the corvette and take his seat in her but Commodore Blowhard himself. In fifteen minutes he came puffing up the gangway-ladder to where Captain Marvellous was waiting (all smiles and bows) to receive him, though at the bottom of his heart he wished him at the de— I should say up the Archipelago hunting pirates.

"I am sorry, my dear sir," said the captain, "that I had not time to have the officers and crew ready to receive you; but the fact is, sir, you took us all by surprise. We did not make you out until you were right upon us, and I really had not time to man the yards and dress the officers. I will take some other opportunity to introduce *my* officers to you."

"Ah, Marvellous," said the broad pennon, "I thought you knew my way of doing business. I always come and go like a beam of lightnin'; and, my dear sir, it only shows you the importance of guarding against all precautions. By the time you are under my command one month you will apprehend the necessity of sleeping always with one eye 'tight open,' for if you don't you'll find that I'll sprawl the party.

"As to manning the yards," he continued, looking around at the sailors who had congregated about the mainmast, "that will do for the 'parleyvous,' 'Queen Ferdinand' of Naples, or his holiness

176   THE ADVENTURES OF HARRY MARLINE.

the 'Carnival' of Rome; but I despise all such demonstrations myself, and should feel quite as much complimented if you let it alone. As to the officers, I make it a rule to know them at once, so do me the favor to invite a dozen or two of them to dinner, including some of those rosy-looking midshipmen riding on the spanker-boom. I like children, Marvellous, and you seem to have a lot of them; they take me back to my days of midshipmanship. 'Ah, happy days! who would not wish once more to be a boy?' as Milton says in his 'Paradise Lost.' Ain't it Milton who says so, Shy?" said the commodore, turning to his secretary, a mild, innocent-looking youth of twenty.

"Byron is the author of the lines, I believe, sir," replied Mr. Shy.

"Well, Byron or Pope, it don't make no difference; I know it was one of the ancient historians; only give us a good lot of 'em at dinner, Marvellous. I like the little fellows mightily."

It would have puzzled any one not acquainted with the commodore's style to find out whether he wanted a lot of "ancient historians" for dinner or the "little fellows he liked so mightily."

The captain understood fully what the commodore wanted, though an invitation to a midshipman was an act of courtesy (or what he would have considered a breach of discipline) of which he was never known to be guilty (the commodore knew this), and in the proposition he could only perceive a blow aimed at the discipline of the ship; he twisted and turned like an eel on a hook, ahem'd and haw'd two or three times, and looked as doleful as the Knight of the Rueful Countenance, whom he at times resembled.

"Why, really, commodore," he said, "I'm not exactly prepared for company to-day—didn't expect you, you know; stores rather short, and all that; and if you will permit me—"

"Oh, don't make any excuses, Marvellous; give 'em salt horse and duff. We don't care about kickshaws, entrées, or pat de fo grass; let us have a flow of reason and a feast of soul, as the poet says. Ain't that what the poets say, Shy, eh?"

"Something of that kind, sir," answered the modest young man.

"And, Marvellous," continued the commodore, "if you are hard pushed for something to eat, send on board the Gingerbread and help yourself to my stores; you will find everything you want there, from a sucking pig down to a nut-picker. And, Shy, just jump into the boat, go alongside the sloop of war, and bring *all* my stores on board this ship, and don't forget to bring my cook, Pierre

Poison, with you; he will cook us up the 'entremets' in no time. No excuses, Marvellous" (perceiving the captain about to speak); "I always go well provided; I always guard against all precautions." And he walked into the cabin.

The captain could have bitten a scupper-nail in two; his ears were laid back like those of a vicious horse just going to bite, and his thin lips had lost that pleasant smile with which they were wont to be adorned when he was telling the story of his good dog "Snap." He lingered behind a moment, and when the commodore was fairly out of sight he "hazed" us all from the poop, and gave strict orders to the officer of the deck never to allow us up there for the future.

The modest secretary returned in a very short time, bringing with him the commodore's cook, Pierre Poison, and all the commodore's stores, said stores consisting literally of one very thin, small, black pig, a dozen skewers, a few nut-pickers, one frying-pan, one string of onions, a paper of macaroni, a quart-pot full of dried apples, and a French coffee-pot.

The commodore had evidently been watching for the return of his messenger, for the moment the boat touched the gangway he came strutting out to receive Pierre Poison, who made his appearance on deck with the little black pig thrown over his shoulder, while the remainder of the stores were festooned about his person. He cast a searching glance around him as he stepped on board to see if he could trust his valuables among the present company; his eye soon caught the commodore's, and he advanced with an air of confidence; while old Blowhard was looking at him with an air of triumph, his eye said as plain as it could speak, "There's a cook for you!"

"Sacre bleu," said Pierre, laying his stores on the deck, "reste tranquille, mon petit cochon—reste ici, ma belle macaroni," and, "Bon jour, Monsieur Admiral, I av brought ze pic, an all ze oser store, sair, je demande votre plaisir."

"Ah, Pierre," said the commodore, "that looks something like. Now get down below, you rascal, to the galley and cook us up a dinner for twelve or fourteen. Lay out your talents, you old son of a sea-cook, and see if you can't sprawl the whole party. Give us the 'entremets,' Pierre, the 'bonbon,' and the 'pat de fo grass.'"

"Oui, monsieur," he replied, "you shall see what you shall see." And with that he descended to the galley, where he took entire possession of the premises, shook all the wind out of the sails of Jean Julien de Baptiste, and made old Gumbo Chaff even open his eyes in astonishment. That intelligent old "colored pusson" was fain to admit that Pierre was the most "missible stronary good cook he hab eber lay his eyes on"; and he did "actelly believe he knew enuff to make a stew out ob de debble's horns."

To give any description of the appearance of Pierre Poison would defy my humble abilities. In height he was about three feet six inches, his body about the size of a wasp's; in appearance he was between sixty and a hundred and fifty years of age. His head was incased in a red worsted night-cap, surrounded by one of the commodore's cast-off hats, said hat being a mile too large and being indented with innumerable cable-tier pinches. He had evidently a disposition to step into the admiral's shoes, for his legs were incased in a pair of high top-boots, which were formerly worn by the commodore in his natty days, and were presented to Pierre on an occasion when he had more than excelled himself in getting up a dinner. Add to the above a long linen coat, something on the Shanghai order (only a little more so), said to have been presented to him by the modest secretary "Shy," and you may have a faint idea of this remarkable *roi de cuisine.*

While he was stumbling down the hatch with the "leetle pic" upon his shoulder, Mr. Barnacle stood observing him with no very pleasant smile upon his countenance; the wart on his nose was flattened out most alarmingly, and turning to Mr. Bluff, who had relieved Mr. Teazer, he said, "In the name of tar, pitch, and turpentine, Bluff, what do you call that thing?"

"That," said Bluff, "is the commodore's broad pennon; he hoists it on every ship he goes in. They tell me he takes up more room at the galley than ten ordinary cooks, and in less than twenty-four hours your decks will be greased from one end to the other."

"Humph!" growled the first luff, "a pretty kettle of fish; but just let him drop any of his slush on my clean decks, and d—n me if I don't tie him and his little pig to the chain-cable and veer away until they go through the hawse-hole. Pipe down, Mr. Bluff."

"Pipe down what, sir?" asked the lieutenant, in some surprise.

"Why, pipe down all those boobies who have crowded to the gangway to see a d—d dirty French cook and a hungry-looking pig. Here, boatswain's mate, take out your colt and clear those booms.

Lean off those guns, young gentlemen. Mr. Bluff, send those young gentlemen on the cross-trees; *they* won't be so anxious to see a d—d dirty French cook another time. You, messenger-boy, stand clear of that paint-work or I will give you a dozen. Humph! a pretty state of affairs indeed, when Commodore Blowhard's cook throws a whole frigate into a state of confusion! It's abominable, Mr. Bluff."

"Sir?" said Mr. Bluff.

"Set the blacklisters to scrubbing the copper outside, and keep 'em at it until sunset."

"Ay, ay, sir," answered the lieutenant.

"And, Mr. Bluff—"

"Sir?" said the jolly lieutenant.

"Never mind, sir. D—n all French cooks! that's all I have to say." And Mr. Barnacle descended to the wardroom in a state of mind not to be described.

CHAPTER XIV.

INVITED OUT TO DINNER—SIXTEEN KINDS OF DISHES MADE OUT OF A LITTLE BLACK PIG.

I WAS sitting very quietly on the main-topmast cross-trees, whither I had been sent by Mr. Barnacle as a punishment for being one of the number who were admiring Pierre Poison and his "leetle pic," when I was hailed by the officer of the deck and told that the captain wanted me. I was so pleasantly employed at the time with my own thoughts, dreaming of old Uncle Abe and his horses, fondly imagining myself at home basking in the sunshine of my dear old grandfather's smiles, that I wished the officer of the deck in Piccadilly when he disturbed my reveries. I was somewhat compensated, however, for being disturbed by receiving the information that I was invited to dine with the commodore.

That liberal old sailor had instructed the captain to invite the surgeon, purser, marine officer, and master, three lieutenants, and four midshipmen, to say nothing of Shy, who was always considered as master of the ceremonies.

The wardroom officers were invited *en règle*, a separate messenger being sent to each one; but when the old negro steward asked the captain, "Who shall I hab de honor, sar, of inwitin' from de steerage ?" he replied, "Invite four of them—I don't care a d—n which."

So the following invitation was delivered to the assembled middies by " Conk " in his most effective manner :

"Gempleum, de capen, Massa Marvellous, will do himself de pleasure of inwitin' four of de midshipmates to do him de felicite ob giben dar kompany to dinna, whar dey will hab de honor ob meetin' de commander-in-chief ob de 'Merican navy in dese har sea. De capen say he don't care a d—n which ob you come so he hab got de 'quired number of gempleum. If," he continued, "de gempleum permit dis har old nigga to make a segestin, he would observe dat it's allers 'spectful to 'pear in de full-dress coat."

This speech was received with loud applause by all the midshipmen. No one felt the least hurt at the manner in which the invitation was given. Old " Conk " had materially softened the rough edges of it by the bland manner in which he had conveyed it.

The party was selected by "cutting in a book"—first letter, left-hand side nearest A, dines with the commodore. And it fell to the lot of Bibb and Tucker, little Jemmy Block and Harry Marline, which, as it turned out, was the very selection the commodore would have made himself.

Suffice it to say that we were all togged out in our best, and soon found ourselves (overcome somewhat with awe) in the presence of the respected commander-in-chief "ob de 'Merican navy," as " Conk " styled him.

The other officers had already assembled, and, each one having taken the seat allotted to him, soup was handed to the guests, and the play began. A description of the dinner will not be necessary ; it will be sufficient to say that Pierre Poison acquitted himself with infinite credit ; that the "leetle black pic" yielded sixteen different courses, among which were representations of woodcock, partridges, and pheasants, turtle stew, and, in fact, everything that the most fastidious epicure could have desired.

Where the six dishes of vegetables came from I never could imagine ; it is possible they were all manufactured from the string of onions mentioned in the catalogue of the commodore's stores, and it was strongly suspected that the calves'-feet jelly and blanc mange were the results of Pierre Poison's old boots, as they mysteriously disappeared that day, and were never seen since ; certain it is that Jemmy Block found a copper boot-tack in his plate.

Wine was handed to the company, and the tongues began to wag. I noticed one thing, however: "Conk" handed to the midshipmen a bottle the liquid of which was much paler than that handed to the wardroom officers; it was strongly suspected of being molasses and water; but "Conk" reassured us on this point, for he whispered to us as he poured out the sickly-looking beverage, "Don't drunk too much ob 'em, young gempleum, 'cos it's berry 'trong, an' you must neber put de enemy in de mouf to 'teal away de brain, as Massa Shickspur say." We consoled ourselves for the thin fluid by drawing wisdom from the moral of Conk's quotation; and if we felt a little malicious toward him for treating us so gingerly in the wine line, he disarmed our anger by filling our plates with nuts and raisins.

There are two or three persons who appeared at the commodore's dinner not mentioned heretofore in these pages, and I should be doing injustice to the world if I did not pay them the compliment of a passing remembrance. Poor old fellows, they have nearly all passed away, and have long since been gathered unto their fathers; one or two of them still cling to life, as decayed fungi stick to a rotten log, but there is little or no vitality in them—they only serve as mementos of the past, and point out to the officers of the present day what "odds and ends" the service was made up of in 18—.

The post of honor I must e'en give to our surgeon, Mr. Hitybelteser, a gentleman whose knowledge was considered so deep at that time that no one could fathom it; his erudition no one doubted, for his library consisted of books into the pages of which no one on board had the temerity to dive. The officers of the Thunderbum never blunted their faculties by reading *heavy* works. He was a poet, a linguist, and a painter, for his room was hung around with scenes sketched by his own hand. The uninitiated in pictures might, perhaps, have had some difficulty in ascertaining which was the sky and which the water, but a connoisseur would have detected their value at one glance. His grand *chef-d'œuvre* was a Highland soldier, copied while the original was on post at Gibraltar. One spiteful person was malicious enough to say that the said Highlander looked as if the ramrod had gone down into his legs and the bayonet had stuck in his throat, judging from the air of agony expressed in his countenance.

The surgeon was, besides all this, a geologist, conchologist, ichthyologist, and entomologist; in fact, as Mr. Bluff expressed himself, "he was the very officer to paint the expression of a dead fish's eye, after a navy officer have cotch him."

"Hity," as he was familiarly called, had a very bad habit of using very hard words in affording an explanation on any question relating to his profession; his sick report, in particular, was generally made out in scientific language, in which he selected the largest words to convey the meaning of the most common disease. These sick reports were a great source of annoyance to the captain, who, if he took any delight in anything, delighted in reading over the sick report; he pored over it with as much eagerness as a politician would over the election returns. The Latin terms put him out of all patience, and he asked the doctor once or twice to write it in plain English, which Hity absolutely declined doing.

The first sick list I ever saw made out by Mr. Hitybelteser was about three months after joining the service, and it was such a remarkable production that I kept it for future reference. I give it to the reader, who may derive both amusement and instruction from it.

"John Smith (sea.), Swelling of 'globus major epididymis.'

"Phelim Adze (carpenter), Inflamation of 'genio-glossus.'

"Mr. Coil (master's mate), Irritation of the 'ganglion cervicale primum.'

"Mr. Hank (sail-maker), 'Hippus pupillæ.'"

No wonder the captain was exercised when trying to decipher it. He read it backward and forward, without deriving any information from it. He closed the cabin-doors, and gave orders to admit no one for an hour, and then he sat down deliberately to study it out, and at the end of that time he rose no wiser than he was before. He took Johnson's Dictionary, looked over every page of it without success; he then appealed to Webster and Walker without any better fortune, and, throwing them aside in despair, he opened the doors and sent for the surgeon.

"Pray, doctor," he said, "may I ask what is the meaning of these words? This is the first ship I ever commanded where I could not make out the sick list. You either write a very bad hand, sir, or else you spell horribly."

"Neither one nor the other, I beg you to understand, sir," replied the doctor; "that is Latin, the only legitimate language in which a sick report should be written, and it will afford me pleasure at any time to explain anything which to you may seem obscure. Why, sir," he continued, "this sick list is as plain as sailing on a mill-pond. I wonder you should have had any difficulty in deciphering it. 'Globus major epididymis' is, sir, the name applied to the upper end of the 'epididymis,' which is of great size, owing to the large assemblage of 'convoluted tubes' in the 'coni vasculosi,' so the lower portion of the 'convolutions of the vas deferens'—"

"Stop, for heaven's sake, doctor!" cried the captain. "Your learning does you great credit, but pray skip that and come to the next."

"Well, then, sir," said the doctor, "the second is inflammation of the 'genio-glossus,' a muscle situated between the tongue and the clavicle of the jaw; it is also called 'genio-hyoglossus,' from its being inserted in the 'os hyoides,' and by some persons it is yclept 'polychrestus,' et cetera, et cetera—"

"Ahem!" said the captain, looking in despair.

"The third case," he continued, "is irritation of 'ganglion cervicale primum,' which is the superior 'cervical ganglion,' situated under the base of the skull, remarkable for its size and the regularity of its occurrence. Under the term of great sympathetic or intercostal nerve are commonly associated all the 'ganglia' which occur from the upper portion of the neck to the lower part of the 'sacrum,' et cetera, et cetera."

"Now, doctor," said the captain, "you have made it all as clear as mud to me; just enlighten me on the last item."

"Ah, sir! Hippus pupillæ, you mean?—a peculiar movement of the iris occurring in amaurosis; it is derived from the Greek language, ιππος, a horse, and pupillis, a pupil, and this disease—"

"Never mind going any further, sir," said the captain; "I am perfectly satisfied, and won't trouble you any more—I really feel very unwell, and I would not wonder if those hard words had stuck in my gizzard. Good-morning, doctor; if I am ever at a loss again I will send for you, you explain everything so clearly."

The doctor, who was the very pink of good manners, bowed himself out, the doors were closed after him, and the captain was not seen for three days.

When "Conk" was asked by the officers if anything was the matter with the captain, he would reply, in a solemn manner and with a grave shake of the head, "Doctor sick list, sar, doctor sick list, sar." "What's he sick of, Conk?" "Sick ob hog-Latin, sar; can't ondigest dem ononcomprenseinable big word dat de doctor am for eber a aggrewatin' him wid; an' it make him cross as a bear wid a sore head. I ain't done had no comfort for two days; it's a mizzible life for old nigga to lead, you may be sure."

I must now introduce Mr. Flint, the marine officer, a worthy son of Mars, who commanded the formidable force of fifty marines which composed the guard, and it seemed to require all his attention to get them into anything like discipline.

Mr. Flint was an old officer, and had done his country some service, if not in the field, at least upon the broad bosom of the ocean. He had, according to his own account, used up more pipe-clay than any other officer in the corps, and had always kept his gun-barrels so clean that he used one to shave by every morning. He was a strict disciplinarian, was as neat as wax in his person, and looked so straight in the back that you would have sworn that he had swallowed a dozen of the marines' muskets, or else been fed on ramrods.

It was very instructive to hear him talk about his "battalion," his forming his fifty brave fellows into a hollow square, "forming line from a column closed up in mass," "forming line on the reverse flank," "countermarching a column at full or half distance," "moving in column of route," and fifty other scientific movements too tedious to mention, all of which was Greek to me at that time, though it elicited my warmest admiration.

Unfortunately, our quarter-deck was too small to admit of any but the most ordinary evolutions, and whether it was from that cause or some other reason, Mr. Flint never succeeded in getting his troops beyond the preliminary steps. I believe he did on one occasion manage to make his marines pass from two ranks into one; he also, toward the latter part of the cruise, tried with a "column right in front" to form line faced to the left, but it was a sad failure, and was never afterward attempted; but, in the "balance step," "oblique step," wheeling, and stacking arms, his marines showed to greater advantage; they could perform the latter manœuvres as well as any marines I have since seen in service.

Mr. Flint, I know, was brave, for he adored the ladies, and no man ever adored the ladies who was not brave.

"Is there a heart that never loved, or felt fond woman's sigh?"

was a favorite song of his; and, although his voice was a little squeaky, the ladies loved to listen to him.

"They hopped in his walks and gamboled in his eyes,
Fed him with apricots and dewberries."

And when he took his after-dinner naps in their bowers,

> "They plucked the wings from painted butterflies
> To fan the moonbeams from his sleeping eyes."

Alas, poor Flint! he has gone with the rest, mourned by many a fair Titania. He died one day from over-exertion, trying to throw a corporal's guard into a "hollow square." His last words were,

> "Charge, Chester, charge!
> On, Stanley, on!"

Showing the ruling spirit in death's last agonies.

CHAPTER XV.

A DESCRIPTION OF SOME OF MARLINE'S SHIPMATES, AND A VERY LONG SONG FROM OLD SHACKLEBAGS.

Mr. Tape, the purser, being a weighty character, we will give him a new chapter.

Mr. Tape was a very modest, unassuming gentleman, and a great politician—remarkable features to be found united in one person. I had never yet heard of a politician who was ever accused of modesty, and but for the oft-repeated asseverations of the "gun-room" officers to that effect, I would not have believed it of Mr. Tape. His modesty did not, however, prevent his getting an office. He danced attendance in his youthful days on Mrs. M., who appointed him to office, because, she said, he was the only truly modest man she had ever met with, and he deserved some reward. It was hinted in some circles that he had presented her with a real Cashmere shawl, but that was all envy and malice. He got his office through his modesty.

Mr. Tape was a cautious man, and weighed every word he uttered; he weighed everything, in fact. And even when a sailor died, he weighed all the tea and sugar in the mess, and took out what belonged to him, even if it was the last day of the month; he made no difference whatever between sea time and civil time. Oh, he was scrupulously exact in all his transactions with the sailors, though extremely obliging to them in supplying their necessities. He would advance them belcher handkerchiefs with which to adorn their fair inamoratas' heads in Mahon. He would let them have yards of English cloth, which they sold to the tailors at half or quarter its value. He fairly forced them, by his insinuating behavior, to accept all kinds of fancy articles (which, of course, were charged for in their accounts), yet never asked for a cent of the money until the ship's company were paid off on her return home. Dear, good, modest Mr. Tape! And then to think how kind he was to the midshipmen also! His chief clerk, Mr. Slippery Elm, had orders to let us have whatever we wanted out of the store-room in the shape of buttons, cigars, razors, penknives, etc. And then the dear, good-natured clerk, who thought of nothing else but how to please us, introduced a very exciting game (of cutting in a book) for our amusement; but then, as he said, it was so much better to be spending our time that way than to have money to spend on shore. Money, he argued, would eventually lead us all into trouble —such, actually, was the case with our good purser at the end of the cruise.

He reaped a net profit of eighty thousand dollars, and, finding himself so rich, he invested it all in a wife; like many persons who have toiled for years to make themselves comfortable, they are sure to do something to knock their comfort into "pi."

Purser Tape got married one day. How his modesty allowed him to pop the question was a problem to every one; it was generally supposed that he got married owing to the force of circumstances. He thought he was marrying a buxom girl of thirty; but he neglected, unfortunately, to weigh her beforehand. He was fortunate in one respect—he got more than he bargained for. He not only wedded himself to a woman, but to a laboratory of prepared chalk, a wheelbarrow-load of whalebone, a dozen coffee-bags for skirts, three trunkfuls of cheap novels, one poodle-dog, and a set of miserable weak nerves, which kept six servant-girls running about the house all day, and two servant-men running for a handsome young doctor, who had lately come in that neighborhood. After marriage, Mr. Tape found that his wife was not buxom, but most of her was "a tale of fiction founded on fact"; and though "it is a providence that shapes our ends, rough-hew them as we will," her mantua-maker was her providence, and shaped her most lamely and unfashionably.

Mr. Tape was no great addition to a small tea-party; and to look at him sitting quietly at the captain's table, holding no converse with any one, you would suppose him to be dumb; he was, indeed, scarcely ever known to speak, but, like the owl, he kept up "a devil of a thinking." He was just then asking himself if Mr. Slippery Elm could not induce Pierre Poisson to buy a pair of new boots and a belcher handkerchief. Pierre was transferred, with a pile of money due him, and the purser was calculating the easiest method of reducing that pile.

The next in order was Mr. Shacklebags, the sailing-master, who was one of the old school, and "an out-and-out sailor," every inch of him. He thought and dreamed of nothing but the sun's altitude and setting up the rigging. He considered it a hanging matter ever to have a seizing put on with an unequal number of turns, or to make a mistake of one second in the ship's longitude, though at that time ships were navigated by lunar observations altogether, chronometers not having been universally introduced. When running for the land, Mr. Shacklebags was up on the fore-topsail yard, with a superannuated-looking spy-glass under his arm; and when he did come down, Mr. Shacklebags smiled with an air of great satisfaction. He had likely predicted that land would be in sight at ten minutes and fifty-three and a half seconds of twelve o'clock, and Mr. Shacklebags was not more than one second and a quarter out of the way.

Mr. Shacklebags had not a very intimate knowledge of the English language, but what Mr. Shacklebags did know he knew strong. His favorite expressions were, "luff upon luff," "topmast backstay lanyards," and "dead-eyes." He had written two or three treatises on ranging sheet-cables, and stowing ground and riding tiers of casks.

His room proclaimed him a virtuoso, though, unlike the surgeon, he festooned his walls with professional articles in place of pictures. His bulkheads were resplendent with serving-mallets and prettily arranged balls of spun-yarn; a sister-block at the foot of his bed to remind him of his favorite sister "Briny" (an affectionate heart had Shacklebags). A harpoon and a pair of grains were secured at the head of his bed, ready to strike the dolphins and porpoises when they ventured to come gamboling under the bows of the ship; and the only thing in which Mr. Shacklebags may have been said to show any touch of fancy was in having two chain-hooks crossed over his wash-stand, and the name of "Sally Splice," formed in one-and-a-quarter-inch thimbles, over his looking-glass.

Mr. Shacklebags had a little weakness for displaying the articles belonging to the master's department; but it was an amiable weak-

188   THE ADVENTURES OF HARRY MARLINE.

ness, and more suited to a master's room than scent-bottles and white kid gloves. Had he been promoted he would have ornamented the ship with various devices. He once had the temerity to propose to Mr. Barnacle to put a pipe in the mouth of the starboard cat-head, when Mr. B. politely told him to "chaw his rope-yarns and walk off."

Mr. Shacklebags's taste for the ornate and beautiful was so well appreciated by his messmates that, on an occasion of giving a ball, he was appointed as one of the managers to dress the ball-room. Mr. Teaser, who was also one of the principal managers and had a weakness for flowers, had gone on shore to despoil some lady's garden and to cut some beautiful evergreens from a neighboring hillside. Mr. Shacklebags (tasty Mr. Shacklebags), who in his heart was always thinking how to make people happy, got up an agreeable surprise for Mr. Teaser on his return.

He emptied his entire store-room, and had the contents transferred to the quarter-deck in less time than one could well imagine. The motto "E Pluribus Unum" was beautifully arranged over the front of a chaste temple, which Mr. Teaser had executed on the poop at great pains and expense; but Mr. Shacklebags's motto cost nothing, and was simple and unpretending, as everything should be relating to our republic—he had formed the letters of iron thimbles, hooks, and marline-spikes on a ground of blue, red, and white bunting.

A female figure (rather rudely cut out of wood), which belonged to an English vessel, and was picked up by us at sea, was placed at the entrance to the temple, a pair of stuffed arms were fastened ingeniously to it, and the left one was leaning on the largest kedge-anchor in the ship. "This figure," said Shacklebags, "represented the figure of Hope"; and by way of economically representing two figures in one, her right hand held his favorite harpoon, on the point of which he stuck a red flannel cartridge-bag. "Ah!" said Mr. Shacklebags, "that's Hope and Liberty all in a heap."

Who was there in the ship who could more feelingly illustrate the character of "Hope" and "Liberty" than Mr. Shacklebags? Was not hope the star that guided him by day and by night? Does the good reader suppose that he had no higher aspirations than to be a sailing-master all his life? Did he not hope, and had he not been hoping since he first entered the navy, twenty years back, that he would one day be a lieutenant? Indeed, had he not stowed away at the bottom of his sea-chest a brand-new copper-gilt epaulet wrapped up in tarred parceling? Dear good old Shacklebags, he had, but he never lived to wear it.

He always swore (did Shacklebags) by the "goddess of liberty." He venerated her as one would a rich old aunt who was full of ailings and was shortly expected to die. Liberty to him was a golden vision. He dreamed of her, and talked of nothing else; I presume from the fact that he was never allowed to go on shore, except on duty, nor permitted indeed to go outside the ship unless it was to stay the masts. Mr. Barnacle very properly remarked that a sailing-master had no right ever to go out of the ship on liberty until the mainmast went on shore.

But to return to Mr. Shacklebags's ornamental designs. After he had made all out of the figure-head it was possible to make, he festooned the hose (tastily intertwined with blue, red, and white bunting) around the ball-room, and had gone so far as to get the spare cat-block upon the capstan "rampart" supported by two deep-sea leads and four small grapnels "couchant"; an hour-glass was hung to the cat-hook, and the blade of a cutlass, ingeniously fastened to the end of a boat-hook, surmounted the whole. This was intended, as Mr. Shacklebags said, to show the company the value of time.

Mr. Shacklebags was about explaining to a delighted audience of midshipmen his allegory, as he called it—it was something about "faith, unity, and the swiftness of time"—when Mr. Teaser returned to the ship and knocked all his beautiful creations into "pi." The manner in which Shacklebags was hustled off the quarter-deck was a caution to all future masters. The poor old fellow took it very hard, and I don't think he ever fairly recovered from the effects of the mortification. He consoled himself by writing an ode to liberty, the concluding lines of which were—

"Oh, liberty! you're everything that's nice;
The picture of you lives in Sally Splice."

"Sally Splice," it will be remembered, was the young lady whose name was festooned in one-and-a-quarter-inch thimbles over Mr. Shacklebags's glass.

Mr. Bluff and Mr. Teaser, both already introduced to the reader, composed the rest of the commodore's guests.

And now "the flow of reason and the feast of soul," as the commodore facetiously called it, began to pass around the festive board. He was himself all life and animation, and had a word for every one. He talked learnedly with Dr. Hitybelteser on the subject of pathology. He told of a wonderful cure that had been performed on him when he had "two buckles" on his lungs, and a "hermitage" of the lungs at the same time. He spoke of another case when his life was saved by a "homopathos" Jew doctor. He was suffering with a severe "newrology" in the head at the time, and also from excruciating pains of the "embargo" in his back, all of which was removed in ten minutes by taking one grain of coffee diluted in a hogshead of water. He was just as familiar with the treatment of a man who had got a marline-spike in his "sarcofagus" as the doctor himself, and when he described the time he saw a "jocular vein" sewed up, when an English lieutenant cut his throat in a fit of "delirious tremblins," you could have sworn that he had the whole materia medica at his finger-ends.

He startled us all by informing us that he was not afraid of poison, not he! He could swallow a pint of "chlorosive supplement" without any fear at all, and sling his hammock to the branches of the deadly upas-tree and sleep as sound as in his cot on board ship. He had "anodines" for all kinds of poisons, and always carried a box of rostrums along with him. He had once lived a whole month on poisonous berries, but felt no ill effects from it, always having his "anodines" at hand.

No one for a moment doubted the commodore's word, not even when he related to the captain how he had once started on a journey across the great desert on an old camel; how the old camel died and he had to foot it three thousand miles; how he had boiled his boots and made soup enough of them to last him the whole of the journey, drinking only at such times as he came across the "well" of a dead camel; how he lived on a pickled head-stall and a hide belly-band, and how he made salad out of some green shavings that he procured from an old saw-mill.

To the purser, whom he mistook for a "virtuoso," he spoke in elegant language of his visit to Rome; how he had stood upon the "Terrapin" rock, and had seen the very spot where the geese cackled when they saved Rome. "He had spent days in the Yatigan of the Pope, examining the vast expositions of the arts, which were lying all about as thick as mush," and he had seen as many as twenty "carnivals" dressed in full costume, their heads covered with a beautiful "taira," and all of them bending to kiss the Pope's toe.

He told us all what a beautiful time he had in the "Colly-see-um," the finest "empty theatre" in the world, though he regretted to say there was no performance while he was in Rome. He described in words of fire how he was overcome when he stood before the temple of "Panther," which he concluded was a building "dedicated to the heathen mythologists."

He quite delighted Mr. Teaser, who had never been in the Mediterranean before, with his account of the beautiful "mosyaks," and cheap "konkilly's," and presented for the inspection of the company a chaste and pretty seal ring, representing a donkey "rampant" with a hamper "couchant."

He was pleased to inform us that the seal in question was an "antiquary" of great value, having been made for an English nobleman by a celebrated "lapilazuliss" in Florence, who sold it to him for mere good-will, and he intended to have it handed down to his "progenerators," and declared that it was worthy to "be embalmed in a sacryfogos, like Cheops of old."

I never in my life witnessed such a versatility of conversation. He seemed to know intuitively the subject that would most interest each one at the table. To the marine officer he spoke of war, the "tented field," the midnight charge, and the forlorn hope. He spoke of movements by the "right and left plank" as if he had been performing them all his life, and as to forming a "holler square," it was as easy as boring square holes with an auger. He did not omit to pay the soldier a well-deserved compliment for the manner in which the marines had stacked their arms on that day.

He even drew the master (good old Shacklebags) out. It was quite enough to speak on the subject of navigation, when Shacklebags's countenance was as bright as a sunbeam. Life was dark and lowering with him, the clouds of disappointment had long shut out the heaven of hope, his mind was oppressed with gloomy shadows, and at times there was neither fire in his heart nor warmth in his pea-jacket, but speak to him about his idols, the sun, moon, and stars, and he felt as if he could take the whole world in his arms and embrace all creation.

Mr. Shacklebags actually stared with astonishment at the amount of information possessed by the commodore on nautical affairs, and more particularly the science of astronomy; he spoke of lunars and treble latitudes as if he had been brought up on nothing else, and as to the eclipses of "Jupiter's stellactites," he never measured the longitude in any other way.

Speaking of the transition of Venus across the moon's disk, it was quite a common affair, and he had quite an original method of his own for obtaining the latitude by "Rory Borealis."

When the master (dear old Shacklebags) hesitatingly asked him if he had ever found a ship's position by assuming two latitudes, he was rather startled when the commodore informed him that the only time he remembered ever to have assumed two latitudes was when he was crossing the equator he assumed the "Topic of Cankir" for three weeks, and after crossing the line he assumed the "Topic of Peppercorn," and the sailors were allowed so much latitude that they shaved every greenhorn in the ship.

When he spoke of "the evolutions of the sun around the earth," "the motion of the earth on its axles," the reasons why cold existed at the "Tartaric and Calthartic poles," I am sure the master must have been confounded—the commodore had it all at his finger-ends, and more besides—but when he began to talk of the "magnetic contraction," the "variegation of the compass," "volcanic batteries," "electric pentegraphs," and "notary perpellers," the master was all adrift—he innocently asked if they were fitted with "lashing eyes, or went with a mousing."

After the champagne was passed around the commodore became more brilliant than ever; he evidently began to "feel his oats." He had a good set of listeners, and he determined to make the most of them. He dived headforemost into natural philosophy and "chymistrey"; he spoke of "ox-gin," "nitre-gin," and "hyder-gin" as if they had been his most favorite liquors; he alluded to the great importance of keeping an account of the "pacific rarity of volatile substances," and spoke of fogs and "humurous vapors" as being "diogenes" to the Banks of Newfoundland.

I remember that he wound up with an interesting account of the Temple of "Jupiter Toenails"; mentioned the fact that "he intended taking the ship to Moscow, so that his officers could say they had seen everything in Italy," and finally announced it as his intention to lay the ship up in Vienna for the winter among the Ostriches, and give his officers an opportunity to learn French!

After all, I look back to that dinner as the most pleasant I ever sat down to in the navy, for I never yet witnessed so much intellectual conversation. To be sure it all came from the commodore, but what is the use of being commander-in-chief if you don't monopolize all the conversation? The object in inviting officers to dine is not for the purpose of drawing them out and making yourself acquainted with their acquirements and character; the object is

MR. SHACKLEBAGS IS INDUCED TO SING.

to impress them with a great idea of your own intellect and importance, and on the occasion alluded to the whole of the officers were entirely subdued.

As to the captain, he was whittled down to the "little ind of nothin'," as the down-Easters say. He had not been able to say a word, though in the absence of the commodore he generally monopolized all the conversation. It must have been a relief to him when the commodore called on him for one of his best stories.

"Why, really, sir," he replied, "I am a poor hand at telling a story, and don't think I know one." Here the commodore winked his eye at the company and stuck his tongue in his cheek. "You had better call on Mr. Shacklebags to relate one. He has sailed a great deal, and no doubt has a dozen at his finger-ends."

"Me, sir?" said Shacklebags (dear old Shacklebags), looking perfectly aghast at such a proposition, while the wine which had mounted to his nose settled immediately into his coat-pockets. "Why, I never told a story in my life, sir. I can't do it, sir; impossible." And the wine flew back to his nose again with such a sudden rush that the old fellow liked to have fallen off his chair.

"Well, then, Mr. Shacklebags," said the commodore, "you must sing a song, for a sailor can always do up a song or a story; so heave ahead, Mr. Shakylegs, and then you will have the right to call on the captain. You can sing, can't you, Mr. Shacklelegs?"

"No, sir, I can't sing," said dear old Shacklebags.

"Can't sing, sir?" said the commander-in-chief, with the greatest surprise expressed in his countenance. "Well, then, no wonder, Mr. Shacklerags, that you have never been promoted to a higher grade. What officer would ever interest himself in another's promotion when he found he could neither sing nor tell a story? I expect my officers to do one or both, I don't care which. Why, sir, if when we go to Moscow the emperor should invite us to dine with him, I should be very much annoyed if, when he asked one of the officers to sing a song or tell a story, he was told 'I can't sing, sir.'" And the commodore settled himself back in his chair with an air of offended dignity.

This was a staggerer to poor Shacklebags; he felt as if the best bower-anchor had been let go right on his head and the whole length of chain veered over his body. He determined not to lose his last chance for promotion, and he said to himself, "Here goes for a song if I burst my boiler"; so ahemming two or three times to clear his throat, growing a deal paler in the face and nose, and brushing his hair well over his eyes, he timidly said, "I will try and sing, commodore."

"Ah!" he said, "I knew you could sing, Shacklepins. Well, heave ahead and save your tide, and then we will have the captain's story."

So Shacklebags, bidding adieu to fear, emitted the following song, to no particular tune, and without regard to any particular meter:

THE SAUCY THUNDERBUM.

To the music of the " Guerriere Frigate bold."

I.

The saucy Thunderbum was a-sailin' on the sea,
With her sails all full aloft and a frigate on her lee;
Says the capting to her master, "There's an enemy close by;
I'm goin' for to capture her, at least I'm going to try."

II.

"Oh, capting," said the master, "I fear that can not be;
We'll have to leave that frigate a-sailin' on our lee,
For the lanyards of the riggin' is rotten, every one,
And our breechin's would not stand the fire of a gun."

III.

"Oh, master, how is this," said the capting in a rage,
"That *we* are all so rotting when a ship I would engage?
My breechin's are so wuthless I can not fire a gun,
So put the ship about, clap on sail and let us run."

IV.

"Oh, capting," said the master, "I fear that can not be;
We can neither run nor fight with that frigate on our lee;
The lower riggin's stranded, and the backstays one by one
Would snap off just like pipe-stems if we pressed the ship to run."

V.

"Oh, master," said the capting, "what are we then to do?
We can only run in port, let go anchor and come to;
When protected by that fort looming up upon our lee,
We can overhaul our riggin' and once more put to sea."

VI.

"Oh, capting," said the master, "it can't be done at all,
For all our anchors washed away, you know, in that last squall,

And our cables is so rotting, each yarn won't hold a pound;
If we trust unto our anchors we soon will be aground."

VII.

"Whose fault is it, oh, master, that such dreadful things can be?
We can't fight, nor run, nor enter, when a port is on our lee;
I'm sure no ship was ever before in such a way.
Let's send for the first lufftenant, and see what he will say."

VIII.

Up came the first lufftenant, and touching of his hat,
Says he, "Capting, do you want me?" Says the capting, "Look at that.
There's a frigate on our lee, we can neither fight nor run;
Oh, tell me, Mr. Ginblock, can we fire airy gun?"

IX.

Then up spoke Mr. Ginblock, "The thing can not be done;
I am sorry, Capting Skareall, we can't fire airy gun,
For the touch-holes is so large, they is bigger nor the bore,
And the shot are all too big that they sent us from the shore."

X.

"Can't we board her?" said the capting. "Oh, Ginblock, don't say nay.
My blood is bilin' over, I am crazy for the fray;
The boarders you shall lead, while the master works the ship,
I will run down with false colors, and have them on the hip."

XI.

"We've no cutlasses on board that would cut a rotting cheese:
A baby two years old can bend them up with ease;
And the pikes are all so rusty, they are brittle as a reed,
If they get into an enemy they would not make him bleed."

XII.

Then the capting went below, not knowin' what to do;
So he took his pistol out and shot himself clean through.
The master tied the cat-block to his leg below the knee,
And exclaiming "Farewell, Polly!" he jumped into the sea.

XIII.

When Ginblock saw the master and the capting go away,
He jumped upon the poop and said, "Oh, dear! I can not stay.
Hoist up the 'Merican flag," he cried, "and nail it to the mast!
I'll go below and take a drink, 'twill be my very last."

XIV.

The ossifers rushed on deck to see what the muss could be—
When they see'd the capting's body they all leaped in the sea;
And the crew were all so petrified, seein' they couldn't run,
They struck the 'Merican colors and fired nary gun.

XV.
MORALE.

Now the moral of this song, as every one must see,
Is not to get an enemi so close upon the lee,
Unless your riggin's good and your breechin's fit for use,
For if you otherwise should do your ship you'll surely lose.

XVI.

And your balls should all be fitted before you leave the shore,
And the gunner should be careful that each one fits the bore;
For an inch of windage is better, although the balls be small,
Than to have them all so large that they will not fit at all.

XVII.

If masters do their duty such things can never be
As havin' rotting riggin' with a frigate on your lee;
They would right off rig new shrouds and get them in their place,
And then the 'Merican colors would meet with no disgrace.

XVIII.

And fust lufftenants always should keep away from gin,
For to see a drunken first luff it is a cryin' sin;
They should examine of their touch-holes to see they warn't too large,
And never put the balls in before they put the charge.

"Good, by Jupiter!" said the commodore, after Shacklebags had finished the song. "I never heard anything better in all my life. Why, it beats 'Billy Taylor' all holler" (here the wine rushed up from Shacklebags's boots and took possession of his nose again); "why, that song inspires me. Beat to quarters at once, Captain Marvellous. Let us see if the backstays are all fitted right over the lower mast-heads, and get your shot and see that they fit the guns; if they don't, file 'em all down to an inch windage." And the captain was about to rise and execute the order when the commodore cried, "Avast, there, Marvellous! let us have that story first; we will go to quarters some other time. Come, Mr. Shacklewind, call upon the captain for a story."

The blood instantly vanished from Shacklebags's nose and retired into the mournful shade of his boots once more. He had never taken such a liberty with his commander. He would rather have taken hold of a conductor while the lightning was passing down it or swallowed a live rattlesnake. Fortunately, he was relieved by the captain's volunteering to comply with the commodore's wishes. "I will give you," he said, "the story of the sea-serpent; an old story, it is true, but this is a story the incidents of which I witnessed myself." As it is rather a long one, it shall have the benefit of another chapter. If the reader don't believe in sea-serpents, let him omit it.

CHAPTER XVI.

VERY SNAKY INDEED, AND SHARP PRACTICE WITH SHELLS—THE DEVIL ON THE HORSE-BLOCK, AND SHIP GOING TEN KNOTS UNDER BOLT-ROPES—STRANGE IF TRUE.

"WELL, then, gentlemen," said the captain, fixing himself as if for a long story, "you want to hear about the sea-serpent. No doubt you think there is no such thing as a veritable sea-snake, or that it only exists in the imagination of wonder-telling travelers. Believe what you will on the subject, but what I am about to tell you now is as true as that the sun rises and sets every day in the week.

"When I was a midshipman sailing with Captain Crabapple in the frigate Viper, we were cruising off the island of Teneriffe with the peak plain in sight. The day was hot and sultry, the barometer had fallen from $30\cdot90°$ to $20°$, and the appearance of the sky foretold a heavy gale. So sure were the indications of the barometer that it never failed to let us know what the weather was going to be, and the captain, who had been anxiously watching it, came out at four o'clock in the afternoon, ordered all the light sails to be taken in and sent down from aloft, sent down topgallant and royal yards, close-reefed the fore and main top-sails and furled the mizzen, furled the courses, and got the storm-sails ready for setting, all of which was done in less time than it takes me to tell of it.

"At this time the atmosphere was as 'clear as a bell,' and those who were no judges of weather laughed at the precautions old Crab-apple was taking. The lieutenants thought that it was one of the methods the captain sometimes took to work their old iron up by keeping them busy, but old Crab (as he was always called) knew perfectly well what he was about. He even took the precaution of having his 'nor'wester' secured under his chin with strong ratlin stuff, for, said he, 'there will be some hair blown out by the roots to-night, and no mistake.'

"At sunset the peak of Teneriffe was lit up most beautifully with the rays of the setting sun. Its snow-capped top showed as white as milk reflected on the clear blue sky in the background, while flashes of light were playing around it like the flames of a volcano. A long black line could be distinctly seen with the naked eye extending down the side of the mountain. It was thought by some to be a shadow cast by the sun, others said that the mountain emitted smoke, and that it was melted lava running down from a crater, but an old quartermaster, who was never known to err where sight was concerned, declared that the object moved and had life. He declared that he could see the twinkle of its eyes, and pronounced it a large 'boar-constructor.'

"Old 'Bunting' was heartily laughed at by the bystanders for making such a foolish assertion, which he had no way of proving, for the sun dipped below the horizon at that moment, and as in the tropics there is little or no twilight, the top of the mountain was almost instantly hid in the gloom."

"Yes, Marvellous," said the commodore, "I noticed that in the Topic of Peppercorn the moment the sun went down it was as dark as pitch."

"At this time," continued the captain, "it was a dead calm, there was a stifling feeling in the atmosphere that almost suffocated one, the sound as of very heavy thunder in the distance faintly struck upon the ear, and an ugly swell came rolling along (increasing every moment) from the northward.

"'Ah!' said old Crab, 'we'll have it presently, and you officers who have not left an allotment-ticket at home will likely repent it, for, if my senses don't deceive me, some of us will lose the number of our mess to-night.' And the old fellow chuckled with delight at the idea of losing some of his lieutenants. There were heavy charges hanging over his head for fraud, cruelty, and oppression, and he would not have minded going to Tophet himself, provided he could have sent his enemies on the same journey.

THE CAPTAIN'S SEA-SERPENT STORY.

"With all his faults, old Crab was a thorough sailor, and knew all about a ship from the laying of her keel to the pointing of a rope, and the officers all had confidence that he would take his ship safely through a gale, no matter how severe it might be.

"At eight o'clock at night the rumbling noise that we had heard ceased all of a sudden; the silence of death, almost, reigned throughout the ship, while every eye was fixed upon the northern horizon. There a little speck of cloud had appeared no larger than my hand; it spread and increased with such rapidity that the deepest darkness overspread the sea; it was impossible to see the mainmast three feet off. Suddenly the clouds opened like the mouth of some huge cavern, and the vivid lightning leaped forth like a demon of destruction, followed by such terrific peals of thunder that I shall never forget them as long as I live. It knocked down every man and officer flat upon the deck."

"Pretty good thunder that," said the commodore. "It is well you had no milksops on board, or it would have turned them all sour. I was in a ship once when it thundered so loud that it completely ruined our cow ever afterward. She never gave anything after that but 'bonny-clabber,' and that was as sour as vinegar. Two ladies we had on board with sucking babies had to feed their little ones on arrowroot for a week, as their milk was perfectly sour for some time after."

The captain, without noticing the interruption, continued: "Old Crab shouted out, 'Stand by!' There was not a moment left for us to think, for the tempest was upon us, and it came like an avalanche, sweeping everything before it. Away went the topsails out of the bolt-ropes, the storm-staysails followed, carrying stays and all along with them, the topgallant-masts, though housed, were snapped off like pipe-stems, and the jib and flying-jib booms were hanging by the rigging under the bow.

"The Viper bent to the blast and laid her lee bulwarks so deep in the sea that a whole school of porpoises were landed on the deck, and two of them actually swam into the steerage-mess, being carried down by the rush of water.

"During all this dreadful time the captain was as cool as an iced cucumber. He waited until the tempest struck us, and then he cried out, in a shrill, clear voice, 'Hard up the helm!' But the ship was, for the moment, past paying any attention to her rudder, and she lay so like a log upon the water that we all expected to see her go down every minute.

"The tempest raged so furiously that it was impossible to hear any orders. It was every man take care of himself, and we could only put our trust in that divine Providence which is our only sheet-anchor in the hour of need. I recollect clinging wildly to some living object that came swimming by me in the lee gangway, and was very near being carried overboard on the back of an old sow belonging to the captain. The old grunter had broken out of the manger with a litter of twelve pigs, and the last I saw of her she was going over the top of the waist-nettings with her entire family following in her wake. Strange to say, she landed safely on the island of Teneriffe, and we are indebted at this time to that circumstance for the fine hogs raised on that island."

"I say, Marvellous," put in the commodore, "that was rather a sorry sheet-anchor Providence sent you that time. I presume the twelve little fellows were thrown in as kedges."

"Kedges or no kedges, sir, all I know is that I was swept aft on the quarter-deck, and faintly heard the captain singing out for the first lieutenant.

"'He is gone overboard, sir,' shouted the quartermaster. 'He is drownded, sir.'

"'Good!' yelled old Crab. 'I hope he may get on shore on his charges and specifications; they'll float him. Where is the second lieutenant?'

"'He was knocked down the main hatch by one of the porpoises, sir,' yelled the steward, 'and broke his collar-bone.'

"'Good again!' shouted old Crab. 'I wish it had been his neck.'

"'Good heavens!' I exclaimed, 'will God permit such men to live?' And, as the lightning broke forth from the clouds, I could see his diabolical face beaming with delight as he witnessed the torture of his fellow-men. He was actually dancing a hornpipe on the horse-block, while every other man in the ship was holding on to keep the wind from blowing him away. If ever the devil showed himself on earth, that man Crabapple was him. He shrieked, he shouted, he danced, and seemed to revel while the forked lightning was playing about his hoary locks.

"The ship had remained knocked down with her lee gunwale under water for about the space of ten minutes, when the fury of the tempest passed over her, and at length, to the great relief of every one, she slowly righted, shaking herself like a Newfoundland as he comes out of the water, while tons on tons of water were discharged down her open hatches.

"'Stand by to work ship, every scoundrel of you!' shouted old Crabapple. 'Move, you whelps, or I will flog all the skin off your backs to-morrow. Why don't you d—d lazy, cowardly officers show the men an example? Where are the officers?' he yelled. 'I hope they are all drowned.'

"No answer came to his call for the officers, and only a few men obeyed his order; not one lieutenant was left; all had been washed overboard. 'Good again!' he fairly screamed when it was reported to him, 'and I hope they and their specifications are burning in the lower regions.' My blood runs cold when I think of it now, even after the lapse of so many years.

"The ship began now slowly to obey her helm, and gathered rapid headway as she fell off before the wind. In a few moments she was rushing madly through the water at the rate of sixteen miles an hour. The entire surface of the sea was covered with one sheet of white foam, and the wind as it whistled through the rigging sounded like so many demons shrieking with joy over our anticipated destruction. In the midst of the storm I heard a fiendish laugh at my elbow, and by the flashes of lightning I could see the demoniacal captain throwing his arms wildly in the air, and hear him invoking the gale to blow harder; he laughed as if it was fine sport.

"Suddenly I heard him yell out, 'How does she head, quartermaster, and be ——— to you?'

"'South-southwest, sir; a little southerly, sir,' answered the quartermaster.

"'Thunder and furies!' he exclaimed, 'she is running exactly for the east points of the island. Ha, ha, ha! there will be more nuts for the devil to crack.' Again the lightning flashed out and showed me his dreadful-looking face, and I have always been convinced that I smelt sulphur at that moment.

"'Ready, about!' he shouted, in tones of thunder. 'Send the boatswain to me, somebody.'

"Mr. Fid, the boatswain, made his appearance, his arm in a sling, and presenting by the lightning's glare a very battered appearance.

"'Jump forward, Mr. Fid, you old sand-bag,' he said, 'and stand by the sheet-anchor; have axes ready to cut when I tell you. I am going to club-haul her.'

"'What, sir!' inquired the boatswain, 'club-haul her under bare poles and bolt-ropes? Do you know the sails is all blown away, sir?'

"'Do you know the road to the devil, sir?' roared the captain. 'Jump forward, you old catamaran, and obey the order, or I will send you below for mutiny.' Old Fid vanished in a minute, and returned in a short time to report everything ready.

"'Have a quartermaster in the chains,' said the captain, 'and try and get soundings.'

"'Ay, ay, sir,' faintly came from the lee gangway.

"'Ready, about! now, men!' shouted old Crab; 'and you scoundrels work for your lives; for if you don't obey my instructions quickly the sharks will have you all before daylight.' The ship was still madly rushing through the water toward the island of Teneriffe; it seemed like madness almost to bring her by the wind, but, nevertheless, the order was given as soon as the captain could get the men to their places.

"'Brace up the after-yards; hard a-starboard; cut away the wreck of the jib-boom,' were the orders given, in a calm, loud voice, and executed almost as soon as given. The ship, obedient to her helm, came to the wind rapidly, and I expected to see her lay her lee rail again under water. The yards and masts fairly bent to the weight of the blast, and the mizzen-topmast, unable to bear the strain, came tumbling down on deck, smashed the wheel into a thousand pieces, and knocked the binnacle into the lee scuppers. Again the voice of the captain was heard, ordering the lee head-braces hauled in, lifts and trusses overhauled. The order was promptly obeyed, and there we were, braced up sharp on the larboard tack, close at it, and going along under bare poles and bolt-ropes at the rate of ten miles an hour.

"'Haul the bowlines,' shouted old Crab, 'and hook the relieving tackle! Blow away, old Boreas; we don't care the snap of a finger for you!'

"Every one, you may be sure, was struck with amazement when they saw the ship working in so wonderful a manner, and running close-hauled in such a tempest, without any sail. We had no time to think, however, for the order came through the trumpet, 'Ready, about!'

"The men had seen such curious things performed that night that they took their stations with implicit confidence and trust in the man who held control over their lives; the most perfect silence reigned throughout the ship among the crew; they waited with breathless anxiety to see what was to come, and but for the howling of the storm and the creaking of the yards and masts, you could have imagined yourself the only one on board.

"Suddenly the appalling cry of 'breakers' was heard from the forecastle, and under the lee bow and all along under the lee beam could be seen a streak of light, while the waves were lashing themselves furiously over the reefs; dismal sounds came up from the sea, appalling the stoutest hearts on board—sounds that were anything but human; many of us thought it the spirits of the damned singing our death-knell.

"Calmly the captain gave his orders, and quickly were they obeyed. Cruel as was his discipline, he had obtained the obedience of all under his command.

"'Stand by the anchor, Mr. Fid,' he said, 'and cut when I tell you.' And then he coolly gave the order to put the helm down handsomely, haul over the spanker-boom, and check the lee head-braces. The ship came up gracefully to the wind, as if she had all her sails on her; she was head to wind (oh! anxious time), when the words 'Haul taut' made the men lay their weight upon the braces; then 'Main-topsail haul' was thundered through the trumpet, and the yards flew round like magic, the captain gave one shout, and the lightning showed him at that moment shaking his trumpet at some object to leeward. Perhaps it was the ghosts of his enemies the lieutenants, whom he may have seen frolicking on the backs of the porpoises.

"'Let go the anchor!' he cried out. The sheet was cut from the waist, the hemp cable went rushing through the hawse-hole until one hundred fathoms had run out; the ship, obedient to the strain, brought the wind a little on the starboard bow. At this moment the cable snapped off by the hawse-hole like a rotten rope-yarn, and then the ship went fast astern. 'Shift your helm and let go and haul!' thundered the captain, and there, gentlemen, was the ship about. Slowly she gathered headway and went bounding through the water as before close at it. 'Haul the bow-lines,' said the captain, 'and lay up the ropes.'"

"I will tell you one thing Captain Crabtree forgot," said the commodore; "he forgot to overhaul his weather main-lifts and lee main-truss, sir."

"Oh, no, he did not, sir," said Captain Marvellous; "it was an omission of mine. I distinctly remember his giving the order.

But to continue my story. At that moment my ears were saluted with a fiendish shriek, like the sound of a locomotive steam-whistle, the lightning flashed out and illuminated the whole ocean for miles round, the light was vivid for at least two minutes, and during the flashes I saw, close under the lee quarter, the most frightful object my eyes ever beheld.

"This object was the huge head of a serpent on a body standing sixty feet erect in the water. He was making direct for the ship, and I at once recognized the dreaded sea-serpent from the descriptions I had seen and read of it. The captain saw him at the same time, for he gave one of his sardonic chuckles, and said, 'Ah! that fellow has had a good supper to-night; he has four of my lieutenants in his belly, and be d—d to them!'

"Again we were left in darkness, and the horrid animal was lost to view. I'm sure, though, I smelt sulphur. I had but little time to think over the strange events happening around me, for again breakers were discovered on the lee bow and beam, and the same light and lashing of the waters was plainly to be seen.

"Now the captain ordered the larboard sheet-anchor to be got ready for club-hauling, and just as it seemed to every one that we were on the point of madly rushing on destruction, he performed the same evolution as before, cut the cable when the ship came head to wind, hauled the head-yards, and we went once more bounding on our course. Again the lightning flashed forth, and again I saw the horrid monster of the deep peering over the quarter with his devilish, wicked eyes. I am as certain that I smelt sulphur that time as I am now telling the story.

"Nothing was left us now but the chain-cables and the bower-anchors, and the order was given to unshackle the chains at sixty fathoms and stopper the ends on deck. Suffice it to say that twice more we approached what appeared to be the breakers, and twice more we club-hauled the ship. We had gained off-shore; we were safe. Each time we went about I saw that horrid serpent, and the last time he gave us a lick with his tail that made the ship shake in every timber; then, lashing the sea with his body and giving one unearthly shriek, he disappeared in the darkness.

"When the serpent struck the ship with his tail the men cried out, 'We have struck a rock!' and all thought they were lost. 'Silence!' shouted old Crabapple through his trumpet; 'it's nothing, men,' he said, 'but an old sea-serpent with two hemps, two chains, two best bowers, and two sheet-anchors in his belly, to say

THE CAPTAIN'S SEA-SERPENT STORY. 205

nothing of my four lieutenants, and my old sow and her litter of pigs.' And he laughed so loudly at his own wit that his voice echoed among the blocks and ropes.

"The crew began to look at him with some fear and much doubt, and for the first time the idea began to prevail among them that the devil was on the 'horse-block.' Some two or three smiled faintly, and seemed to think it strange that the captain could have heart to be facetious at such a moment. Old Ben Cuttlefish swore to the last day of his life that he had plainly seen the captain's horns and cloven foot, and I verily do believe he did.

"It was about midnight when the tempest began to abate, but still the wind blew too hard to show any sail. Even when it did moderate we had to keep the boats lashed down to prevent their turning bottom up, and the men stood in groups under the weather-bulwarks, holding on fearfully to each other to prevent being blown away. Yet the good ship flew along under close-reefed bolt-ropes and bare poles, going through the water ten knots an hour. Like the captain, she seemed to bid defiance to the blast.

"The sea now began to set in heavily from the northward; the spray was flying over us like heavy rain; the 'Corpo Santos' with their unearthly light were flitting about on the yards, first alighting on one boom-iron, and then, as if some new fancy had taken possession of them, they would dart off to another spot; sometimes there would be one on each truck, and again they flew to the night-heads or the end of the spanker-boom; so unearthly were the appearances that night, no wonder we all thought the world was coming to an end.

"Daylight broke slowly upon us; it was a joyful sight to us all, though it presented to our eyes a most melancholy spectacle of death and destruction. Not a sail was to be seen aloft, the courses had been blown from their gaskets when the tempest first struck us, nothing was left above the topmast-heads, and the fluttering of small shreds of canvas still attached to the top-sail bolt-ropes were the only signs of our ever having had sails on board.

"The lee gangway was a perfect charnel-house; there were to be seen sailors and marines firmly locked in the embrace of death: they were drowned when the water rushed over the lee gangway. A cow and several sheep that were generally kept inside the launch on the booms were lying stiff and dead among the crew, and there were two or three porpoises that had been washed inboard still flapping their tails on deck—one of them had a harpoon in him with a line attached—while at a short distance old Joe Finback (a prime old sailor) was laid out a corpse, with his head resting on a shot-rack and his feet propped against the bulwarks to support himself; he was found holding on to that line as if he had ventured his all in that one cast.

"I was afterward informed by an eye-witness that when the ship was hove down and the porpoises were washed inboard, Joe Finback, who was an old whaler, jumped to his harpoon and threw it into a fish that was rushing madly up and down the lee gangway; just, however, as he was about to haul in his prey, he received a blow over the head from some unseen object that killed him on the spot.

"On a close examination of the dead men and animals it was perceived that they were terribly mutilated: some had their arms wrenched from their bodies, some were without heads, others without legs, and the entrails of nearly all were more or less mixed up with the rigging about deck. As to the cow and sheep, they seemed to have been torn literally to pieces by some voracious animal. It was a horrid sight to look upon, and I shall never forget it as long as I live.

"When the state of affairs was reported to the captain, he fairly shouted for joy. 'Glad of it,' he exclaimed; 'the infernal fools will know better how to take care of themselves another time; get up holy-stones, you scoundrels, and clean the decks, heave overboard the dead and wounded, and see that not one drop of blood is left on the deck, or I will keel-haul every mother's son of you.' What a time was that to holy-stone decks! But the crew had to obey that old devil or be keel-hauled.

"Just as they were in the act of throwing over the dead bodies, a cry of horror burst from the lips of the sailors, and leaving the duty unfinished, they fled in dismay down the hatches into the cabins or wherever they could find a place to hide their heads; the captain was the only one who stood unmoved, and he laughed like mad.

"Turning around from the place where I stood to see what was the object that caused so much fear to the sailors, I beheld looking over the bulwarks the same dreadful serpent that I had seen during the gale. O God! I shall never forget that sight; my teeth chattered and my legs refused to do their duty when I tried to run and hide myself in the lowermost recesses of the ship.

"You can imagine my horror, gentlemen, when I tell you that

THE CAPTAIN'S SEA-SERPENT STORY.

the head of the monster was as large as our first cutter, his eyes were as large as the dead-eyes in the lower rigging of a three-decker, and so frightful to behold that I shudder to think of them. His great, wide, blood-stained mouth was armed with three forked fangs, and a long tongue cut at the edges like a saw ; with these things, as you presently will hear, he seized his prey and masticated his food.

"The back of this hideous serpent was covered with scales that looked like burnished gold, and from the back of his head as far down his body as I could see he had a roached mane of skin and bone, something like that you see in the pictures of ancient sea-horses ; how many feet he had I won't pretend to say, but I think about a thousand, each foot armed with long, sharp claws like those of a crocodile.

"His pestiferous breath was so hot that it seemed to carry death and destruction wherever he turned his head to breathe, and many a poor fellow sank down fainting on the deck, either through fright or owing to the dreadful odor emitted by the serpent.

"The only place of escape I could see close at hand was the poop, and in my despair I rushed up there, intending to hide myself under the thwarts in the stern boat. I cast my eyes over the taffrail, and, oh, horror! I could see the entire body of the sea-monster, extending for more than four hundred yards in our wake, his tail all the time lashing the water most fearfully. The largest part of the body was certainly as large as that of a whale, tapering down to a point resembling the barb of an arrow.

"I was about to rush down again for the purpose of seeking some other shelter, but I nearly fainted with fright when I found my retreat cut off by a smaller-sized serpent, whose head was just coming over the bulwarks forward of the mizzen rigging ; and, on jumping to the other side of the deck, I found that a smaller one still had climbed up the mizzen rigging, and had taken a turn with his body around the cross-jack yard, while his head hung down within six feet of the deck, his ugly mouth wide open ready to seize upon his prey.

"I saw nothing but certain death before me, turn whichever way I would ; and as a last chance I jumped into the stern boat, and seized a boat-hook to defend myself with. Nothing daunted, however, at my defiant attitude, the devilish creature on the cross-jack yard commenced letting down his head, and approached me with evident intention of swallowing me down, boat-hook and all.

"A fortunate idea now struck me, and saved my life. The captain kept his vegetables and some other sea-stores in a netting over the stern, and among them was a bundle of stinking codfish and five or six bunches of onions and garlic. It took me but a moment to fix them to the end of the boat-hook, and, as the reptile approached me with his mouth wide open, I rammed the mixture down his throat. He closed his jaws upon it with a snap louder than the explosion of a twelve-pounder, and swallowed down the boat-hook, fish, and all.

"The medicine took effect on him immediately, and I was not called upon to repeat the dose. He squirmed and wriggled like a worm on a hook; turned as blue as indigo under the gills; made a noise like fifty thousand geese hissing together; and, sliding down from the yard, he made his escape forward. The last I saw of him he was going down the main hatch, and (as it afterward appeared) he coiled himself away in the starboard cable-tier, where he tried in vain to digest the captain's codfish and garlic. If he succeeded in doing so, it was more than any one on board the ship had been able to do; for I think old Crab was the only one who had been known to eat it with impunity.

"The serpent on the larboard quarter seemed rather disturbed at the retreat of his brother, or sister, I don't know which; but the old one in the lee gangway was committing most dreadful ravages. It had taken possession of the middle part of the ship, and was licking up the dead bodies of men and animals, and sawing them into chunks with her saw-tongue, after which they were transferred to the monster's capacious belly.

"We could now account for the manner in which the dead bodies had been so disfigured. This was not the first visit the serpent had paid to the ship; it had evidently been on board the night before, but had not been seen in the confusion.

"All this time the captain was laughing like mad. He seemed to enjoy the fun very much, and rubbed his hands together in great glee whenever a dead body of man or animal was transferred to the serpent's maw. 'That's the fellow for clearing up decks!' he shouted. 'Only let him alone, and he'll holy-stone decks for us afterward.'

"The old boatswain ventured to approach old Crab, and informed him, if he did not know it, 'as how the ship was being boarded by a sea-sarpint,' and wanted to know if he should 'call away pikemen and boarders, and stand by to "repel."'"

THE CAPTAIN'S SEA-SERPENT STORY.

"'No, you old fool!' he replied, 'don't you see he ain't done his breakfast yet; you wouldn't disturb a gentleman before he has done his breakfast, would you?' And he laughed louder than ever.

"'But, sir,' the boatswain respectfully said, 'he's a-eatin' all the dead bodies and swallerin' all them holy-stones you ordered on deck, to say nothing of the squilgees and swabs, which is goin' down his throat by dozens.'

"'The devil he is!' shouted the captain. 'What! swallowing my holy-stones and squilgees? That will never do, Mr. Fid; we must stop that at once. Clear away two of the quarter-deck guns and run 'em forward here.'

"I immediately ran up to the captain, though on ordinary occasions I would as soon have faced a ghost. 'I know what will drive him away, sir,' I breathlessly said; 'give him raw codfish and onions.'

"'Raw codfish and onions?' said the old sinner, looking at me in astonishment. 'What do you know about it, you young brat?'

"'Why, sir,' I replied, 'I tried it on one of the young ones; I gave it some of that stinking codfish and those onions, in the stern netting, on the end of a boat-hook; he swallowed boat-hook and all, sir, and immediately fled down into the hold.'

"'What, sir!' he cried out in a rage, 'you gave him my codfish and onions and my brass boat-hook, did you? you spawn of the devil's dam!' And with that he jumped down from the 'horse-block' and threw his heavy brass speaking-trumpet right at my head. It struck me with great force in the temple and knocked me for a moment senseless upon the deck, and, rolling forward, it brought up within a few feet of the serpent's mouth. The reptile was just lowering his head to pick up the carcass of a dead sheep, when the glittering trumpet met his eye; turning his head a little on one side, and looking at it in a contemptuous manner, he snapped it up and crunched it as flat as a pancake, not, however, before he pointed it toward the captain and gave the most unearthly scream through it I ever heard.

"'Ha, ha, ha!' laughed old Crabapple. 'Good again, you devil; you want metals, do you? and metals you shall have. Here, Mr. Prime,' he said, calling to the gunner, 'pass up half a dozen shells and a lighted port-fire. I'll see what the lining of his stomach is made of.'

"The order was instantly obeyed; the shells were handed to the captain, who walked straight up to the serpent with one under his left arm and a port-fire in his right hand. Lighting the fuse, he pitched the shell right into the monster's mouth, who swallowed it as if it had been something good to eat. Presently he shook his head and made a wry face, as if he had swallowed a bitter pill, but it did not seem to disturb his equanimity in the least; he commenced eating away again with the most perfect *sang-froid*.

"'Oh,' said the captain, 'you will not take it so easy when that shell reaches your powder-magazine, my boy.' And, sure enough, he did not, for at that moment we heard an explosion some short distance astern, and saw the water thrown up in a large jet under the lee quarter. The serpent wriggled and squirmed as if he had the belly-ache; he dropped the dead body which he held in his mouth, but did not retreat one step; he only seemed to be preparing for a deadly encounter, and looked as if he was going to destroy everything within his reach. Opening wide his mouth, and showing a throat as big as the main hatch, he gave himself a shake which made the ship tremble under him. He looked daggers at the captain, and the glance of his eye seemed to say 'Come on with your iron pills; I don't care a snap for them.'

"'Fetch along the shells and load up the two quarter-deck guns with grape and canister,' the captain ordered. And as fast as he could light the fuses and pitch them into the serpent's mouth he did so, yelling all the time like a maniac.

"Explosion after explosion took place inside the serpent without any apparent effect other than to make him snap his jaws together, which sounded like the cracking of the main-yard when it parts in the slings. At last, in a fit of desperation, I ran off, picked up a bundle of the stinking codfish and a string of onions, and pitched it into his mouth just as a shell exploded in his beastly throat. My practice was too much for him, and he caved in at once; his eyes closed, the color left his jaws, and his head began to droop upon the deck as if he was mortally sickened.

"'Stand by to fire the grape into him now,' said the captain to Mr. Prime, and off went the guns in quick succession; but, although the splinters flew out of him, he did not give up; on the contrary, the grape-shot seemed to revive him, when, seeing how matters stood, I pitched in another dose of codfish and onions, and he immediately began to back out. Before he went, however, he seemed to gather himself up for a last effort, and, bringing his head around violently against the lee main rigging, he swept away every

He looked daggers at the captain, and the glance of his eye seemed to say, "Come on with your iron pills; I don't care a snap for them."
Page 210.

shroud at one blow; then giving one devilish hiss and a blow with his tail under the counter (which stove in all the dead-lights), he disappeared under the waves.

"We had to be quick and secure the mainmast with 'pendant' tackles, and it is a wonder that it did not go over the side.

"We all breathed freely once more when we got clear of this dreadful sea-monster; not a man in the ship expected to escape death, and for my part, I have never grown any since."

"That serpent was rather hard on the pills," remarked Commodore Blowhard. "Pray, Dr. Belteazer, how do you account for that fellow's swallowing those shells so easily?"

"It was all owing to the peristaltic action of the intestines, sir," replied the doctor, "produced by the iron on the long intestines of the snake."

"Ah! I suppose so," answered the commodore. "Suppose we take a drink all round, gentlemen; that story of the captain's makes me dry in the throat. Mr. Shacklesnakes," he said, "you must set that to music."

Captain Marvellous suggested, as the story was rather long and not half finished, that he should postpone the remainder until some other time, but the commodore would not hear of such a thing, so he continued. But we will follow the story in the next chapter.

CHAPTER XVII.

CODFISH AND ONIONS BAD FOR SEA-SERPENTS—SEA-SERPENT IN CABLE-TIER—PATENT ANCHOR AND CABLE—DEATH OF OLD CRAB, ETC.

"To describe the destruction which everywhere met the eye would be impossible. The ship never recovered from the effects of that adventure, for to the last day of the cruise she bore the marks of that sea-serpent; many a poor fellow was laid low and met his tomb in the maw of that insatiable monster; nearly all the officers were killed or drowned, for the second lieutenant was the only one alive, and he was laid up in his cot with a broken shoulder-blade.

"A new danger now stared us in the face. The wind had died away, and the sea was still running mountains high, and although the ship worked so beautifully under the bolt-ropes and spanker-boom, we found them insufficient to steady her. Gun after gun broke adrift from the lashings, and we had to pipe down hammocks and throw them under the trucks before we could secure them. The lower part of the ship was deluged with water, and all hands were kept at the pumps twenty-four hours before they could clear her.

"All this time, so great was the confusion that every one had forgotten the small sea-serpent I had seen going into the hold; no doubt it was unseen by most of the crew, who were all busy witnessing the proceedings of the greater monster.

"Thinking that he might be there still, I crept quietly below with a light, and, as I entered the hold, there was his snakeship coiled up in the starboard cable-tier, as much in appearance like the cable we had lost as anything could be. I was going to scud up the hatch again in affright, but I was arrested by the filmy look of his eye and his languid expression. He had codfish and onions marked on his countenance as plain as day; there he lay, with his head hanging down over the coil of his body, to all appearances dead; and his tail was lying in the center of the hatch, for all the world like a cable ready to go up for bending.

"I had seen so much during the gale that I had become perfectly fearless where sea-serpents were concerned, and I even had the temerity to take the candle out of my lantern and apply it to the tip end of his tail. The thing, however, never moved at all except to raise his head a trifle, and then he looked at me in the most piteous manner, as much as to say, 'Go away, young man, and don't trouble me; don't you see I have been eating some of the captain's codfish?'

"I immediately went on deck and reported the presence of the serpent to the captain, and the old fellow was highly delighted to hear such good news. He considered it a streak of good luck to catch a live sea-serpent, even though it was a young one, and only about two hundred and fifty feet long. He immediately ordered all the hatches in the hold to be fastened down, and, after his snakeship was well secured, all hands went to work to repair damages and get up a new set of sails.

"All this time the ship was drifting in to the land very rapidly and making no headway, there not being a breath of air, so old Crabapple set to work to make an anchor, and a very ingenious one it was.

"He first took our stream-anchor and broke the shank as close

THE CAPTAIN'S SEA-SERPENT STORY.

to the stock as he could (it was already cracked there), and he shoved it into the muzzle of a long 32-pounder; it fitted as snug as if they had been made for each other. The anchor was securely fastened to the gun by cross-lashings around the crown to the breech of the gun, and finally secured with frappings behind the trunnions; the whole was covered with thick hide to keep the lashings from chafing against the rocks.

"Then the broken mizzen-topmast was taken for a stock, and sawed down through the middle, and fitted so nicely over the cascabel that it could not move in any direction; add to this a couple of iron crow-bars, lashed along the gun and secured to the stock, and we had as complete an anchor as it was possible to get up under the circumstances. The gun was run forward on its carriage, the yard and stay tackles were hooked on, and in a very short time it was out of its bed and hanging to the cat-head, ready for letting go.

"The captain superintended all the arrangements himself, and all the time he was at work he seemed to be full of glee; something evidently pleased him mightily; he was never known to be so long without knocking down a sailor or cursing an officer.

"'I don't know where the cable is to come from for that ere anchor,' said the boatswain to him (touching his hat respectfully). 'The stream, you knows, sir, was used up for a messenger in place of the one as parted t'other day, and the new messenger is so rotten that it's stranded in twenty places.'

"'And who in thunder asked you to know anything about it, you old chowderhead? Do you suppose,' said the captain, 'that I am such a fool as to rig an anchor without knowing where my cable is to come from? Come along with me, Mr. Fid, and I will find you a cable.' And he went down on the berth-deck, and, sending for the captain of the hold, he ordered him to take the hatches off.

"'There ain't no cables down there,' said Mr. Fid, timidly; 'they all ran out to the bitter end; and the chain-cables, you know, sir, went out when we club-hauled the two last times.'

"'Ha, ha, ha!' laughed the captain; 'you are a pretty fool for a boatswain not to know there was a spare cable in the ship. Get a chain-rope down here, sir, and stand by to rouse up that cable the end of which is lying in the hatch.'

"The boatswain turned his eyes in the direction of the captain's finger, and beheld the moving tail of my friend the sea-serpent lying on the orlop-deck. 'Good God, sir!' he exclaimed, the blood leaving his cheeks, 'that ain't no cable; that's a living beast, sir; it's one of them varmints as cleared the decks in the gale.'

"'Varmint or no varmint, you old bunch of rope-yarns, send down the chain-rope and hook on to it. You are a pretty boatswain to be so drunk at eight o'clock in the morning as not to know the difference between a hemp cable and a sea-serpent; don't you see it's a cable? You worthless old marlinspike, I'll break your back, sir.' And with these words the captain looked thunder.

"The poor old boatswain was completely dumfounded; he had not a word to say to the captain's last remark, though he did say to Prime, the gunner, that the breakfast grog was rather strong and made things look a little queer.

"To show his alacrity, Mr. Fid jumped into the hold himself, took the hook of the chain-rope in his hand, took a turn with it around the tail of the serpent, and was proceeding to half-hitch it so that it would be sure to hold, when the reptile moved his tail suddenly and knocked his legs from under him. He was out of that hold in no time and upon the berth-deck again, his usually rubicund face pallid with fright.

"The captain laughed heartily at his cowardice, and then, to set an example, he jumped down himself and secured the chain-rope properly, the serpent making desperate efforts all the time to serve him as he had served the boatswain.

"'Now, Mr. Fid, go on deck,' said the captain, 'and send all the starboard watch down to haul up and bend this cable. See that you make a handsome bend, sir; and when you have finished, bitt and stopper at twenty-five fathoms.'

"'Ay, ay, sir,' said the bewildered boatswain, who really thought the captain must be the old one.

"It was with no little difficulty that the tail end of the *cable* was roused on deck and pointed fairly through the largest hawse-hole. He wriggled and twisted like an eel in his dying moments, and, although there were three hundred men on the ropes and tackles, he sometimes resisted all their efforts, and would get eight or ten fathoms into the hold again before they knew what he was up to. At length, after six hours' hard work, they managed to bend him to the anchor, and, after eight hours' harder work still, the boatswain reported the cable bitted. He was very particular in calling it a cable."

"It is my opinion, Captain Marvellous," said Commodore

THE CAPTAIN'S SEA-SERPENT STORY.

Blowhard, interrupting the narrative, "that if it had not been for that codfish and onions of yours the sea-serpent would have sprawled the party."

"*I* think so, sir," said the captain, "and so did every one else on board the ship with the exception of old Crab, and I thank divine Providence for making the suggestion to me. After everything was right once more," he continued, "we stood into port and made preparations to anchor, the cable was well stoppered in four or five places, and sand thrown on to make the stoppers hold; the sea was still setting in heavily as we ran into the open roadstead, and it was considered very doubtful by many if our patent cable would hold. The inhabitants were all assembled on the shore to look at us, for they had considered us as lost, having seen us in the gale without any sails, and some of the persons who were drowned were drifted on the beach, among them the body of our first lieutenant. The old sow and her litter of pigs were also thrown on shore, but every one of them alive and unhurt.

"We clewed up and rounded to at a safe distance from the beach, and the captain gave the order to let go the anchor. Away it went, the *cable* running out very nicely until it came to the bitted part, when it would not 'render.' The anchor had not more than reached the bottom, and the ship was slowly dragging it in shore. Old Crab jumped down on the gun-deck, and sang out to them to veer to the cable; but the serpent refused to veer an inch.

"'I'll make him veer,' said the captain, 'and teach his snakeship a lesson. Bring me a powder-horn, Mr. Prime, and a portfire.'

"The powder-horn and port-fire were brought, and a thick train laid all along the serpent's back.

"'Now stand clear, my hearties,' shouted old Crab; 'I will promise that he shall veer out fast enough this time and be glad to go.' With that he touched the port-fire to the train of powder, and, sure enough, the cable began to render around the bitts in earnest, the fire flew from the bitt-heads, and the scales flew from the reptile's body like hail—he was going out, you must know, against the grain.

"When it came to the stoppers, they all parted like so many fiddle-strings, and the only thing that prevented the serpent's going out altogether was his head getting jammed in the hawse-hole; it was too large to go through, so there he stopped, at the bitter end.

"As his head came up the hatch, Captain Crabapple made a

lick at his mouth with a lighted port-fire, which so enraged him that he threw his mouth around in his agony and caught the captain by the middle of his body. In one instant the old sinner was deprived of life—he left the world without repenting of a single sin. He even laughed to the last; and his dying words were, 'Veer to, you scoundrels, or I will flog every one of you to-morrow.' Around the bitts he flew in the serpent's mouth, and when he reached the hawse-hole he was a mangled corpse. The serpent had still life enough left in him to hold on to the body, and it gradually disappeared into his stomach.

"The ship now brought up by this curious contrivance, and I expect we were the first and only vessel that ever used that kind of cable. With the death of old Crab our disasters seemed to end, and winds and waves ceased to trouble us.

"We remained at anchor off Teneriffe six days, and there the most wonderful things of all came to pass. On the second day the great monster sea-serpent that had committed such ravages on our decks drifted on shore, dead. He was discovered by some fishermen, who informed our second lieutenant (now our captain), and he proceeded to the spot where the body was lying. He tried hard to preserve the skin, but it was so torn with shells that had exploded inside, and so mutilated by the sharks, that to save it was an impossibility.

"On an examination of the body, strange to say, our two sheet-anchors, the two bowers, and all the cables were found snugly coiled away in his maw. One of the sheet-anchors was partly digested, being minus an arm; while both the hemps had been very much injured and decomposed by the acids in the sea-serpent's stomach. They were never fit for anything but swabs afterward. Getting some camels down to the scene of action, we managed to have everything transported to the ship. We had but just got the anchors in their places, ready for letting go, when a heavy squall came off the land, and the sea-serpent, by which we were riding, snapped off close to the hawse-hole. We lost it altogether (with the exception of the head), as we were driven out to sea. The misfortune was, we lost the finest opportunity of procuring the only living specimen of a sea-serpent that had ever been on board ship.

"The head was preserved, and, after sundry adventures, came into the possession of a wealthy gentleman by the name of Shoemaker, who lives near Germantown. He got it under the impression it was the head of a whale, and it can be seen at any time

THE CAPTAIN'S SEA-SERPENT STORY.

among the curiosities of his extensive grounds. At present it is set up as an arch over the entrance to his hot-house, and in summer the pretty morning-glories and Madeira vines are trained over it, and almost hide it from view.

"And now, gentlemen," said Captain Marvellous, "my story is done, and, notwithstanding it has been a long one, and perhaps a dry one, I am sure you never heard anything like it before."

"Well, Captain Marvellous," said the commodore, "you have told that story well, and it does credit to your head and heart. It has what I like in a story—it has no circumlocution, it is full of incidents, and is right up to the point. Why, the incidents come down like ambulances from Mount Blank. There is one thing, however, that may throw a little incredulity on your story, and that is the 'discomposition' of that sheet-anchor while in the serpent's 'die-phram.' How is that, doctor?" he said, turning to old Hitybeltcser. "Give us your 'dog-noses' of this disease."

"Well, sir," said the doctor, clearing his throat and delighted to have an opportunity of showing his learning, "the active agent for chemefying elementary substances in the body is an organic compound called *pepsin*, though Liebig considers that it is nothing else but a proteine compound in a state of change. It has also been ascertained that the saliva and pancreatic fluids have an equally soluble power when acidulated. In the acid state they act like the gastric fluid upon azotized matter; its operation on starch, for example, is precisely that of diastase. In so doing it acts in a fermentitious manner, having the power of exciting a change in another substance in which it does not participate."

"Hold on a minute, doctor," said the commodore; "I want to make a note of what you say; this thing is presented to me in an entirely new light. I'll sprawl the navy commissioners on this subject the next time I write to them on anchors."

The commodore took out his pencil, and, after writing a few moments, he told the doctor to proceed.

"As I was going to say," continued the doctor, "this is exactly the nature of the operation of pepsin on azotized matters, on which it produces an incipient change that so alters their condition as to dispose them to solution in hydrochloric and acetic acids, with which they form chemical compounds; the substances forming the oleaginous class do not."

"There, that will do, doctor," said the commodore, "I understand it all perfectly."

Notwithstanding it was getting late, the commodore insisted on the captain calling on some one for a story, and the captain gratified him by calling on him.

"Well, I will tell you one," said the commodore, "although it is not exactly ship-shape to make such an attack on the flag-ship; and as I never saw a sea-serpent, I must tell you a story of a monkey, which I consider next door to a sea-serpent; and, moreover," said the commodore, "you must promise to believe every word of it, and more besides. Pass the wine around, Conkshell, and fill the gentlemen's glasses."

Just at this moment the door of the cabin opened and the orderly announced Mr. O'Classics, the school-master, who wished to speak to the commodore.

"Tell him the commodore is engaged, and he must wait for some other opportunity," said the captain, frowning dreadfully.

"Let him come in," said the commodore, "let him come in; my heart is as wide open as a cellar-door, and I feel in one of my most liberal moods to-day. Send the school-master in, orderly." And in marched Mr. O'Classics, dressed in full uniform; that is to say, he was dressed in what the middies had told him was full uniform; he had on a white hat with a blue, red, and white ribbon around it, representing the American flag; a soldier's pipe-clayed belt slung over his shoulder with a putty-knife stuck in the frog; his legs were incased in a pair of leather gaiters coming up as high as the knee, and his coat was embellished with a blazing red star on the collar; he looked for all the world like the figure of St. Patrick wrapped up in the American flag.

"And pray, sir," said the commodore, "what can I do for you this evening?"

"If you please, sir," said Mr. O'Classics, "I would like to obtain your lave to travil a bit. I've jest met an auld friend of mine from Killarney, an' he's on a bit of a tramp, an' faith he's jest axed me to join him, an' if yev no objection, Mr. Commodore, I would just give the midshipmates a vacation an' take lave of 'em for a short time, the divil's brats as they are."

"And pray, sir," said the commodore, "where might you be going? and where do you intend to rejoin the ship?"

"Well, sir, I have an idea fairst an' foremost of goin' through France, then through Italy and Germany, take post-chaise for Vienee, spind a pleasant time wid the emperor, go down the Dan-

THE STORY OF JOCKO AND A LONG TAIL.

ube to Constantinople, take a 'kibob' wid the Sultan, an' join the ship whiniver it will be most expadient."

"Why the devil don't you go to Vienna by sea?" inquired the commodore.

"Is it by say, you ask?" said the school-master, opening his eyes; "faith an' sure yer ballaganterin' me, commodore. Divil a bit of say there is to go there wid that I know af."

"Then, sir," he replied, "you had better study your geography, for I am going there with this ship myself," said the commodore.

"You have a very pleasant trip before you, Mr. Antics," he continued, "and you have my full permission to go." And the school-master bowed himself to the door, quite delighted with his success. "But I wish to impress one thing on your mind, Mr. Antics" (the school-master was all smiles and attention), "and that is, you must be back by sunset."

"Shut the door, orderly," he said. "Now, gentlemen, that's what I call sprawling the party, and so here goes for my story," which, reader, is entitled to another chapter.

CHAPTER XVIII.

MUCH GEOGRAPHICAL KNOWLEDGE DISPLAYED, AND A LONG TAIL.

The commodore, having settled himself comfortably in his chair, commenced his story as follows:

"You must know, gentlemen, that on the confines of 'Timbertoes,' in the empire of Sorrocco, there exists a monkey known to travelers as the red-horned ape. The animal is mentioned by Herodotus, or in Ovid's 'Metamorphoses,' I don't remember which; but this I do know, that the same kind of ape is still to be found in the great deserts of that oasis, and has been identified by the late travelers Mungo Park and Captain Riley.

"Among a tribe of Africans called the 'Woomerangs' these monkeys are brought up as members of the family, and treated with great consideration; indeed, their intelligence is so great that they exercise a good deal of authority in the domestic arrangements of the family; they make the fire, dress the children, tend the hoe-cake while it is baking, and catch the fish for dinner. Their favorite amusement is catching clams, and on a moonlight evening you may see hundreds of them walking along the beach at low tide, with their baskets on their arms, digging for the delicious shell-fish, which on the coast of Africa excels anything of the kind known in any part of the world.

"During a war that was waged against the 'Woomerangs' by the 'Samboshins' (a neighboring tribe) the latter devils were victorious, and the vanquished were, according to the customs of that country, carried into captivity and sold to foreign dealers as slaves; to this custom are we indebted in our Southern States to that great institution commonly called 'the negro'—the institution that has made us what we are, that has abolished rags in Europe, and permitted almost every lazzaroni to wear a clean shirt once in six months; it affords people east of sunrise (especially Bostonians) opportunity to *speak* virtuously about its abolishment, when at the same time they are building ships for the further importation of the 'Institution,' knowing full well that its destruction would ruin them root and branch; it would stop the wheels of their factories, and pull down their free schools, which they so well know that they treat all the negroes so badly who go there that the 'Institution' at the South is afraid to run away and seek their protection.

"Just study that 'Institution,' gentlemen; you will find that it rules the world. Great Britain may rule the waves, but the 'negro Institution' rules Great Britain. Let the 'Institution' say England sha'n't have any cotton, and where would be your Great Britain in six months? Why, sirs, they would have to take all the spare duck in his Majesty's navy to clothe themselves with—but that has nothing to do with my story.

"The negroes I mentioned as having been licked had the misfortune to be sold to a Spanish slave-dealer; they were crowded into a small schooner of American build, and it was whispered that she belonged to old 'Abhedam Philanthrofister' of Boston, though she sailed under Spanish colors, and carried two or three sets of papers. Among the negroes was a red-horned ape, who preferred sharing the captivity of his family to be digging clams on his native shore.

"In the confusion incident to the embarkation of two hundred and fifty slaves, it was easy for 'Jocko' to pass by unobserved, especially as the marker put him down on the list as a 'red nigger,' and flattered himself that he had one more than he paid for.

"I suppose you have all heard of the horrors of the slave-trade; how the poor blacks sicken and die from grief and despair; how the brutes of captains, indifferent to their own interest, treat them to the worst kind of fare, and keep them penned up like sheep in the lowermost recesses of the vessel; how, when driven almost mad with hunger and thirst, mothers eat their own children and suck their blood; husbands eat their wives, uncles eat their nephews, and grandchildren so far forget the respect due to their elders as to eat their grandmothers; I do believe they would eat an admiral, even, if they could get hold of him, and that, too, without pepper and salt.

"The captain of the Dolores (so the schooner was called) was the worst tyrant that ever stepped a deck; his name was Fernando Comesangre (which in English means blood-sucker), and I was told that the appearance of the wretch corresponded exactly to his name. I saw the scoundrel after he was dead, and had his brains blown out, and a more hideous-looking wretch I never laid my eyes on.

"Captain Comesangre, although a great brute where others were concerned, took care of number one; and when he left port he laid in a good supply of plantains and bananas, to say nothing of a netful of delicious oranges, which were kept hanging over the stern. When half drunk (which was every day), he used to make his appearance on deck with a handful of fruit, and, taking a seat on the hen-coops, he proceeded to regale himself; the inside he took for himself, but gave the skins to his chief mate (whose name was José Carnero, or Joseph Sheep); a most befitting name it was for the wretch, for he swallowed the skins down as if they were bacon and greens; and usually he received a kick from the captain, accompanied with the endearing expression of 'quita maldonado,' which means, in good English, 'Get out of the way, you ugly son of a gun.'

"Mr. José Carnero was the only one out of all that crowd who ever had a taste of the fruit, although it was spoiling every day before his eyes, and the smell of one even was not offered to the poor little sick children, who were dying by dozens of the scurvy.

"The schooner had been at sea twenty days, and was lying almost becalmed to the south'ard of Bermuda, when a rakish-looking brig was seen standing down before the wind. The expert eye of Captain Comesangre detected the man-of-war in the stranger's taut-looking masts, his square-fitting sails, and other indications not to be mistaken. 'José,' he said, 'go aloft, you malcriado, and see if you can make that brig out; if she is American, we need not trouble ourselves about her, but if she is English, we must run, "porque los Ingleses son demonios por los negros."'

"José reported he could see her quarter-boats, and that was quite enough for Captain Comesangre, who had no relish for any closer acquaintance with her guns. The sheets were eased off, light sails set and wet down, and the schooner commenced moving quickly through the water. 'Adios, malcriado,' said Captain Comesangre, shaking his fist at the Britisher.

"But don't be so fast, Mr. Comesangre, for that brig is bringing down a spanking breeze with her, and will be alongside of you before you know what you are about; and, sure enough, the brig came within gunshot in a very short time, Captain Comesangre swearing at all the saints in Christendom for bringing him such bad luck.

"He thought, perhaps, that the brig would pass without taking any notice of him, but, oh, no! John Bull is too great a philanthrofister for that. He has a nose for a slaver, no matter if she is ten miles dead to leeward, and his 'oilfactories' have been very much sharpened up since they have been allowed ten dollars a head for every darkey they recapture.

"Up went the British flag, and Comesangre flew the American at them, but John Bull was not satisfied with that; he sent his compliments in the shape of a twenty-four-pound shot, which went skipping along like a young lamb in a turnip-patch, and threw up the water a few feet from the counter of the Dolores.

"'Malcriado,' muttered Comesangre, but he never hove-to.

"The next shot John Bull fired was better aimed, for it struck the schooner right under the taffrail and knocked over a poor sick negro who was sitting in the bow.

"The only notice Captain Comesangre took of this was to give José Carnero a thundering kick behind, and mutter his usual 'malcriado.'

"In the mean time the brig was gaining upon the schooner fast, and the shot began to fly in earnest; five or six had already passed through the stern-frame, and had committed sad havoc among the poor negroes below.

"Finding that the schooner would not heave-to for solid shot,

THE STORY OF JOCKO AND A LONG TAIL.

they commenced firing shell from the brig. At that time we knew nothing about the Paixhan shell, and we used the fuses made of match-stuff; sometimes they went off, sometimes they didn't; on this occasion, however, they were fired with great accuracy, and, exploding among the slaves, knocked them into flinders. The most awful screams came from the lower deck, but the only notice Captain Comesangre took of it was to throw a rotten orange at Carnero's head, and mutter 'Malcriado Ingleses.'

"Presently a shot, or rather a shell, landed on the quarter-deck and bounded on to the forecastle, where the fuse commenced fizzing at a most tremendous rate. No one dared go near it, and every one sought some place to 'hide his diminished head.' Even Comesangre jumped into the cabin, giving José Carnero a kick as he went below, muttering 'Quitase, malcriado.'

"I must now introduce my hero to you, gentlemen," said the commodore, "and must apologize for not having done so sooner; but this is the first opportunity I have had to bring him upon the stage. He was like many of those great men we read of in history who are brought before the world by the force of circumstances, and the circumstances that brought out Mr. Jocko were of the most forcible kind, in the shape of gunpowder.

"Just as the last-mentioned shell landed on the deck, a curious-looking figure, about four feet high, and blood-red from the crown of his head to the sole of his feet, was seen to emerge from the lower deck. On his head, and nearly in the center of his forehead, he had two short horns, black as ebony; and his tail was so long that it looked like a coil of rigging when it was flemished down.

"Captain Comesangre, who was looking out of the cabin-door, sung out, 'Que malcriado negro colorado es eso, José Carnero?' meaning, What infernal red nigger is this, Joseph Sheep? But Joseph Sheep had disappeared down the hold, and no answer came to the captain's call.

"His wonder was suddenly turned into admiration for the 'malcriado colorado' when he saw Jocko jump to the bomb-shell, seize the fuse in his teeth, tear it from the shell, and then, jumping on the rail, let it drop into the water; his teeth chattered and his little sunken eyes glistened like a tiger's; he looked as if he meant to defy a whole battery of bomb-shells.

"'Bien hecho malcriado,' shouted Comesangre, though he was convinced in his heart that he saw the devil. 'Hit him again, red jacket,' he cried out, though the only answer he got was an angry growl from the ape, who seemed to be fighting on his own hook, and wanted no interference.

"Shell after shell was thrown upon the schooner's deck by the English brig, but the moment they landed, Jocko, as before, hauled out the fuse and threw it overboard. He seemed to be in a perfect frenzy of delight, and chattered and shouted like fifty niggers at a banjo dance. Presently a shell lit right in the main-top and laid there fizzing like mad; but Jocko was up aloft before you could count one, and, seizing the fuse in his mouth, he ran out on the yard and dropped it into the water.

"This was the first time during the excitement that Jocko had shown the length of his tail, and its length was enormous; when he was in the top the end of it hung down two or three fathoms on the deck. Any one would have supposed it to be a useless appendage, but you will see presently that it was a most invaluable tail.

"Comesangre, who had witnessed the surprising feat above mentioned, gave a perfect yell of delight. 'Bien hecho carajo malcriado,' he cried, 'bien hecho,' but the monkey, instead of receiving his congratulations in an amiable manner, again seemed to evince great anger at the captain's interference; and, before Comesangre had time to think, he threw his tail around his neck, lifted him fairly off his feet, and let the bomb-shell fall directly on his skull. But for a thick Spanish tarpaulin-hat he wore, he would have had his brains knocked out; as it was, he was knocked perfectly insensible, and remained so for three or four days.

"Jocko, quite delighted with his feat, chattered and shrieked like fun, and, diving down into the stern-boat, where the captain's bananas and plantains were kept, he shouldered a bunch of each and disappeared down the hold, where he divided them with the family to whom he belonged. These things were told me by Carnero, who was taken prisoner by us afterward, for causes which I will presently relate.

"Conkshell," said the commodore, interrupting the thread of his story, "tell Mr. Saddlebags that I will drink his health with great pleasure. What do you think of that purchase around the captain's neck, Mr. Saddlebags?"

"Timber-hitch, sir, I presume," answered the master; "tail selvaged at that, no doubt, sir; or else mayhap it was a running bowline."

"Wrong, sir," said the commodore, "quite wrong, sir. How

do you account for it, doctor? I expect now that you can rig a better purchase than the master?"

"There is no purchase about it, sir," said the doctor, who was quite proud of being called upon to settle this momentous question. "The power in the tail is owing to the exercise of that vital property of contractibility belonging to the muscular tissue, which, in this case, is called into action by the cerebrum and medulla spinalis, causing contraction of the muscles of the back and caudal extremity, especially the quadrati lumborum, the spinales dorsi, and the coccygeus. A portion of this contraction, in this instance, was induced by reflex action, and involved only the medulla spinalis; while another portion, being undoubtedly voluntary, called into play the cerebral function and the co-ordinating and regulating power of the cerebellum, if, as in the opinion of most physiologists of the day, this important organ possesses that function," and the doctor threw himself back in his chair after this lucid explanation, and seemed quite overcome.

"That's what I call an opinion as is an opinion," said the commodore. "Your views agree with mine perfectly," he said; "it's all as clear as mud, and, after drinking your health, doctor, I will get on with my *tail*.

"A breeze now sprung up," continued the commodore, "and carried the schooner out of reach of the shell, but still the shot told, and many of the poor slaves were killed or horribly maimed. The command fell upon José Carnero, in consequence of the accident to the captain, and, exerting all his skill and energy, he managed that time to escape. He became quite fond of the ape, for he knew that but for him the schooner would have been blown to the devil. In four days' time the captain recovered his consciousness, and the moment he was able to move he was carried on deck. His anger knew no bounds when he found that the English shot had committed such horrible devastation among his cargo; the shot that had entered through the stern had killed twenty captives and wounded one hundred and twenty more, many of them so badly that they were beyond cure. Their moans were so pitiable that it would have pained the heart of any one to hear them, with the exception of Comesangre, who had not any heart to pain.

"'What devilish howling are those devils keeping up?' he said to Carnero. 'Smoke 'em a little with the stink-pot; see if that won't quiet the malcriados. How many killed and wounded are there?'

"When told the number by the mate, he fairly shouted with rage, and swore that he would take vengeance on the first English ship he met with of inferior force, and well the scoundrel kept his word.

"He ordered the killed and wounded on deck, and had them all thrown overboard, with the exception of those he had the slightest hope of saving, and the savage delight he showed on seeing them go to the bottom, or in witnessing the struggles of the wounded, was only equaled by the cool brutality by which his orders were executed by his savage crew—men who were the offscourings of all nations, who respected no law, human or divine, and who only obeyed the captain so long as it suited their convenience.

"Three days after this a sail was made out from the mast-head, and reported to be a merchant-vessel standing toward them. The captain's eyes glistened with delight as the idea of some diabolical plan ran through his prolific brain. Sore as he was, he arose from his bed and buckled on his sword and pistols and ordered the boats got ready for service with full crews. 'And now, malcriados,' he said (addressing his cut-throat-looking crew), 'if that is an Englishman we will make up for our losses, and for every slave they have made us lose, I will take the life of one of the malcriados, if there are enough on board.'

"'Como Vmd. quiere,' they replied, and then walked coolly to the grindstone to sharpen their knives.

"In an hour's time the stranger was quite close, and, unfortunately, proved to be an English vessel bound to Honduras, loaded with dry-goods, and carrying a crew of nine men; she also had on board fifty passengers (emigrants bound to Honduras), among whom were many women and children.

"The vessel approached so incautiously that, before they were aware of it, the schooner luffed up under her stern, poured in a fire with her long gun and small arms, and then, running right alongside, the ferocious crew, with Comesangre at their head, rushed on board. Carnero was left to take care of the schooner, for, as that worthy scoundrel afterward admitted, he was too great a coward to go on any expedition, and this the captain was well aware of.

"To describe the scene of butchery that ensued would be impossible," said the commodore. "I was on board the brig three hours after the thing occurred, and I fainted at the sight my eyes

THE STORY OF JOCKO AND A LONG TAIL. 227

witnessed; never shall I forget it as long as I live; I even grow faint now when I think of it. Conkshell," he said, "give me some champagne, and enable me to get through the horrors of this story.

"After massacring every man, woman, and child they could find on board, the pirates proceeded to rifle the brig of her cargo. They had broken open the hatches and had transferred a great many valuables to the slaver, when, on board the schooner to which I belonged, the quartermaster reported a brig on the lee beam with her sails all flying about, and a rakish-looking schooner alongside of her. At the same time, we saw the smoke from the gun, and heard the faint report of a cannon. You may depend upon it, gentlemen, that in less than a minute things were in a state of commotion on board the Quickstep, which was the name of our vessel, and you never in your life saw sails go out so fast; in three minutes by the watch we had everything set low and aloft. We carried thirty-two different sails in the Quickstep, not including the save-alls and wind-sail steering-sails, and whenever the Quickstep undertook to overhaul the vessel she looked at, the party was soon sprawled."

"May I ask, commodore," said Mr. Shacklebags, timidly, "what the save-alls are? I don't think I have ever seen them in the service."

"Why, Mr. Shacklebags, I am astonished at you," he replied. "Not know what save-alls are? Why, I thought every ship in the navy carried them. If they don't, they ought to. Save-alls, sir, are sails that are tacked over the hawse-holes to catch the wind that comes through the cabin-windows; perhaps you never saw wind-sail steering-sails either?"

Shacklebags answered in a faint voice that he had not, and blamed his own curiosity for instigating him, in the first place, to ask any questions at all.

"Well, then," continued the commodore, "the Quickstep carried lower and top-mast steering-sails on her wind-sails, besides those at the end of the yards, and these steering-sails were nothing more nor less than the midshipmen's table-cloth tied on to a squilgee-handle, and triced up to the wind-sail bowlines."

The commodore continued: "We gained on the schooner rapidly, and, fortunately, they were so busy robbing their prize, and committing acts of horror too terrible to relate, that we were within four miles of them before they saw us; and then, leaving the brig in a great hurry, they got on board their schooner and made all sail to escape from us. They did not wait even to hoist their boats up.

"It was doubtful for a time whether we gained on the slaver or not. It was the first time the Quickstep had ever met her match in sailing, and even save-alls did not seem to get her along. The schooner at length began to gain on us, when suddenly we saw her top-mast steering-sails come down by the run and drop into the water; then down came her royals and topgallant sails, the top-sails followed suit, and in less than three minutes her foremast was almost stripped of the sails.

"We did not know what to make of the manœuvre, but we could evidently see that there was great confusion on board, and we could also see, with the aid of our glasses, a small figure skipping from yard to yard, and wherever he appeared a sail was sure to drop. At the same time we could see the smoke and hear the report of firearms, and we presumed that a mutiny had broken out on board among the crew or slaves, for it was evident that she was a slaver. The little man aloft had, after cutting away all the sails on the foremast, shinned up the fore and aft stays and commenced the work of stripping the mainmast, jumping about all the time like a monkey, and dodging the shot from below, which were evidently aimed at him. I might as well tell you now," said the commodore, "that the little man who was doing us such good service was no other than my hero Jocko, the red-horned ape. Instigated by more than brute sense, he had jumped aloft when he saw that the schooner was chased, and with his sharp teeth soon cut adrift the halyards of the sails, and in less than ten minutes (notwithstanding the fire of the musketry) had placed the slaver completely at our mercy.

"All these details I received from the scoundrel Carnero.

"About this time the wind died away and left the sea perfectly calm. The schooner got out all her sweeps, and once more commenced moving away from us.

"Our captain ordered all the boats out, and the men were armed and in them before you could say Jack Robinson. It was not then as it is nowadays when you call away a boat to arm for an expedition; now it throws the whole ship into confusion. The pistols are in one arms-chest, the belts in another, and the cutlasses stuck up in some out-of-the-way place where no one can get at them; the cartridges are stowed in the magazine, the percussion-

THE STORY OF JOCKO AND A LONG TAIL.

caps ditto, and the pistols are so filled with oil that they won't go off when you want to fire them. In those days we kept everything at hand, the pistols were kept loaded, and the belts attached to them and well filled with cartridges ; the boats were always ready for *any* service, and the crews were properly instructed by the officers, who all knew their business, though they had not studied the classics, and were no way scientific at that.

"We made a dash in the boats at the schooner, the launch leading with a six-pounder carronade in her bow, with which we opened fire the moment we got within range. It is needless to say that we met with little resistance, for our volley was only returned with a few straggling musket-shots, which did us no harm and only excited our men to greater exertion.

"When within two hundred yards of the slaver a snake-like looking boat was lowered from her stern and hauled up to the gangway, into which five or six men jumped, headed by the captain. He had intended to escape to the island of Eleuthera, about five miles distant. No doubt the wretches would have succeeded but for an unlooked-for prevention.

"The red-horned ape who seemed to befriend us throughout the chase again came to our aid. Just as I dashed up to the side, in hopes of catching the rascals before they left, I saw the boat shove off, and the captain, turning round, fired his pistol right at us, fortunately wounding no one ; and, giving one shout of exultation, the slavers sprung to their oars.

"Their triumph was of short duration, for just at that moment I saw what I took to be a little darkey dressed in red flannel jump into the main rigging with what I supposed to be a coil of rope in his hands. With great dexterity he caught the captain around the neck and brought the boat up all standing, for, as the men pulled and he held on to the thwarts, the boat could not move an inch ; it enabled us to board her and secure the crew, with the exception of the captain, who, being choked almost to death by the little red ape, let go his hold and was dragged overboard.

"Comesangre at length got breath enough to enable him to seize the tail in both hands and haul himself, hand over fist, to the vessel's side, where he clung to a chain-plate, more dead than alive.

"It was now (for the first time) that I discovered the little red darkey to be a monkey, and what I took to be a rope was his long tail, which he had thrown with such dexterity around the pirate's neck, and kept it fastened there, by the contraction of the parabolum antilles and crocodile extremities, as the doctor so lucidly explained to us."

"I beg pardon, sir," said the doctor; "I mentioned the words 'cerebellum' and 'spinales,' also '*caudal* extremities,' but I don't think I said anything about the antilles."

"Well, it's all the same," continued the commodore; "all I know is, that the captain had a great timber-hitch around his throat, and was well-nigh choked to death. I saw him trying to draw his knife from his belt, and, intending to do my friend the monkey a service, I pointed my pistol at the slaver's head, fired, and broke his jaw; but I was a minute too late; his knife flashed in the air, and with one wipe he severed poor Jacko's tail from his body, and, having got a pretty good coil in his hands while he was hauling himself in, he only left Jocko about twenty feet of his caudal extremities.

"Jocko screeched and chattered like a devil incarnate, and, making a dive head-foremost on to the deck, he disappeared from sight. I was so enraged at the villain for his cruelty that I fired again at his head and lodged a ball right under his eye. He shook his knife at me while the devil himself looked out of his eyes, and shouted "Carajo, malcriado Yankee." I was about loading up to give him another broadside, when to my surprise the red monkey appeared in the chains with a cocked pistol in his hand, and, pointing it close, to the wretch's head, he pulled the trigger and bespattered the vessel's side with his brains.

"The hands of the scoundrel relaxed their hold, and down he went, brandishing his knife in the air to the last. One of the men happened to catch hold of the coil of monkey's tail that was timber-hitched around his throat, and took a turn with it around the boat's thwart, which prevented Comesangre from sinking, and we finally landed his ugly carcass on deck.

"We had been so much occupied with the chase that we had not paid much attention to the English brig, and now I saw that thick smoke was issuing from her hold; the pirates had set her on fire to hide their villainous deeds. The boats from the Quickstep that had stayed by the schooner put out to her assistance, but did not arrive until she was almost burnt to the water's edge.

"The *pirates* were taken into New Providence, delivered up to the authorities, and there hanged, while the negroes (all who were left alive) were apprenticed out to some planters in the British West India Islands, and when called for had all died, and been de-

THE STORY OF JOCKO AND A LONG TAIL.

cently buried, as could be seen by looking at their neat graves, every one of which was adorned with a wooden head-board, with the purser's names of the occupants inscribed thereon!

"I took the monkey as my share of the prize, and he became the pet of every one on board, though he was the greatest rascal in the way of playing tricks I ever saw.

"I recollect once his snatching the doctor's wig from his head, and, shying up to the main truck, he stuck it on the spindle of the conductor and amused himself combing the curls out of it, for which the doctor never forgave him.

"Another time he got into the cabin (where the captain had a globe of beautiful gold-fish that he was taking home to his sweetheart in Charlestown), and, picking them out one by one, he deliberately threw them into the sea. Fortunately it was calm, and the little fish, knowing that they were in a salter element than they were accustomed to, swam to the starboard gangway, and, putting their noses out of the water, asked, as plain as could be, to be taken on board. This was immediately done, and, lowering down the glass globe to them, they all swam in. The captain was in a terrible rage at Jocko, and swore that he should leave the ship at the first port; but he changed his mind in a day or two, and offered me two hundred dollars for him, which, of course, I refused.

"On another occasion the captain got his pistols out to shoot him, but Jocko again disarmed his anger and set him to laughing heartily.

"The captain had on board a parrot which he prized very much, not only for its cleverness in talking and mimicking, but for its beautiful plumage. This was also intended for the young lady in Charlestown, notwithstanding it swore most awfully.

"It could say almost anything; called the 'Officer of the deck' in the captain's voice, and sang out 'Quartermaster of the watch' in the different officers' voices. He would sometimes crawl to the hatch and, imitating the boatswain's whistle, call 'All hands to stand by their washed clothes,' or 'All hands reef top-sails,' and kept the vessel in a continual uproar. There was no end to his talking; there was nothing he could not say. The captain would not have parted with him for the world, and every day he took the greatest pains to smooth his feathers with a camel's-hair brush; he wanted them to be perfectly smooth when he presented him to his Dulcinea.

"One day the parrot had hobbled to the main hatch, and had

just commenced calling 'All hands to witness punishment,' when Jocko, who was lying asleep under the launch, jumped out and seized him by the leg, and, before he could be prevented, he made his escape with his prize to the main top-sail yard, where he sat and chattered as if he had done the cleverest thing in the world.

"The parrot screamed out 'All hands ahoy,' 'Where's the officer of the deck,' 'Quartermaster of the watch,' and 'All hands shorten sail.' He swore some terrible hard oaths at the same time, but they were all lost on Jocko. When he called 'All hands shorten sail,' the monkey commenced picking him with both hands, the parrot crying out all the time, 'Oh, you rascal, I'll cut your life's blood out of you!' The feathers were flying all over the ship, and the captain, who happened to come on deck at the time, saw his dearly prized plumage all scattered to the wind.

"He swore, he raved, and stamped upon the deck, and at last got up his pistols with which to shoot the hero of the Dolores.

"The parrot now began to pipe 'Belay' in his shrillest whistle, and Jocko, apparently in obedience to his call, stopped stripping him, but, unfortunately, not until he was as naked as a three-days'-old blackbird. He held him at arm's length for the admiration of the crew, who, in spite of discipline, could not repress a loud shout of laughter. Poll was no favorite on board. He was too fond of calling 'All hands to witness punishment,' and the sailors thought that was a reflection on them.

"I verily do believe that the captain would have killed the monkey, but every time he pointed the pistol, Jocko would hold the parrot in front of him, and look as much as to say 'There's a target for you; fire away,' and the captain was afraid of killing the bird. In despair, he rushed into the cabin, when Jocko, seeing the coast clear, descended to the deck with the parrot under his arm. He pinched him until he was as blue as indigo, every time he did so the parrot singing out for the 'officer of the deck.'

"Just as Jocko landed on the deck the captain came out of the cabin and told the first lieutenant to send all hands up and 'catch that monkey,' when Jocko immediately stepped forward and, making him a polite bow, laid the parrot at his feet. Up jumped Poll and waddled to a gun-slide, the captain looking on in astonishment and sorrow. Hauling herself up by her bill, Poll looked around with great dignity upon the lookers-on, and screamed out, 'Ain't I a beauty? Officer of the deck, pipe down.' The first words the captain had just succeeded in teaching her, which he wanted her to

THE STORY OF JOCKO AND A LONG TAIL.

repeat when he made his appearance before his lady-love, to whom he had written about this wonderful bird.

"The whole scene was so ludicrous that every one burst out laughing, and the captain, who had an eye for the ridiculous, joined in heartily. Jocko seemed to enjoy the fun as much as any one, and sat looking on in the stern of the launch, having taken possession of a small messenger boy's hat, which he wore on his head cocked sideways.

"Fortunately, Poll's feathers grew out once more, and the captain had the felicity of presenting her to his sweetheart, with plumage more beautiful than ever.

"Poor Jocko met his death at last in the most singular manner, and I grieve to think that I could not have the satisfaction of getting him to the United States. Barnum would have given ten thousand dollars for him alive, and no doubt half as much for his skin, but I lost that also.

"We had on board a great number of marmosets—a very small kind of monkey—that had been bought by officers and men on the Spanish main. There were over forty in all, I think.

"Now, these little fellows had a favorite spot on the booms, where they clustered together, like merchants at an exchange, to discuss the morning news. Here the men were in the habit of feeding them with bananas, plantains, sugar-cane, and other delicacies, which they carefully stowed away in their jaws ready for future use.

"Latterly I had run very short of bananas, and Jocko felt the privation very much, for he had to resort to the men's messes, particularly on duff days, when he obtained a plentiful supply of plums. He had been noticed to take his seat in the slings of the main yard, watching the little marmosets as they were fed by their owners, and cocking his ears knowingly whenever one of them stowed away his banana in his false jaw. Those who were acquainted with Jocko's habits knew that he had some deviltry in his head, and were looking forward for fun; they knew he was not watching the marmosets for nothing.

"One morning, when the marmosets had all been fed according to custom (Jocko watching them all the time), and had assembled in a group to digest their food, the monkey quietly arose from his hiding-place in the slings of the yard and noiselessly slid down the main-stay until he was right over the marmosets. Then, throwing down his tail, he caught a couple of the little fellows in a running bowline, and hauled them up to the stay, the marmosets screaming and kicking with all their might and trying to get away. Of course, every one who saw it nearly killed themselves laughing, while Jocko knowingly winked his eye to all around, and then taking one of the little monkeys by the back of the neck, and squeezing his mouth open, he put in his finger and pulled out the contents of his false jaw, which he immediately transferred to his own stomach.

"To add insult to injury, Jocko laughed so immoderately that it frightened Poll from her nap, and she sang out, 'Silence; all hands witness punishment,' and swore round oaths enough to sink a ship of the line. Jocko quietly dropped the marmosets on the mats in the launch (which were put there to dry), and proceeded to haul up two more with his tail, and they received no better treatment than did the first. So he continued until he had made a good meal of the bananas they had stowed away in their magazines, and which had been so piously kept by the owners of the little brutes—"

"Beg your pardon, sir," said the doctor, "but I thought (if I am not mistaken) that you remarked that the monkey had lost his caudal extremity, and, if so, he must have lost the property of contractibility belonging to muscular tissue."

"Not at all, doctor," the commodore replied; "the tail grew out again after I got him, and he possessed in a greater degree than ever the contractibility of the 'cherrybum pinealehouse' and the back action of the 'pinealehouse cock-eye sea-horse,' as you were kind enough to explain to us."

"Permit me to correct you, sir," said the doctor, who seemed to be a little annoyed; "I spoke of the 'cerebrum and medulla spinales,' the 'spinales dorsi,' and the 'coccygeus.'"

"All the same," said the commodore; "a rose, you know, smells sweet if you call it an onion, as the poets say.—Isn't that so, Mr. Shacklebags?"

"Ay, ay, sir," said Shacklebags, who had fallen asleep in his chair, "all ready to cut, sir; let go the anchor," and poor old Shacklebags woke up, mortified to death to think that he should have gone to sleep while the commodore was telling a story. He saw his promotion further off than ever, and the wine in his nose actually forced itself out through the toes of his boots.

"Well, gentlemen," continued the commodore, "I see *some of you* are getting sleepy, and I must bring my story to a close.

"The monkey continued his attacks on the marmosets every day, and, after filling himself with bananas, would retire to the lee

THE STORY OF JOCKO ENDED.

main yard-arm, stretch himself out, and take a comfortable nap. The poor little devils were harassed to death, and dwindled away to mere specters for the want of food, while Jocko grew fat on his ill-gotten plunder.

"One evening, just after sunset, the officer of the deck noticed a great excitement among the marmosets. They seemed to have assembled together for some particular object, and one in particular, who seemed more excited than the rest (which he evinced by his chattering), seemed to be addressing the crowd. They kept it up until after dark, Jocko meanwhile slumbering peacefully on the end of the mainyard, little dreaming of the danger hanging over him.

"Suddenly the little fellows, apparently moved by one impulse, rushed up on the yard, by stays, shrouds, or any rope they could lay hold of, and, before Jocko was aware of it, they attacked him *in the rear* and pushed him overboard into the sea, and then, giving three cheers in the marmoset language, they slid down to their places and kept up the chattering all night.

"The officer of the deck, who had witnessed the whole scene, immediately cut away the life-buoy and luffed the vessel up in the wind, but, though a boat was lowered, the body could not be found, and that was the end of poor Jocko.

"The parrot, which seemed to have been a looker-on, waddled to the launch, where the little monkeys were assembled, and, mounting on the stern, sang out, 'All hands witness punishment,' which so frightened the marmosets that they dove down under the booms and chattered louder than ever.

"Now, gentlemen," said the commodore, "my story is ended, and I flatter myself that none of you ever heard of such a monkey before. Conkshell, give us some champagne, and, Mr. Shacklelegs, I want you to set that to music."

CHAPTER XIX.

VERY FISHY AND STUPID—THE STORY OF A WHALE-SHIP.

The commodore's story was much applauded by every one, and I thought Captain Marvellous looked a little chop-fallen at having the wind taken out of his sails. Two or three glasses of champagne, however, soon restored his equanimity, and he joined with the rest in praising the commodore's yarn.

Mr. Bluff was now called upon to afford his share of amusement, and the jolly lieutenant's eyes lighted up with fun as he set his wits to work ransacking his brain for what he called a "smasher." About this time Mr. Bluff had taken more than one glass of champagne, and rolled about in his chair like a wood schooner in a calm off Cape Hatteras; his little eyes twinkled like diamonds, and his pursed-up mouth gave a very comical expression to his whole face.

"I could tell a story, commodore," he said, "that would make your ear ache, but with such a dry throat as I have at present I don't think I could get through with it without going on the doctor's list. I ain't drank nothin' this half-hour" (Mr. Bluff was not remarkable for his grammar) "and I feel now exactly like a pump-bucket must feel after it has been lying idle for two months, or a half-live fish after it has been carried on a string for a couple of hours."

"If that's all," said the commodore, "we can soon trim ship. Here, 'Conk,' bring some more ammunition, in the shape of champagne and sherry, and place it at Mr. Bluff's elbow—"

"And" (put in Bluff) "don't forget a cigar. 'Conk,' a little brandy and water to rectify the champagne, and a bottle of olives to rectify the brandy; throw in an anchovy and a toothpick by way of making everything snug, and then I'll make sail."

Everything being brought to Mr. Bluff's satisfaction, he sheeted home and hoisted his top-sails (to use his own expression), and, "cutting the waves with his taffrail," he let his yarn run out.

The Whale-Ship.

"When I was seventeen years of age," said Mr. Bluff, "I ran away from home and shipped on board a whaler called the Train Oil, bound to the Pacific.

"The captain's name was Tekel Blubber, the first mate Hezekiah Whalebone, the second mate Bill Sternall, the cook's name was Jim Fluke, and the supercargo's name was Jeremydidler Harpoon— very appropriate names they were for the business in hand. Whether they were purser's names or not I don't know, but I presume not, as many families of those names still live in and about Nantucket. The crew of our vessel consisted of sixteen besides those I have already mentioned. Their names were chiefly Smith, Jones, and

MR. BLUFF'S WHALE STORY.   237

Brown. They were a slab-sided-looking set of fellows, and each one had a share in the profits of the trip, provided they ever came back again. It is not my intention to go into the history of our voyage out round Cape Horn to the Pacific. Suffice it to say that we rounded the Cape in the southern winter, and it was as dreary and uncomfortable as a voyage could well be. The captain was a perfect Tartar, and the mate, who was drunk nearly all the time, led the crew such a life that they would have thrown him overboard if they could ever have got a chance. For my part, I often wished myself at home, and nothing but the hope of seeing a whale taken kept my spirits up.

"Among the crew was one good fellow—an out-and-out Irishman named 'Barney O'Blazes.' He and myself were sworn friends from the beginning, because I did not join with the crew in running rigs on him. I had not forgotten the lesson taught me by Mr. Brutus Coriolanus Nat when I was so jocose as to call him 'Sambo.'

"Barney O'Blazes and myself kept together all the time. He was a powerful fellow, and could handle any two men in the ship. The mate never ventured to molest him, and I kept in the wake of so good a friend to be under his protection. If Mr. Whalebone had been ever so desirous to try his tyranny on me, Barney O'Blazes would have served him out right handsomely had he done so.

"We were three months and a half getting around Cape Horn to the neighborhood of our cruising-ground without having seen a single whale. The skipper swore at everything right and left, the mate kept beastly drunk, and the scurvy began to make its appearance among the Smiths, Browns, and Thompsons.

"It was at the latter end of September, late in the afternoon; the crew were all half-asleep on the deck, and the wind was scarcely strong enough to shake a lady's veil, when the cheering cry of 'There she spouts' came from the lookout in the crow's nest, and it so electrified the captain, mate, and all hands, that the face of the former brightened up, the mate ceased to stagger, and the crew simultaneously jumped for the boats. The deck, that for months had shown nothing but an apathetic crew, was now alive with bustle and excitement, harpoons were seized hold of by unpracticed hands, and the boats' crews were busily at work in clearing away their lines for present use. 'Where away is she?' shouted the captain to the lookout. 'One point on the larboard bow, sir,' was the reply. 'Starboard your helm and let her go off a point; lower away the boats, boys, and let us put out after her,' said the captain. No sooner said than done, for in less than five minutes the boats were lowered, with the captain in one and the mate in the other; the cook, second mate, supercargo, and carpenter were left to take care of the ship, which was ordered to steer after us, and away we went for the whale as fast as six stalwart arms in each boat could row us.

"I had no right to be in the boat at all, being of no use whatever; but my friend Barney O'Blazes being one of the oarsmen, I jumped in the mate's boat without saying anything to any one. The mate had not seen me in the bustle and excitement of the moment, and it was not until we were five or six hundred yards from the ship that his drunken, blood-shot eyes fell upon me.

"'What in thunder are you doing here, you young villain?' he shouted; 'jump overboard and be smashed to you, and swim back to the ship.'"

At this part of the story Mr. Bluff looked around and found that every one had fallen asleep; the commodore had leaned back in his easy-chair and was snoring loudly with his mouth wide open; Shacklebags had fallen under the table, and most of the others had composed themselves to rest in various positions—in fact, I was the only one awake.

"Conk" even had fallen asleep, leaning against the cabin sideboard.

I did not wonder at it all, for the bell had sounded past midnight, and the hoarse "All's well" of the sentry was a signal for decent people to seek their repose.

"Youngster," whispered the lieutenant to me, "let's slip off quietly and leave these stupid fellows to sleep away their senses. They do not deserve to hear a good story.

"I will tell you some other time what befell me at the island of Papia with the pretty queen Tawa, who met a most dreadful fate; how we reached the United States, and, being then fit for nothing else, how I got appointed a midshipman."

We accordingly slipped out and left the sleepers to themselves, and I was told that next morning, when the midshipman went to report eight bells, they were all in the same position.

The commodore was exceedingly dignified all that afternoon; the captain looked bilious as a vinegar-bottle; the master broke his comparison-watch in winding it; and Mr. Teaser nearly set the midshipmen crazy with the messages he sent down to the first lieutenant.

WE SAIL FOR NAPLES.

Soda-water was in great demand, and the commodore, not having any on hand, sent down to ask Mr. Bluff if he had any. The jolly lieutenant sent him word that he had none himself, but would make some in half an hour from salt water and Seidlitz-powders.

CHAPTER XX.

SAIL FOR NAPLES—FIRST GALE—NOTHING IN PARTICULAR— FAMILIAR POETRY.

Two days after the commodore's dinner the ship was ordered to be ready for sea, and Naples was said to be our port of destination. How our hearts bounded with delight when this joyful news was announced to us, and we were about to realize all the visions of pleasure we had formed for ourselves! I could already in my imagination hear the orchestra at San Carlos, laughed to myself o'er the anticipated witticisms of "Punchinello," and all night long dreamed that I was standing on the top of Vesuvius, the crater belching forth fire and smoke, and throwing huge bowlders of heated lava at my head. Reckless had told us so much about Naples that we knew it by heart, and only wanted to see it to realize it.

On the third day we were sailing out of the Bay of Gibraltar with all canvas set, making rapid headway through the water, and in a few hours the crouching "Lion" was lost to view. "Ape's Hill" (or the "Pillars of Hercules") faded in the distance, and the coast of Spain loomed up in all its grandeur. The high hills of Sierra Nevada, covered with snow, formed a delightful contrast with the vine-clad and smiling villages at its foot. Old Moorish towers, standing out like sentinels on rugged promontories, reminded us that Spain did not always possess these beautiful districts, and that the once valiant Moor had degenerated into something less than a donkey-driver. The days of the Cid were no more, and the Alhambra was but a faint resemblance of what it was in the days of Boabdil. We flew so rapidly along the coast that before sunset Cape de Gat was seen looming up in the distance, and three or four hundred vessels, from the full-rigged ship down to the little xebec, were lying idly flapping their sails where the wind had left them. We flattered ourselves that we were bringing up the breeze along with us, and soon would lead all the small craft a dance around the cape;

but our hopes were soon to be destroyed. One sail after the other began to hang idly against the masts; "All aback forward!" cries the officer of the forecastle, and in a few moments the steering-sails all came in, the yards were braced up, and there we lay like a huge shark among a parcel of minnows.

There is a tradition among sailors that no ship can pass Cape de Gat without paying toll to the "Witch of the Winds," who holds her court in some of the deep caverns with which this coast is indented. Binnacle shook his head when any one spoke of getting round the cape, and said, "Ye'll catch thunder before daylight," quoting at the same time the following piece of doggerel:

"Mackerel skies and mare's-tails
Make lofty ships to dowse their sails"

(which is attributed to Moore, Shelley, or Byron, I don't know which). He shook his head knowingly and walked off.

The captain also began to look uneasy. He would stick his finger in his mouth and hold it up for the air to blow on and indicate its direction. The barometer, sympiesometer, and aneroid were consulted every ten minutes; but as these distinguished authorities seemed to differ materially on the subject of the weather (which they invariably do on board of an American ship of war), the captain was nonplussed, and had to appeal to the standard authority of the ship, Ben Binnacle. The captain had been rather off speaking terms with Ben since the little difference of opinion about the sloop of war Gingerbread, and had failed to consult him on any little matter about which heretofore he had been invariably guided by Ben's opinion.

"I say, Mr. Know-everything," said the captain, "the sympiesometer's down: what do you think of that?"

"I think as how, sir," said Ben,

"'That mackerel sky and mare's-tails
Makes lofty ships to dowse their sails;
If lofty ships should fail to do it,
I'll bet my grog they're sure to rue it.'"

"Give me a plain answer, you old fool!" growled the captain, "and when I ask you anything give me an answer in prose; d—n your poetry, sir!"

"Well, then, sir," said Ben, "I meant to say 'that mackerel sky and skirries stratiyes,' as the chaplain calls it, will make lofty ships to lower of their canvas, and if the lofty ships shouldn't lower of their canvas, why ten to one that lofty ships won't have a chance to lower of their canvas, for the winds will blow it all away."

"Get down off the poop, you old scoundrel, and tell the first lieutenant to close reef the top-sails and make things snug for a gale!" shouted the captain; and down he went to see if the barometer, sympiesometer, and aneroid had come to any final settlement on the subject of the weather. The barometer still stood up as stiff as a "cuffie," and evidently seemed determined not to yield an inch, while the aneroid had gone so low that by rights we should have been scudding before the wind. The little sympiesometer, hanging between the two with an eye on each, seemed undetermined how to act. It feared the huge, blistering old barometer with its fierce face, and feared to displease its more modest friend the aneroid, which it felt was mostly right; it would consequently rise and fall according to the looks of the instrument on either side of it. "Don't you see," said the Aneroid, "that the storm will soon be upon us with royals on the ship, and our friend Barometer is evidently out of sorts (Barometer was always out of sorts), otherwise his usual wisdom would not forsake him?" "And don't you see," said Barometer, in his loud, imperious tone, "that that little timid Aneroid is so shaken in her nerves that she is for ever getting up a panic? We will never get to Naples at this rate, and, if you ain't a fool, Miss Sympiesometer, you will do as I do—show fair weather even when it's going to be foul."

Sympiesometer really had weak nerves, and they were so shaken by the fierce words of Barometer that she began to fall very rapidly, much to the joy of her sister Aneroid, who had no desire to lose her reputation. It was well she did so, for the wind commenced fluttering over the surface of the calm ocean, then it sighed heavily through the rigging, again came a puff that made the canvas belly out, and in a few moments the little craft in all directions were bending to the fury of the blast. The trampling of feet on deck, the rattling of the cordage, the shrill whistles of the boatswain and his mates, the clear voice of old Barnacle through the trumpet, the shouting of the men on the yards—"Haul out to windward!"—and the squeaking voices of the midshipmen passing some order, made "confusion worse confounded." Old Barometer even, with all his pride, could not stand it, and he gradually came down from his high horse and "acknowledged the corn." So ashamed was he of his former proceedings that he even fell lower than was required of him, and it was some hours after the gale was over that he condescended to rise again. Sympiesometer no longer heeded him, but went hand in hand with her gentle sister Aneroid, who had never deceived her. So much for truth, and so must truth always conquer.

When the gale did set in to blow, it seemed to have let loose all its fury, and tried what damage it could do to our strong, stanch ship. Sails split into a thousand ribbons, masts bent and cracked with the violence of the blast, guns tore away from their fastenings and drove wildly about the decks, and in the midst of all the confusion one of the seamen was washed overboard. The life-buoy was cut away, which he fortunately seized upon and went floating astern, vainly endeavoring to catch the numerous ropes that were thrown to him. I never shall forget the poor fellow's look of wild despair when he saw that the ship was leaving him, and he felt his last hope was gone of ever seeing his messmates more.

A hundred willing hands jumped aft to the tackles, and a dozen officers sprang into the boat and were willing to be lowered to save a shipmate's life; but what hope was there in such a hurricane, "for the ship lay motionless and seemed upset"? "The water left the hold and washed the decks," "and made a scene men do not soon forget."

"Wait for orders!" shouted Mr. Barnacle, "and don't lay a finger on that boat's falls till I tell you, you boobies! Why, no boat could live a minute in such a storm, and the poor fellow will have to stand his chance of being picked up by one of those coasters."

Poor, frail little barks! they seemed more intent on saving themselves than looking out for shipwrecked sailors, and were scudding away before the wind, hoping to reach some safe haven before the sea got higher.

The last I saw of poor Tailblock he was hugging the life-buoy wildly with one hand, and holding his hat high in the air with the other, his hair blown off his face, his silk handkerchief streaming in the wind. When he saw that no boat was lowered for him, no kind hand held out to save, his look settled down to one of sullen despair, and, casting his eyes heavenward, he was soon lost to view in the thick spray that was thrown up from the water by the angry winds.

Heavens! how my heart ached when I saw that fellow being launched upon the wild waves on his frail boat! I thought of some good old mother, who most likely depended on him for support, reading his last letter from Gibraltar, and smiling over the words of love and kindness he bestowed upon her ; or I thought of some old father, whose pride and pleasure were all centered in an only son, the guide and prop of his old age ; or I thought of a fond sister, whose only hope of happiness was clasping that brother to her breast after long years of absence ; and finally I thought of the bereaved wife, who sat with tearful eyes looking to heaven for consolation, the little ones at her side.

> "In vain seek pleasure from a mother's love,
> In lieu of that the Father did bestow,
> And silent kneel with lips that scarcely move,
> Praying for him by sudden death laid low."

Alas! poor Tailblock, these lines are likely the only ones your fate has elicited ; you were perhaps mentioned in the log-book as having "fallen overboard" ; or perhaps at the end of the quarter your name may have been sent to the Department as "lost at sea." But are there many among the hundreds who witnessed your sad fate who an hour after cast a thought upon you, or depicted to your friends in heartrending language the agonies of your last moments ? Who is there can tell how many weary hours you buffeted manfully against the storm, or whether, unnerved by despair, you sank the moment the ship was lost to view ? Oh ! sad, sad is the sailor's fate who falls overboard at sea ; men there are always willing and ready to risk their lives to save him, but the stern dictates of duty must be obeyed, and the feelings of the officer who gives the order to let a fellow-being perish must be ten times more agonizing than the feelings of those who are willing to go to the rescue. Poor Tailblock ! I have seen many a seaman fall overboard in my time, but none do I remember that bore with him to the grave that last agonizing look which rested on his features.

. . . .

"'Twas twilight, and the sunless day went down over the waste of waters like a veil,"

and all night long, and for weary hours thereafter, we rolled and pitched until everything seemed to have gone to destruction. At length, after three days of such weather as I have never witnessed since, the gale began to break, and

> "Now overhead a rainbow, bursting through
> The scattering clouds, shone, spanning the dark sea."

Wild breakers were rushing still in anger against the rugged cliffs of Granada, while the rich fields of Almeria seemed smiling in derision at the futile attempts of the ocean to break its bounds.

Well, will the reader exclaim, how uninteresting is all this digression about the storm! Storms are a common event in a sailor's life, and why make so much of this? Because, good reader, it was my first heavy gale at sea, and you can have some idea of its force from what Captain Marvellous said of it when he fell in with Captain Lollipop, of the frigate Limbo. "Lollipop," he said, "it was fearful; the topgallant-mast bent so that the spindle at the main truck bent over and took my cap off; the commodore had the hair blown off his head (the commodore always wore a wig) and all the gold plugs out of his teeth; a large sow weighing six hundred pounds, with a large he-goat (horns six feet long), was blown through the scupper-holes; the monkey-tails were sticking in the bulwarks like so many arrows, and the two long forecastle 32-pounders, carriages and all, were landed in the maintop."

"Dare say so," said Lollipop; "it often happened so off Cape de Gat," and then he sang—

> "At Cape de Gat I lost my hat,
> And where do you think I found it?
> At Port Mahone, upon a stone,
> And all the gals around it."

So from Captain Lollipop's admission Cape de Gat must be a d—l of a place.

Many accidents occurred to the men during the gale; the surgeons were quite as busy patching up cuts and splintering up fractures as after a battle, and that storm became the memorable event of the cruise.

Reckless, also (that head-over-heels fellow), must go and fracture his ankle in endeavoring to get a running bowline around Mr. O'Classics' neck while they were reefing topsails (that greenest of all school-masters having succeeded, in his fright, in getting halfway up the main rigging, where he stuck fast, and remained clinging to the shrouds until Mr. Barnacle had him lowered down). Reckless had carried him an order (which he said came from the captain) that "O'Classics must go to the weather-earing on the main-topsail yard." "And now, Mr. O'Classics," said Reckless, "the eyes of the whole ship are on you; let 'em see what a son of

AFTER THE GALE.

Erin can do." It is needless to say that Mr. O'Classics never got more than half-way up, but there he stuck, shouting out, "Reef away, me boys, down with the yards! I'll be wid ye in a jiffy." Poor old Barney! his trousers were blown so high up his legs that he never got them down again.

Mr. Reckless was taken below after spraining his ankle and lodged in a cot at the head of the cock-pit hatch, but his wild spirit could not be tamed even by an accident that promised to keep him in bed two months at least.

The gale was abating (though the sea was running high), and the different mess-rooms were clearing away the wreck and damage caused by the water running into the air-ports. Many were the old boots and the new boots and old caps and new caps that were mixed together in one indiscriminate mass; three or four pairs of good cloth pantaloons were there also entirely ruined; a new cocked hat perfectly shapeless was lying affectionately alongside of an old wet swab, and a fine Spanish cloak with a red velvet collar, seemingly ashamed of the company it had got with, had stowed itself away in a dirty slop-bucket. There never was such a mess in all creation, and Scantling, with a troop of mess-boys, was endeavoring to get matters ship-shape once more, though the labors of Hercules were mere child's-play to what he was doing.

All the trash was thrown out of each mess-room under Reckless's cot (that being the most convenient place to hide it for the present), and he, being asleep at the time, took no notice of it; but when, however, he did awake, he immediately discerned that he was being very badly treated. At this moment Mr. O'Classics was regaling himself with a piece of old cheese and a pot of good English porter, and was about to send it to "that bourne from which no cheese or porter ever returns," when Reckless, imitating the voice of old Barnacle, called to him to keep less noise.

"Is it me ye're spaking to, Mr. Barnacle, or the mess-boy?" replied O'Classics, and with that he popped up the hatch, with Ned Smitherins, the captain's clerk, and Doctor Gallipot, the surgeon's mate, at his heels.

The first salute he got was a pair of damp boots alongside the head; Smitherins got the wet swab in his mouth, while Gallipot got the visor of a wet cap right in his eye, and Ventriloquist Riggs, the purser's clerk, who was just putting a mug of porter to his mouth, had the pewter flattened against his nose by the heel of a thick wash-deck boot, and his beauty was spoiled for the rest of the cruise. This was a source of regret to us all, as Riggs was a general favorite (when he was sober), and would amuse us by the hour; he was the best ventriloquist I ever heard, and some of his imitations of people's voices were so inimitable, and his faculty of throwing his voice into anything so wonderful, that we thought he might have made more by his talents than by his clerkship. I never shall forget the day when the hot duff on our neighbor's mess-table commenced crying out, "Murder, murder! Thieves, thieves, thieves!" (we didn't know then that there was a ventriloquist on board), and, seizing on to the knives, every one rushed in upon the pudding to liberate the captive supposed to be imprisoned there, when, lo! there was a silver spoon that had been stolen from the wardroom two days before. It is needless to say that the pudding escaped eating at dinner-time, and was eaten cold that night by Riggs and some others who had been let into the secret. If Riggs had not been in bad company his nose would not have been smashed.

The party assaulted immediately retreated, but for a moment only, for they attempted a sally, which was met by such a shower of filthy things that a Jew must have knocked under to it; and finally, when the school-master made a rush up the ladder the third time, the Spanish cloak, fresh from the dirt-bucket, was slipped over his head and the end stuck in his mouth. There was too much fun going on for Reckless to go it all alone, and by this time all the young midshipmen in the steerage had joined in.

There was dreadful swearing in Irish, and some loud "Well, I nevers!" from Smitherins, and in the midst of all the uproar who should come down the ladder but old Barnacle; at the same moment a wet swab was flung at Smitherins, which fell at the feet of the first lieutenant. Mr. Barnacle picked it up, as he always picked up everything (Mr. Barnacle was of a very inquiring mind), and shouted out, "Silence!"

At that moment a wet pair of pantaloons were thrown around Mr. O'Classics' neck, and he rushed up the ladder during the intermission and faced the first lieutenant.

"What do you mean by all this uproar here, Mr. O'Classics?" he said, frowning his darkest frown.

"Och! ye innocent auld divil," said the master, "ye look as if butter would not melt in your mouth! Off wid ye, for a baste of a first lieutenant!" and with that he slapped him right in the face with the wet trousers, saying, "Take that, ye auld divil, and may the cat fly away wid ye! Ye're so fond of dirty breeches, take yer

MR. O'CLASSICS IN DIFFICULTY. 247

bellyful av them," and again began hammering away at old Barnacle with all his might and main.

The assault was quite unexpected to the first lieutenant, but he was not a man to be taken aback without being ready for the occasion, and, holding in his hand that familiar belaying-pin (which he always carried with him), he brought it down on O'Classics' head with such a crash that it was a wonder the Irishman's brains were not knocked out. It sent him tumbling into the cock-pit, and meeting Smitherins and Gallipot (who were coming up the ladder) in his fall, he carried them down with him on to the deck, where, clinching Smitherins by the throat with one hand and Gallipot with the other, he knocked their heads together until they were nearly blind.

Mr. Barnacle knew from the strength of the blow that it would be some time before the teacher came to, and, ascending to the quarter-deck, he ordered a file of marines below to bring the mutineer on deck. Presently O'Classics appeared, very shaky in the legs, looking very wild about the eyes, and the blood streaming in profusion over his face.

Captain Marvellous had been sent for, and the commodore, who was walking the poop, came down, he said, "to see the fun."

The investigation was a long one, and much interesting evidence was elicited, though I regret to say that the interesting-looking O'Classics was fast going to the wall.

He accused the first lieutenant of throwing dirty swabs in his face down the cock-pit ladder, and pitching all his "dirty auld boots" into a mug of porter which he was in the act of drinking, "as he belaved he 'ad a parfect right to do in a frae country," and all the bad luck he wished "auld Barnacles" was "dat the cat might fly away wid him the next gale of wind we 'av'!"

Both the captain and Barnacle saw that there was something *sub rosa* which they could not get at, and would likely have gone the cruise without being any the wiser if a dirty little midshipman named "Babble and Squeak" had not come forward and turned state's evidence. "He had no idea," he said, "that the whole steerage should bear the blame for dishonorable conduct committed by one person," and then he drew himself up nearly three feet and a half high. Alas! poor "Babble and Squeak," that was the unluckiest day's work you ever committed, and Sindbad, with the Old Man of the Mountain on his back, was in paradise compared to you. I well remember that your hammock would never stay on the hooks (even the hooks took a dislike to you); your "slapjacks" that were saved for you when on deck somehow always got foul of the mustard-pot; you never slept with your mouth open but it was sure to be mistaken for a spit-box by some of the men on deck, of course, and one night (poor "Babble and Squeak!") I remember so well your getting up to drink (which you always did about midnight), and, putting the can to your head, found that some one had —but never mind what. Every dog has his day, and you had yours; but, if I am not mistaken, many of your days were equal to any two other dogs' days I ever saw. The whole affair in hand so injured him in the estimation of his brother officers, and followed him through the navy, that he got his name changed by an act of Legislature, and is known now as "Squabble and Beak." He married a respectable apple-woman's daughter named Tabitha Flimsey, and after having about a dozen little "Squabble and Beaks," or "Babble and Squeaks," he settled down as one of the Moral Reform party of the navy, and was one of the *élite* who were retained when the navy underwent a pruning.

After Babble and Squeak's *exposé* Reckless was regularly done for in the captain's estimation, though the commodore thought it the greatest joke in the world. "D—n that fellow Reckless!" he said, "he shall be my aid, if he has to go on crutches." As to "Mr. Buckle and Sneak," as he called him, he would order him to the first schooner the Government sent on the station.

But what did poor old Barney O'Classics do when he found that the "auld first lieutenant" was innocent? "Faith!" says he, "Mr. Barnacles, if ever I want to study astronomy, I'll go to you an' yer belayin'-pin; for may the auld cat fly away wid me, but ye made me see more stars, suns, moons, and comets than I iver seen in my born days, an' if ye're so agreed, I'll cry quits wid ye! I flapdadled the wet trousers in your face, and ye gave me the worth av it in belayin'-pin. So, Captain Marvellous, if ye'll be agreed, I'll think no more of what the farst liotinent's done to me. I know he's a relation of the McBarnacles, away up in Tipperary, from the way he handles the shillalah, and I'm third cousin to Matty McBarnacle, whose aunt's sister married the second cousin of my wife's grandmother, named Grawler McBarnacle, an' faith I hauld no ill-will," and with that he held out his hand.

Old Barnacle was not proof against the magnanimity of his new-found relative. He had punished him rather more severely than he at first intended, and, as the whole matter originated in a mistake, he let Barney's breach of discipline pass, not, however, without a reprimand to the teacher for leaning against the paint-work, which that gentleman could not very well help, considering his then enfeebled condition.

In the mean time the wind has been drawing fair, the sea has been going down, and the ship running at the rate of twelve knots on her course. Ivica, Majorca, and Minorca are dropping out of sight behind us, a fresh breeze carries us safely through the Straits of Bonufacio, and in twenty-four hours thereafter we are running, with all steering-sails set, into the Bay of Naples.

I must refer my readers to many, if not all, of the European tourists who have written books for a description of this beautiful bay. I never was good at description; it is not my forte, although I am an ardent admirer of Nature in all her aspects. A midshipman stationed on the quarter-deck going into port has little or no opportunity to indulge his observations on scenery; for to look through a port would subject him to a banishment to the lower recesses of the ship, where the air-ports are arranged something like the glasses of a panorama, but infinitely more obscure, very thick and very dusty, and scarcely serve to show whether the elbow of the mess-boy has removed the remains of the first course from the plates.

To get on a gun and look over the bulwarks would be the highest breach of discipline known in the naval service, and if a middy should escape the keen eyes of the first luff, he would likely be reported by the gunner's crew, who have an affection for their Long Toms little short of what they feel for Sally Baker or Polly Bowline when they meet after a three years' cruise.

The first chance, then, a middy gets to indulge his admiration of the beautiful in nature is when, by chance, he can get liberty on shore; and then his observations must be cut very short if he would see the inside of a billiard-saloon, for the sun, traveling rapidly to his nest, warns him that the boat will be at the wharf at sunset, and he must concentrate a great many pleasures in a few hours if he would be up to time.

I once recollect going to see the opera of "Masaniello," and was much struck with the grandeur of Mount Vesuvius in the back scene of the theatre. It was vomiting forth fire and brimstone enough, and had such rivers of lava running down its side that fifty cities like Herculaneum and Pompeii must have knocked under to its fury. The spectators applauded more at the pyrotechnic display than they did at the sweet sounds of the orchestra (which I was afterward told was a most unharmonious set of instruments), and it was well that the stage-manager hit upon so happy an expedient as Mount Vesuvius to draw off the attention of the audience from the wretchedly executed opera. Suffice it to say that the representation I then saw was far superior to the original mountain, and "Old Hickory" was not far out of the way when he threatened to put it out by sending over the Falls of Niagara.

One can readily imagine what a catastrophe that would have been. What a fizzing and a sputtering there would take place with the Niagara, going at the rate of thirty miles an hour, leaping into this heated caldron; not a pig in the kingdom of Naples would have had a bristle left upon its body, and it is rather probable that the macaroni would all have been boiled to a jelly.

I never shall forget the day, however, when, in company with other midshipmen as ambitious as myself, I attempted the ascent of Vesuvius; it was a broiling day in June, and we had not the foresight to make any preparations in the way of creature comforts to carry us through, though we did procure, about half-way up, a bottle of sour stuff they sold to unwary climbers for "Lachryma Christi." We fell in with an English family bound like ourselves to get scorched. Some were unkind enough to say that they were button-makers from Birmingham, but Mrs. Dumpling Growler (a fat old lady of forty) talked freely of her intimate friends "Lady Milkwater" and the "Countess of Heatherdown"; old Frowsy Growler said it was the very thing Lord George Donkeypate would like, and the sweet little Biddy Growler (we always called her Bid after that for shortness) declared "if she could honly 'av' the Duke of Liverwhite's heldest son hat 'er side, that hit would be the 'appiest day of 'er life." She thought, however, that six rather good-looking midshipmen would do at a pinch, and I remember tugging away with a silk handkerchief around her waist until the pretty Miss Biddy was safely landed on the top. "O my! Mr. Marline," she exclaimed, scarcely able to speak from exhaustion, "'ow I should like to 'av' a little fresh hair!" and I consoled her by telling her she had the prettiest and freshest-looking ringlets in the world, and she need not wish for any others. "La!" says she, "but you Americans do blarney one so; but if you will promise not to mention hit to the Duke of Liverwhite's heldest son, I will give you one when pa ain't looking." At that time old Frowsy Growler, Esq., was about a hundred feet below us, singing out, "'Old hon, my 'earties, we'll soon be hup to the top!" and Mrs. Dumpling Growler was with her back to us, telling "her heyes what a 'ot place it was," when I out with a penknife and robbed the sweet little Biddy of the dearest little curl in existence, in doing which our lips came— but never mind that; I remember now nothing but Miss Bid. Stones from the crater were flying thick around me (they may have been the bowlders I dreamed of, for what I know), and I was called to look a dozen times at the beautiful prospect at our feet—the city of Naples away below us, and the milk-white clouds resting on the side of the mountain; but I saw it not—I saw nothing, good reader, but a pair of pretty blue eyes, bluer far than the heavens above us, and the pearliest teeth, whiter far than all the corals of Naples; and then such cheeks, bursting with health! the finest tint in an Italian sky was nothing when compared to them; they beat Mount Vesuvius all hollow, though some of my messmates did say she looked like a milkmaid, and showed their want of taste by saying that the intelligent-looking nose of my charmer was of the order of snubs. Ah me! perhaps if I had married the old button-maker's daughter, if old Frowsy Growler had not been decidedly opposed to a connection with a warrior (old Frowsy was a Quaker), I might have been a better and a happier man, but fate has willed otherwise, and now in my forty-eighth year I still cherish, among numerous other mementos of the same kind (of black, auburn, and flaxen), that lock of golden hair, and often wonder if, like mine, her's are sprinkled with streaks of silver-gray. I wonder if Miss Biddy ever looks at the lock I slipped into her hand on the way down the mountain, and I wonder if it will be any consolation to her to know that I remained single (perhaps she will think for her sake), and devote myself to some fourteen nephews and nieces, as all old bachelors should do. "And yet I find a comfort in the thought that these things are the work of fate."

The next day we arrived in the Bay of Naples, where we anchored off the king's palace; the quarantine-boat came alongside, and we were informed that we were quarantined for twenty-four hours, which, however, did not deprive us of a bumboat full of delicious fruit, or the pleasure of witnessing the performance of Punch and Judy alongside, all kinds of conjurors in boats, dancing monkeys, and some of the sweetest singing girls I ever met with anywhere.

CHAPTER XXI.

A CALL ON THE KING OF NAPLES—MR. BLUFF'S ADVENTURE WITH A COUNTESS.

The morning after we arrived at Naples was one of Heaven's own days, if I may use the expression, and everybody counted on going ashore by nine o'clock, or as soon as morning inspection was over.

The ship was in a great state of excitement, and Mr. Barnacle was as cross as a bear with two sore heads, or two bears with a sore head—he was unbearable. It was, "Keep off the paint-work, you booby! Young gentlemen, keep your hands out of your pockets. You lazy marine, I'll get a post for you to lean on. Here, boatswain's mate, out with your colt and start that boy Fiddler up the main rigging, and, Mr. Marline, go to the mast-head for looking at me so disrespectfully. Gentlemen of the watch, get the fire-hose out and squirt it on that hand-organ alongside, and that infernal Punch and Judy. We can never get the ship in order so long as those devilish things are allowed to come alongside. The first man I see looking over the side at that fellow making a fool of himself standing on his head on the point of that knife, and that other fool cutting his head off and putting it under his arm, will get a dozen at the gangway. Here, quartermaster, bring me a belaying-pin to throw at those dancing jacks alongside."

The old fellow was about to put his threat into execution by hurling a belaying-pin at poor Punch and Judy, when the commodore appeared at the cabin-door clad in a rich silk dressing-gown and with a Turkish fez upon his head and a pair of green embroidered slippers on his feet.

"Hold on, Barnacle, hold on; don't go off half-cocked and involve the two nations in war. Why, sir, you are about to commit a 'cassus belly,' and just when I come here expecting to enjoy myself at the opera, I may find myself involved in hostilities, and be called upon to open my broadside on Mount Vesuvius, and very likely have to send home for Niagara Falls to extinguish the damned mountain altogether, for I believe that would be the only way to bring these lazzaroni to terms. No, no, Mr. Barnacle, don't make a 'cassus belly'; that is a horse of another color. In throw-

MR. BARNACLE'S ACQUIREMENTS.

ing your belaying-pin at Punch and Judy you hit his majesty the King Ferd., and her majesty the king's wife. Don't you see, Mr. Barnacle? Besides that, you expend one of Uncle Sam's belaying pins, which you can not account for except by saying it was expended on Punch and Judy. When that is put in the returns it will bring a letter from the navy commissioners asking an explanation, which will keep me two days in my cabin writing the answer and explanation, and deprive Mr. Shy of the pleasure of going on shore the moment we get into port. No, no, Mr. Barnacle; think a bit and save your belaying-pin. Now, Mr. Barnacle, although you're a tip-top sailor, and could, no doubt, work a ship under bolt-ropes, dead to windward, through the Dardanelles against the eight-knot current, yet you know no more about international law than my grandmother. So don't touch Punch and Judy while I have command of this squadron."

During all this harangue Mr. Barnacle did not wince under the commodore's fire. His wart was a little larger, and there was a smile about the corners of his mouth, so that he seemed half-way between getting mad and getting pleased. Good humor won, and he told the commodore that after such a lucid explanation of international law the rights of Punch and Judy should be respected. "Belay the hose, young gentlemen, and don't interfere with the international rights of that fellow trying to cut his throat alongside. Mr. Reckless, stop throwing coppers overboard to make those small lazzaroni dive for them. One fellow has already been under water an hour, and we shall have a case of international law on our hands before we know it. Mr. Babble and Squeak, haul in that fish-line and stop hooking that fellow's oranges. Go to the mast-head and study Puffendorf and Vattel for two hours. And you, Mr. Brace, let that monkey alone; you'll be involving the nation in difficulties before you know it." With that old Barnacle walked away, looking as smiling as a basket of chips.

The commodore looked quizzical, and, calling the midshipmen to him, said, "Now, young gentlemen, I want to show you the force of genius. There goes the best sailor in the United States navy, and also, much to my surprise, the best posted officer in international law that I have ever met. He has learned it intuitively, and, although he never heard the principles expounded until within the last half-hour, he sucked in the whole subject as an infant does his mother's milk. It shows that seamanship is the root of all evil. I beg pardon. I meant the groundwork of all knowledge. Now, young gentlemen, you will never be good officers until you sleep with a volume of Pastell and Demidorf's International Law under your pillow. Send Mr. Shy to me. By the way, young gentlemen, there is another remarkable man. When I first took him he knew absolutely nothing; now he has all the international law at his finger-ends. He speaks seven languages and can write fourteen, writes three kinds of short-hand, and is so modest withal."

All this time the commodore was standing on deck in his remarkable costume, the officers and sailors gazing in astonishment at this desecration of the quarter-deck.

Such matters, however, never troubled Commodore Blowhard; he considered himself a compendium of all that was wise, and cared not twopence what anybody thought.

"Mr. Babble and Squeak," he sang out, "tell Captain Warhorse I want him—Captain Mavellous, I mean—and hurry up Mr. Shy."

The captain came rushing on deck buttoning his coat, for he had stopped to put on his epaulets before entering the commodore's presence, and his eyes grew as big as saucers when he saw the commodore on the quarter-deck in fez, morning gown, and slippers. "Great heavens!" he thought, "the service is indeed going to the devil, and I expect to see the midshipmen in morning gowns before the week ends," but he smiled pleasantly on his chief, and would have sported a dressing-gown himself had the commodore requested it.

In the mean time Shy, the secretary, had come on deck and awaited orders. "Ah, Captain Marvellous," said the commodore, "glad to see you this April morning. We must call to-day on the king and invite him on board, but before I go myself I must send and call on him. Mr. Sneezer" (addressing Mr. Teaser), "send for Mr. Bluff. I want him to call on the king. He has had so much to do with Bourbon that I think this Bourbon king will take a fancy to him; they look something alike."

Mr. Bluff soon appeared, looking red in the face.

"How are you this morning, Bluff? I hope you are well."

"Not very well, sir," said Bluff.

"Well, you do look red in the face."

"Yes, sir," said Bluff, who had retired to rest full of Bourbon whisky, "I slept with my air-port open last night, and it always makes my face red."

"Why, Bluff," said the commodore, "it was only yesterday

morning, when I remarked that you were paler than usual, you told me that sleeping with your air-port open always affected you so. You must have been speaking metaphignatorily."

"Yes, sir," said Bluff, "that word expresses my situation exactly."

"Well, now, Mr. Bluff," said the commodore, "reposing special confidence in your ability, patriotism, and knowledge of international law, I am going to send you on shore to call upon the King of Naples for me. Shy will go with you; he speaks ten different languages, including the Italian, and writes eighteen. He will do the interpreting."

Here Shy put in a modest disclaimer, and said, mildly, "I don't speak Italian, commodore; I don't even understand it."

"Oh, yes you do, Shy. You don't know yourself what you understand. Go into the cabin and commit the following messages to heart and translate them into Italian: First, 'How is your royal majesty's health?' Second, 'Commodore Blowhard has just arrived in the waters of your dominions, and is commander-in-chief of all the American forces in the Mediterranean, Archipelago and on the coast of Syria, besides the vessels stationed on the coast of Gibraltar, Spain, and Africa, and in the Empire of Morocco' (the entire squadron consisted of the frigate Thunderbum, sloop of war Gingerbread, mounting four 'Pisen guns,' and the schooner Jackal, of two guns). Third, say to the king, 'I have come to settle all our international questions,' and just hint that, although Mount Vesuvius is a mighty volcano, Niagara Falls would put it out in half an hour. Fourth, say to him, in the way of conversation, that we once whipped the British out of their boots and destroyed the entire nation of Qualla Battoo for eating one of our missionaries, besides making them pay twenty dollars damages. Speak to the king also in French, Shy, and say that I hope to have him come and dine on board. Just tell him what a cook I have in Pierre Poisson, who can make twenty-four dishes out of one little pig."

Here Shy put in a mild protest that he couldn't speak a word of French.

"Oh, yes you can, Shy," said the commodore. "You don't know yourself what you can do. That mind of yours is stowed chock-full of things, like an old garret. You don't know what's there until you break it out. Lastly, tell the king I want to send my sailors on shore to see Punch and Judy on a large scale, and will get the minister to negotiate with him for permission to export one of the party to the United States, where he will make a fortune and be the means of cementing the union between the two nations; and, Mr. Bluff, take Mr. Carlin" (meaning Marline) "on shore and let him see a full-rigged king. Come, Shy, move into the cabin and put all that into Italian, and carry on all sail while you are about it."

Tears stood in poor Shy's eyes as he moved off, but there was no remedy, and he had to hunt up his Italian dictionary, with which and his knowledge of Latin he hoped to get through his heart-rending job.

"Mr. Bluff," said the commodore, "tell his majesty I will salute him, gun for gun, and tell him that little story how we threw over the British tea in Boston harbor. Tell him how we licked the Britishers at Bunker Hill; that'll sprawl him. And now, Mr. Bluff, get off as soon as Shy commits all that Italian to memory, which will be in about ten minutes."

It took Mr. Bluff and his escort but a short time to get ready, and we shoved off, Shy looking very sad and studying very hard a sheet of paper on his knees, containing the messages to the king. We landed at the foot of the stairs leading to the palace, which we ascended, surrounded by all the lazzaroni of the city, bawling and turning somersaults like mad. I thought of Mr. Spicy, the chaplain's, Africans, whose capers were somewhat similar, and concluded that Mr. Spicy would work out a theory that these lazzaroni were descendants of those self-same Africans.

The king received us in his reception-chamber, with the queen at his side, and we were all surprised to find a plainly dressed, handsome man, whose only indications of rank consisted in a double-breasted frock-coat, with navy buttons, and a red ribbon at his button-hole.

We made our bows in stately American style, having previously determined not to kiss his majesty's hand, when the king advanced and said, in excellent English, "Glad to see your ship in our bay, sir, and hope your captain is well." Mr. Bluff was taken completely by surprise, and Shy beamed all over, for he had not committed the Italian to memory, and could never have done so. No one can tell what a relief it was to the poor fellow to find the king could speak English.

Mr. Bluff acquitted himself with credit, delivered the commodore's compliments in good style, and made arrangements with the king to receive that officer next day, after which we took our leave, all of us sorry that we had not kissed the white hand of the queen and the prettier white hand of the king's sister, a handsome young lady, who afterward married Dom Pedro, Emperor of Brazil.

We retreated in true courtier style, or, as Mr. Bluff expressed it, "We backed and filled until clear of the royal presence, when, boxing short upon our heel, we squared away and ran into the offing."

We had no sooner regained the street than we were beset with crowds of beggars, who turned somersaults and begged for coppers. "Please give it one penny, Mr. Officer; poor blind man nix mangere for sixteen week; give it one penny for buy a little macaroni."

A very genteel-looking fellow, an Italian in appearance, sidled up to the lieutenant two or three times and tried to whisper in his ears, and finally got close enough to do so. I heard him say, "One berry pretty countess want see you come he house; he berry much in lub wiz he."

"The devil he is!" said Bluff. "He may go to thunder. If it was a she now, I'd go and see your countess."

"Well, sair, he is a she," said the Italian. "All the same is 'Merican countess; me no speak Englis too much."

"No, I should think not," said Mr. Bluff. "You were away from home when English was served out, weren't you?"

"Oh, very much; yes, I speaky all same 'Merican frigate. You come see countess, Mr. Count gone way; only sixteen year old. She berry much in lub wiz you; say you berry handsome man; want you come eat macaroni and chocolate wis her. Say bring some 'Merican officer; come take some macaroni long wiz she."

"Oh, no," said Bluff; "in time of war I'd rather cruise singly. I never divide prize-money if I can help it. But, old fellow, duty is duty, and I can't come to-day, but look out for me to-morrow, and I will go and take macaroni with the countess; and remember, if the count comes home you let me know in time."

"Si, signor, guardito a me per domani."

"Domani yourself," said Bluff, which he concluded meant goodmorning.

So we took our way to the boat and returned on board, reporting the king's wishes to the commodore. The commodore was quite disappointed at hearing the king spoke such good English, solely, he said, on Shy's account, who would have had such a fine opportunity to show off his Italian; but the secretary took a different view of the matter, and said, when he got below, "If the commodore is determined to make me a great linguist in spite of myself, I shall take passage in the first ship for home."

Orders were given for Mr. Bluff, Shy, and myself to hold ourselves in readiness to accompany the commodore and captain on shore next day to visit the king, and then seven or eight of us formed a party to visit Mount Vesuvius, and passed a pleasant day, as do all midshipmen on their first visit to Naples.

We met a party of English people going up the mountain, old Mr. and Mrs. Growler and a pretty girl, Miss Biddy, formerly mentioned, and received a kind invitation from the Growlers to visit them at the Rue de Vermicelli, where they had apartments. I went back to the ship with no shoes on my feet and very tired. We had no sooner got on board than I put a plan in operation to play off a joke on good old Mr. Bluff.

I had been an attentive listener to his conversation with the Italian, and remembered all that had passed between them. I sat down and dictated the following note in very bad Italian without considering it necessary to call in Shy to assist me:

"NAPOLI, *Abril 10. Rue de Rosas, No. 20.*

"CARO UFFIZIALE AMERICO: Io te he veduto caro mio en la strada, y a la primera volta yo mi ha inamorata con vuestro excellensa, vuestro bella ojios—vuestro bella figura y vuestro suave voce, tutti mi ha cautivado, dio mio, non he dormito anchi una hora, desde questo tempo no mi dormíré piu si no mi dormi dentro vuestro bracchi. Vuestro veramente amante,

"DONZELLA."

This effusion, written on scented paper and folded "cocked-hat fashion," was sealed with blue wax, and Mr. Bluff being below, I took it down to him, saying that a man had left it alongside and had immediately shoved off, and that, as near as I could distinguish in the twilight, it was the same person who had accosted him in the street that morning. Mr. Bluff smiled all over as he took the note and carefully broke the seal, and his disappointment was great on finding the missive written in what he supposed to be choice Italian.

I was looking at him from the steerage, through the wardroom blinds, watching the emotions of his face, which were very pleasant, even although he could not read the note. Presently he directed the steward to call Mr. Marline, and when I appeared he stepped into his room and, directing me to follow, shut the door.

MR. BLUFF'S POWER OVER WOMEN.

Pointing to the note, he said, "Can I trust you, Mr. Marline, in a little matter that requires secrecy?"

"You can trust me to the death, Mr. Bluff," I replied.

"I believe it, my boy," said Bluff. "Well, here is the same old story; go where I will, all the women fall in love with me. There is a certain magnetism about me that is irresistible, and if I once give chase to a craft she backs her main-topsail immediately. Six women have died of broken hearts for me, Mr. Marline, and one committed suicide because I wouldn't marry her. I feel very sad when I think how heartless I have been, and here is another beautiful creature dead in love with me at first sight."

"Why," said I, "Byron must have had you in mind when he wrote 'Don Juan.'"

Mr. Bluff scrutinized me closely, but, finding I looked serious, he continued: "Why, Mr. Marline, Don Juan wasn't a circumstance to me; his loves were mere bagatelles to mine. You remember that story I once told of Maya; it was every word of it true. And I can tell you another thing, Mr. Marline: the Queen of Portugal was once so dead in love with me that it was five years before she got over it. It affected her in the shape of a lameness that made one of her legs six inches shorter than the other, and they had to feed her on humming-birds and attar of roses the whole time she was ailing. But, sir, he continued, this note is all Greek to me, although I know it is written in Italian, and I must get you to translate it."

I took the note, and, pretending to have much difficulty in making it out, I finally gave Mr. Bluff a literal translation of my own Italian. During the reading I had the breath nearly knocked out of me by Mr. Bluff slapping me on the back, which demonstrations he accompanied by explanatory remarks.

"I knew it, my boy! The women can't help themselves when I heave in sight. She's not over sixteen I'll bet. I wonder if she has a duenna? I'll dress her in midshipman's clothes and take her to America."

"But," said I, "she would have to sling her hammock with the midshipmen, which wouldn't do."

"God bless her," he said, with a sigh. "I will devote my life to her and give up all other loves for the future. I'll ship her as an Italian boy and stow her away in my state-room—no one will suspect it." And so Mr. Bluff went on in ecstasies, while I could scarcely keep from laughing; but here is a translation of the note which so excited the lieutenant:

"MY DEAR AMERICAN OFFICER: I have seen you, my love in the street, and at the first sight of you I surrendered my heart to your excellency. Your beautiful eyes, your beautiful figure, and your sweet voice have captivated me. My heavens! I have not slept a wink since I laid eyes on you; I shall never sleep more if I do not sleep with my head upon that breast.

"Truly your love,
"DONZELLA."

"Now, Mr. Marline," said Bluff, "if I do not return her love that woman is wretched for life, for she will no doubt have a shrinking of her leg just like the Queen of Portugal, and have to be fed on the same diet. What's to be done? How am I to find her? I want to fly to her right away."

"Leave it all to me, Mr. Bluff," I exclaimed. "I will fix it to your satisfaction. I will go ashore to-morrow and find the lady if she is in Naples." With that assurance I left Mr. Bluff to sleep on a bed of roses in the shape of a hair mattress and sought my hammock, with a promise from Mr. Bluff that I should "sleep in" all *his* watches as long as we sailed together.

At eight o'clock next morning I went on deck to take my day's duty, and there was Mr. Bluff walking up and down and beaming all over. I never before saw him so neatly dressed. He wore his best undress coat, with a bran-new epaulet, and sported a shirt-ruffle big enough for a jib. For the first time within my recollection his hands were incased in white kid gloves, and he was trying to hum an opera air which sounded like a medley of "Yankee Doodle" and "The Campbells are Coming."

A dozen men had assembled at the mast to prefer some complaint or await some order, matters to which Mr. Bluff generally paid strict attention; but the Bluff of last week had undergone a transformation, and we could see Cupid on a dolphin tickling him with a small harpoon. He was in the seventh heaven, and did not even notice that the ropes were not "flemished down" about the deck, and that I was the only midshipman in sight; he seemed to be in high good humor, dreaming away his entire watch.

Two hours passed, and still Mr. Bluff seemed sunk in revery. The boatswain stood at the gangway waiting for the order to square yards, when suddenly Bluff turned to me and said, "Mr. Marline, go down and ask Mr. Shacklebags to send me up word what is the greatest *lusus natura* he ever heard of."

"Aye, aye, sir!" cried I, and down I went to Mr. Shacklebags, whom I found in his state-room bending over a plan of the main hold, and glancing occasionally at that magic name worked in copper thimbles over his washstand.

When Mr. Shacklebags had anything weighing upon his mind he always contemplated that name—it seemed to relieve him of all his difficulties.

"Mr. Shacklebags," said I, "Mr. Bluff wants you to send him word what is the greatest *lusus natura* you ever heard of."

"Lusus what, sir?" said Shacklebags.

"*Lusus natura*, sir," I replied.

"Lord bless me!" said he, "I never heard of any in this ship; leastwise, I don't remember any on the list of stores. Gracious heaven! I hope the captain don't want any. I must make out a requisition at once for it."

Poor Shacklebags saw dim visions of a blowing-up from Captain Marvellous and no more going on shore till the mainmast and ballast went.

"Tell him, Mr. Marline," said he, despondingly, "I am sure there is none in the ship." And I accordingly delivered that message.

Mr. Bluff chuckled at this answer and seemed to inwardly enjoy it. By this time about fifty men had congregated at the mainmast and were getting a little impatient, which exhibition of feeling was contrary to the discipline of a ship of war in those days.

Presently Mr. Bluff turned to me again and said, "Go and tell Mr. Shacklebags that the answer to that conundrum is, 'when Mary had a little lamb.'" I jumped down, almost splitting with laughter, and communicated this information to Mr. Shacklebags.

"Bless my soul, sir!" said he, "who is Mary, and what have conundrums to do with her lamb? I don't understand all this, Mr. Marline. I must go up and see Mr. Bluff. There's no Mary on this ship's books as I knows of, though I remember an allotment made out to a person of that name, but I don't think it was Mary Lamb."

"Mr. Shacklebags," said I, "Mr. Bluff is full of his fun this morning, and this is a conundrum and answer he has sent down to you."

"Bless my soul!" said Shacklebags, "that man would joke if

he was dying, and wouldn't even respect his grandmother's corpse. I thought when he went on deck with so much head-sail set he would be yawning about the quarter-deck all day. Tell him, Mr. Marline, I say that if he will haul down his jib and set his foretopmast stay-sail he won't steer so wild." And old Shacklebags laughed at his own conceit.

I delivered Mr. Shacklebags's message to Mr. Bluff, who said, "Well done for Shacklebags; it's the first joke he ever brought forth. And speaking of conundrums, I want to get an answer to the one that came from the countess, and, as you would like to go on shore to-day, I propose that you take a pilot and beat up to that young critter's anchorage and signal to her that you want to communicate, and send a boat on board with my compliments, you know. Mr. Marline, tell her I'll take her in tow."

"Aye, aye, sir!" I replied; and, after rigging myself in Brace's best toggery, I was landed in the dinghy at the palace-stairs.

As may be supposed, I didn't bother myself about the countess, but went to a house where they hired out masquerade costumes and made arrangements for obtaining the use of two female and four bandit suits. This done, I sauntered around the city. While walking in the Rue de Vermicelli I saw a familiar face at a window and two pretty blue eyes twinkling with pleasure as they recognized me. It was my mountain friend, Miss Biddy Growler, and as I stopped to say "good-morning" my heart palpitated like a wooden clock.

Miss Biddy invited me in—an invitation I was not slow in accepting; and entering the house, found myself in the presence of my charmer and a nasty little spaniel and an equally nasty Skye terrier, both of whom yelped like mad as I seized the young beauty around the waist and imprinted a kiss upon her rosy lips.

"Lauk me, Mr. Marline," said she, "'ow unansome of you! even the dogs are ashamed of ye; they hain't used to such things."

"The sooner they get used to them the better, Miss Biddy," I replied. "That is American fashion." And with that I kissed her again.

"Lauk, there you go hagain, Mr. Marline; you Hamericans can't behave yerselves. Lor, if mar was to know hof it she'd 'av' a nervous hattack, and pa 'av' han hattack hof gout; he halways does when hany one tries to kiss me."

"Ah!" said I, "does any one ever try that?"

"Well," said she, blushing, "Lord Meekly does sometimes;

but he haint tried it since the Skye bit 'im in the leg. I wonder he don't bite you; but he don't seem to mind it."

With that I kissed Biddy again, who only exclaimed, "Lauk, Mr. Marline, 'ow you Hamericans do carry hon."

I found Miss Biddy very agreeable, and half an hour slipped away in a twinkling. Her hand and mine became so well acquainted that they didn't care to part company, and were so mixed up you couldn't tell t'other from which.

Miss Biddy and I became like brother and sister, only a little more so. I swore I adored her, and she swore she'd follow me "hover the hocean" and "live for love in a cottage in the 'ills hof Hamerica."

My pleasant interview was suddenly interrupted by the voice of old Mrs. Growler, who sung out from up-stairs, "Bid, hit's time them dumplin's is hon, and, has Lord Meekly will be 'ere this hevenin', you've got to sew a new back to that poplin dress hof yourn."

Poor Biddy blushed scarlet, and only said, "Lor, mar, Mr. Marline his 'ere, and he don't want to know hall hour 'ouseold matters."

Thinking, however, that I had stayed long enough, I took an affectionate leave of my charmer, who invited me to return in the evening with some of my messmates and take tea, which I promised to do about ten o'clock. The nasty little dogs yelped after me as I departed, and the terrier actually put his teeth through my boot while I was giving Biddy a last kiss at the door. I thought to myself that I would reform those dogs' manners when I became more closely connected with the Growler family.

I then took a boat to go back to the ship, and could see Mr. Bluff, while I was a mile away, watching for me through a spy-glass.

No sooner was I over the side than Mr. Bluff wanted me to tell him everything in a breath.

"Well, sir," said I, "I have seen the loveliest creature my eyes ever beheld. Her name is the Countess Guiccioli." (I trusted to Mr. Bluff never having read Lord Byron's life.) "She is about seventeen years old, and is too beautiful to describe. She is madly in love with you, and will meet you at eight o'clock this evening, accompanied by her maid, at the entrance to the Villa Reale. Thence she will accompany you to the house of a friend, as she is afraid to go to her own palace, and a palace it is. You will know the lady by a striped silk dress and lace mantilla, and she will hold a white handkerchief in her hand. The maid will be plainly dressed, with a simple white mantilla on her head. You can't mistake them, Mr. Bluff. How I do envy you, sir!"

"Never mind, Marline, your time will come soon enough—as soon as you mount an epaulet—then all the girls will be after you; and remember, as long as my name is Bluff you shall want for nothing that I can give you. You are a trump, and will make your way in the navy. There's no knowing how this adventure may end. Perhaps I shall get leave of absence, elope with the countess, and travel through Italy. Lord, won't those lieutenants envy me?" With that he went off snapping his fingers as though the world belonged to him.

The midshipmen said that Bluff had been behaving in a most unaccountable manner all the morning, his chief occupation being to propound conundrums to Mr. Shacklebags and then sending that old innocent the answers thereto.

One of these I remember. It was, "Who was the inventor of butter stamps?"

Shacklebags, who had forgotten the morning's experience and was busily occupied in rearranging the thimbles over his wash-stand, sent back word that it was the navy commissioners or the naval committee of Congress, he had forgotten which; but Mr. Bluff informed him that it was Cadmus, as he "first brought letters into Greece."

"Ah, yes," said old Shacklebags, "now I remember. I sailed with that fellow in the schooner Wildcat, and he ate more butter than any man in the mess."

I had formed my plans for the evening. Baby Drinkwater, Slinky Slapjack, Reckless, and myself were to act the part of banditti, while Brace was to play the part of countess and little Block that of lady's maid.

Brace knew Italian words enough to deceive Bluff, who did not understand a syllable, and no doubt depended on the universal language of love to carry him through, if indeed he wasted any thought on the matter; but the chances were, he expected the countess to understand his English while he fully comprehended her Italian.

Just before sunset we saw Mr. Bluff depart for the shore, his shirt-ruffle standing out so prominently that you might have hung a hat on it. His white kids were a trifle large on account of his seldom wearing them, and, notwithstanding his ridicule of the

British officer at Gibraltar, he was steeped in cologne from truck to keelson.

The conspirators followed shortly after, and, repairing to the costumer's establishment, we were soon rigged out to our entire satisfaction. The individual who dressed us exclaimed, when Brace and Block were arrayed, "Que dui bella regatzi Americani bellissima!" Indeed, no one could have looked handsomer than those two boys in women's clothing.

Quarter before eight found us on the spot, the countess sitting in a seat where the light of a distant lamp revealed the beautiful proportions of her figure. Her mantilla was drawn so as to conceal her features, while the maid stood at a little distance. When all was ready, the four banditti concealed themselves in the adjacent shrubbery.

The only thing we were afraid of was that something might occur to prevent Mr. Bluff from coming, or that he might fall in with convivial friends and get to calling for "punchi caldi per dui," in which event we felt that the countess's attractions would be forgotten; but, true as the needle to the pole, Bluff was there to the minute, and as he passed through the gate the countess signaled with her handkerchief, and he walked to the spot where she was sitting.

How little one knows his own shipmates! When you see a man day after day and month after month with a speaking-trumpet in his hand, interesting himself in tar and rope-yarns, thrashing the messenger-boys and damning the berth-deck cooks, you can not associate such a man with anything sentimental. What, then, was our surprise when we saw Mr. Bluff kneel down before the lady and press her hand to his lips.

Here we feared an *eclaircissement,* for Brace's hand was none of the softest; but the lieutenant was so much infatuated that he saw nothing but the loved object of whom he had been dreaming for two days. Titania was not more enamored with Bottom than Bluff with his countess.

"Beautiful lady," said Bluff, "you have stowed my heart so full of love for you that I have two strakes list to port. You see before you the most faithful sailor that ever trod a ship's deck, and although I say it, who perhaps oughtn't to say it, I can tack and veer a ship, close reef a topsail, work ship in a tide-way, and handle one in all weathers as well as any man in Uncle Samuel's navy."

Mr. Bluff expected the countess to strike her flag at once on hearing this lover-like speech, but she only sighed, and said softly, in *Italian*, " O Dio mio ! wha tanas sthis lieut enant is ma king of hims elf ! "

" Si, señora," said Bluff, " until death. Yes, you'll find me so until death. I know it, because in all cases of this kind I have always died at my post."

" At repponde Americano mulli bono Americani prache macaroni."

" Oh, we, mossu," said Bluff. " Yes, this is a great country for macaroni and no mistake, but you have a little too much of it here ; indeed, I may say, beautiful creature, that you rather run it into the ground."

The countess sighed audibly and uttered the most piteous " Dio mio " I ever heard.

Meanwhile, the banditti were gradually closing in upon the loving and unsuspecting Bluff, and, though hardly able to keep from laughing, they drew their wooden swords and prepared for action. Just at the moment when the amorous lieutenant had slipped his arm around the waist of the shrinking countess she exclaimed, "Marito mio !" which was the concerted signal for the assassins to advance. Baby Drinkwater jumped forward, knocking the lieutenant's hat over his eyes and singing out, " Masaniello liberta, lazzaroni !" all of which the bewildered Bluff took for orders to murder him.

The shrieking countess took to flight, followed by her trembling maid, while the lieutenant, in endeavoring to protect her from the bravos, fell floundering under the bench, with his hat so jammed over his eyes that he could see nothing.

In this condition the four assassins had given him sundry murderous gashes in his coat and pantaloons, and had emptied over him a bottle of bullock's blood mixed with water, tinging his shirt-ruffle and giving him the appearance of one covered with wounds.

All this did not occupy a minute ; but Mr. Bluff, though temporarily *hors de combat*, soon regained his feet, tore his hat from his head, and delivered a blow from the shoulder right between the eyes of Baby Drinkwater, who happened to be the assassin nearest to his hand, and sent him flat on his back. As the Baby lay stunned for an instant, the lieutenant might have captured him but for the exertions of the rest. Slinky had brought a wooden rifle to bear on him, Reckless was trying to lasso him from behind, and

I was pelting him with pomegranates from a bush near by, so that altogether Mr. Bluff had his hands full.

I am sorry to say that at this stage of the affair Baby Drinkwater showed the white feather, running away as fast as a weight of one hundred and ninety-six pounds would permit, and never stopping till he reached the ship, where we found him crying when we got on board, his head swollen out of all proportion.

Mr. Bluff, seeing himself surrounded and the tallest assassin leveling his gun, determined to die game. Striking an attitude, he threw open his coat and said, in a firm voice, "Fire, you d—— macaroni! and fire quick, or I'll be into you!" And he made a desperate rush at Slinky, who took to his heels, Reckless and myself following his example.

Mr. Bluff, left master of the field, was too disgusted to follow us far, but returned to get his hat and search the shrubbery for his countess. He soon found that she had disappeared, no doubt frightened by the assassins, whom he supposed had been set upon him by her jealous husband.

Bluff sat down despondingly, exclaiming, "'Twas ever thus from childhood's hour; I never dropped a slice of bread and butter that it didn't fall buttered side down. Just as I had grappled that craft and was about to carry her, in come those infernal pirates and recaptured her; no doubt, blast 'em, they'll claim salvage."

All this time I was hid away listening in the bushes.

"Well," soliloquized Mr. Bluff, "what a trim little craft it was! Her hand a little hard, owing, probably, to her having to wash up the tea things—that's what all the countesses in this country have to do; and then I smelt garlic; that must have been the chambermaid; they all eat it. But this is a bad business; here I am wounded and bloody. My wounds don't hurt me yet, but will when I get stiff. What a joke Teaser would make of this if he ever heard of it! But no one shall know anything about it. Ah me! I never loved a dear gazelle to glad me with her mild black eye, but when she came to know me well some infernal dog was sure to eat her."

While Bluff was indulging in reverie, a Swiss guard of three men came hastily up and addressed him in German.

Hearing the outcry, they had entered the Villa Reale to see what was the matter.

Mr. Bluff listened to the unfamiliar German sounds, and replied, "No speaky Italian."

"Betrunken," said the corporal.

"Nicht betrunken," said another; "ich habe ihn gesehen."
"Kennen sie Deutsch?" said a third.
"No parle vous Italiano," said Bluff.
"Kennen sie Italienisch?"
"No polly vous Italiano, mossoo," said Bluff; whereupon the guard clapped him on the shoulder and beckoned him to follow them, which he did as quietly as possible. Bluff was quite heart-broken. While he thought his prize in danger he fought the assassins like a tiger, but now that he had lost his countess, perhaps forever, his heart sank away down to his boots and there was no more fight in him.

The guard took their prisoner to the American minister's, who, considering it a case of "larking," sent Mr. Bluff on board ship. As he went over the side Mr. Teaser was on deck, but Bluff went quietly below to his room, a sadder if not a wiser man than when he went on shore.

Teaser, who was always ready for a talk, was surprised at Bluff's taciturnity, and, having heard of the conundrums propounded by the latter to old Shacklebags, he called out, "Stop, Bluff, I want to give you a conundrum. Why are you like a ship in the middle of the Atlantic?"

"Don't bother me!" said Bluff, as he darted below; but Teaser bawled after him, "Because you are half seas over."

This was too much for Bluff, who came back and gave Teaser a conundrum: "Why are you like a man who has a room next to an idiot?"

"Oh, bosh!" said Teaser, "that's no conundrum at all."

"Yes, it is," said Bluff; "because you are next door to a fool," which was so much crosser than Bluff had ever before been known that Teaser was quite puzzled, and it took him all the rest of the watch to work out the problem.

After our adventure in the Villa Reale the party, minus Baby Drinkwater, who had so ingloriously fled, returned to the costumer's and assumed our proper clothing. Then, after discussing a bottle of champagne, we repaired to Vermicelli Street to spend the evening with Miss Growler.

At the door we were met by a pretty English maid with rosy cheeks and eyes as blue as turquoise. It was as much as she could do to keep those nasty dogs from biting us, and indeed one of them tore Reckless's trousers, which he had borrowed for the purpose of coming on shore.

When shown into the parlor, we found the family assembled, consisting of old Mr. Growler, reading *Galignani's Messenger* with the aid of a huge pair of horn spectacles, Mrs. Growler with a scrap-basket, from which she was concocting a patch-work quilt, and pretty Miss Biddy in a blue silk dress sitting beside a gaunt-looking Englishman, who was no other than Lord Meekly. His lordship surveyed us from head to foot with his eyeglass as we entered the room, as much as to say, "What the devil animals are these?" while Miss Biddy received us with great *sang-froid*, merely nodding to me and not deigning to notice my companions.

She undertook to introduce me to Lord Meekly, but remarked, "Ah, I've forgot your name, sir, and 'ope you won't be hoffended at my not remembering it. I think I met you hon the mountain."

I was very near saying, "Biddy, I am the young man who kissed you so often this morning," but, determining to pay her off, I bowed coolly and took a seat alongside old Mr. Growler, inquiring what was the news, while the other midshipmen commenced making friends with the terrier, King Charles spaniel, and a cat with six kittens, that were gamboling on a mat in the bay-window.

Old Growler, in answer to my inquiry, informed me that there was a great demand for 'orn buttons hon the Continent, and that 'orn had riz; pork was dull and nominally easier; the coffee market had opened with one cent decline; butter was a shade stronger, and lard at good prices; flour was without decided change, though round hoop shipping Ohio barrels brought the best prices; small lots of domestic molasses changed hands within the range of yesterday's quotations, etc.

I don't know how long the old fellow would have continued in this line if I had not suddenly inquired the price of soft soap. Soap was not mentioned, he said, but tallow was decidedly dull, which information was extremely interesting to me.

I then took a seat alongside Miss Biddy, determined to force the conversation with her and throw Meekly in the shade.

"I took the liberty," said I, "of bringing one or two friends to tea with me in accordance with your kind invitation." Here his lordship looked daggers.

"Lauk, Mr. Whatsyourname," said Biddy, "hi don't think hi ever hinvited you to tea; you must be mistaken. We 'av' done tea, hand I ham going to the hopera with Lord Meekly, hand, my lord, hit's time to go."

Ah, thought I, is that the way the wind blows?

Biddy then went to the door and cried out, "''Orton, fetch me my hopera-cloak hand my 'at."

The pretty maid soon appeared with the things in her hand, when I stepped forward and took them from her, saying to Miss Biddy, "Let me relieve your sister of these things and help you on with them."

"My sister hindeed!" she exclaimed, her face growing scarlet. "My maid, sir. Hand I shan't hask you to 'elp me hon with my hopera-cloak; Lord Meekly can do that." And she looked into his eyes confidingly.

"Aw, yes," he said, "'pon my soul, I'll 'elp you hon with your coat, aw, hand think hit devilish aw hintrusive for hany one helse to try it."

"Sir," said I, "I will call upon you, if you please, in the morning. There is my card, sir," handing him one of Mr. Bluff's, which had been given me in the morning by that gallant sailor to leave with the countess.

"Aw, bless my soul!" said his lordship, "'ow very hextraordinary! Aw, yes, aw, 'pon my soul—very glad to see yar—yes, 'pon my honor."

Biddy gave a little scream, hurried on her traps, and saying, "Good-night, mar, set hup for me," she and Meekly bolted from the room.

Old Mrs. Growler had for some time been watching Reckless and little Block, who were busily engaged in tying the kittens' tails together, while the mother cat was looking anxiously on, wondering what all the proceedings meant. Old Growler, deep in *Galignani*, saw and heard nothing.

Mrs. Growler suddenly remarked, "I hain't going to sit 'ere, Mr. Growler, hand see them cats' tails a-tortured so. If as 'ow them gentlemen can't behave as sich, hi'm not hagoin' to sit hin this room." And out she went.

"Aw, 'pon my soul," said old Growler, "you mustn't mind 'er, young gentlemen; she's allers so, a little cantankerous, as you Yankees say. She's got Meekly hon the brain to-night; don't mind 'er. Bid will be 'ere hin han 'our, hand she'll make hit hagreeable to you. I must go to my banker's hand see the price hof shrimps hin market, hand whether periwinkles 'av' gone hup. Henjoy yourselves till Bid comes 'ome, and then hit will be hall right."

So saying, Mr. Growler departed, leaving us alone with the cats

WE DISPOSE OF THE DOGS AND KITTENS. 271

and dogs, the latter looking rather uneasy at being shut up with such strange company.

We all shouted when we heard the street-door close, and concluded it was the jolliest tea-party to which we had ever been invited. What were we to do? All the household had departed, and we felt as if Meckly had gone clear to windward of us.

"Well, boys," said Reckless, "let's make a good lark of this." So stripping the covers off the sofa-cushions, he commenced stowing the cat and kittens away in bulk, while I did the same with the two dogs, which barked like mad and struggled hard to escape from us. We turned the room upside down, and when old Growler returned he found that sofas and chairs "had declined," cushions were a "trifle lower," pictures had "riz," as we had shortened all the hangings, curtains were "rather tight," as we had tacked them to the windows, and bookcases were "flat," as we laid them all on the floor, and then we departed.

We hurried to the wharf, took a boat, and proceeded on board with our plunder. When we arrived alongside we didn't know what to do with our prizes, but Reckless, who never wanted for ingenuity, proposed taking out the tompions of the spar-deck carronades and slipping the dogs and cats into the guns, which was done, and each of the nine guns on the larboard side had a cat or a dog stowed snugly within it.

Thus ended our day's frolic.

CHAPTER XXII.

THE COMMODORE VISITS KING BOMBA—A WIG ADVENTURE—THE COMMODORE'S EXTRAORDINARY ADDRESS TO THE KING—CAT AND DOG SALUTES—WHAT BEFELL US AT THE BANQUET TO THE KING.

NEXT morning I was up betimes, determined to put the finishing touch to my fun. I knew how much Mr. Teaser would be delighted to hear of the adventure of Mr. Bluff and the countess, and that I could get several "sleeps in" by telling it to him. Bluff had played Teaser so many tricks that I felt sure the latter would never let him up.

I waylaid Mr. Teaser, therefore, at seven bells on the gun-deck, for, as he was going on duty for the day at eight o'clock, I knew that was my only chance with him.

"Excuse me, Mr. Teaser," said I, "but I have the best joke in the world to tell you about Mr. Bluff, if you will promise never to let any one know you got it from me."

"Good!" said Teaser, his eyes sparkling. "Tell it, Mr. Marline, and I promise to keep your secret till I die."

Whereupon I told him all about our adventure of the night before, with the exception of that part relating to the Growler family.

"Now," said Teaser, when I had finished the recital, "Bluff won't say his soul is his own while this cruise lasts. He has run me ever since he came on board, and I'll pay him off," and Teaser laughed till the tears ran down his cheeks.

"Now, Mr. Marline, run up and see if the bumboat has brought off the morning paper." I soon returned with a little sheet twelve by fourteen inches, printed in Italian, with which Teaser repaired to the wardroom.

The mess were at breakfast, and Mr. Bluff, looking very serious, was quietly sipping his coffee, and his messmates looked in vain for his usual humorous sallies.

Mr. Teaser was apparently absorbed in the little newspaper, when all of a sudden he exclaimed, "Great heavens, how awful! I never read of such a thing before in all my life!"

"What is it?" cried all the mess.

"Why," said Teaser, "the most horrible assassination of a beautiful young countess and her maid. The murderers can not be found. One of those implicated is an American officer."

I was looking down the hatch, and shall never forget the expression of grief and horror on poor Mr. Bluff's countenance. He was white as a sheet; but so anxious were his messmates to hear the particulars of the affair that they did not notice his excitement.

Then Mr. Teaser read the imaginary article, making it up as he went along, commencing, "Horrible Atrocity! Dreadful Assassination of a Young and Beautiful Countess! Escape of the Murderers!

"Last evening, at eight o'clock, shrieks were heard, mingled with cries of 'Help!' 'Murder!' near the east gate of the Villa Reale, and the guard promptly rushed to the direction of the outcry. The noise, however, was so soon hushed that the guard were for a time misled, and some moments elapsed before they could get on the track of the assassins.

"At gate No. 4, near the image of Santa Agatha, two females were discovered, both having been murdered by blows with a knife. One of the bodies was evidently that of a lady of rank, while the other was dressed like an attendant. A large concourse of people soon assembled, and the bodies were recognized by the agonized husband of the lady, Count Guiccioli, who had just returned from his estate in the country. The whole affair is shrouded in mystery, and, strange to say, an officer of the American frigate is implicated. As one of the guard ran toward the north entrance, to cut off persons attempting to escape in that direction, he came upon a stout man in the uniform of an American officer, apparently struggling with two smaller men dressed as banditti. The officer broke away at that moment and ran rapidly toward the water, followed by his persecutors, leaving his hat and one of his shoes behind him, which it is hoped will lead to his identification; but he ran so rapidly that it was impossible for guards or assassins to keep up with him."

"It's a confounded lie!" said Bluff, bringing his hand down heavily on the table; "and whoever says it isn't I will cut out his tongue and put my heel upon him. I never ran from any man, much less an infernal lazzaroni. I knocked one fellow down, and the rest ran like a flock of sheep."

Here Bluff paused, dumfounded to think how he had committed himself.

"*You*, Bluff!" cried all the officers in chorus; "in the name of heaven, what had *you* to do with it?" for no one suspected that Teaser had not been reading a veritable extract from the newspaper, forgetting for the moment that his knowledge of the Italian language was rather limited.

Poor Bluff was in a sad quandary. The horrible story read by Teaser made him feel badly enough, but to be accused of running away from an Italian robber was more than he could bear, and he rushed to his room and shut himself in.

About noon the American minister came on board to accompany the commodore in his visit to the king. The first thing he asked was concerning the poor lieutenant whom he had sent on board the night before very much battered, and who seemed to have been drinking freely. The minister said that the officer had been brought to his house by some Swiss guards, who reported finding him intoxicated and bleeding in the Villa Reale. Here was a mystery which time alone could unravel, and Bluff seemed to be getting deeper and deeper into it. He did not emerge from his room that day, but went on the doctor's list, Mr. Teaser being appointed in his place on the commodore's staff when the latter visited the king.

At a little past one we left the ship, the commodore, captain, and officers in full uniform and the minister in court dress—a gorgeous affair, which threw the navy costumes entirely into the shade.

We disembarked at the palace-steps, where the king's chamberlain was in waiting, who conducted us to the royal palace, a large and handsome building fronting the great square. A guard of Swiss soldiers was turned out to receive us—tall, splendid-looking men, a striking contrast to the sallow macaroni-eaters that composed the Neapolitan army.

The Bourbon kings, having little confidence in troops raised from the people over whom they ruled, had from time immemorial imported these Swiss mercenaries to serve as their body-guard, who had always proved faithful to their employers even unto death. The King of Naples had two thousand of these foreigners in his employ at high wages, and allowed them every indulgence, while his Neapolitan soldiers got eight francs a month, with an allowance of five cents a day for rations. But this would purchase a daily supply of macaroni sufficient for an anaconda, and provide them with half a pint of *vin ordinaire*, which was sour enough to turn the stomach of an ostrich.

The King of Naples carried on his court in great style, and seemed outwardly to be the happiest of monarchs; but his was really no bed of roses, for he stood in constant fear of assassination.

The Swiss soldiers constantly surrounded the palace, one thousand of them being always on guard. Mounted men were kept stationed at every street-corner, who at a signal galloped to the palace and formed in squadrons. All the forts around the city were manned with picked soldiers commanded by Swiss officers (for none other could be trusted), and the portcullises were kept closed night and day. The king's prime minister was always watched by a spy to him unknown, and that spy was watched in his turn. The waiters in the public houses were detectives to report the conversation of the guests when it had the slightest bearing on the political situation. Often before a man had time to finish his breakfast he was carried to prison to answer for some unguarded speech made at table. Private families were not exempt from this system of espionage. Sons watched their fathers, brothers watched each other, and young women have even been known to consign their lovers to the Castle of St. Elmo for some unguarded expression. In fact, a reign of terror prevailed in Naples such as was unknown in any other part of the civilized world at that time, unless it might have been in Spain.

When the king rode out it was in a close carriage surrounded with guards; that is, he was supposed to be in the close carriage, though in reality it is said the supposed king was only a clever dummy, dressed and padded to a perfect resemblance of his Majesty, and the real king followed at some distance behind clad in a more unpretending manner.

The royal party always went at a gallop, preceded by fifty dragoons to clear the street, and people were frequently run over and killed or maimed; but life was of little account in Naples compared with Bomba's convenience, and nothing pleased his soldiers better than to trample over the lazzaroni sleeping about the pavement.

Yet this great city, where tyranny in its worst form held sway, where the prisons were filled with political offenders, the streets swarming with soldiers, and a citizen could not say his soul was his own, where fathers, mothers, brothers, and sisters were playing the part of spies on each other, appeared to an uninitiated person the happiest place on earth. People seemed to have but one idea, and that was amusement.

The brilliant skies and balmy air invited all the world to come out of doors, and the streets of Naples were filled with as gay a throng as those of Paris.

In the evening some fifteen theatres, from the grand San Carlos, where you paid your dollar for a seat, to the little establishment where the "Marionettes" performed for a quarter of a carlini, were in full blast, and crowds assembled to witness the still cheaper performances of Punchinello, where the vulgar wit of the performers afforded constant amusement to the audience. Yet all performances were watched over by detectives, and if by any accident a word was uttered that could be twisted into political significance, the offender very soon found himself locked up in the castle.

The king had evidently imitated the policy of the Roman emperors, who lavished vast sums on the amusement of the people, so that they should not interfere with politics; and although, unlike some of his prototypes, he did not make the fountains run with wine, he ordained the cultivation of the grape to such an extent that the exhilarating beverage was placed within the reach of the poorest inhabitants, and people could hardly die of starvation when half a penny would buy a good meal of macaroni.

Cold and hunger are great promoters of revolution, especially in a country where all good and evil are supposed to emanate from the head of the government; and no doubt but for the soft, enervating climate and the small quantity of food required to fill the stomach, the revolutions in Naples would have been frequent. When, however, there was the least appearance of rising, the populace were ridden down like sheep.

I did not intend to touch upon politics when I commenced this chapter, for the subject of these pages is more properly of midshipmen's frolics; but no doubt the same ideas would strike any one on a first visit to Naples. A short sojourn there, however, will break a stranger of the habit of indulging in such speculations; he soon learns to be indifferent to the political sufferings of the people, and finds that as long as he minds his own business and does not mix himself in affairs of the government he will enjoy himself and receive every indulgence from the authorities.

While I was musing I was keeping the commodore waiting, and he at length good-naturedly asked me if Captain Marvellous ever sent me to the mast-head, at the same time giving me a profound wink.

At length we were all ready to advance. The guard at the palace-gate presented arms, and the commodore and suite took off their hats, bowing low. Unfortunately, a brisk sea-breeze was blowing, when the wind caught under the lee-clew of the commodore's wig and carried it down the street at the rate of ten knots an hour. All the little lazzaroni at once started in pursuit, and the commodore, left bald-headed, with scarcely a sprig of hair in sight, turned coolly around, lifted Captain Marvellous's wig, and, putting it on his own head (hind part before), marched into the royal presence.

The captain stood astounded. No one had ever before seen him without his wig; in fact, nobody on board ship knew whether he wore a wig or not. Go into his presence at any time or place, and Captain Marvellous had always a bushy head of hair, and in gales of wind he had never been known to call any one to hold his hair on, yet here he was exposed before his officers and the entire Swiss guard.

"Come on, Marvellous," sung out the commodore; "you've got to scud under bare poles for a little while. I expect it isn't the first time you've done it, judging by the looks of your truck. Mr.

Marline, go back and fetch up my sky-scraper, if you can get it from those beggars, and give it to the captain, who will want it, while I sail in to hail his Majesty," and the commodore walked on, accompanied only by the minister. He turned around once more and hailed the horror-stricken captain, saying, "Marvellous, when you bend that sky-scraper of mine see that the clews are well toggled, for I think it rather large for you, although about the right color."

Poor Captain Marvellous stood with his cocked hat on over his perfectly bald pate, which shone like a looking-glass, while the Swiss guards presented arms and wondered why he didn't move on. They would have stood there for ever under the same circumstances.

In the mean while I had recaptured the fugitive wig and brought it in triumph to the captain, expecting to receive his heartfelt thanks, but Marvellous took hold of the old sunburnt appendage with his thumb and finger, and with an awful wry face transferred it to his head. The wig was much too large for the captain, who looked, as Teaser expressed it, like a rat peeping through a bunch of oakum.

At length we found ourselves in the presence of royalty. The king, queen, and all the court were waiting to receive us. The commodore, with his old red wig hind part before, contrasting with his coal-dyed whiskers was the observed of all observers, and I was forcibly reminded of the passage in Milton—

"Where perhaps some beauty lies,
The cynosure of neighboring eyes."

Perhaps the Neapolitan court took these two officers for specimens of the Whig party, for Captain Marvellous was now presented with his red whiskers and black wig, which looked, if possible, worse than the commodore's.

The Italians could with difficulty restrain their mirth, for they have a keen sense of the ridiculous; but their strict decorum finally prevailed, although one young lady to whom I was introduced said she would like *so* much to visit America, they made such beautiful wigs there.

After the preliminaries had been gone through with, Commodore Blowhard, to the astonishment of everybody, produced a paper and read an address to the king, which it seems had occasioned him several days of hard study.

"I come, your Majesty," said old Blowhard, winking his eye as usual, "by order of my Government, to make your royal Majesty's acquaintance, and to endeavor to cement the existing friendship between the two countries. Founded, as our Governments are, on the same principles, and sympathizing, as we do, in all political matters, there is every reason why the warmest friendship should exist between us. We are each in a measure necessary to the other; what one requires the other can supply. We have the coldest climate in the world, and our ice crop is the largest in creation. You have the softest climate on the face of the earth, and groves of lemon- and orange-trees teeming with delicious fruit. You want our ice to cool your lemonade.

"Ours is a practical and money-making people. Every man in America is a millionaire, and there are no laborers, while you have thousands of idle lazzaroni wanting occupation. We open our arms to them and invite them to come and build our railroads and dig our canals, while our native population are all awaiting an opportunity to come to your delicious clime and spend their wealth. Yours is the land of the poet, the painter, and the sculptor. The names of Fanny Ellsler, Cracovienne, and Masaniello are household words with us. In our granite hills we want to adorn our palaces with their works of art, and shed the refulgence of their rays over the rude landscape that nature has bestowed upon us.

"You have a Mount Vesuvius, which often gives you trouble, and sometimes destroys your cities; we have the Falls of Niagara, which could extinguish it in half an hour. You have music and the drama, and Punch and Judy in all their perfection. Our people desire to imitate you in all these things. Your climate is enervating, and you require a change to one where you will be invigorated by the blasts from our snow-clad hills. Our institutions are marvelous, our people the most go-ahead of any in the world. They will show you how to climb a rainbow, slide down a streak of lightning, scalp an Indian, grin a panther to death, and, in short, whip everlasting creation.

"We want your statuary to adorn the steps of our Capitol, the greatest building in the world; we want your pictures to adorn its rotunda, the largest rotunda in existence—not but what I think our painters and sculptors are quite equal to any you have ever produced in Italy.

"We welcome you, one and all, to America. Come by railroad, come by sea, whichever way you please, for our motto is *E Pluribus Unum* (the eagle's flight is out of sight).

"In conclusion, your Majesty, I will say we are two great countries. The web of our existence is of a mingled nap, good and evil together. Like water and whisky unmixed, the one is too weak, the other too strong; but, when properly stirred together, a most invigorating drink. You are like a ship sailing on a great lake with all sail set, and with a crew too weak to shorten sail in a squall, while we are like a ship under double-reefed top-sail and foretop-sail, stay-sail set, snug as a bug in a rug."

During this speech the company seemed paralyzed; they had never heard the like before, and only two or three of the court understood a word of it. When the commodore finished, the king bowed low, and said, "Thank you, commodore; walk in to collation. Do me the favor to hand in the queen. Captain, do me the favor to hand in madame the Countess Catanna," and the courtiers and ourselves all followed in the wake.

The commodore was, to use his own expression, "flung flat aback" at the king's not responding to the speech, which Shy and himself had been three weeks preparing, though the last touch was all his own, and he had even thought of getting Shacklebags to set it to music.

"Well," he said, as he left the presence, "these people are macaroni in all their institutions, and could never rise to a republic half as easy as we could come down to a monarchy. They are not a go-ahead people, and can't imbibe our ideas, while we imbibe all theirs, imitate their corrupt practices and enervating customs.

"We show a strong liking for monarchy, which would fit us like a purser's shirt on a handspike. I wouldn't be surprised to see Congress import a Swiss guard for the President before I die. Captain Marvellous, do you understand a pun?"

"Yes, sir," said the captain, bristling up; "I think I understand a little of everything. You might as well ask me if I know how to make a drumstick."

"Well, then," said the commodore, "what would majesty be without its externals?"

"Well," said the captain, "it would be the naked truth."

"No, no!" said the commodore. "Majesty without its externals would be *ajest!* Do you see it?" But Captain Marvellous couldn't see it at all.

"Now, captain," continued the commodore, "how do you make a drumstick?"

"Well, sir," said the captain, "I would send for the carpenter and tell him to get a piece of ash two feet two inches long, shape it like the lower joint of a turkey-leg, and put a knob on the end."

"Bosh!" said the commodore. "I could do it easier than that. I would take a drum and put it into a barrel of glue, and it would stick fast enough." And in this intellectual conversation they whiled away the time.

The collation lasted just an hour. Everything was kingly and decorous in the extreme. Captain Marvellous in vain endeavored to introduce his favorite toast—

> "Naples and America,
> Always weak and never strong."

When the king wanted us to go he bowed, and the minister pulled the commodore's coat-tail, and we finally got away.

The commodore invited the king to visit the ship next day, and said, "I hope your Majesty won't forget to answer my speech." The king smiled, and said he would be on board at 1 P. M.

Just before reaching the ship the commodore said, "Here, captain, is your wig; please give me mine," and the captain had to change wigs in the boat before the whole crew, much to his chagrin. The commodore did not mind it, as he made no secret of his bald pate.

"Marvellous," said he, "you will find your sky-scraper a little too large just now after I have been carrying sail on it so hard. Take a single reef in it for a day or two till it gets its set. Mr. Teaser, make a note in the log of this exchange of sky-scrapers between the captain and myself, for this is a historical day." Then we ascended the side and sought our respective quarters.

Next day everything was got ready for the king's reception. The decks were holy-stoned till they looked as bright as a kitchen dresser, the sails were neatly furled, life-lines got upon the yards for the men to hold on by when manning them. The officers were in full uniform, and the sailors were dressed in white.

Preparations were made for firing a salute; the spar-deck guns were carefully loaded, the cartridges being sent softly home to prevent their breaking.

So carefully was all this done that the dogs and cats were not disturbed.

Just at two bells a beautiful little corvette, under the Italian flag, was seen standing out from the mole, with royals set and the king's standard at the main. As soon as she passed the point of

KING BOMBA PAYS US A VISIT.

the mole she hauled on a wind, braced sharp up, and steered for our stern, jumping over the water like a thing of life.

As the corvette approached us it could be seen that the king himself, in undress naval uniform, was at the helm, and he seemed to handle the vessel with the ease of a veteran tar.

Just before the corvette's bow reached the line of our stern the king signaled with his hands, the courses were hauled up, the main-top-sail flew aback, and the ship lay quiet in the water.

"Well done, king!" sung out the commodore from the horse-block. "I couldn't have done it better myself." The king bowed, though he couldn't hear exactly what the commodore said.

The deck of the Calliope, for such was the name painted on the stern of the corvette, was crowded with officers in splendid uniforms. Two large barges towing astern with well-dressed crews now hauled alongside, into one of which stepped the king and his ministers, and into the other the twelve royal chamberlains, bedizened with gold lace, and each having a large gold key embroidered in the middle of his back.

At this moment our crew jumped into the rigging and sprung into their respective stations aloft. Every man stood as firm and square on the yards as if on *terra firma*, and the ship presented a most beautiful appearance. "Ah, bellissima," said the courtiers, "queste Americanos sono bello marineri!" The royal standard of Naples and Sicily was run up at our main royal mast-head, and it fluttered aloft just as the king came alongside. Then eight tiny side-boys ran to hand his Majesty the man-ropes, which he boldly laid hold of, and sprung up the ship's side with the agility of a midshipman.

When his Majesty stood on our deck, in his neat undress navy uniform, he looked every inch a sailor.

He was received by all the officers, headed by the commodore and captain. The marines presented arms, and the first lieutenant sung out in a stentorian voice, "Starboard, fire!" and the gun belched forth its ringing sound. When three seconds had elapsed Mr. Barnacle gave the order again, "Larboard, fire!" but this time there was no response. Then the order "Starboard, fire!" was quickly given, and the gun went off at the word.

But when the order "Larboard, fire!" was again repeated without eliciting a sound, "the devil was to pay and no pitch hot." Up to this time everything had worked well, but here was a *contretemps* of which very few understood the cause. However, the first lieutenant, nothing dismayed, went on firing the salute all from one side, for none of the larboard guns answered the summons until the nine guns on the starboard side were all discharged, when they had to fly to the gun-deck, where, fortunately, the guns had been kept loaded and the shot drawn. Finally Mr. Barnacle managed to get through with twenty-one guns, but it was the most bungling salute ever fired from a ship of war.

The commodore stood unmoved, but his eye twinkled, showing that he enjoyed the fun. The captain tore up and down the quarter-deck like a madman, while Mr. Barnacle seized a belaying-pin and stood like a bull at bay, as if wondering whom he should pitch into. The midshipmen, who understood the whole matter, turned pale, for they saw visions of mast-head in the distance.

The quarter-gunners were filled with dismay. In their minds' eye they saw nothing but disratings and stopped grog, and altogether the ship presented such a scene as is seldom witnessed on board a man-o'-war.

"Your Majesty," said the commodore, "must excuse this salute; it's what Captain Marvellous calls the French touch, but I will make it up to you. I will send the sloop of war Gingerbread down here on purpose to show you how a salute ought to be fired—she does such things up brown." In the mean time the commodore expected the king to answer his speech of the day before, but the latter probably distrusted his ability to meet the commodore's expectations. At all events he said nothing, and the company walked aft to take a look over the spar-deck.

Meanwhile Mr. Barnacle had ordered the cartridges drawn from the larboard guns. When the cartridge-bag was drawn from gun No. 9, near the gangway, it was noticed that the priming-wire had not touched it. "There must be a wad in this 'ere gun, Somers," said old Tomkin. "Put in the worm and see what is the matter." So in went the worm again, which encountered something soft, and the most unearthly screams came from the bottom of the bore. At this moment the commodore was passing forward with his Majesty to inspect the ship, and stopped suddenly, attracted by the sounds.

"By George!" said the commodore, "there must be a ventriloquist in your party. I never heard a carronade scream that way before, though I have often heard them bark. There must be a mongoose in there. Screw him out, quarter-gunner, and let his Majesty see what queer things we load our guns with." With that

THE KITTENS MAKE A SENSATION.

the quarter-gunner hauled out the worm with Mrs. Growler's old cat sticking to it.

Here was an explanation of the mystery. The old mother of the six kittens, squirming and caterwauling like mad, worked herself loose, flew aft, and disappeared through the cabin skylight.

The commodore laughed heartily. "Split my top-sails, Captain Marvellous," said he, "but this is the awfulest category in which I ever saw a ship. Your Majesty must see that the captain was on shore last night, and must be troubled with rats. Here, Mr. Barnacle, let's see what you've got the rest of the guns loaded with. I should think your Majesty would enjoy this. You can say when you go on shore that you saw the cats served out in handsome style on board the Thunderbum."

In the mean time the quarter-gunner had screwed out a kitten, which, though half dead for want of its mother's milk, arched its little back and seemed determined to fight to the last.

The captain was furious, the king calm but amused, the commodore bursting with laughter, and the Italian officers astonished. "Capito!" said one, "che sono mulli gati davero le Americani sono brave gente."

Cat after cat, or kitten after kitten, were extracted from the carronades, all more or less exhausted, and the commodore suggested to Captain Marvellous that he thought it would be more convenient to serve out this cat-soup in a ladle, and give the company a chance to taste it, whereupon the captain walked away, looking daggers.

"I am sorry we can not give your Majesty a greater variety," said the commodore; "but there are two more guns, and I never knew a cat to have over six kittens. Perhaps we shall find a grizzly bear in the next one, so let's enjoy the fun while it lasts." The Skye terrier next appeared, yelping and bloody; and as soon as he could get clear of the screw he rushed aft, setting up such a frightful howl as was never heard before.

"I knew we'd find a grizzly," said the commodore, "although that is a very small one. Your Majesty, they are common in America, where they weigh two thousand pounds; this fellow must have been boiled down so as to get him into a gun. I expect we'll find an alligator next. Go ahead, quarter-gunner, let's have an alligator."

Just then the King Charles came forth, the most dilapidated animal ever beheld. Poor Biddy Growler would have been heart-broken could she have seen him hanging on to the screw of the worm.

"There!" said the commodore, "that accounts for the milk in the cocoanut. His Majesty King Charles determined to surprise you and meet you on board with his suite, and the trouble is they all got into the wrong box. Mr. Teaser, make a note of all this in the log-book. I must make a full report of the transaction to the navy commissioners. This is the best cat and dog story I ever heard. Mr. Shacklebags, I want you to set it to music."

The excitement on board the ship was intense; all hands were dying with a desire to laugh outright, which none dared to do. The men kept aloft all this time were wondering what was the matter, while the sailors caught up the little kittens, which were turned into pets, the King Charles and the Skye terrier meanwhile having their wounds dressed preparatory to adoption into messes No. 4 and No. 13.

"Well, your Majesty," said the commodore, "I don't think Captain Marvellous has any more of his menagerie to show you at present, unless he has his old Berkshire sow in the manger, which supplies him with milk and butter all the year round."

"Dio mio!" said the king, "I never heard of such a sow as that before"; and he explained this extraordinary circumstance to his astonished courtiers, who exclaimed, "Cospetto! que maravillio." The captain wanted to deny the truth of the commodore's story, but saw that it was useless to contend against old Blowhard, who could never be stopped when once under headway.

All the events of this never-to-be-forgotten day were minutely chronicled in the Thunderbum's log-book and signed by the commodore, for, said he, these transactions are historical, and he often spoke of the day when Captain Marvellous got into a category, and his guns went off so dogged nicely.

After the commodore had bothered Captain Marvellous as much as possible, he proceeded with the inspection of the ship, which was very satisfactory, the king declaring he had never before seen a vessel half so clean, and recommended his naval officers to notice the efficiency of the Americans—"especially in firing cat salutes," remarked one of the Neapolitans as he fell out of the king's hearing.

When the galley was reached every one stopped while his royal Majesty tasted the ship's soup, an example which was followed by the court. Some of them, indeed, took a ladleful, and wanted more.

PIERRE HOPES TO ASTONISH THE KING.

After the inspection the party returned to the quarter-deck, where the captain and first lieutenant seemed to be carrying on a lively altercation. Old Barnacle, with his wart spread out larger than usual, held on to the inevitable belaying-pin, as if he would like to give the captain a clip over the head. I only heard him say, "Cats and dogs, Captain Marvellous, a first lieutenant can not be expected to run round with a worm and ladle looking into guns for unexpected animals, and, sir, I shall send on an immediate application to leave your ship," which last remark brought the captain to terms.

I had nearly forgotten to mention that Pierre Poisson, the commodore's cook, had been set to work to astonish the king when he should visit the ship. The commodore had said to him, "Now, Pierre, you must outdo yourself. Let's have such *entremets* as were never seen before; give us something original. If you do the thing well and astonish the king, you shall be presented to his Majesty."

Pierre was allowed *carte blanche* to get what he wanted for the grand occasion, but, to the astonishment of everybody, he returned from market bringing with him only a little pig and a string of onions. Some one said, "But, Pierre, this is a live king that's coming on board, and you must let yourself out, and not disgrace the American flag."

"Nevaire mine," answered Pierre, "you sall see zat wich you sall see. If I no make zat king happee, zen you no call me ze fus cuke in ze Unised State. You vill zee everyzing in ze worl on zat table, an ze king vill zee someting zat vill him astonis." And Pierre shook his head and went to work.

A long table had been set in the cabin, and, in truth, it was beautifully arranged. There were boned turkeys, partridges *à la* Mount Vesuvius, patés, jellies, *méringues*, whipped creams, etc., but the grand *chef-d'œuvre* was the center-piece, of which the design was a combination of the Capitol at Washington and the Castle of St. Elmo in Naples. The idea of this classic composition originated in the fertile brain of Commodore Blowhard, and it was beautifully carried out by the artistic Pierre.

This center-piece covered nearly the entire breadth of the table, about six feet, was eight feet long and four feet high.

Imagine the center of our Capitol with a Castle of St. Elmo added to form each wing, surrounded by lakes, fountains, and forests, and you may form a faint idea of Pierre's *chef-d'œuvre*.

The dome, which was modeled after that of St. Peter's, was

movable, and at a certain time, when a music-box in the depths of the center-piece began to play, an unseen wire would lift the dome and out would fly canary-birds, while the fountains would spurt champagne.

Had this all been carried out in the spirit in which it was conceived, nothing like it would ever have been seen on shipboard.

We left the king much gratified with his visit to the berth-deck. The officers and courtiers had lighted their cigars and were lounging around the decks, while his Majesty reclined on an ottoman that had been brought from the cabin.

The sea-breeze was blowing freshly, and volumes of fresh air were carried by the windsails to the lower regions of the frigate.

The bedizened old chamberlains had been poking around in every direction, and two of them, seeing the distended windsail like a huge post invitingly before them, yielded to the temptation, leaned against it, and, before they could think what was the matter, the windsail gave way and precipitated them both to the lower deck.

There was a rush to see what had happened, and the decorum of the quarter-deck seemed for a moment forgotten. Horrible yells issued from below, mingled with cries for the doctor, who, hearing his name called, ran with his instruments to the scene of the accident. The officer of the deck commanded silence, and summoned the quartermaster of the watch, and old Ben made his appearance with a spyglass under his arm.

"Quartermaster," said Mr. Teaser, "find out what all that row's about, and let me know the particulars."

Old Ben took a survey of the hatch, but, finding nothing to elucidate matters, proceeded to the lower deck, where the two wounded officers were stretched out under the care of the surgeon and his mates.

Ben saluted the surgeon and said, "Dr. Betteser, the ossifer of the deck wants to know wot's all the row about, and please inform him who's dead."

"Well," said the surgeon, "there's no row at all, but two of his Majesty's attendants have accidentally fallen down the hatch. One of them has splintered the clavicle of the shoulder-blade and has received a compound fracture of the skull. The other has a compound fracture of the left leg and a severe contusion of the epigastrium and region of the diaphragm, besides breaking the tympanum of the ear, which has left him deaf."

"Aye, aye, sir!" said Ben, who at once returned to report to

AT THE BANQUET.

Mr. Teaser, who anxiously inquired, "Well, quartermaster, what is the matter down there?"

Ben, touching his hat and drawing himself up to his full height, responded, with a gravity suited to the occasion, "Two of them 'ere kings what come aboard in that 'ere Tialian cravat have tumbled down the hatch and broke their limbs. Dr. Betteser says one of them have broke the span shackle of his shoulder-blade, and has besides been very much confused on a fracture of his upper works, and has smashed his tin pan, which was stowed in his overopagus. The other king," continued Ben, "has a confounded faction of his left leg taken off, and has been very much injured in his upper gas streak and drop haim, and it's the saddest case of homicide the doctor ever knew or heard of."

"Bless my soul!" said Captain Marvellous, who at this moment made his appearance, "what a day this has been for accidents! This king will think we have some design on him. So much for bringing his bed-chambermen on board ship. If he had brought his chambermaids instead the midshipmen would have looked after them, and there would have been no accidents."

"Yes, sir," said Mr. Teaser, "and the lieutenants also would not have objected to looking after them."

The king took the accident to his chamberlains very coolly; "stoopido," he said, and then gave orders in Italian to the prime minister, who had the sufferers transferred as soon as possible to the corvette. Dinner or *dejeuner* was then announced, and the commodore conducted the king to a seat at table directly in front of Pierre Poisson's masterpiece. The king seemed much pleased with the happy combination of St. Peter's, the Capitol, and St. Elmo, and remarked to the prime minister, "Davero queste gente Americani sono uffiziali, brave."

All were seated; knives and forks clattered, Mount Vesuvius and partridges had begun to disappear, jellies, whips, patés, and Pierre's *entremets* generally, as Commodore Blowhard called them, rapidly taking their places among the things that were, when the time to astonish royalty with Pierre Poisson's great work at length arrived.

The captain rose to give his great toast:

"Naples and America,
Always weak and never strong,
Never right and always wrong."

"Cut that short!" said the commodore. "Shy, make the signal," and with that the dome of St. Peter's was raised as if by magic from the classic center-piece. As was intended, about fifty frightened canaries flew out and made for places of safety, while the building began to heave in a most extraordinary manner, the left wing opened, and Miss Biddy Growler's old cat appeared, her eyes gleaming like coals of fire, a dead canary in her mouth, and looking as if she would jump in the face of any one who disturbed her. The king looked particularly distressed, for the old cat eyed him savagely.

"Catch her by the tail!" yelled the commodore, and he made a movement as if to carry out this idea, when the cat started full tilt for the other wing, and the whole fabric began to totter. The champagne fountains burst their pipes, the trees fell as if swept by a hurricane, and the cat, rushing around the table like a demon, finally landed in the captain's wig, which, apparently mistaking it for some animal, she dashed off with and conveyed it to the lower regions of the ship.

The commodore remarked, "Well, if this party ain't sprawled I never saw one that was," and he shouted, "Call away the boarders!"

The party was completely broken up; the king had seen enough of cats. "Allons!" said he, "nous avons eu beaucoup des chats, si nous restons ici longtemps ils nous donneront le chat à neuf queues." And he rose and said to the commodore, "My boat, if you please. I have enjoyed myself very much, notwithstanding all the *cat*astrophes of the day. Monsieur Commodore, why did you not mention in your speech the virtues of the American cat, for I am sure I never saw such remarkable animals in my life? *Au revoir!*" And out he went, followed by his suite.

The yards were manned, the officers and marines drawn up, and the king, bowing and smiling to the last, stepped into his barge. When he reached his little corvette he once more took the helm, at the instant when a salute of twenty-one guns was fired from the Thunderbum, which the commodore pronounced equal to any ever fired from the Gingerbread.

There were no cats and dogs in those guns, for every one had been carefully loaded in the presence of Mr. Barnacle, who stood by, belaying-pin in hand, ready to knock down anything or anybody.

Captain Marvellous went on the doctor's list, but, fortunately, his wig was found on the berth-deck next morning, and he rapidly recovered. The commodore was happy, and never ceased laughing. He ordered that all the events of the day should be inserted in the ship's log-book, and wrote a long report of the same to the navy commissioners.

An investigation now took place as to how the cat got into the center-piece, when the old cook explained the matter as follows:

"Wen dat cat start for to run, sar, an' jump down dis here hash, dis ole nigga was a standin' by dat table, an' de top of dat ere constructin was off, so we mought be ready to put dem canary prebious to closin' up de dome.

"De hole was mighty large, sar, an' wen dat cat jump down, sar, she done lit right inter it, an' dar she remain as quiet as any cat I eber see, sar. My first impulshun was to cotch her by de perlongation ob de spinal marrer, which stuck berry permiskus out ob de constructin; but den dis ole nigga considered a bit, an' says he to heself, 'If dis 'ere ole nigga should catch dat animal by dat perlongation, dat animal will endebber to act catawaciously, an' dar will be de debbil to pay, an' dat ar constructin which Peter Poisson hab so much trubbel to make out ob dat little pig will be so knocked around dat none of dat constructin will be leff.' So I conclude it bess to leff her be, an' I put in de dome, an' de cat done quietly haul in her tail and stow herself in de cable-tier ob dat constructin.

"Den we put in dem canary-bird. I tell Peter Poisson he better leff dem out, an' he say, 'Mon jew! dat wuff noffin' widout dem bird'; an' so I agree to dat; and wen dem bird done been put in dere dis ole nigga heard a skrimmagen inside, an' sez I, 'So much de better; dat cat keep quiet arter eatin' a dozen ob dem,' an' so she did. An' dat's all dis ole nigga knows ob dis bizness. All he knows is dat only half ob dem canary-bird done fly out ob dat constructin, an' dat's all dis ole darkey knows ob de unfortnit bizness."

"Well," said the commodore, "that accounts for the milk in the cocoanut. You have explained the matter so satisfactorily that I will give you five dollars, with permission to visit the opera."

"Yes, sar," said Cook. "I reckon dat I elucerdate de hole ob dat subjec'."

There was a lull after the storm. The ship had been in a hubbub all that day, and it was a comfort when the boatswain piped down the hammocks, and the officers could quietly assemble forward on the gun-deck, smoking their cigars and cracking their jokes. A thousand stories were flying about the ship, and Jack

Martin, of the foretop, "allowed" that he knew the captain would suffer from the cat before he died, he was so fond of serving it out to others.

Old Ben said he had often played poker, but never before saw three kings so badly beaten out. And old Cook declared, "Dem was de mose unaccountable doin's dat ebber dis ole cullered pusson see."

All this time Mr. Bluff kept his state-room, thinking of his lost countess, and dreading the result when the whole story should become known. As for the midshipmen assassins, they were trembling in their boots, for Mr. Barnacle, with the scent of a sleuth-hound, was on the trail of the authors of all this mischief. His visits to the cabin were frequent, and he was in constant consultation with the master-at-arms and ship's corporals.

Our only hope was in the old commodore, whom we knew would befriend us in case our misdeeds ever came to light. We retired to our hammocks very shaky, and glad to lose the sense of anticipated troubles in sleep.

CHAPTER XXIII.

A DEMAND FOR THE ABDUCTED CATS AND DOGS—A COURT OF INQUIRY—A TRANSFORMATION—A DUEL BETWEEN TEASER AND BLUFF.

NEXT day I was listening to a story Mr. Spicy was telling (which I could plainly hear through the wardroom slats) of an old fisherman (it may have been the celebrated Sam Jones for what I know) who was much addicted to catching eels, in pursuit of which interesting animals he used to go long voyages in the smack Sarah Jane.

It seems that the aforesaid fisherman was one day exploring the intricacies of Fire Island Inlet, and spent some time in filling his boat with the products of his eel-pots, when he suddenly disappeared, or at least his smack was observed to be sailing about the bay and performing various evolutions not familiar to the denizens of that locality, when at last the other fishermen, thinking that Sam Jones had been drunk long enough, put out in their boats and finally succeeded in overhauling the Sarah Jane. Much to their astonishment they found no Sam Jones, and concluded that he had either gone on shore or fallen overboard and got entangled in the eel-grass. But where Mr. Jones had fallen overboard was to them difficult to conjecture, for the smack had been seen for several days in various parts of the inlet acting so strangely that it was evident her mother didn't know she was out. The boat was filled with eels, and the master had evidently left in a hurry. All went to work to drag for the body, and after several days' exertion they pulled it up.

Sam Jones had evidently been some time in the water, for the eels had taken considerable liberties with his person. He had persecuted them in life, they persecuted his body after death. In fact, most of the flesh was missing from his bones, and more than six dozen fat eels were coiled away in the pea-jacket pockets of the lamented Jones, where they were quietly dozing off the effects of a surfeit on his flesh.

Meanwhile, Mrs. Jones was not at all uneasy at Sam's non-appearance. "Let him alone," said she, "he'll turn up. The Sarah Jane always comes into port all right."

When his comrades found Sam Jones's body they took it home tenderly to the bereaved widow, who was duly informed of all the heartrending circumstances of the case, and also of the six dozen eels found in her husband's pockets. She smiled at the recital, and after a few moments' consideration said, "Sam makes a capital eel-pot; he'll pay better dead than living. Set him again; it's such fun."

This story set me to thinking whether it was not possible to set that cat of Biddy Growler's again, and, while I was still laughing at the story of Sam Jones and his affectionate wife, Reckless came down, saying, "Here's a go, Marline; the fat's all in the fire. Here's old Growler and Mrs. Growler, and Miss Biddy and Lord Meekly, and the pretty chambermaid all on board to prefer charges against the midshipmen for carrying off their property, and they are now in the cabin with the commodore, captain, and Mr. Barnacle. We are in for it this time, and no help for us."

I must confess that upon the receipt of this alarming intelligence I felt my knees shake and my face grow pale; all my blood ran to my boots; but before I had time to do much thinking an order came for all the midshipmen to repair at once to the cabin, and so we had no opportunity of concocting any plans to meet the charges against us.

When we reached the cabin we were confronted by the whole

Growler family, Biddy in tears, with a handkerchief to her eyes, and old Growler looking as indignant as if the whole British nation had been insulted in his person. As we entered I heard him say, "I 'av hinformed my government hov this haffair through the minister hof 'er Majesty (God bless 'er) hat this court."

"All of which was unnecessary, sir," said the commodore, "as I assure you the republic of the United States will deal out strict justice to all malefactors, and strictly observe the treaty stipulations with every nation on the face of the earth. I, sir, am the representative of my country, with full authority to settle all international difficulties; and you will see that republics, though considered ungrateful, will yet mete out strict justice to all offenders. Mr. Grunter, please take off your hat in presence of the court."

"Growler is my name, sir. I ham a Quaker, hand halways wears my 'at. Hit's a Briton's right."

The commodore, not wishing to raise an international question, waived the point.

It appears that when Mr. Growler first came on board to make his complaint the commodore was so indignant that he immediately ordered a court of inquiry, with himself as president, Captain Marvellous and Mr. Barnacle members, and Shy judge-advocate. The table was covered with books on international and military law, including the naval regulations and the Constitution of the United States. The marine officer was acting as provost-marshal, and a sentry was on hand to take charge of the prisoners.

"Let the prisoners walk in and be seated," said the commodore. "Provost-marshal, take charge of their swords."

"Don't you think, sir," said the captain, "it would be better to call them the accused until they are proved guilty of the charges, although I have no doubt every man of them will be convicted?"

"Captain Marvellous," said the commodore, winking at the midshipmen, "you are too fond of leaning toward leniency. Shy, what does Puffendorn say on that point?"

"Puffendorf says nothing about it, sir; but these gentlemen are neither accused nor prisoners, as no charges have yet been preferred against any one in particular, and there is no proof that these gentlemen had anything to do with the matter."

"My heyes!" broke in old Growler, "don't you suppose I knows a man has as done me ha hinjury when I see 'im only one day hafter he's a done hit, hand don't hi know them here gentlemen hif has so be they his gentlemen?"

MR. GROWLER TESTIFIES.

"Silence in the court!" roared the commodore. "Don't prejudge the case, Mr. Grunter." Here Miss Biddy began to cry.

"Growler, if you please," said the Briton.

"Now, Mr. Growler," said the commodore, "stand up and give your evidence. Judge-advocate, swear the witness on Vattel in the usual form. Mr. Growler, our laws are all founded on those of Great Britain, who, you know, was our ancestor before we turned her off. Somehow or other we have never been able to get rid of her laws, although, I believe, they are not original with the English, all being founded on the laws of Moses."

"Hi don't think you will find that hin hany British 'istory, sir," said Mr. Growler. "We makes hour hown laws. Hi don't swear, sir; hi 'olds hup my 'and." Whereupon Mr. Growler then and there declared that he would tell the whole truth, and nothing but the truth, and the examination commenced.

"Now, witness," said the commodore, "tell us all you know about this case."

"Well, sir," said Mr. Growler, "three hevenings hago, hon the third hof the month, hat twenty minutes past ten o'clock, seven young midshipmen came to my 'ouse to spend the hevening. I know the time to a minute, has hi looked at my watch to see hif hit was time to go to the hexchange to learn the state of the markets, being hinterested hin the price hof periwinkles hand shrimps."

"Stop a moment," said the commodore; "pick out the culprits." And Mr. Growler pointed out myself, Reckless, Brace, Block Slinky, Baby Drinkwater, and Babble and Squeak; the latter of whom was not with us at all.

"Provost-marshal," said the commodore, "take charge of those prisoners."

"Accused, if you please," put in the captain.

"Well, accused, then," said the commodore. "Now, Mr. Grumbler, go on."

"Growler, if you please, sir. Well, sir, when these young men came to my 'ouse hi treated them with great 'ospitality hand hentertained them with the prices current from *Galignani*. I remember telling that one," pointing to me, "that pork 'ad riz, hoats 'ad gone down, that lard was flat on the market, hand that hoil was ha drug. Hand then my daughter 'ad han hengagement with my Lord Meekly for the hopera, hand they went; hand Mrs. Growler, not liking the men's tying 'er cats' tails together, flounced hout of the room, hand hi, hafter hentertainin' them to the best of my hability, left them to go to the hexchange, hand when hi came back hi found my 'ouse hall turned hupside down, hand hall my wife hand daughter's dogs, cats, hand kittens which they had himported from hold Hengland, hand which 'ad been many years in the family, were gone."

"Stop a minute, Mr. Growler," said the commodore. "I want to ask you one question. You say you have imported those dogs, cats, and kittens from England, and they have been in your family many years. How long have you been in Naples?"

"Six months, sir," said Mr. Growler.

"How old are the kittens, Mr. Bumper?"

"Growler, sir, if you please. Six weeks old. They were born in Naples."

"Then," said the commodore, "they are not British kittens unless they were born under the British flag."

"No, sir," said Growler; "but they were born in my 'ouse."

"That will do, Mr. Grumbler. You can sit down."

"Growler, if you please, sir," said the witness, as he retired from the stand.

"Here, Mr. Bubble and Squeak, come forward. Take the book and swear. Put him through, Shy." And Shy administered the oath.

"Now, witness, tell us the whole truth, and nothing but the truth," said the commodore. "You fellows are in a bad scrape, and nothing short of an alibi will save you."

"Before I am examined, sir, I would like to call in a witness—Mr. Teaser—in whose watch I was on the night in question," said Mr. Babble and Squeak.

"All right," said the commodore. "Shy, make out a subpœna for Mr. Teaser. Provost-marshal, bring him into court." And Mr. Teaser accordingly appeared.

"Now, judge-advocate," said the commodore, "swear in the prisoner, Mr. Teaser."

"Neither prisoner nor accused," said the captain. "Mr. Teaser is simply a witness."

"All the same," said the commodore. "Swear him in."

"Now," said Babble and Squeak, "I want to ask Mr. Teaser a question."

"Pitch in," said the commodore.

"Mr. Teaser, will you please inform the court where I was on the night in question from six till twelve?"

"Well," answered Mr. Teaser, "this gentleman was at the mast-head from six to eight P. M.; from eight until nine he was sent to ride the mizzen-stay; and from nine until twelve he was standing by the horse-block holding a twenty-four pound shot in his hand."

"Did you send me down twice in the wardroom during the watch to mix you a gin cocktail?" inquired Babble.

"Yes," said Teaser, a little confused, "I think I did."

"Does he mix good cocktails, Mr. Teaser?" said the commodore.

"Yes, sir," said Teaser, "pretty fair; only he makes them rather strong."

"Captain Marvellous," said the commodore, "put Mr. Bubble in my barge hereafter. I will teach him how to mix cocktails perfectly. Now, Mr. Teaser," he continued, "could Mr. Bubble and Squeak have gone on shore and been absent two hours without your knowing it?"

"No, sir," said Teaser, "he couldn't have been away two minutes."

"Well, by jingoes!" said the commodore, "this looks like an alibi. Mr. Growser, what do you say to it?"

Here Miss Biddy spoke up. "Pa, that midshipman warn't there, but them hothers was."

"Still an alibi, proved by two witnesses," continued the commodore. "Mr. Grinder, allow me to say that we have given this case a fair and impartial trial, and the more we investigate the plainer it appears that these young gentlemen were not the culprits. We are trying the case by your own laws, and in every instance have proved an alibi. Now, sir, strict justice requires me to dismiss all further proceedings against these persons, except that they shall all go to the mast-head to-morrow for allowing themselves to be suspected, and that will be the extent of their punishment. Now, Mr. Grumbler, we will be equitable to the last, and allow you to identify your property if it is on board this ship."

"But, sir," said Growler, "these hother ones hain't been hexamined, hand Biddy says them's the ones."

"It wouldn't be a particle of use, Mr. Grumbler, to examine them," said the commodore, "for they would all prove an alibi just as Mr. Bubble has done, and we can not waste our time in frivolous investigations. Let me ask for a description of the animals you lost."

"They were hall my hanimals, sir," said Miss Biddy, "hand I can hidentify them heasily. My King Charles his black-hand-tan, with long silky 'airs, ha silky tail, hand long 'air hall hover 'is legs hand hunder 'is stomach. My Skye hiz a dapple-gray, with bootiful moostachers hand hover'anging heyebrows, hand his rather cross to strangers. The hold cat hiz tortoise-shell, hand so hiz the kittens, hand hall of them would know me hin a minute."

"Bring them all in here, provost-marshal," said the commodore, "and let these good people identify their property. I hope, Miss Growser, your animals won't prove an alibi also."

It took about an hour to collect the animals, during which the court took a recess. The commodore chucked the pretty chambermaid under the chin, and Miss Biddy and I got on good terms again. I laid all the blame on Reckless.

Lord Meekly looked awfully huffy, and Mr. Growler threw himself on his reserved rights.

When the commodore asked the old fellow how he liked the looks of the frigate, he said she wasn't "'alf as 'an'some has the British frigates"; but the commodore knocked spots out of him by telling him that we had captured the Thunderbum from the British, and had never altered her a particle, after which old Growler subsided.

At last in came a troop of sailors, each one bearing in his arms a specimen of the animal kingdom; but, oh! how different from the pets of which the Growlers were in search! for when the men ascertained that a party of English people had come to claim their dogs, cats, and kittens, they exercised their utmost ingenuity to alter them so that they could not be recognized.

All the animals were shaved behind like French poodles, and the kittens, with little tufts on the ends of their tails and little ruffles around their ankles, looked for all the world like the children's toys one sees in a shop-window.

The two dogs were so changed that their mothers would never have known them. All their hair and eyebrows had been shaved off clean, and they resembled the dogs of which the Chinamen delight to manufacture patés. The old cat's tortoise-shell color had all changed to black by using nitrate of silver, and the two dogs had been so plied with grog that they would not have recognized their best friends.

Miss Biddy jumped forward to embrace her pets, but there was no sign of recognition on the part of the dogs. She looked sorrowfully at them and said, "Them hain't mine, hor hif they his they hav' taken hall the 'air hoff them; they'd know me hanywhere." And she burst into tears.

"It's another alibi," said the commodore, "as clear as mud; and, Mr. Growler, we must dismiss the court; but I shall punish all these young gentlemen severely for laying themselves under suspicion. Dismiss the court, Shy, and, Mr. Barnacle, pipe down."

Mr. Growler was highly indignant. He remarked to the commodore, "Your court's ha 'umbug, sir, hand there's no justice hon board han Hamerican ship of war." And Lord Meekly remarked that it was "devilish hunandsome hin Hamerican hofficers to beave hin that manner."

"I will make it up to you, Miss Growler," said the commodore, "when I go to Japan, where I will get you some black-and-tans only four inches long, and weighing but two ounces, and Skye terriers that you can only see through a magnifying-glass."

And the party took their departure, Miss Biddy weeping, and old Growler and his wife not noticing anybody.

Said the commodore, "This is the clearest case of alibi I ever saw, and no man ever had a fairer trial than Mr. Grumbler."

But it seems that Mr. Barnacle was of a different opinion. He sent for us, and said, "Young gentlemen, I see through all this thing, and, though it is the pleasure of the commodore to prove an alibi, you can't deceive me. Now I won't have any cats and dogs in this ship, and you go on shore to-night and leave those animals at the owner's house, and let there be no mistake about it, or you'll live at the mast-head for six months." And Mr. Barnacle clinched the belaying-pin in his hand with more than usual vigor.

We carried out Mr. Barnacle's directions, glad enough to get off so easily, but couldn't resist the temptation to dip the dogs' tails in the tar-pot and give them a lick of tar over the eyebrows.

We deposited the pets at the Growlers' door, rang the bell, and ran away as the pretty maid came to the door and gathered them all in.

The commodore made an official communication of this whole transaction to the American minister, who laughed heartily over the matter, and promised that her Britannic Majesty's representative at the court of Naples and Sicily would make it all right with the home government. We never heard of the Growlers again.

The captain next sent for us to his cabin, and gave us fits. He never stopped to inquire who were the delinquents, but he tore up and down that cabin like mad, taking good care not to interfere with us until the commodore had left the ship. He only regretted one thing, the captain said, and that was that he could not cat-o'-nine-tails us all, and he would not rest until he had procured the passage of a law authorizing captains so to punish their midshipmen.

"I'll teach you to bring cats on board my ship." Here the captain clapped his hand to his wig to see if it was safe. "Now, leave my cabin! Conk, never lend these young gentlemen my No. 2 table-cloth and napkins again when they have company."

Next day the following doggerel, evidently the production of some of the crew, was picked up at the cabin-door. It was sung *sotto voce*, and old Marvellous never could discover the author:

I.

There was a bully frigate, her name the Thunderbum,
Commanded by a capting who kept beneath his thumb
A crew of galliant seamen who worked that vessel's guns,
And officers who whisky drank and brandy by the tons.

II.

Now the capting warn't a beauty to make a lady stare,
He wore a larboard glass eye and all of his own hair,
Exceptin' wot he bent wen he set out for the shore,
And then a handsome bob wig this galliant capting wore.

III.

His ears were rather mulish and deep red was his nose,
His face had the carnation of a full-blown tuber-rose;
His voice was so melodious 'twas like a donkey's bray,
And when he sang he frightened all the women folks away.

IV.

He was werry fond of floggin' mornin', noon, and night;
His steward, he use to say. he rose from bed half-tight,
Which was the why he catted so; yet the old wretch often swore
He'd like to give the frigate up and flog his men no more.

V.

And then he'd call the bosen his nine-tail for to bring,
And four-and-twenty lashes into some chap he would fling;
And havin' thus relieved his mind of all his earthly cares,
He'd call all hands to muster and meekly say his prayers.

VI.

One day poor Billy Bowline, our smartest chap aloft,
Was catted by the capting, who'd catted him full oft,
Took sick and on his death-bed said, "This catting you will rue;
I'll tell you now, the cat, sir, will be the death of you."

VII.

And from that time this capting he had no peace at all,
Go where he would by day or night he'd hear cats caterwaul;
And one day with some ladies, when steppin' from his gig,
A cat jumped on his shoulder and clapper-clawed his wig.

VIII.

Now imagine his dilemma with them ladies standin' by,
Who never knowed he wore a wig, much less a neat glass eye;
And they turned away disgusted and stepped out from his gig,
Because he'd tried to fool 'em all by wearing of that wig.

IX.

And then those lively critters they treated him with scorn,
And looked on him with hatred—he wished he'd ne'er been born;
He took a bunch of codfish and tied it to his knee,
And jumped from off the taffrail right into the sea.

X.

A splash, a shriek, a splutter, then a rippling of the wave,
As the briny waters closed above the catting capting's grave,
While a thousand cats in chorus a requiem o'er him sang,
And the burden of their music was, "Better drown than hang."

Mr. Bluff had now been invisible for four days—that is, he had kept his state-room and saw no one except the wardroom steward, who made him frequent mysterious visits. At the end of four days the voice of Mr. Bluff was heard singing, in a husky voice:

"Pensez à moi, ma chère amie,
Saw off my leg close up to the knee."

There was a shout in the wardroom when Bluff's voice was once more heard singing so cheerily. All knew that he was recovering his spirits, and hoped soon to hear his interesting yarns again.

Old Shacklebags was the only one up and dressed when Mr. Bluff emerged into the wardroom, singing out in a humorous voice,

"*Ponche caldi per dui!* Ah, Shacklebags, how are you? You look as fresh and rosy as a woodpecker! Now I am going to give you a conundrum; see if you can guess it."

"Oh, please don't, Mr. Bluff," said Shacklebags. "I never could understand your conundrums: they exercise my mind too much; and then you give such scientific and historical ones that they lay me out on my back."

"Well, now," said Bluff, "what's the most terrible blow that you know of?"

"Ah, now," said Shacklebags, "that sounds more reasonable; that is coming home to a fellow. Well, now, Mr. Bluff, they say the last blow is always the heaviest; but I think the most terrible blow I ever saw was off Cape Horn, or rather after we had got round the cape. We were in about the latitude of Magellan Straits, and the wind, which had been fair, chopped round right in our teeth and blew great guns. We never showed a stitch of canvas for eighteen days, and at the end of that time we had drifted right on to Cape Pillar, at the entrance of the straits, having narrowly escaped the Twelve Apostles, as we were under bare poles. There was no help for it but to put the helm up and run through the Straits of Magellan, and we finally brought up in York Bay, where we let go all four anchors, veering away equal strain on all, and—"

"Bosh!" interrupted Mr. Bluff. "What a long yarn you are making! I asked you a conundrum, and you are giving me the history of a cruise. The question is, What's the most terrible blow you ever heard of?"

"Well," said Shacklebags, "I thought that one was; but perhaps it wasn't so hard a gale as we had while I was attached to the Mary Ann, when we were off Nantucket Shoals, with all sail set and—"

"Oh, there you go again," said Bluff. "Better 'give it up,' as the minstrels say. Why, the worst blow is 'b'low zero.' That's as terrible as anything I know of."

Shacklebags pondered a minute, then shook his head and exclaimed, "Ah, yes, I see—very good." And out he rushed on deck, thinking to surprise Mr. Teaser.

"Mr. Teaser," he said, "you are very fond of giving me conundrums. Will you please tell me the most terrible gale of wind you were ever in?"

"Why, yes," replied Teaser; "in 1824, in the Boxer, when we lost all our masts, and the vessel foundered, and we got off in the boats, and the boats capsized in sight of land, and we had to swim to the shore ten miles off, the sea running mountains high, and I was the only one who got ashore, for all the others were drowned. That's about the worst gale of wind I remember; at least it was the most inconvenient one."

"That's not the answer," said Shacklebags. "When the thermometer stands at sixty degrees below zero point, that's the answer, though somehow it don't seem quite so funny as when I heard it from Mr. Bluff; but I'll go down and get it again."

But when he got below Bluff was in a full gale of another kind. He was saying that instead of being in his state-room he had been on shore all the time; that the story Teaser had read from the paper was false, that the countess was alive and kicking, that he had spent the previous evening with her, "and," said Bluff, "I tell you I had a good time; you ought just to have been there, you'd have seen times, I tell you."

"Why, what did you do, Bluff, that was so nice?" said two or three in chorus.

"You'd like to know, wouldn't you? Well, then, I'll tell you." And he put on a quizzical expression.

"We first got well acquainted by mutually playing with a pet porcupine the countess has brought up by hand. It follows her up and down stairs, comes when called, and dances the polka. Then we drank cider through a straw, and ate pop-corn and peanuts. Then we had four kinds of sweetened water, camphor, and milk, music on the andirons. Then we told conundrums, and finally wrapped the dog in the table-cloth and hauled him around the table, while the chambermaid told ghost-stories that made our hair stand on end. I stayed to supper, and we had cauliflower and apple-sass flavored with garlic. I ran my boots down at the heel, and the countess broke her tortoise-shell comb, and then let me out through the cellar-door, and I came off to the ship in a balloon. If you want to hear the rest, go ask the cook."

And old Bluff assumed such a comical expression that all the mess roared with laughter.

"Steward," said the lieutenant, "I am very particular in my eating after dining with the nobility. Take away this beefsteak; it's tough as the leg of a missionary I once dined on away out in Viti Levu, one of the Fejee Islands. During a snap there once it became so cold that the thermometer stood at one hundred degrees below zero, and the missionary meat froze so hard that we couldn't get a fire big enough to thaw it. Get me some *poulet à la chartreuse.*"

"What!" said the marine officer, his mouth wide open at hearing of this wonderful degree of cold, "a cold snap at the Fejee Islands? Why, that's away down under the equator, somewhere in fifteen south latitude."

"Well," said Bluff, "don't you suppose they can have cold snaps at the equator just as easy as they can have hot snaps at the north pole? Why, I have seen it so hot in Spitzbergen that you could fry an egg in the sun."

"What!" interrupted the marine, "fry an egg in the sun at Spitzbergen?"

"Yes, sir," said Bluff, coolly, "provided you had a frying-pan and plenty of fire."

Which turned the laugh on the marine officer. And so they went on until the wardroom looked like old times again.

At eight o'clock it was Mr. Bluff's turn to relieve Mr. Teaser in charge of the deck; and when Bluff appeared Teaser came smilingly toward him and said, "Hullo, old fellow! Glad to see you about again. Some hard stories about you and a certain countess."

"Stop, sir," said Bluff, "do not mention that angelic creature. You and I have a little matter to settle; therefore please confine yourself to delivering the day's orders, and I shall require nothing further of you at present. As soon as I get through with the day's duty I shall call on you for satisfaction."

"Why, Bluff, you must be joking; you can't mean it, certainly," said Teaser, looking somewhat alarmed.

"Yes, sir," said Bluff, "I do mean it; and as there is one too many in the wardroom mess, I intend to diminish the number."

"Well, just as you please," said Teaser; "perhaps you'll not fare so well yourself."

And down he went, boiling over to think that Bluff should be such a fool.

That day's duty over, Bluff called on the master, Mr. Shacklebags, to act as his "friend," at the same time informing that gentleman he was going to quiz Teaser before all the mess, as he knew the master was utterly opposed to dueling. Bluff was to challenge Teaser, there was to be but one pistol loaded with blank cartridge, the parties were to toss up for weapons, and Bluff was to get it and was then to play his part.

Teaser chose for his friend the marine officer, poor, innocent

BLUFF AND TEASER FIGHT.

old fellow, whom every one could deceive, and Dr. Hitybelteser was to accompany the combatants on shore to dress the wounds, etc.

At the appointed time, all the arrangements having been made, the party started for Castellamare—a long pull in the hot sun. Teaser had tried in every way to accommodate matters, but the miserable Bluff would accept of no apology. So Teaser made his will and had it witnessed by the first lieutenant and chaplain, who wondered why he was so particular in making this disposition of his effects, when, as everybody knew, he had not a hundred dollars' worth of property in the world. They had no idea that Teaser was about to fight a duel, the matter having been kept secret.

Before leaving for the field of honor Bluff sent for Reckless, and said, "Now, my young friend, if you want your mother's monkey to get out of a bad scrape you must do as I tell you, or your name will be cut on the main-topmast-head so often that you can't put your finger down without touching it." He then told Reckless the whole story of his challenge to Teaser for playing the newspaper joke on him. "Now," he said, "I want to serve him out, and you must help me do it. I propose to frighten Teaser, who likes the smell of powder about as much as a monkey does the crack of a coach-whip. My plan is to have one pistol loaded with blank cartridge and get the right to use it. This must be arranged in the toss-up. You have been in four duels, and are quite notorious on board ship in that line. The marine officer, who acts as Teaser's second, knows nothing of such matters, and is frightened out of his boots by the responsibility of the occasion. Go and offer your services to assist him in this trying ordeal, and he will be too glad to accept. When you get on the ground see that no ball goes into the pistol, and leave the rest to me."

Reckless accordingly proffered his services to the marine officer, who was delighted with the prospect of such valuable assistance.

"Bless my soul! Mr. Reckless," he said, "I can handle any number of marines, and can throw two hundred of them into a hollow square and never make a mistake, but I know nothing about the rules of dueling, so I will avail myself of your assistance and trust everything to you."

Reckless informed me of his arrangements, as I was officer of the boat. As we proceeded across the bay Mr. Bluff was very taciturn. He would shut his hand, stick out his forefinger as if pointing at some object, and count, slowly, one, two, three. Sometimes he would appear to aim at a gull flying through the air, and sometimes at a fishing-boat's mast, all of which made Mr. Teaser still more nervous and irritable. The marine officer suggested to Mr. Bluff that it wasn't fair to practice beforehand when his opponent did not do it, whereupon Bluff stood up in the boat and went through the pantomime of wheeling and firing, and this he continued until we reached the shore. Once he whispered audibly to the doctor, asking where was the best place to shoot a man so as to have him die a lingering death ; to which the doctor replied that a man shot in the aorta might linger for some time, and finally die of gastritis or nervous prostration.

The terms of the meeting were as follows : To fight at ten paces ; to have but one pistol and toss up for the choice ; to count one, two, three, and fire when you please after the word three was uttered, but not before.

Once on the ground, the surgeon produced his instruments, which were contained in three mahogany cases. He laid out three saws of different sizes, six knives, as many probes, a number of long forceps for extracting balls, a quantity of bandages, a bundle of silk to tie up ligatures, a bottle of ether, and a bottle of brandy.

Bluff then divested himself of his upper clothing, while Teaser looked the picture of despair ; next he proceeded to take off his boots and trousers, and finally stood clothed only in his shirt and drawers. Mr. Teaser was invited to follow his example, which that gentleman declined to do until informed by his second, prompted by Reckless, that such a proceeding was absolutely necessary in order to comply with the regulations of the code. So the unhappy Teaser was obliged to strip, and stood in a pair of tight-fitting red flannel drawers, his legs looking about as big as pipe-stems.

The day was cool, and this, together with nervous excitement, caused Teaser's teeth to rattle like a pair of castanets ; while Bluff, who had taken the precaution to wear a double set of underclothes, felt quite comfortable and not a bit nervous.

When the toss-up was made, Bluff, of course, got the pistol, and, the ground being measured off, the combatants were placed in position, Bluff with a curious expression in his eyes and humming his favorite tune, "A wet sheet and a flowing sea," while Teaser looked like a man in the pillory, his hands clinched, his knees knocking together, and his face pallid with the fear of the certain death he saw before him.

The word was given, "Ready!" when Bluff called out, "Stop

Bluff took deliberate aim for about a minute, then, lowering his pistol, said, "Doctor, whereabouts did you say the aorta was?"
Page 305.

THE DUEL ENDS TO THE SATISFACTION OF ALL. 305

a moment. I would like to ask Mr. Teaser if he does not wish to write a note to the countess in his best Italian asking her forgiveness?" Teaser faintly declined the offer, and word was slowly given, One! two! three! At the word "three" Bluff took deliberate aim for about a minute, then, lowering his pistol, said, "Doctor, whereabouts did you say the aorta was?"

"Fire, sir," said the unhappy Teaser, "and end my misery. This is cowardly."

"Ah, yes," said Bluff, "you think so, do you? Well, sir, the understanding was that we could fire any time after the word 'three,' and I intend to fire when it suits me. I won't shoot you now, sir, but will keep you for my own particular shooting. Remember, you are my meat when I choose to cook you."

The whole party were rather surprised at this, and the doctor was terribly disappointed in not being able to show his skill. Teaser was glad to get out of the scrape, and determined in his own mind that he would never again go ashore at the same time with Bluff. The seconds were pleased, and the two midshipmen highly amused.

The party now returned to the ship, and you may depend it was not long before the officers got wind of the affair.

In the boat Mr. Bluff seemed very anxious that Mr. Teaser should not take cold, offering him his pea-jacket, which was gruffly declined, and whispering audibly to the doctor, "Let him have some brandy; I don't want to lose him," which made Teaser furious.

That night Mr. Bluff called the midshipman of the watch, and said, "Go and knock at Mr. Teaser's door, give him my compliments, and ask him if his air-port is closed. Tell him to remember the interest I have in him, that he must always be ready for my call, and must be exceedingly careful of his health."

Next day Teaser was confined to his bed, and Bluff sent fifty times a day to inquire about him, with always the same injunctions not to neglect his health, and always to be ready when he (Bluff) wanted him.

Teaser never actually recovered from the effects of this joke, and years afterward Bluff used to write and caution him to take care of his health, as he might be wanted at any moment.

Teaser was never known to perpetrate any more jokes. He became very intimate with Mr. Spicy, the chaplain, who induced him to become an honorary member of the "Society for the Diffusion of Brass Warming-pans among the Heathen Tribes of Africa"; and he would listen by the hour to Mr. Spicy's adventures in that country, and about the two queens, Raka and Kringleoo.

Mr. Teaser also became a strict member of the church, and nobly forgave Bluff for the unchristian hoax which the latter had played upon him, and which was now known to the whole ship's company; but Mr. Teaser's new-born piety did not prevent his hazing the midshipmen, which he doubtless considered a religious duty.

CHAPTER XXIV.

ABOUT MATTERS AND THINGS IN GENERAL—AN IRRUPTION OF TERMITES—MR. SHACKLEBAGS GETS SOMETHING IN HIS EYES AND A BLOWING UP—CAN'T GO ON SHORE TILL THE MAIN-MAST GOES—THE CAPTAIN GETS OUTWITTED BY TWENTY-FOUR MIDSHIPMEN.

I DID not set out with the intention of writing a description of Naples and its environs, nor is it my intention to do so now, but I would have the reader to think that I was not indifferent to the many works of art for which Naples is celebrated, and that I appreciated the beauties of nature which attract the eye, let it look where it may; suffice it to say that I followed the routine laid down in the best received guide-books, and "did up" everything after the most approved fashion. Were I so disposed, I could discourse most learnedly about these matters, but that intelligent chaplain, Mr. Spicy, is coming out with a book, and I have no desire to forestall him.

I must refer those persons who take any interest in the matter to the letters I wrote my respected grandfather about that time; he was kind enough to be pleased with them, and, indeed, paid me the compliment of showing them to those persons who took any interest in my welfare.

A glowing description of the famous Punchinello from my pen also appeared in the "Babylon Tittle-Tattle," a paper of considerable reputation and some circulation. Its rival, the "Independent Sneak," severely criticised my composition, and was somewhat indignant at my grandfather for permitting such a silly article to appear in the "Tittle-Tattle"; but the animadversions of Mr. Squint, the editor of the "Independent Sneak," were dictated by unworthy feelings. He did not hesitate to say that the "Tittle-Tattle" could only boast of a circulation of one hundred sheets per day, when it was well known that the "Tittle-Tattle" was decidedly the best paper of the two; it possessed one of the best corps of foreign correspondents in the Union, among whom the editor did me the honor to rank me as a shining light.

Had I felt so disposed, I might have made a very interesting work on matters and things in general appertaining to the kingdom of Naples, the most interesting of which would have been the study of the moral and physical condition of the lazzaroni, their liberal sentiments with regard to things that don't belong to them, and their capacity for forming a government of their own on the model of our own glorious republic.

At one time I thought of writing a novel (in the style of the "Last Days of Pompeii"), and proposed to lay the scenes in the "Grotto del Cane," or the "Sibyl's Cave," but on consideration I gave it up. These things are overdone nowadays, and no one cares about reading a novel unless it contains something very spicy. All the twaddle about "hearts and feelings," "concealment like a worm," etc., don't go down with a go-ahead country like ours; they have no time for sentiment, nor any desire to cry, and novels, they say, only burn out candles and bring on the dyspepsia. One reason (I said to myself) why I didn't write on the above subject was that I saw the pages of a work, written by a brother officer of mine, pasted inside of a trunk that was for sale on Broadway, and my attention was drawn to it by the author himself, who was very *unwisely* leaning over and reading his own productions, heedless of the boy who was bellowing in his ear, "Do you want to buy, sir?" Taking everything into consideration, I think I was sensible in sticking to the narrative of my own adventures, and, as the Italians say, "*Ognium faccia il suo maestiero è farrallo dadovero,*" which is a good proverb; but far more to the point is that wherein they say, "*Chi lava la testa dell' asino, butta il tempo e la lisciva.*" I take it for granted my readers understand Italian or I would not quote it.

Of all the foreign ships that visit Naples, and indeed all the ports in the Mediterranean, none are so overrun with visitors as the ships of the United States; the English and French, as a general rule, are very exclusive, though some of the English commanders throw their ships open to visitors as we do. John Bull generally comes to Naples to settle some matter in dispute between him and the somewhat tricky old king who has figured in these pages, and our good progenitor generally brings his Majesty to a proper state of reflection by anchoring two or three ships of the line in front of the palace-stairs (on the water side), with a polite intimation of a Paixhan shell for breakfast, or a hot shot at night as a warming-pan. Need it be said that his Majesty generally finds it convenient to apologize? While negotiations are going on ships are not likely to be troubled with visitors, and John Bull escapes many of the annoyances that Brother Jonathan is subjected to, and is not pestered to death by people of all classes.

I say pestered (knowing that this will not likely be translated into the Italian, as Mrs. "Beecher's toe" was, and that no Italian lady will ever feel indignant as she reads it), for of all the pests in the world the greatest is a crowd of Neapolitans on board of a ship. If they came by the hundreds even, or at stated hours, there might be some toleration, and I can compare them to nothing else but an irruption of the termites, little white ants that suddenly make their appearance among the West India Islands, overrunning and destroying everything they come in contact with. If anything, they are more desirable friends than the Neapolitans, as they clean up everything over which they pass, and have been known to leave nothing but the clean-picked bones of a sick person who was caught in bed; the Neapolitans, on the contrary, stick daggers into the heart of an old first lieutenant by littering the decks, smuggling grog to the sailors, and leaving a smell of garlic sufficient to knock down an albatross on the wing.

I have seen as many as ten thousand on board during the course of twenty-four hours, poking their inquisitive noses into every hole and corner of the ship, and taking liberties with us plain republicans that they would not venture on, on board of a European vessel of war. There the crown, that symbol of "might makes right," stares them in the face on their first entrance to the quarter-deck, and the sight of it exercises so wholesome an influence they don't seem to forget where they are.

With us, however, there is no spot so sacred but they will intrude; the captain gives up his cabin, while the steward locks up his silver spoons; the lieutenants, if they would be private, retire to their hot little state-rooms and suffocate over a candle, while the midshipmen, who live (as it is styled) "in the country," are driven away from their shady retreats and sequestered groves to the open road, where they are hustled about by fat old women and sleek-looking friars, or grim-looking school-masters with a score of equally grim-looking scholars at their heels.

I well remember, the day after our arrival, when we sat down to dine at the usual hour of twelve, our dinner that day consisted of "salt horse" and bean-soup and a famous dish of macaroni, got up in Scantling's best style—the side-dishes it will be unnecessary to allude to ; suffice it that we were doing ample justice to the fare before us, and even Mr. O'Classics pronounced the "pae-soap" to be the best he had ever eaten, and was stowing it away as if he was bound on the tour of Europe with the expectation of being back by sunset.

Crowds began to flock in from the berth-deck, where they had been witnessing the surprising efforts of Jack to stow away the good things provided for him by his good old "Uncle Sam"; and one old lady carried, wrapped up in her cotton handkerchief, a huge hunk of duff (sufficient to swamp a yawl-boat), presented to her by some benevolent sailors, who thought, perhaps, that she required ballast to keep her in trim ; another held a piece of salt beef wrapped up in brown paper, and one or two little fellows were trying to break their teeth on some huge biscuit that had been furnished them gratis from the bread-bags.

"A' queste sono gli uffiziali," said the first-mentioned old lady, "mangiano macarone."

"È curioso davvero," said an old fellow, leaning over the table, and with an eye-glass looking into the soup-tureen.

"Mamma," said one of the little fellows, "mangiano manteca gli uffiziali ?"

"Manteca," said the old lady, "mangiano tutte le cose che son buona ; queste Americani son richi come principi, ce molto oro in America, sono bravo gente, tanto polito. Mangia macarone, Eccellenza ?" she said, addressing O'Classics.

"Faix, no, marm ; there's nothing mangy about it at all—it's pae-soap," said the teacher, "and devilish good at that. Won't you thry a few, marm ?" And with that he handed her, in gallant style, a plateful and a spoon, and the old lady fell to with an appetite that would have done credit to a quarryman.

"O Giacomo !" she said, looking at the old fellow, " gusta de questa ; è veramento saporosa, veramento ste Americani sono milordi, i Francesi e gli Inglesi non han zoppa come este." The old fellow took a mouthful, and, shaking his head approvingly, said, "Esta gente sono bravo davvero, e mangiano roba buena."

"Mamma," said the little fellows, "darrime un pochetino."

"Sst, sst, sta quaglione non vedi che esta roba è per gli uffiziali, certamente, e sono polito?" said the old lady, swallowing spoonful after spoonful, while her dear Giacomo was putting down two to her one.

"Ah," said O'Classics, "the lazy roony don't 'av' such soap as that iviry day, ould leddy, I'll bet sexpance."

"Si, signore," said the old one, who had heard the word lazzaroni (pronounced in Irish, to be sure), "abbiamo multi lazzaroni in Napoli, molti, moltissimi."

"A gli uffiziali Americani, sono bravo gente," said old Giacomo, patting the teacher on the back, and he made a sign at the same time with his spoon at the macaroni-dish.

"An' is it macky roony ye'd be afther 'atin'? Wal, help yoursel', auld boy, an' ye may be fond of it for me, but divil a bit it comes up to the stapple comodity 'av' auld Ireland, the blissed pretaty, ony how."

With that permission, in went the spoon, and the contents of the macaroni-dish disappeared down the old fellow's throat.

"Ah, Giovanima," he said, "che buono. Gustato. Ah! queste Americani sono da-vero brave," and Madame Giovanimi dipped in her spoon and soon used up what remained of the macaroni.

"Ah, ye're divils at macky roony, an' no mistik," said the Irishman. "Giv' the leddy a glass of water, Scantlin', to wash it down wid"; but she declined, and, as the crowd began to assemble, she bundled up her duff and piece of salt horse, and, wishing us a "bon giorno," took her leave, with her dear Giacomo and the little ones.

Now on, on come the termites, and the same scene is gone over again; the "pae-soap" is among the things that were, and the macaroni and salt horse have vanished, leaving

"Not a wrack behind";

the bread-bag is laid under contribution, and the termites stow the bread away in very deep pockets, and even in their hats, and one old fellow, who could not succeed in getting near the table, reached over and secured a cucumber-pickle, which he stowed away in his vest-pocket, and, for fear some one should rob him of his treasure, he buttoned his coat up tight, and kept his hand on the sacred spot.

At last there was nothing more to offer, but there they stood, looking at us as if we were wild beasts, scarcely speaking, until an old hag came rushing in from the berth-deck, misery depicted in her countenance, singing out, "Nikolaki! Nikolaki! oh, mio figlio, mio Nikolaki! oh, dov'e Nikolaki! ho perduto Nikolaki! oh, Nikolaki è perduto!"

"Che Nikolaki," said an indignant Italian; "per che veniti a seccarci con Nikola? non vedete che questi sono tutti uffiziali?"

"Nikolaki!" screamed the old thing, "ah, mi povero Nikolaki!" and, seeing the teacher looking at her in rather a benevolent manner, she laid hold of his arm, and, with the most imploring countenance, asked him, "Signore, l'aveto veduto il mio figlio Nikolaki? O Nikolaki! Nikolaki!"

Had Mr. O'Classics been addressed in Latin he would have been at home, but he had not been long enough in the country to learn more than two words—one was macky roony and the other was lazy roony. He looked a little puzzled at first, but at last the idea struck him.

"Faix, an' I hav' it now, gentlemen: the poor woman's a starvin', and she'd be afther 'atin' somethin', an' she thinks she'd like to hav' some Nikolaki. I say, Mr. Scantlin', is ther' ony in the mess? for may the cat fly away wid me if I know what she manes!"

"O Nikolaki! Nikolaki! dov'e sta, Nikolaki!" shouted the old woman. "Mio figlio Nikolaki! Nikolaki! Nikolaki!"

"Oh, tunder and blazes, old woman! Divil a bit must ye make that noise here," said the kind-hearted Irishman; "for if Mr. Barnacles (that auld gintlemin, marm, wid a wart on his nose) should hear till ye, he'd whap ye as sure as ye'r a lazy roony."

Nevertheless, the old hag continued to sing out, "Nikolaki! Nikolaki! oh, mio figlio Nikolaki!" and was joined by half a dozen others of her family, who sang Nikolaki in chorus.

At last it was discovered that Nikolaki was the old woman's son, who had been lost in the crowd, and, after shouting for him in the hold and spar- and main-decks, she finally came to the conclusion that he had been boiled in the coppers by "gli infami Americani" and made soup of. She carried off the crowd with her, who, no doubt, deeply sympathized with her at the tragical end of her beloved Nikolaki, and one old fellow, who could not get near the table, was heard to affirm that "gli Americani sono republicani infame, y gli Francese y gli Inglese sono bravo gente."

Thus it was, day after day, all the time we were anchored in the Bay of Naples, and at last, when it had ceased to amuse us, we determined to put a stop to it. We complained to "the auld gintlemin wid a wart on his nose," and asked for a sentry to keep our apartments clear; but that was out of the question, and we were told to bear it patiently, as it would only be for two or three weeks longer. O heavens! thought we, all the Punchinellos and San Carloses in the world would not compensate us for what we underwent, so we determined to clear the termites out on our own hook.

It is astonishing how fertile midshipmen are in expedients when necessity or other circumstances call forth their powers of invention. Miserable is the fate of any poor wretch who comes within the circle of their displeasure, and even a captain or first lieutenant, with all his power to inflict punishment, can't do otherwise than quail before a well-arranged system of annoyance on the part of the midshipmen. How unenviable, then, must be the fate of a greenhorn or a spooney who falls into their clutches! Mr. O'Classics about hit it when he said, "Arrah, macky roony and lazy roony, if the divils of midshipmates 'av' got hauld av ye, ye'd better be afther saying yer prayers at onst. May the cat fly away wid ye, but ye'd better kape in your own climate!" But as the Italians did not understand Mr. O'Classics' brogue, they did not profit by the advice.

I recollect on one occasion the twenty-four worthies who comprised the different messes went to work deliberately and with one concerted will to annoy the captain, and well they succeeded, for the point in question was never raised again after that trial of midshipmen's skill in circumvention.

It's a good story and worth telling, and if the reader will excuse the digression, I will relate it.

Captain Marvellous had taken it into his head, all at once, that the sun was not properly cared for by that amiable and distinguished luminary of science, Mr. Shacklebags, or else he wished to instruct the young gentlemen in the rudiments of navigation, which instruction the aforesaid young gentlemen had made up their minds not to receive. He accordingly issued an order that they should repair to the quarter-deck every day at seven bells, and then and there proceed to bring down the sun's image to the horizon, whence the latitude would be ascertained at twelve o'clock, and the Thunderbum's position be accurately known.

Now just imagine twenty-four midshipmen going on deck at one time to take the sun. I wonder that Old Sol would venture to shine under such circumstances, and I think it likely that he would have declined doing so had the twenty-four midshipmen been obliged to comply with the captain's order, but, fortunately for the sun, they got off.

The first thing they did was to make out twenty-four requisitions on Mr. Shacklebags's department for twenty-four quadrants, to the great horror of that amiable person, who had never heard of such a thing in his life, and he had been in the service, man and boy, forty-four years. He had but three sextants in the ship altogether, and one of those was of no use. "Good heavens!" said Shacklebags (more excited than he had ever been known to be before), "I can't possibly supply you, gentlemen, with twenty-four quadrants, 'cause I ain't got none 'cept what I'm a usin'." They showed him the captain's order, "that they should all go up at seven bells and take the sun." "Sure enough," said Shacklebags; "how kin you take the sun without nary thing to do it with?" And he, poor soul, sent in for the captain's approval the requisition for twenty-four quadrants, to be bought at the first port. What he got in consequence of that rash act you may be sure he kept to himself, but some one did hear the captain tell him that he should not go on shore until the mainmast went, and poor Shacklebags knew that such an event would not take place until the ship went home, and he had made arrangements already to have a glorious time at the first port. The captain not only refused to approve the requisitions, which was considered an arbitrary display of despotism, but he ordered that the midshipmen should be roused up every day at seven bells, quadrants or no quadrants, to look at the master take the sun, if they could not do it themselves. "I'll work 'em up," said the captain, in the hearing of old black Conkshell, his steward; but that old nigger shook his head very mysteriously, and said to himself, "Betta leff 'em be, Massa Capen, betta leff 'em alone, 'cause dey're a werry wexin' set, and no mistake, leastwise de midshipen wos in de mos' ob de ships I done sail in. Betta lef 'em alone, sar; dey is werry aggrawatin', sir, werry." Unfortunately for the captain's peace of mind, he did not hear his old steward's remark, or he might have saved himself some trouble.

There were among the twenty-four midshipmen only two old

quadrants, supposed to have belonged to the Bonhomme Richard, of Paul Jones's time, and they had for many years been laid upon the shelf as useless.

That worthy gentleman, Mr. Shacklebags, had no sooner fixed himself on the horse-block when these two old quadrants were industriously brought to bear upon him in such a manner that the reflection of the sun from the horizon-glass was continually playing on the retina of his eye, and so annoyed him that he saw nothing but little spots on the sun's image. He thought there must be something wrong about the sun. He rubbed his eye, and then his glasses, and squared himself off to give the sun "fits"; but just as he congratulated himself on getting the reflected luminary in a proper position, those two old quadrants of the Bonhomme Richard were brought to bear on his top-lights, and he was all adrift again.

Poor old Shacklebags! How he rubbed his eyes and burnished his glasses again! but it was of no use; the enemy was too strong for him, and the Serapis was not worse riddled by the Bonhomme Richard's shot than he was by the Bonhomme Richard's quadrants. He was blinded completely, without having the least idea that there were two quadrants on each side of him, illuminating his face until it looked like sunrise. That fertile mind of his was so busily at work inventing a new kind of glass that would defy the sun's rays altogether that he never thought of looking to see what the midshipmen were doing. He immediately built up a theory of his own, and he wondered that Sir Isaac Newton (of whom he was a great admirer) had never thought of it before him. He concluded that portions of the sun's surface were becoming fused, and that the vitrified parts acted as heliotropes and threw a stronger light on the retina of the eye than it could bear. He entered into a long calculation, by which he proved satisfactorily (to himself) that such a reflector must be ten million six hundred thousand miles in area, and that the light must travel six hundred thousand miles per second. Electricity was a mere circumstance compared with it.

Thinking, perhaps, that his sextant might have been deranged, he ran below to get another; but the twenty-four were as hard-hearted as a thirty-two-pounder: they went below, also, and reappeared with innumerable small pieces of looking-glass, with which they opened such a fire on old Shacklebags that the two old quadrants of the Bonhomme Richard sank into insignificance, and the vitrified spots seemed to the master to have increased very much since he left the deck—so much so that he was heard to exclaim,

"God bless me, but the sun is melting up!" That day (and do I live to chronicle it?) Shacklebags sent in his reckoning with a remark, "No observation at noon, sun in a state of fusion."

How different was it with the two old quadrants of the Bonhomme Richard! They sent in the latitude "observed," and the rest of the twenty-four copied after them. That day twenty-four neat little *billets-doux* were laid on the captain's table, folded up in various shapes, cocked-hat fashion, squares, stars, and octagonal; and it would have puzzled the great magician Blitz himself to have opened them without damage to the envelope.

The captain was really furious with the master for not getting the sun at twelve o'clock, and had the heartlessness to ridicule his theory to his face, and insinuated that Mr. Shacklebags had something else in his eye besides vitrified spots. Picking up the twenty-four *billets-doux*, "Look here, sir," he said, "all the midshipmen even have caught the sun, and you, a master, could not get it. Get out of my cabin, sir; you are not worth your salt!" And with that poor old Shacklebags went below and sadly contemplated the initials of a certain young woman that were arranged with hooks and thimbles over his looking-glass.

The captain, being more out of humor than usual, was disposed to find fault with everything; he suddenly cast his eye over the twenty-four *billets-doux*, and calling to "Conk," bade that respectable colored "pusson" to go below and inform the midshipmen that he wanted no more colored paper sent in to him, and that hereafter they must send in their day's work on cartridge-paper, which was quite good enough for midshipmen; moreover, they were to send in their reports done up in official form, and he wanted no more cocked hats, squares, stars, or octagonals.

That was nuts for the twenty-four. Down sat they all and made out separate requisitions for ten quires of cartridge-paper, one bottle of ink, one bunch of quills, one penknife, one slate, and one pencil. "O heavens!" said Shacklebags, when he found the requisitions lying on the table, "who ever heard of such a thing as serving out two hundred and fifty quires of cartridge-paper, unless when going into action?" But he sent it in to the captain, as in duty bound, for his approval, and that gentleman cut it down to one sheet apiece, and one bottle of ink for all, and nothing more. There was no mistake, he exhibited a great deal of meanness on the occasion, and was severely talked about when the twenty-four were in caucus.

The next day, when seven bells struck, the twenty-four were on deck, backing the two old quadrants of the Bonhomme Richard, and poor old Shacklebags was more bothered than ever with the vitrified spots on the sun—he was fairly blinded, and tears ran down over the end of his nose like water over the Falls of Niagara. It was no go, he could not get an observation, and again, with the sun shining out fair, he sent in his dead reckoning with the additional remark, "No observation at noon, spots on the sun densely vitrified."

At 12.30 twenty-four official documents (two feet long and one foot wide) were laid on the captain's table, each one announcing the latitude observed, and differing considerably from the dead reckoning; but the captain was in a great rage at finding that each one had expended his entire sheet of cartridge-paper, and there was another requisition for a bottle of ink, the first one having rolled off the table. The master was sent for, and received such a "blowing up" that even old Conk pronounced it "mizzable hard doin's," and poor old Shacklebags went down into the cable tier, and was not seen until next morning.

The midshipmen were all sent for into the cabin, and, after a severe lecture about their wasteful extravagance, were told that they might go to the devil their own way, and that he, Captain Marvellous, washed his hands of them. "As to your day's work, gentlemen," he said, "don't send me any more of 'em; and get out of my cabin; I never want to lay eyes on any one of you again. Conk," he said, "see that my cook don't ever make anything for the midshipmen again when they have visitors, and don't lend 'em my two decanters and the tin dish-covers, which they are in the habit of borrowing. I wish they were all overboard; they will worry my life out of me."

"Yes, sar," said Conk. "I tought you find 'em a werry aggrawatin' set, sar; dey is alwis so, sar, at leastwise dey alwis is on dem ship on which I done hab sail in. I ain't done lent 'em de dish-cobers, sar, for dis long time, 'cause dey ax me to lend 'em two pound of sugar, and I tought dey wos gittin' too big for dar briches, sar."

"Shut your mouth, you old nigger!" said the captain, "and don't offer any of your observations until they are called for."

"Yes, sar," said Conk, and thus the affair ended; but after that the mast-head was frequently adorned with the young gentlemen's persons; but with a novel or two, however, and a lunch in their pockets, they found it preferable to learning navigation, which they looked upon as a useless branch of their profession.

CHAPTER XXV.

WHICH CONTAINS AN ACCOUNT OF A WONDERFUL MIRACLE, AND DESCRIBES A VERY IMPOSING CEREMONY.

Revenons à nos moutons, or, Let us return to our sheep.

About the time of our sojourn in Naples Bay, Mr. Spicy, the chaplain, had gone on his travels, and his cassock and surplice being left behind, they were borrowed from his boy on the plea that we were going to have a private masquerade; he hesitated a little about the propriety of letting out his master's property, but a bribe of a dollar settled all his qualms of conscience.

In the above-mentioned vestments we incased the portly person of one Deepwater (a large, fat reefer, weighing about two hundred and sixty pounds), with a large tin trumpet on his head; he was generally known as Baby Deepwater, from the fact that he would cry for hours over a tale of fiction, and also when the midshipmen would toss him in a blanket, which they frequently did; we also secured the services of four smooth-faced little messenger-boys to act as his acolytes in the approaching ceremony, and provided each one with a deep spit-box, which was to be used as a censer. Baby looked the padre to perfection, but refused to have his hair shaved from the top of his head, being very vain of his curly locks; the midshipmen were going to insist on his having it done, but when they witnessed the tears standing in Baby's eyes they very magnanimously desisted and substituted the trumpet as head-gear; the next thing we did was to procure twelve candles, which were placed in as many junk-bottles, and then we laid a large leaf of a table on four camp-stools and hung up a flag to keep out intruders.

While one gang of middies were engaged fixing a block and rope to the cross-piece over the midshipman's hatch, another party were hard at work making up a stuffed Paddy of great proportions; some hours were passed in these edifying proceedings, and when the Paddy was done, it could not have been beaten by some of the best figures in Madame Tussaud's wax-work establishment. It looked for all the world like the person for whom it was intended, even to the face, a good mask having been bought on shore for the occasion.

Among the "twenty-four" there was a very tall fellow, of pale and cadaverous countenance, called Slinky Slapjack, a nickname he obtained from the fact of his being able to coil himself away on one camp-stool, put a clothes-bag under his head, and sleep undisturbed for hours; and also from the circumstance of his having been known to eat four dozen pancakes (called slapjacks in the navy) at one sitting, and then wanted more. He was a regular Calvin Edson of a fellow in appearance, and on this occasion acted the part of corpse on express conditions that the said corpse should be fed during the approaching ceremony with an unlimited number of slapjacks and molasses.

About twelve o'clock, when the greatest number of Neapolitans were about collecting to "see the animals feed," Slinky was escorted (or rather carried) to the inclosed spot, where he was laid out; his face was daubed over with flour, his head and jaws tied up in white handkerchiefs, his arms crossed over his breast, and a wide white sheet thrown over all; being six feet four inches, he made a very respectable-looking corpse, and looked a deal sight more imposing than when he was alive; the candles were now lighted and placed at his head and feet, and standing around him, in various costumes, and with solemn mien, the midshipmen waited until the steerage was full (almost to suffocation) of the termites.

When no more could get in, and they were hustling, quarreling, and crowding each other, so as to get a full sight of what was going on, soft music was heard in the cockpit, and the faint tinkling of a little bell announced the approach of Baby Deepwater, who ascended the ladder dressed out in all his robes; he was attended by two of the midshipmen dressed in fancy rigs, one having adorned his head with a large coffee-pot, the other had selected a large pewter mug, which was tied on his head by a string under his chin, and the four acolytes with their spit-boxes brought up the rear; in one hand Baby held Bowditch's Navigator, and in the other a larger pair of wooden compasses; as he approached, the flag was suddenly removed, and there lay the dead in solemn repose, waiting to be committed to the deep after the last ceremonies were performed over his mortal remains.

The termites all crowded in, looking on with the most intense

AN INCANTATION.

curiosity, and to watch their faces it could be seen that they were deeply impressed with the ceremony.

Tinkle, tinkle, tinkle, went the little bell, and the acolytes commenced swinging about their censers, which were filled with tow, sulphur, and asafœtida, while Baby Deepwater commenced in a deep, sonorous voice to chant—

"Wax gobiscum, roar o no probis, cockuli, cockulorom e pluribus unum. Hilino sopholatibi squidii A B Squee, oh! mater vocabulorum, Canistavenising Tituri two. Pat you lie, recubans, sub tegmine fagosimi, snactissime, investus non est comatibus, roar o no probis, roro o no probis."

And the little acolytes swung round their spit-boxes (*alias* censers), and already the company began to cough.

"Ah!" sighed a fat old lady close to me, "questi sone brava gente, sone catolici, come noi altri."

"Aime povero uffiziale, che buon prete, e che bel giovane era il defunto, rassouriniglia a mio figlio," said another fat old woman, "non mangiera piu de macaroni, povereno," that being in her estimation the greatest calamity that could have befallen him.

"Parla bene il latino," put in an old fellow of about a hundred, with very long tails to his coat, and very short waist, "anch io parla latino, il prete lo parla benessimo."

Here Baby put an end to their remarks by chanting again—

"Wax gobiscum gloriam, fecit miraculum, mortuum, hocusi pocusi pitsacas bocas, puntum sosenum, mellio uno grosso, caponi que uno magra gallino, sanctum sancteriorum sanctiroryborum." And the censers went to work like young steam-engines.

There was an immense deal of coughing about this time, almost enough to interrupt the ceremonies; but curiosity kept the strangers below, and respect for the rites going on before them kept them quiet; one of the fat old ladies began to sing out, "Aqua per l'amor di Dio." "Sangre di San Gennaro," shouted an old fisherman. "Che puzzo, che puzzo, il cadavero puzza come il diavole." "Sst, sst, sst," said the crowd, "va pregare el prete"—

>"In hoc signo conquerorum
>Wax gobiscum, Slappy Jackum,
>Roundum squareum dorem borum,
>Ipse dixit, up and at um"—

low murmurs of applause on the part of the crowd, and much coughing, the censers smoking rather strong about this time.

Scantling now approached with a large covered dish, and a small pitcher holding a thick, dark fluid, and Baby Deepwater, dipping his fingers into the pitcher and raising his eyes in the direction where the main truck was supposed to be, while one of his assistants commenced reading the rule for double altitudes in Bowditch, touched the end of the sick man's nose, and in a solemn voice exclaimed,

"Arise, dead man, and eat."

At this summons the music struck up a lively air; the dead man slowly opened his eyes and sat up in bed, staring wildly about him.

"Un miraculo, un miraculo," murmured the Italians; "madre de Dio, un miraculo Americano." "Ah!" said the old fellow of one hundred, "io capita, il prete si e servito del Sangue di San Gennaro, io capita quando ha parlato latino."

"Sst, sst, silencio, Spazzino," said the crowd, "va mangiare il cadavero." If they considered the resurrection a miracle, what must they have thought when they saw Scantling approach the resurrected with the covered dish containing a large pile of slapjacks, which the said resurrected dipped into the molasses and gobbled down like magic!

"Ah! guarda come mangia le frittati," they exclaimed, "questo e davvero un miraculo." But their astonishment knew no bounds when a fresh dish was brought in, and the resurrected proceeded to eat four dozen without winking.

"Ah! povero uffizziale," said the fat old lady, "no mange niente per sixteen week, ai che puzza dio mio andiamo via, andiamo." And indeed the smell was terrible, and the resurrected began to cough so badly that we feared, at one time, he would have a relapse.

The crowd could stand the smoke and smell from the censers no longer, and began to murmur, "Che puzza, che puzza, ai che miraculo, queste sono christiani l'istesso che noi altro, ai che puzza."

The acolytes were doing their best, at this moment, to raise more smoke, though the atmosphere was so thick already you could cut it with a knife; tears were streaming down the men's and women's cheeks, not from sympathy, but from pain caused by the smoke.

About this time the resurrected had finished his slapjacks, and popping out of bed and dipping his hand into a pillow-case along-

THE SHIP IS CLEARED OF VISITORS.   321

side of him, he took out a handful of flour and slapped it in the face of an Italian dandy, who was already half suffocated with foul smells.

"Cazzo," shouted the dandy, "questo e el demonio!" another handful of flour in the face of an old woman who was shouting out "Nikolaki, Nikolaki, dove sta Nikolaki!" It was the same old woman, previously mentioned, who had again lost her darling Nikolaki, who, it appears, had not been (as was formerly supposed) boiled in the coppers.

Now came the crowning scene, which was to strike terror into their breasts and drive them out of the ship. The resurrected was becoming excited and unmanageable, and was thumping the crowd most unmercifully with his flour pillow-case; some were singing out, "Ladros, ladros, un borsainlo borsainlo, scroccone, scroccone!" and uttering all the expletives they could think of. The offender was seized by the midshipmen and rolled off into a recess in the steerage, while his counterpart, the stuffed Paddy, was hauled to the hatch, the rope quickly put around his neck, and before the Italians could think what was to be done they saw the body of the resurrected, apparently, dangling in the air. "Ai che omicidios, sono queste infami Americani," "Piratos, corsaros," "Che cogliohi appiciale un giovane," were the numerous expressions; "Andiamo! andiamo!" And, horror-struck and frightened, they rushed up the ladders; the only one left behind was the old woman who had lost her son, and who was still shouting, "Nikolaki, Nikolaki, dove sta mio figlio? Nikolaki."

For the first time during the week we had a clear ship; the Neapolitans, having no desire to see such curious performances more than once, confined themselves thereafter to looking at the outside. Baby Deepwater divested himself of his robes, and Slinky called for something to drink to keep the slapjacks quiet, while acolytes and censers were sent out of the way; we suffered almost as much with the smoke as the enemy did, and so did the lieutenants, who were looking through the wardroom blinds and enjoying the fun; lucky was it for us that the captain was out of the ship, or some one would likely have adorned the mast-head.

Mr. O'Classics was the only person who animadverted on our proceedings. "Ah, micky roony and lazy roony," he said, "ye got in the divils midshipmates' hands, did ye? Faix then ye were fools to lave your own deleceus cloimate to go bally-waggerin' over a ship; an' afther all, I don't know but it sarves you right. For

21

my part," he continued, "I like the paple, I like the cloimate, an' I loike the Punch and Judy, but divil a good pretaty av I seen since I been in the counthry; an' as to their buther, it's all crame." O'Classics was liberal enough, however, to admit that "San Carlos bate onything they iver had in Tipperary," and that "Mount Vesuvius was big enough and hot enough to roast all the pretatys in auld Ireland at one clip."

CHAPTER XXVI.

A TEDIOUS DOG-WATCH, AND A TOUGH YARN FROM A QUARTER-MASTER.

A NIGHT or two previous to our departure from Naples I had the second dog-watch on deck, after having passed the day roaming through the adjacent hills; I was standing near the taffrail, watching the full moon sailing quietly along through the deep-blue firmament, and casting a soft and mellow light on all below. It was such a moonlight as is only seen in the Bay of Naples, for nowhere does she shine so bright, or does the landscape seen by her light seem to rest in such quiet repose; the tiny fishing-boats, with numerous lights, studded the bay as thick almost as the stars of heaven, and one could well have imagined, while looking at the reflection of the moon in the still, polished surface of the sea, that there were two firmaments, one above and one below.

I was thinking of home, as who will not think of that dear spot, let him be even where Nature wears her brightest smile? Who is there who will not invest the home of his childhood with all that is beautiful around him, and perhaps deceive himself with the idea that the same moon is shining sweetly o'er the hallowed spots he so much loved, and the friends of his heart are at that moment keeping company with him looking at it as it performs its nightly course? My reveries were suddenly interrupted by Old Ben, the signal quartermaster, who had been working up to me for some time past, evidently disposed to talk his dog-watch away.

"What are you looking so melancholy about, Ben?" I asked him. "You look as though some one had broken your best spy-glass."

"Me, sir?" said Ben; "look melancholic? Oh, no, I ain't

one of them; my natural dispersition is quite the rewerse, sir, though I have gone through enough in my lifetime to make me never smile again." And the old quid shook his head very solemnly.

"Come, Ben," I said, "I shall go to sleep presently, and get mast-headed for doing so, if you don't do something to keep me awake. Come, give me an account of your adventures; I know you have many a tough yarn stowed away in your ditty-bag."

"I never tell tough yarns, Mr. Marline," he replied; "it would be very unbecoming an old man like me, who ought to be thinking of slinging his hammock in a better world than this; but I can tell you a story that will bring tears to your eyes, if you have the heart I give you the credit for. It is a tale of murder and crime, such as was never perpetrated on this earth before nor since, and, if you would like to hear it, I will tell it to you. It will serve to pass away the dog-watch at any rate, and may make you reflect seriously on the ways of Divine Providence, and the wondrous means it adopts to bring to punishment those who offend against the laws of God. Now, my good young sir, listen to me."

And divesting the story of some of Ben's phraseology, which was not in the main very ornate, I give it as he told it to me, as near as I can recollect it. It helped to pass a weary dog-watch, and may perhaps do as much for the reader.

THE PIRATE PARRICIDIO.

"I was but fourteen years old when I first went to sea," he began. "I sailed out of Liverpool in a brig of three hundred tons, commanded by Captain McGregor; we were bound to the island of Martinique, and had on board ten or twelve passengers, mostly French people, who were going there either for profit or pleasure. Among the passengers were a young Frenchman and his wife, who had been married about three years, and they were supremely happy in the possession of a beautiful little daughter just beginning to run about; her innocent prattle was the delight of her too fond parents, and the child was adored almost by every one on board. One old Frenchman in particular, Monsieur Pierre Girard, would hug and kiss little Antoinette all day long, and swore that he would work his fingers' ends off to make a fortune for her, though she was in no way related to him.

"Nothing could be more interesting than the affection existing between Mr. Laroche and his beautiful wife. They were always of a pleasant day to be found sitting aft on the weather side of the quarter-deck, and little Antoinette gamboling like an innocent lamb about their knees. He would read to his lady while she was working on some pretty dress for their beloved idol, every now and then interrupting him to draw his attention to something the little angel was doing; then they would smother her with kisses, and the fond mother, dropping her work on her knees, would regard her with silent happiness, while the husband would continue his reading. Ah me, sir," said Ben, "that was thirty years ago, but I can in my mind's eye see that happy couple and that innocent child as plainly as if they were now before me, and many a tear it brings to my old eye when I remember the many hours of misery and unhappiness through which they passed.

"Monsieur Laroche was one of those who had escaped out of France during the early period of the revolution. He was of a respectable family, and his father, who was a good royalist, had died, leaving him a handsome estate; but his own brother, who was an unscrupulous and avaricious villain, not being satisfied with what he had (though he was equally well provided for), and hating his brother for espousing one on whom he had also placed his affections, proclaimed him to 'les Terroristes,' and he was too happy to escape with his wife and child and find an asylum in England; there, on a small pittance, but happy in each other's love, they managed for a year to live in a cheap and modest little cottage. His estate was finally confiscated and fell to the lot of his villain brother, who was one of the leaders of 'les Buveurs de sang,' 'Chevaliers du Poignard,' and everything else that was horrible and bad. Monsieur Laroche, with what remained from the sale of his wife's jewels and a few hundred pounds he had invested in the English funds, was now bound to Martinique in search of a living, and was fortunate enough to make the acquaintance of Pierre Girard, who was already established there in business, and who, loving the little Antoinette as if she were his own child, promised himself the pleasure of assisting the father in the pursuit of fortune. He had already formed an idea in his own mind of the dowry he intended to bestow on his little pet. A gentle dignity distinguished the mother, though she was very gay at times and playful with her husband; she alone could make him smile and laugh when the memory of departed wealth would come to cast a shade of sadness o'er his handsome brow, for he loved her as tenderly as ever man loved woman, and all his happiness seemed to center in those two beings, his wife and little daughter; strange indeed would it have been had it been otherwise, for never on this earth were there two human beings more calculated to call forth the strongest feelings of attachment.

"It would have done your heart good, sir, to see the fondness shown by the old weather-beaten sailors for little Antoinette, and the respect they evinced for her father and mother. Sailors are a hard, weather-beaten set of fellows, but with all their roughness there is a well of human kindness within their bosoms, and when they take a fancy to any one (particularly a child) there is no end to their affection. I do believe there was not a man on board the Blue-eyed Mary (that was the name of the brig) who would not have divided his last plug of tobacco or given his allowance of grog to any of the Laroches if they had expressed half a wish for it, and that, I think, sir, is the strongest proof of kindness a sailor can show.

"Those were the happiest days of my life, for Captain McGregor was a kind man, and made every one about him as happy as circumstances would admit of. I was taken into the cabin as cabin-boy, and had nothing whatever to do but take care of little Antoinette and wait on Mr. and Madame Laroche. I found my duties almost a sinecure, for I was seldom called upon to do anything, and my greatest happiness was running after the little girl and gratifying all her whims. Sometimes when I was building block houses for the sweet little creature, or letting her ride on my back, Monsieur Laroche would pat me on the head and call me 'Bon garçon Benny,' and almost every day I received some kind token of regard from his sweet lady, which always made my heart bound with delight.

"But this happiness was of short duration, and the scenes through which I afterward passed brought me so much misery and sorrow that I almost forgot that I had ever been happy at all.

"We had been at sea twenty-five days, and had been gliding along quietly with a pleasant little breeze, had passed the island of Madeira, and had just got a snuff of the trade-winds, when in the first dog-watch a sail was seen on our weather beam, and when we could make her out she appeared to be steering for us. She proved to be a large two-topsail schooner with all kinds of sail set, and the rapid manner in which she neared us showed her to be no ordinary sailer.

"Those were the days, sir, in which it was not desirable to meet a clipper-looking schooner at sea, for the ocean was swarming with pirates, and the British navy, instead of being employed in protecting British commerce, was lying idly at Spithead looking out for the divine right of kings or something of that kind, and lending a helping hand to keep some infernal despot on his throne—or perhaps they were watching the French, who were always jumping into a war with them. The merchant service had to look out for itself; and, indeed, we would as lief almost have met the devil at sea as a British man-of-war, for all the protection we got was to be removed on board by a press-gang, and had to fight for old England whether we liked it or not. Those things were, however, so much a matter of custom that no one thought anything of it, but at the same time sailors preferred the hard work of a trader to the easy times and strict discipline of a man-of-war, and when they saw a rakish-looking vessel they gave her a wide berth, no matter what she was.

"Captain McGregor cracked on sail the moment he saw the stranger standing toward us, and the Blue-eyed Mary began to dance along over the sea as if she knew that some hard customer was after her. She was not a bad sailer, and for a time we thought we held our own with the stranger; but that hope was idle, for in a few moments his hull came looming up above the horizon, and then we saw that he was going two knots to our one.

"Our only hope now was to dodge him in the dark, and as the sun went down in a thick bank of clouds, and the weather was a little hazy, the dim outlines of our pursuer became fainter and fainter, until at last we lost sight of him altogether. Old Captain McGregor began to smile again, for his face had an uneasy look upon it as long as the stranger was in sight, and he did not know what his fate might be before morning. The brig was well armed with ten twenty-four-pounder carronades, and we had a crew of twenty men, officers and all, besides the ten or fifteen male passengers, who were all men of mettle and could do good service in time of need; but, Lord bless you! what could a ten-gun brig with her pop-guns do against one long-tom of such a schooner as that? and if she was a pirate, we felt sure that she carried more than one of that sort; but the captain got everything ready for action, and put a few shot in the galley fire to be ready in case their services were needed.

"As soon as it was quite dark Captain McGregor took in the

steering sails and hauled on a wind on the larboard tack, standing in toward the Cape de Verd; he felt sure that the stranger did not see us, and took it for granted (if he was a pirate) that he would follow the course we were steering when he last saw us. Every light in the ship was put out or concealed so that it would not show, and every precaution taken that we might not be seen; so sure was the captain that the stranger would not be in sight in the morning that he dispelled the gloom that had settled on the pale and anxious faces of the passengers. Mrs. Laroche, who had been sitting as pale as death, pressing her darling little Antoinette to her bosom, consented to put the child to sleep and take a little repose herself, while the anxious husband said he would keep watch with the captain until daylight. All that night we turned and doubled like a hare, first standing on a wind with all we could carry, and then running with the wind on the quarter, so as to leave no chance of seeing the schooner at daylight.

"All night the crew were at their posts; there were few drowsy people about, I can tell you, and every old sailor had a yarn to tell about some blood-thirsty pirate that would make your blood run cold.

"At that time there was a story afloat of a dreadful Portuguese pirate named 'El Parricidio,' from the fact of his having killed his own father in the most brutal manner; after committing the dreadful deed he shipped on board of a slaver, and, being associated with a set of villains as hardened as himself in crime, he killed the captain and had himself elected in his place; the next step was to turn pirate and commence a career that would shock the annals of crime. Now and then faint rumors were afloat of a two-topsail schooner with a horrible-looking creature as her captain; but if such a vessel did exist, the pirates left so little trace of their crimes that it was impossible to know whether there was any foundation or not for the reports. A number of fine ships that had left England for the West Indies had been missing, though they had been supposed to have foundered at sea in some of the dreadful hurricanes; but one ship had been left without being properly scuttled or set fire to, the pirate being frightened off by the approach of a ship of war. When the officers went on board the deserted vessel there were too many evidences existing that she had fallen a prey to pirates: the sides were covered with blood, foot-prints of blood were fresh upon the deck, and a female hand with the rings upon the fingers was found grasping the man-rope at the gangway; it had been severed at the wrist, and in the last agonies of death had retained the grasp made while the owner was being dragged to an untimely grave or something worse. There were too many reports of horrors committed in France at that time to cause much attention to be paid to a vague rumor about a pirate, especially as the vessel that boarded the deserted ship was said to be a Frenchman, and no reliable information could be obtained regarding her. Ships, however, went heavily manned and armed, and instances had occurred where some had been reconnoitred by a clipper-looking schooner and escaped unmolested.

"The night passed away slowly listening to these stories, and I believe I was a shade whiter when morning came for fear of seeing a bloody pirate close on board of us; what, then, must have been my feelings when at the break of day we descried a sail, and that sail was the identical two-topsail schooner dodging along after us under easy canvas, and evidently waiting for daylight to pounce upon us. To describe the scene of excitement that ensued would be impossible; the captain took the deck, guns were cast loose, pistols loaded, and boarding-pikes laid out ready for use; the Frenchmen were running about the decks, gathering up swords and muskets ready to defend themselves, while preparations were made to send the women below to a place of safety. Never shall I forget the parting between Mr. Laroche and his wife as the time came for him to go on deck; despair and anguish was written in legible characters on her face, and he, poor man, was pale as the purest marble, while his lips were firmly pressed together, showing a determination that nothing but death could conquer. Alas! they both felt, sir, that it was their last meeting on earth, and even the dear little Antoinette seemed to cling to her father in his last embrace as if she was aware that she should never see him more.

"All this time the schooner was gaining rapidly upon us, and she had now got so near that we could see her men on deck and her long gun pointing over the bow. There was no doubt in the mind of any one about her character, and, if there was, it was not allowed long to exist, for as the sun rose above the horizon a large bloody flag fluttered at her peak, and at her fore there floated a flag bearing the name of the detested Parricidio. There was one look of anguish among the whole of that crew, but it disappeared in a moment when the cool voice of McGregor exclaimed, 'Now, boys, we have got to fight for our lives, and recollect we are Britons, and ought not to fear those rascally pirates.' He had scarcely uttered the words when a shot from the schooner came dancing over the waves and took off a piece from under our counter. 'Luff to and lay the main-topsail to the mast, and rake her as she comes down on us,' said the captain.

"The order was quickly obeyed, and, as the Blue-eyed Mary came to the wind, and the guns were brought to bear, a broadside was poured into the approaching schooner, and the splinters were seen to fly in every direction. This was evidently an unexpected attack to the pirates, who were not aware that they had to do with an armed vessel; the schooner's helm was put a-lee instantly, and she flew round like a top, but not before she had received another broadside, and her fore-topmast fell dangling over the side, struck by one of our shot.

" The pirates evidently did not like this sport, and there seemed to be some confusion on board, for your murderers are always cowards at heart, and only attack when they know their prey is defenseless. For a few moments our guns did good execution, their main-topsail yard came down by the run on to the cap, and the bloody trophy at her peak fell upon the deck, the halyards cut away by our grape-shot.

"The pirate was now busy getting his foresheet aft and his inner jib up, and commenced shooting ahead out of our range. Captain McGregor gave orders to 'wear ship,' and bring the other battery to bear; but just as we were going off before the wind the schooner avoided the effects of our manœuvre by putting her helm down and going about, thereby increasing her distance and getting out of range of our guns; we were, however, in time to give her one broadside, but, though we saw the splinters fly, no serious damage seemed to be done to the hull or spars, and before we could load up again she was out of reach of our short carronades.

"The passengers, who knew nothing about such matters, thought she was running away, but our captain knew better than that, for he judged truly that the villains were only trying to get at long shot, when they would riddle us with the guns of greater range.

" As was expected, she hove to about a mile and a half from us, and opened fire with two long-toms, one forward and one aft, and almost every shot told with dreadful havoc either among our men or on our spars. What could we do? We were a perfect target to be shot at. We fired away, elevating our guns as much as possible, but our shot all fell short, and the devils only laughed at us; to describe the scene that ensued would be impossible: the shot came pounding on our decks like hail, and we could only stand and take it. All hands went to work to make sail on the brig with the hope of escaping or of delaying our capture as long as possible, trusting that some vessel of war might hear the guns and come to our rescue; but these were vain hopes, sail after sail was shot from aloft, and every spar was so riddled that we gave up in despair. Captain McGregor, who never once lost his presence of mind, sent every one below among the cargo, with instructions to stand by to rush on deck in case the pirate should attempt to board us, and, standing calmly at the helm, he bravely waited the worst, having made up his mind to die at his post, knowing what his fate would be when the pirates captured him.

"In the mean time the pirates approached closer, and, taking up a position on our quarter, poured in a fire that swept our decks; one shot cut off the right leg of Captain McGregor, who, though suffering intense agony and nearly fainting from loss of blood, sat down on the deck and steered the brig. Never was there a more heroic man than that. He was an honor to Scotland, of which he was a native, and would have stood as high in fame as Nelson had the same opportunity been offered him. Eight of our crew and passengers were lying dead on the deck, and among them good old Mr. Girard, whose heart was pierced by a grape-shot, and the shrieks that came up from the run under the cabin too plainly told that some sad misfortune had happened there. I could stand it no longer, and went aft to see what I could do for them, though I knew that I could not do much.

"As I passed Captain McGregor he took me by the hand, and, as the large drops of perspiration stood upon his forehead, he said, 'Ben, if you live through this, see my owners and tell them I died at my post and defended their property to the last, and tell them, Ben, to remember that I have a wife and child whom I leave without a penny in the world; God bless you, boy, and may you never want a friend.' Just at that moment I heard a shriek in the cabin as a shot came crashing through the stern, and I rushed below to see what was the matter. I found Mrs. Laroche lying on the floor with her child clasped to her bosom; she had crawled up from the run, and, overcome with fright, lay half dead with fear upon the deck. I tried to console her by telling her that her husband was safe and that we had a strong party yet in case the pirates attempted to board us; she was about to rush frantically upon the deck to join him, when the voice of Captain McGregor was heard calling, 'Away there, boarders!' I looked out of the stern-window, and there was the schooner close alongside of us, and in another instant came a crash, and the two vessels were close together. Then was heard a shout from each vessel, the rattling of small-arms, and in another instant the trampling and stamping of feet on our deck, like men mixed up in bloody fray.

"Seizing a large carving-knife, I rushed out, not knowing exactly what I was going to do, and, O heavens! what a sight met my eyes! A hundred and fifty of the most ferocious-looking wretches the imagination ever pictured to itself covered our deck, cutting and slashing right and left among the small remnant of our crew. One after another of our men fell covered with wounds, and poor Captain McGregor lay at his post with his brains blown out, while a dead pirate, killed by his hand, lay across his body. Mr. Laroche was fighting, sword in hand, against five ruffians, whom he kept at bay with his broadsword, four having already fallen at his feet. His face was covered with blood from a large gash across his forehead, and his left arm hung helpless at his side from the effects of a pistol-shot. The fight was too unequal to last long, for as our men fell, overpowered by numbers, the miscreants rushed upon him, and he fell pierced by a hundred wounds; that was the last I remember, for a stunning blow knocked me senseless, and I only awoke to consciousness an hour after on board the pirate. How I got there or why I was saved (the only one out of all that crew) I did not know, but I was lying, bound hand and foot, on the quarter-deck, and through the port could see the brig not far off, which the pirates were rifling.

"On an arms-chest close to me was seated the ugliest human being my eyes ever beheld; there was nothing indeed human about him, and a recent gash across his cheek, and his blood-stained countenance, added no charm to his features. His arms hung away down, almost touching the deck, and his form was rendered particularly hideous by a large lump on his back. I knew from the description I had heard of him that this was the dreaded Parricidio, and I shuddered when I saw him turn his bloodshot eyes upon me.

"At this moment a boat approached from the brig, and I could see the pirates pass a rope down and lift something up the side. Good God! it was the lifeless body of Mrs. Laroche, all bedabbled with blood, and directly after a huge negro appeared carrying in his arms the poor little Antoinette, pale as a sheet and crying most bitterly.

"'Is she dead?' shouted the wretch on the arms-chest.

"'No,' said the negro, 'she has only fainted because she saw her husband's corpse, and that blood she got from taking a last embrace of him; it was that fellow who gave you the cut, Parricidio.'

"'Ah!' said the pirate, while a gleam of fiendish delight stole over his devilish countenance. 'Is it so? Then I will be doubly revenged. Fling her into the cabin, and pitch the brat after her; when she comes to I will pitch it overboard before her eyes. What booty in the brig, Falsario?'

"'Thirty thousand dollars,' said the negro, 'and a rich cargo of silks.'

"'*Tem dido isso*,' said the captain; 'then get me a glass of brandy, for this infernal cut makes me feel faint. Diavolo, how those English fought! But none are left, Falsario, I trust?'

"'No, Parricidio, not one, with the exception of that brat on the deck there,' replied the negro. 'What you want with him I don't know; you had better let me cut his throat and throw him overboard.'

"'No, Falsario,' said the captain; 'the crew may cut your throat before long, and I want some one to taste my victuals in case of poison, and these fools of English, though they fight hard, are too chicken-hearted to poison any one, so I will train him, and if he won't learn you may cut his throat.' All this was said in Portuguese, but, as I knew the Spanish language, I could understand every word of it, and you may imagine my feelings. The perspiration stood in large drops on my forehead, and my hair stood fairly on end; I could scarcely realize that two human beings could talk so coolly about murder after satiating their appetites with the blood of about thirty of their fellow-creatures. They were hardened indeed in crime, and I thought with anguish of the horrible fate that most certainly awaited the unhappy but beautiful French lady when she should regain her consciousness. Far better would it have been had she shared her husband's fate than to have fallen into the hands of so unscrupulous a wretch as Parricidio; better by far that the husband and wife should have been undivided in death, and that the dear little Antoinette had shared the same fate; it would have been less horrid than a painful awakening to a consciousness of her awful position, and I almost prayed God that she might never revive to see my painful forebodings realized. I wondered why Heaven permitted such villainous wretches to be triumphant over innocence and virtue, and though we are taught that Providence has many ways of working out its ends and bringing malefactors finally to justice, I can not for the life of me understand why a good and beautiful woman—one who never passed a day without adoring her Maker, and whose every thought was as pure as the dew-drops from heaven—should be made use of as an instrument to bring about the final punishment of such a miserable wretch as this pirate. Why should she who was born to shed joy and happiness on all around her be cast into the clutches of such an insatiable monster as this Parricidio? Why did not Heaven take her to itself and place her where she was made for, among the choir of angels who sing the praises of God around the throne of mercy? These are matters, sir, which rather bother us poor sailors, and about which I find it better not to reason, for they sometimes raise doubts in my mind calculated to interfere with my peace and happiness.

"So much was I interested for Mrs. Laroche that I never thought once of myself. I determined in my own mind that I would do all I could to serve her and alleviate her sufferings if she should ever revive, for all this time she lay upon the deck at the feet of the two pirates, to all appearances quite dead, while dear little Antoinette was clasping the inanimate body and calling her mamma to awake, that papa wanted her. It was a heartrending sight, but only served to amuse the two pirates, who had not one drop of humanity in their composition.

"'Falsario,' said the captain, 'loose that boy lying there, and kick him up; he is not insensible, for I saw his eyes open while you were pulling from the prize. Take the woman and her child down into the cabin with the grating windows, for she looks like one of those who would not hesitate to jump overboard when she knows what is in store for her, for you recollect how I lost that beautiful American woman, who jumped through the stern port and strangled herself with her hair; *que pena, isto faz me estremecer.*' And they both set up a laugh that made my blood run cold. 'I shall take better care of this one,' said Parricidio; 'and if she is not very amiable she shall see her own child floating astern on a cork buoy, food for gulls and sharks; while, after letting her feast her eyes for a time on the spectacle, I will turn her over to the crew.'

"'What an inventive genius you have, Parricidio!' said the negro. 'You don't reduce the fair sex by sighs and prayers, that is very certain; but one who showed so much ingenuity in killing his father and getting away with his money-bags ought to be up to anything.'

"'You are right there, negro,' said the other (who seemed to take this last remark as a great compliment). 'I had almost forgotten that event, and I wish you would remind me of it now and then; for it was my first crime, and the cause of all my present happiness and wealth. But, now, Falsario, go below with the woman, and send the English boy down to attend her. She will be less violent when she comes to in his presence, and I don't want the crew to see too much of her or they might claim their rights.'

"With these remarks he came to me, and, turning me over with his foot, ordered me to get up, which I managed to do, though I nearly fell again from a painful sensation running through my brain.

"Addressing me in English, he told me to go below and take care of the lady, and, 'You English dog,' said he, 'if you are not faithful to all my commands, I will salt and pepper you, and roast you before a slow fire. The only reason why I saved your life is that you took no part in the conflict. Had you done so, you would have been food for sharks now, with the other fools who undertook to whip off Parricidio. You are not the first, though, who have tried that, and likely will not be the last. Now down with you into the cabin, and the sooner the lady is ready to receive me complacently the better it will be for you.'

"My first impulse was to seize the knife hanging to his waist and pierce him to the heart; but I instantly thought how little good such an act would do me or those over whom I determined to watch, and I sadly followed the pirate below, who, pointing to a door, bade me enter.

"There I found the unhappy lady lying on a sofa in a richly adorned cabin, with the ports covered with strong iron gratings, and no other egress besides the door through which I came. How many scenes of lawlessness and crime, I thought to myself, have been enacted in this chamber! And with a shudder I recalled to my recollection the fate of the unhappy American lady who had jumped through the port into the sea, and whose sad fate the two pirates had alluded to.

"While standing near the prostrate form of Mrs. Laroche, poor little Antoinette jumped toward me, and I clasped her in my arms, while she cried almost enough to break her heart. 'Mamma sleep,' she said; 'mamma no wake up for Tony. Papa gone away. Tell papa come back and wake mamma up.' And she kissed me a thousand times, and I mingled my tears with hers.

"The poor lady was still insensible, but when I approached her I could see that she still breathed heavily, and that animation was only for a time suspended. I immediately ran to the sideboard, where there were bottles of liquors standing, and, having found some brandy, I proceeded to rub her face and hands, and in a short time was rewarded by seeing her heave a deep sigh; and, renewing my efforts, she finally opened her eyes and stared wildly upon me. 'O my God!' were the first words she said, 'what a frightful dream I have had!' And then, starting up, she screamed, 'My child! my child! where is my child?'

"'Here, mamma,' said the dear little creature. And, clasping her mother round the neck, she smothered her with kisses.

"'Thank God!' she exclaimed; 'then it was only a dream after all. But, O Ben! such a horrid dream, that I am sure I have grown ten years older from the effects of it.' Then, looking at my sad face, and casting her eyes around the cabin, she jumped up in a perfect frenzy. 'Good heavens! Benny, where am I? What place is this?' she exclaimed. 'Where is my husband?' And at that name the most frightful change came over her, and I thought she was going to faint once more. Falling back upon the sofa, she clasped her hands to her forehead and burst into an agony of tears. 'I see it all,' she cried; 'I understand it now. It was no dream after all, but horrid reality. O husband! husband! are we never to meet again on this cruel earth? are we indeed separated for ever? No, no,' she said, turning her eyes to heaven, 'we still will meet there, where nothing will ever trouble us, and this is but one of the trials through which we have to pass to purify the soul ere it seeks the presence of God. My child, oh, my child! you are still left to me.' And, covering Antoinette with her arms, she shed plenteous tears over her, which seemed to relieve her.

"'I see it all now, Benny,' she exclaimed. 'The pirate's first gun, the tramp of feet, the shouts of men mingling in conflict, are all plain to me now. My husband's corpse, disfigured with a thousand wounds, lying trodden under foot upon the deck, will never, never be forgotten; and I sinfully hoped, when I fell upon his body and pressed my lips to his gaping wounds, that our souls were united in heaven, never to be torn asunder.' And again her bosom was convulsed with such grief that I thought it would kill her.

"I was too much overcome to speak or offer any consolation, but, leading her child to her, placed its hand in hers. She raised her eyes mournfully, then, clasping Antoinette passionately to her breast, she exclaimed, 'Poor, dear little one! and who was there to take care of you with father and mother both gone? Who would have healed that little broken heart, and have wiped away the tears of grief? Father of heaven,' she exclaimed, falling on her knees, 'forgive the anguish of a bereaved wife, who, in misery at her loss, knows not what she says. You have left me my child, kind Being, and I am sinful in wishing to be separated from her. But oh, Father of mercy, I loved him so, and did perhaps so cherish his image, that I may have been wanting in duty to my Creator. Thy will be done, good God, and I bow humbly to thy decree, trusting that at your own time we shall be united in heaven.' She arose from her knees, and, drawing her child to her bosom, silently wept over her, while Antoinette said, 'Don't cry, mamma, papa come presently.'

"'No, child,' said the mother; 'father has gone to heaven, and we can not meet him till God appoints the time.'

"'Then ask God to let us go also, mamma; I know papa wants us.' This brought forth another passionate flood of tears, and one could well have imagined the fountain of sorrow had almost run dry. After a while, however, the lady became comparatively calm, and but for the painful expression on her countenance and a lock of her hair grown quite white, no emotion but deep and silent grief was perceptible. Oh, how I wished at that moment that I was a good Christian like that pure being sitting before me! What but a firm reliance on the justice of God, and the certainty of one day resting under the shadow of his greatness, could apparently reconcile one who had met with the greatest earthly loss that could happen—the loss of a beloved husband, whose days were spent at her side, and who was only happy while basking in the sunshine of her smile? Never on earth were there two beings so wrapped up in each other, and little Antoinette was a link that bound them still stronger together.

"'We have fallen on unhappy times, dear Benny,' she said to me, 'and I dread to think of the misery that is yet in store for us; we are of course on board the pirate vessel, for I do not recognize in these splendid trappings by which we are surrounded any of the furniture of the Blue-eyed Mary.'

"'Yes, good lady,' I replied, 'we are indeed prisoners to the most horrid butcher that ever trod the earth, the cruel Parricidio, who killed his own father, and who I heard boasting of the circumstances this morning.'

"She turned deadly pale, if a countenance already pallid with woe could change at all, and clasping her child to her bosom, 'Good God,' she said, 'if I am reserved for a fate that makes my inmost soul to shudder, take, oh! take me and my child from this world of woe. Better far that I should perish in the deep than live dishonored and polluted. My poor, poor child,' she said, 'we will join your father in heaven, for I could not leave you behind me on this earth of sin and wickedness.'

"'Is heaven a nice place, mamma, and has papa got a nice house there?' said Antoinette.

"I thought the poor mother's heart would break at this remark of her daughter; she bowed her head upon her bosom and wept long and silently, while I stood a respectful witness of her deep distress. I can not tell you the effect it had on me in the last hour. I became a man in feeling, though but a child in years, and I determined to watch over the safety of those two dear beings as if they were my mother and sister, and wait patiently the turn of events to see what I could do for their relief.

"At this moment we heard the shout of many voices outside the vessel, and, going to the grated port, I looked out and saw that the Blue-eyed Mary was in flames, and that the pirates, having taken all that was valuable from her, had left her.

"The fire flew aloft, catching the sails and licking up every combustible thing in the way, and in a short time the brig was completely enveloped in the flames. The fire soon reached the magazine, where a small quantity of powder was stowed; it was sufficient, however, to cause a loud explosion, and in a minute the Blue-eyed Mary had disappeared under the waves, and nothing but a few spars and pieces of floating timber remained upon the surface of the water.

"The lady prayed fervently while this scene was being enacted. She knew that her husband's body was on the deck of the ill-fated vessel, and to think that his remains should not meet with Christian burial almost broke her heart. 'Better thus, dear husband,' she said, 'than to be as I am, in the hands of a ruthless murderer. Ah!

Henri, Henri, I feel we soon shall meet again.' And she sobbed so pitifully that it must have touched the heart of the ruffian could he have seen her, if heart he had.

"There was now a noise and bustle on deck, and by the motion I could see that the pirate was once more under sail and going rapidly through the water, like a ravenous shark, having satiated himself with plunder. He was bound in search, no doubt, of a place where he could deposit his ill-gotten wealth; for these pirates have all got their stow-holes, and no doubt many thousands of doubloons and dollars lie hid among the unfrequented islands of the ocean.

"Two days passed away without any notice of us from the captain, Parricidio, during which time none of us had tasted a mouthful of anything but some crackers and cheese that we found on the sideboard, and a little wine. On the third day I went on deck to endeavor to see the captain, for the child was suffering from hunger, and was hot and feverish from sickness.

"I found Parricidio sitting on the deck, propped up with cushions, his face deadly pale, and looking as if he was suffering from his wounds; at his side, close at hand, lay a pair of pistols, and his sword was placed where he could put his hand on it in a moment. Amidst all his boasted wealth and happiness he distrusted it seems, those around him who were sworn to obey his commands, and who were likely only waiting for an opportunity to get rid of their tyrant.

"The deck of the pirate vessel presented a very animated scene, and a painter would have made a good picture could it have been transferred to canvas. The vessel was a large schooner of nearly three hundred tons, and carried twelve brass guns at her sides and two long brass twenty-four-pounders at the stern and bow. She was rather a neat-looking vessel inside, and in any other employment might have done good service; but there were many stains of blood upon her deck, which I fear me, sir, would never come out with all the holy-stoning in the American navy. Our shot had told well upon her hull, for three or four carpenters were at work mending up the holes made in the bulwarks; had the rencontre been at close quarters, the result of the action would have been very different, and all the harm I wish the man who invented carronades is, that he may meet with a pirate who carries two long brass thirty-two-pounders, while he has nothing but his pop-guns to defend himself with.

"The crew of this vessel was composed of all sorts of people, and from all countries. Playing at monte, between two guns, were a dozen cut-throat-looking fellows, who were evidently Spaniards; they played with great gravity, and carried their knives in their belts, ready to defend their winnings. Farther forward were a gang of Portuguese, who were handling their knives and cleaning off the spots of blood that had adhered to them in the affray with our brig; they were boasting of their exploits, and telling of how many they had each killed. They are great boasters and greater cowards these Portuguese, and will only attack a man who is not armed. A knot of Frenchmen were sitting about the long gun, smoking and drinking, and talking of the fun they would have when they returned to 'la belle France.' Two fierce, dogged-looking Englishmen were knotting the shrouds that were carried away by our shot, no doubt being the only good seamen on board, and all the rope business fell to their lot. There were negroes, Lascars, Italians, and Dutchmen, all dressed in the costume of their country, and the language of all those nationalities might be heard spoken at the same time. Among the crew were two men who evidently had little to say to any one around them. They were leaning against the bulwarks, talking in a low voice to each other, unnoticed by any. They were evidently of the Anglo-Saxon race, but whether English or Americans I could not at that time discover. I was wondering to myself whether those two were pressed men or not (for pirates have press-gangs as well as some civilized nations), when a thundering voice close to me shouted, 'Well, whelp, what do you want? If you expect any sympathy from that crowd you are very much mistaken, for they are already grumbling because I won't let them cut your throat and turn your Frenchwoman over to them; but, by ——, I make it a point to thwart them in everything they ask, and your throat sha'n't be cut until I cut it myself, which I will certainly do when I find you no longer of use to me.'

"These words made my blood run cold, but, remembering that I lived for others and not for myself, I replied respectfully to the scoundrel, and told him that I was desirous to please him (God forgive me for lying), and told him that my mistress was really suffering for food.

"'Ah! is it so?' he said. 'Well, she can have plenty of that, and do you see that she wants for nothing; in a day or two I will pay her a visit, and I expect her to be looking her prettiest. Tell her a live lover is worth ten dead husbands, and that she can make a paradise for herself if she so disposes. But look here, boy,' he said (and the most demoniacal expression came over his countenance), 'tell her if she loves her child (as it is said that foolish mothers do) that she must welcome me properly; no sighs, no tears for the dead, but love and smiles for the living. Diavolo! but I have almost had a mutiny on her account already, and I must have a ready recompense for not complying with the wishes of my would-be murderers. Go, now, and keep your ears on your head.' And with that he rang a bell close at hand, and the negro Falsario made his appearance.

"'Falsario,' he said, 'see that the Frenchwoman has all she wants. She has asked to eat already. In two days more she will be ready to wear a bridal wreath and receive a new lord.'

"'If you would only send her your miniature, Parricidio,' he replied, 'she would dry her tears in an hour, you are such a beauty.' And the two wretches laughed heartily at their own conceit.

"I was too full of indignation to speak, had it been prudent to do so, and I walked off sadly to the cabin to comfort the lady, if in my power, and think of some plan for her safety and protection. I determined never to leave her for a moment, and endeavor to get possession of some weapon with which to defend her honor if it was assailed. In the course of half an hour Falsario appeared at the door with a waiter full of all kinds of delicacies. There was nothing wanting to tempt the palate, and everything was served on massive silver, with cups of gold to drink out of. But, alas! could gold, steeped in the blood of a fellow-creature, please the wife of a murdered husband, or all the dainties in creation bring her an appetite after such an agony of tears? She ate not. But the little Antoinette, unconscious of the sorrow that was eating away the life of her mother, ate ravenously.

"Three days passed, and the pirate had not yet paid his promised visit. His wounds still kept him confined to his cushions, and I only hoped that they might continue to torture him. I thought, perhaps, that a man-of-war might fall in with us and take the schooner before an outrage was committed that would disgrace the annals of crime; but day after day passed away, and nothing hove in sight. We steered southwest, and were running along rapidly with the trade-winds, I supposed bound to the West Indies; for it is always a rule with pirates, after plundering a vessel and committing such crimes as I have mentioned, to change their cruising-ground and go to some distant place, where they enact anew their scenes of murder and rapine.

"We had been on board three weeks, and the lady's grief had settled into a calm melancholy which nothing could dispel. She prayed half the day long and fervently, and at night she made little Antoinette kneel down beside her and pray to God for deliverance from the den of pirates. I always took part in these devotions, and truly no sinner ever poured out more heartfelt prayers than I did on those occasions.

"One afternoon, on the twentieth day after the massacre, I went on deck to get something for the lady and child to eat. The captain was not in his accustomed place, and I awaited his return. He had quite recovered from his wounds, and, as he had not been unkind to me of late, I thought that perhaps some spark of humanity still lingered in his bosom, and that he had determined to forego his hellish designs. At that moment a shriek from the cabin struck upon my ear, and, without a moment's thought and almost crazy at the idea of having left my charge, I rushed below. Good heavens! what a spectacle met my sight! The demon Parricidio was standing inside the cabin with little Antoinette held aloft in his left hand, while his right held a knife of glittering brightness to her innocent throat. Mrs. Laroche was on her knees before the monster, begging the life of her child.

"'Give me my child! give me my child!' she cried, 'and do with me as you please; but spare, oh, spare my child!' were the only words I heard, for I was rushing on him to stab him in the back with a carving-knife that I had secreted about my person, when two brawny arms were thrown around me, and I found myself in the grasp of the herculean Falsario. He struck me one blow with his clinched fist that deprived me of my senses, and when I came to I found myself in a dark hole, bound hand and foot. How long I had been there I knew not, and neither could I tell how long after I came to I remained there, for it was so dark there was no means of counting days or hours. A pitcher of water and some crusts of bread were handed down to me every day, and though I had no appetite, yet I ate to preserve my life, thinking it might still be useful to those I loved. The blood almost stood still in my veins when I thought of what might have happened during my absence, and when I remembered the words uttered by Mrs. Laroche, the terrible thought struck me that she might have sacrificed herself to save the life of her child. Whether we ever were to meet again I could not foresee. I had no idea what my fate was to be. It was certain, however, that they were not going to kill me just yet, or they would not have troubled themselves about my diet.

"As well as I could judge, about a week after my confinement the hatch over my head opened, and the voice of Falsario ordered me to come forth. I arose, stiff and benumbed, and when I stood in the fresh air once more I almost fainted with the change.

"'Follow me,' said my conductor; 'and mind, no words, nor any excitement at what you see, or I will plant a knife in your heart as sure as you live. Thank your stars,' he continued, 'that Parricidio did not know of the compliment you intended for him with the carving-knife, or your life would not have been worth a groat. Come to your mistress—I mean Parricidio's mistress, now, for they are as thick as two turtle-doves,' he said, with a sneer.

"For a moment I had to lean against the bulkhead for support, 'Can it be,' I said to myself, 'that my worst fears are realized, and that she still lives? But, alas! poor lady,' I said, 'your cup of sorrow has indeed been full to overflowing, and I shall be the last one to cast a shadow of blame upon you. Happen what may, I will still die to serve you.'

"Falsario opened the cabin-door and pushed me in, and, O God! what a picture of grief and ruin met my eyes! There sat the poor lady, looking twenty years older than when I left her. Her eyes were swollen and bloodshot, and every bit of color had faded from her cheek; there was a maniacal expression about the mouth that told she had met with much sorrow since our separation. She raised her eyes mournfully as I entered, and, holding out her attenuated hand to me, burst into a flood of tears.

"'Don't weep, lady,' I said, 'all will yet be well.' She pointed to the little Antoinette, who was lying on the sofa propped up with a pillow, the shadow of her former self, burning up with fever, her little eyes sunk deep in the sockets. She was tossing restlessly on her couch, and evidently did not know me when I leaned over and kissed her, while scalding tears fell from my eyes when I saw what a change had come over her since I last saw her.

"'Go away, you bad man,' she said to me; 'you sha'n't kill mamma; you sha'n't kill Benny; my papa will kill you.' And so she rambled on in her conversation, while my heart bled to hear her.

"'You see a sad change here, dear Benny,' said the lady, 'since you left us, and I have gone through all that a mortal could go through and yet live. My brain is on fire, and but for that dear child I should be mad. But the love of the mother is strong within me, and Heaven wills that I shall be chastened of all human affections. She will die, Benny' (and her voice faltered as she said it), 'and then I will follow her; but while there is life in her dear form I feel it a duty to live for the sake of the angel God has given me, knowing that my reward will come hereafter; and if I have drank the deep cup of sorrow on earth, I shall drink the waters of Lethe in heaven.'

"I tried to console her, but she told me there was no consolation for her; she was dishonored, and life had no longer any charms for her, and she longed to rest in the bosom of her Redeemer. Then she told me the horrid tale of her wrongs, and I swore, if it cost me my life, I would avenge them on the perpetrator.

"It appears that on the day I went on deck the brutal Parricidio stood before her in her apartment ere she was aware of it. She had never seen the hideous monster before, and could hardly repress a shriek when her eyes beheld his inhuman form. 'Sit quiet, fair lady,' he said to her; 'I come to console, not to frighten you, and I hope to bring back the smile to those sweet lips and the color to those cheeks.'

"'Is it the murderer of my husband who talks of bringing a smile to my lips?' she scornfully replied. 'Out of my sight, you demon, ere an angry God blasts you where you stand! I hate and scorn you, if such a feeling can exist toward so inhuman a butcher!'

"'Ah!' he said, 'scornful, eh? And has your spirit not been tamed by the lessons you have lately learned? My good woman, it is time that you should reduce that lofty air. It won't pass current here.'

"'My spirit, sir, has bowed in submission to my Maker, but can never stoop to the murderer of my husband.'

"'Ha! ha! ha!' he laughed. 'That is very fine, no doubt; but in these arms I intend that you shall soon cease to think of your murdered husband, and learn to receive me as your future lover.'

"'Death sooner!' cried the lady. 'I would sooner be food for sharks than let your hateful hand touch the hem of my garment! Out of my sight, monster! The presence of you is agony to me.'

"'Is it so?' said the pirate. 'Then death you shall have; and I will commence here.' And with that he seized the child, and had the knife to its throat, when the feelings of the mother overcame her, and she who would not beg for herself asked mercy of the pirate for that dear child. She could have borne the thrust of the knife herself and welcomed its approach ; but when she saw the glittering weapon within an inch of her darling's throat her pride gave way, and she shrieked for mercy for her child. The thought of what passed is too painful to relate, and I would fain drive it from my memory.

" 'God, I know, will forgive me for living, Benny,' she cried, 'for I live but for Antoinette. My soul is still pure, and just as acceptable in the sight of Heaven as if that monster had never seen me. I leave him to God's punishment, which will sooner or later overtake him ; and I only pray that my Maker may soon take me to himself and end all my sorrows.'

"Let me pass over the unhappiness and misery of the following three weeks. The life of Antoinette hung by a single thread, and nothing but the most constant attention on the part of that suffering mother prevented the light from going out. At length the little sufferer gave signs of recovery. The fever left her, but, oh! in what a condition ! Her attenuated face and hands were painful to look upon, and it was some days before she could lisp the endearing name of mamma.

"One day she said, 'Mamma, I have been to heaven, and have seen papa. He says we shall come to him there, and be happy in a great mansion, like we were in France.'

"Scalding tears fell from the mother's eyes down her pale cheeks, and she folded the little creature in her arms and silently prayed that God might deliver them from all their dangers.

"During the illness of Antoinette I had frequently to go on deck for medicines and other things that were wanted, and I lost no opportunity of looking around me seeking some means of escape. The dispensary where the medicine was kept was near the second cabin-door, and I always went there alone to get what was required. The pirate vessel was not supplied with a medical man, and every one was his own doctor. Among the medicines were two large bottles of laudanum, kept I knew not for what purpose at that time, but afterward learned that the captain used to drug the crew's liquor when he wanted to secrete his treasure on shore, and he and Falsario could work together unmolested. I noticed the bottles the first time I went to the dispensary, and thought to myself they might be useful to me some day. The crew's grog was set

THE PIRATE PARRICIDIO.

out every evening near the dispensary, and I felt tempted once or twice to empty the contents of the laudanum-bottles into it. No matter, I thought, if I kill them all; they are more or less murderers, and I would only be killing them in self-defense, and to save the lives of those who are dearer to me than my own.

"One night I was standing near the door of the cabin leading to the deck; it was blowing a violent squall, and the sails were flying about in great confusion. The captain was giving orders after orders that no one seemed to obey, and I heard a voice near me say in good English, 'The wretches are all so drunk that many of them can't move from the berth-deck.' The person who used these words was close to me, and by the lightning's flash I recognized one of the two young men formerly mentioned in this story. The few words he had spoken convinced me that he was on board against his will, and I had noticed that he and his companion never had anything to do with the rest of the crew.

"He passed close to me in hauling up a rope, and, happen what might, I determined to speak to him. I knew it could not make our situation worse if it did not better it. 'Who are you?' I whispered to him. 'Are you an Englishman?'

"'Ah! is that the English boy?' he replied. 'Be careful that no one sees you speak to me, and go in the cabin and put your ear to one of the grated ports and I will speak to you. Get out of the way!' he said, giving me a push with apparent rudeness as one of the drunken crew staggered up by us.

"I went below, and after waiting two or three minutes at the port a shadow passed over it, and I whispered, 'Are you there?'

"'Yes,' he said. 'I have only time to say a few words, for I must not be missed. The crew are all so drunk that only a few of us are left to work the vessel, and now is the time for freedom or never. I and my companion are Americans pressed here against our will. If you can get into the second cabin and drug the captain's liquor the ship is all our own, for after this squall is over he and Falsario will go down and drink like fish.'

"'Go,' I said, 'I know what to do.' And he disappeared.

"I immediately went outside to the dispensary, and near the door I saw standing a large can of grog, the crew's evening allowance. In one minute I had emptied the contents of one of the large bottles of laudanum into it, and got possession of the other.

"The voices of Parricidio and Falsario could be heard high

above the squall, encouraging the few men that were able to work to save the sails, which were fluttering wildly in the wind. Now was my time; and, entering the cabin quickly, I drugged every bottle on the sideboard, and retired unseen to our own cabin. Mrs. Laroche was praying as I went in, and I silently joined my fervent prayers to hers for our safe deliverance. When she arose from her knees there was a placid look of serenity on her countenance that I had not seen there for a long time, and, turning to me, she said, 'Benny, my sorrows will soon be over; while sleeping on the sofa, with Antoinette in my arms, I saw my dear husband, and he smiled so sweetly on me, and told me that we would soon be free, and then the noise on deck awakened me, and I knelt down and prayed to God to deliver us from this den of iniquity.'

"'Your prayers have been heard, dear lady,' I replied; 'deliverance is at hand. We have friends on board, and this night I hope we will be free.' I then told her what had taken place, and she prayed Heaven that our plans might succeed.

"I now went on deck to reconnoiter, and found the schooner reefed down close, and only the two Americans doing anything at all. There were half a dozen negroes helping to coil up the ropes, but they were more or less intoxicated. Parricidio and Falsario were standing near the mainmast talking, and I slipped behind the mast to endeavor to hear what they had to say. It was so dark that I was perfectly secure from observation.

"'Falsario,' said the captain, 'you have drugged the men almost too much. Had it not been for those two Americans we should have lost our masts. But it is a fine night for our purpose, and when the moon is down and this squall passes over, we can run in to the island and anchor (it is only six miles off), and, after landing and secreting the treasure, we can slip and go to sea again before any one of the crew can have time to come to.'

"'What shall we do with the two Americans?' said the negro. 'They must not see us.'

"'Why,' said the captain, 'knock them on the head. I am doubtful of those two men. They never will be with us in heart, and you saw that they did not join the boarders when we took the English brig. It is true they work more faithfully than any one on board, but we must get rid of them. I leave that for you to do. My authority with the crew is on the wane, and all owing to that Frenchwoman and her sickly child.'

"'What do you intend to do with her in the end?' said Falsario. 'For I can't see that you derive any profit or pleasure from her company.'

"'Why,' he replied, 'on my saint's day I intend to make the whole of them walk a plank. For that day, as you know, I have always celebrated with some dreadful deed. This is getting to be a tiresome business, Falsario, and, as we have now wealth enough stowed away to make us both rich and comfortable for the rest of our lives, we must escape from the schooner, after drugging all hands and blowing her up.'

"'Whenever you please,' said Falsario. 'For if anything should happen to you, they would cut my throat in an hour.'

"I had gone through so many horrors within the last month that I did not tremble at the terrible revelations I had heard; but, fearing detection, I slipped away (as the two scoundrels walked aft toward the taffrail) and joined Mrs. Laroche in the cabin. The squall had passed over, and a nice little breeze was wafting us slowly onward under the reduced sail. I told Mrs. Laroche to be ready for anything at a moment's notice, and to lie down and take some repose, as she would need the exercise of all her energies. She was, however, too much excited to sleep, and kept a breathless watch with me.

"Presently I heard Parricidio and Falsario descend the ladder, and, putting out the light in our cabin, I crept to the door to listen. They were both talking carelessly, and I could hear the glasses jingle as they poured out the liquor, which they were in the habit of drinking freely every night. Then I could hear them draw their chairs to the table, and they commenced their usual amusement with dice, which I could hear distinctly rattle on the table.

"The can of grog was still standing near the cabin-door, and, seizing hold of it, I quietly ran on deck. The American was at the wheel, and, putting it close beside him, I said, 'The captain and Falsario are drugged. Give this to the rest of the crew.'

"Calling his companion by a sign, he put the liquor in his hands, and he quickly disappeared forward. I ran below again, to listen to what was going on in the pirate's cabin.

"'Another glass of brandy, Falsario,' said the captain. 'The liquor tastes devilish good to-night after that soaking I got in the rain. Fill up for yourself, and we will drink "The pirate's best friend—the plank. Those who walk it tell no tales."'

"'Good!' said Falsario. 'And I will give "The slow-match. It obliterates all evidence."' And then they rattled away with the dice, and laughed heartily. An hour, or longer, perhaps, passed away while I listened to hear how often the scoundrels would drink. Twice I was aware that they had partaken of the brandy, and that, I knew, would settle them for the night, if it did not kill them. They drank deep and often, and at last I heard Parricidio say, 'I am devilish sleepy, and will rest a little while. Do you keep watch down here, and call me in an hour.'

"'Yes,' said Falsario; 'and will amuse myself throwing the dice.' With that the heavy body of the captain fell upon the sofa, and in five minutes he was snoring loudly. The dice rattled on the table without disturbing him. Falsario played, but slower and slower fell the dice. At last I heard him yawn like one overcome with sleep, and then all was silent. I slipped on deck and told the American all that had happened. 'Stand by to leave the vessel when I call you,' he said, 'and in twenty minutes more be certain that they are asleep. Now is our chance or never.' When I went below again there was loud snoring in the pirate's cabin, and I could plainly hear the two scoundrels breathing in unison. Then, for the first time, my heart began to beat so audibly that you might have heard it ten yards off. My knees trembled under me, and I could scarcely stand up. 'Courage, Ben,' I said to myself; 'more lives than one depend on you to-night, and now is the time to show yourself.' With that I prayed fervently for strength to carry me through my enterprise, and soon felt assured again.

"I now opened the door cautiously and peeped in, and there I saw Parricidio stretched upon the sofa, with his head hanging nearly touching the deck; and the villain Falsario had fallen from the chair, and was sound asleep upon the deck. The table was strewed with bottles and glasses, and the cabin was redolent of the smell of cigars, the stumps of which were lying about. It was plain from the appearance of the decanters that they had drank deep, and it seemed to me that they were sleeping their last sleep.

"I touched Falsario to see if he would awaken, but he never moved. I then shook him gently, then harder, and finally pulled his woolly hair hard to see if he had any sensation. 'He is dead,' I said to myself, 'and he died as he deserved, previous to the intended commission of a great crime.' I felt that God would hold me guiltless.

"It was useless to make any experiments on the captain, for there was no mistake about his condition; so, putting out the light and locking the door behind me, I went on deck to see the Americans.

"The moon had just gone down, and there was a light breeze on the water, scarcely enough to make the schooner move along. As soon as I told the American how matters stood he left the wheel, after luffing to and lashing the wheel down. He and his confederate jumped to the boat's falls and quietly lowered her into the water, having already placed in her the sail and oars, and some biscuit and water.

"'Now for the lady and child,' he said; and with that I hurried below and told Mrs. Laroche to follow me. She was as cool and calm as if she were going to an evening party, for the poor lady had passed through so many sorrows that there was nothing left to appall her. Little Antoinette was wrapped up comfortably in some blankets, and giving the lady a bottle of wine that was on the sideboard, and taking the child in my arms, I left that detested cabin.

"'Are we going to see papa?' said Antoinette as we went quietly out of the door.

"'Yes, darling,' I replied, 'but you must not speak a word, for if that bad man hears us he will stop us, and you will never see papa again.' She clasped her little arms around my neck, kissed me, and never spoke another word. In a short time we were quietly seated in the boat, and were about shoving off, when the American said, 'Stop one moment; let me make matters doubly sure.'

"'Commit no murder,' whispered the lady. 'Leave them to God; he will surely punish them in his own time.'

"'My hands are as innocent of blood as yours, good lady,' he replied, 'and I shall commit no act that you will be ashamed of.' And climbing up the side, he was soon lost sight of in the vessel.

"In ten minutes (which appeared hours) he returned, and, quietly taking his seat, cast off the painter and we dropped astern. 'They can't follow us now,' he said, 'for some time, for I cut the tiller-ropes and cut away all the lanyards to the rigging, so that it will be nine hours before that drunken crew can repair damages, even if they live through the drugging they have had, for they seem to me to be more dead than drunk. Now let us step the mast and hoist the sail, and get as far away as possible. You may sleep quietly to-night, lady, for none of them can move for twenty-four hours at least, and you are under the protection and guidance of one who is as much a stranger to crime as you are, and who has served in that craft strongly against his will, and has daily been praying that Heaven would grant him his freedom.'

"A nice little breeze sprung up, and our little bark (stanch and tight) went skimming merrily over the waters, as if she joyed with us in getting away from that vessel. In less than half an hour the faint outlines only of the schooner could be seen, and soon after we lost sight of her altogether.

"Our hearts all beat with rapture at our escape, and we all joined fervently in the prayer put up by Mrs. Laroche. 'Guide us, Father of heaven, through the perils of the deep,' she said, 'as you have this night guided us through the midst of our enemies, and forgive me, Father, if I have murmured at my wretched fate, for I have been sorely tried. I put my trust in thee, good God, to whom all honor and glory is due. Amen.'

"'Oh, for a sight of a good frigate!' I said, 'that we might catch those miscreants as they lie steeped in drunkenness and crime.'

"'Leave them to God, Benny,' she said; 'he will punish them all in his own way, which will be more felt than any punishment that can be inflicted by earthly judges. We are free from them; let us forget them if possible, and hope for happier times.'

"That night the party slept soundly, the male part by turns taking the helm, and by daylight we had made at least twenty-five miles, and the schooner was nowhere to be seen. I am sure we all enjoyed our scanty breakfast more than we ever did a meal on board the pirate vessel.

"During the day the two Americans told us their stories. They were brothers, and had been taken out of an American brig, where the same scenes were enacted as in the Blue-eyed Mary. They told us of a beautiful American woman who was going out to Rio de Janeiro to join her husband, and who was taken on board the pirate, and finally jumped overboard and was drowned in sight of all the crew. This, no doubt, was the same one alluded to by Parricidio and Falsario during the conversation I overheard; they described many dreadful scenes among the crew, but as the recital of them seemed to pain Mrs. Laroche, we came to the conclusion never to mention the subject before her again, and try and make her forget it, if it was possible for her ever to drive those horrible events from her mind.

"It was now two days since we left the schooner, and the sea continued smooth and the breeze moderate, as if kind Providence was watching over our safety. We knew not where we were, but

Edward Atherton, one of the Americans, thought from the course we had been steering in the schooner that we were near some of the West India islands, and we hoped hourly to fall in with some vessel bound to the United States if not to England.

"On the third day our eyes were delighted by the sight of land; a small island was just heaving in sight on our weather-bow, and as the wind was ahead and quite light, the men thought it better to lower the sail and pull for it, though it was a great distance off and might be, for what we knew, the peak of some high island.

"In an hour we neared it quite rapidly—so fast, indeed, that we concluded there must be a very strong current setting toward it, and in half an hour more had succeeded in getting quite close to it, although at first we imagined that it was an all-day's pull.

"When we got within a mile of the island it appeared to be covered with the most luxuriant foliage down to the water's edge, and seemed to be entirely free from rocks or shoals. We all congratulated ourselves on this adventure, and flattered ourselves that we should be able to take some good repose under the shade of those beautiful trees, and perhaps be able to regale ourselves with some of the delicious fruit of the tropics, though the island was not likely to contain a great variety.

"What was our surprise, as we approached, to see the thing rocking and rolling about like a ship in a sea-way, and when within twenty yards of it a voice from the topmost branches of the trees shouted out to us, 'Git out of the way with yer boat, or I reckon you'll be run into.'

"We had hardly time to obey these commands before the thing we took for an island came tearing past us, and we heard the same voice in the branches singing out, 'Boat ho! on the starboard.' 'Luff to,' shouted a loud voice among the trees, and the island appeared as obedient as a ship to her helm, rounded to handsomely, and lay as quiet on the water as a ship with main-topsail to the mast.

"'Boat ahoy!' shouted the stentorian voice from the trees. 'Whar are you from, and whar are you a-goin'?'

"'This must be magic,' said the lady, much alarmed. 'Let us fly, good Atherton, before it is too late, and we get entangled in new toils.'

"'It is rather a strange affair, madame, indeed,' he replied, 'but there may be protection here, and if it is magic, there is no chance of escaping from it. I think we had better pull closer and reconnoiter.' She clasped her child close to her bosom, as if to protect it, and said, 'God's will be done; I am in his hands; do as you think best, my kind preserver.'

"With that we pulled up to the floating island, and, as we got close to it, a man came out on one of the branches which overhung the water and exclaimed:

"'Wal now, I never! Why, if thar ain't a boat adrift with a 'oman and a child intew it! Wal, did I ever! Who are you, anyhow?' said the man to us, 'and what are you doin' of, adrift in that 'ere boat?'

"'We are distressed mariners,' Atherton replied; 'and, in the name of Heaven, who and what are you?'

"'Wal, now, you mought well ax that question, for I reckon the owners wouldn't know the good ship Ichabod just now. We are a guano-ship, my good fellow,' he continued, 'and bound to Bosting, and them 'ere leaves you're a lookin' at now is nothin' but the timbers a-sproutin', that's all. Pull alongside, my hearties, and we'll give you a welcome and the best mess of codfish you set down to for many a day.'

"Strange as this explanation appeared to us, we hesitated no longer, but pulled alongside, having to haul the boat under the branches of the trees to reach the gangway. Many anxious and curious faces were standing around, and, as we handed our charges up, ten thousand questions were asked in a minute; but there was no want of sympathy for the distressed voyagers, and every one seemed to lend a helping hand to get us on board.

"'I reckon,' said the person who appeared to be captain (a bluff, jolly-looking old fellow), 'that you were a leetle frightened at the critter when you first hearn me hail you, and yer not the first ones we have met that have been frightened; this here ship, you must know, was built of green timber, and sent to the Chinchi Islands for guano, and, bless my soul! if she didn't commence sproutin' six days after loading her. We cut and whettled at the branches like fun, but it warn't no use at all, for the more we whettled the more the bushes growed, and it all turned out well, for we came round Cape Horn with a spanking fair wind, and have kept it ever since, and I do reckon we have made the slickest passage that is at present on record — only fifty-four days from the Chinchis, and within eighteen hundred miles of Bosting.'

"This explanation was very wonderful, but there we were, standing on the deck of a large ship of twelve hundred tons, and sur-

THE PIRATE STORY CONTINUED.

rounded by Christian men and American sailors. There was no mistake, the thing was as the captain said."

I had listened very attentively to old Ben's story up to this time, being deeply interested in the fate of the poor French lady and her sweet little child while in the hands of the pirates. Tears of sympathy flowed from my eyes, and when I found that Ben was trying to humbug me about the guano-ship, and knocked all my sympathy into "pi," I could almost have cracked his skull with his own spy-glass.

"Why, Ben," I said, "you can beat Captain Marvellous all hollow; and the story of the guano-ship is ahead of the story of the 'hoop-snake' ten to one. As to your pirates, I don't believe a word of anything you have told me. And an old fellow like you, with one foot in the grave, ought to be ashamed of himself for inventing such falsehoods."

"Don't judge too harshly, Mr. Marline," said Ben, "lest you be judged yourself. All I have been telling you is as true as gospel; and I'm ready to swear to it whenever you please. If you don't like my story, why, let it end. There's no harm done, and your dog-watch is almost out."

"Go on, Ben," I said. "Let us hear how the guano-ship got into port, and I beg pardon for interrupting you. But you must confess that it is rather a marvelous story."

"So it is, sir," said Ben. "And you would have thought it still more marvelous had you seen it as I did. The entire ship was covered in with branches, red oak, white oak, and locust, that had sprouted from the tree-nails. There was hackmatack also, and even the masts had sprouted and were wearing pine-burs. Great attention had evidently been paid to keeping the decks clear; but here and there little patches of weeds might be seen, though a young lad was constantly going about with a shovel cutting them off. The effect of the whole was beautiful, and you might have imagined yourself in fairyland; for the birds of every clime through which the ship had passed had sought shelter in the branches, and built their nests there. Such a twittering I never did hear in all my days, and even the parrots were flying about in flocks among the topmost branches. Not a particle of sun ever got to the decks, and awnings were of no use whatever. The only difficulty the captain had during the voyage was in taking the sun, and to do that he had always to go upon the main-truck. He calculated to make more by his trees and birds than he would by the guano, though the latter was very high in the United States about that time.

"We asked him what he was going to do if he got a head wind. 'I ain't a-goin' to have nary one,' said the old salt. 'I'm just a-goin' to take her as slick into Bosting as if she war a steamboat; and if it does come a head wind, I'm a-goin' to lay to until it changes.'

"The name of this old gentleman was Captain Brownrig, of Pawtucket, and a prime old sailor he was. His wife and two daughters were on board with him, and he had a strong, steady crew of forty-five men, who all looked as if they could whip their weight in wild-cats. The ship was frigate-built, and had been contracted for by the French government; but, as she turned out to be built of green timber, they refused to take her, and so she was put into the guano trade. She mounted a splendid battery of fourteen guns on her spar-deck, eight of which were the long twenty-fours originally intended for her. She had taken all her battery out with her when she sailed, but had sold the remainder to the Peruvians.

"How I wished that she had not sprouted, and had fallen in with that devil Parricidio! She would have made mincemeat of him in no time, though it is likely that the cunning devil would have avoided her when he made out her force.

"The captain, family, and crew all listened with wondering looks to our tale of misery and misfortune, and deep were the curses showered upon the pirate by the sailors for their cruelty to a woman. They only prayed that they might fall in with the scoundrel, and they promised to use him up, hampered as they were with trees and bushes.

"'Lord!' said old Brownrig, 'what a Tartar he would catch if he got our Sal!' (a tall, raw-boned, red-headed girl of about twenty-six.) 'She would harpoon him before he could say punkin-pie.'

"And Sal laughed, and said, 'And Patience could haul in the line after I struck him.'

"As the wind had been light during the last two days, the pirate could not be more than thirty miles off, and Atherton assured us it would take twenty-four hours to repair damages, if the crew had got sober, which he was sure they had not, for the liquor was doubly drugged, and many of them, he thought, must be dead; he also told us that she was completely disabled as far as her armament

THE PIRATE STORY CONTINUED.

was concerned, that he had spiked every gun with rat-tail files, had thrown overboard every pistol that was in the arms-chest, and had knocked a plank out on each side of her two remaining boats.

"'How abouts does she bear, do you think?' said the captain.

"'About northeast,' said Atherton.

"'Then,' said the old trump, 'this wind will do for her. Get your harpoon ready, Sal,' he said. And turning to the first mate, 'Put your helm up and steer northeast, and let Zeb and Ike take turn about at lookout till we see her. Get up shot, Mr. Longjaw, and see everything clear for the darndest fight you ever seen.'

"There was a heavy squall brewing to the southwest, and Mr. Longjaw thought 'the capting had better git the axes to work and wheetle down a leetle;' but Atherton, who was a man of good judgment, said the squall would favor us and surely dismast the schooner if it reached her. We went off rapidly before the wind, and, when the squall did strike us, the good ship seemed to fly through the water and never felt it in her hull, as the wind was right aft. But I thought the trees would be torn from the sides; they bent and cracked like everything. The only damage done, however, was to a few birds'-nests that came tumbling on deck. These were soon replaced again, and we traveled along ten or twelve miles an hour.

"The squall did not last long, and after it was over we had a good, steady, three-knot breeze. That night we had the moon until four o'clock, and not an eye was closed during all the watches, so anxious was every one to get a sight of the schooner; but nothing was seen that night. At early daylight Atherton said we had overrun our distance, and proposed that we should lie to until the sun rose, so that we could see all around the horizon, and the captain rounded to in accordance with his wishes.

"Atherton's judgment proved to be correct, for as the sun rose above the horizon the joyful cry of 'Sail ho!' came from aloft; 'but I fear tain't her,' said Zeb (who was the lucky fellow to first see her), ''cause this here vessel is a small sloop-rigged thing, and hain't got no sail set.'

"'That's her!' said Atherton, his face beaming with joy; 'she has lost her mast in a squall, and the pirates have not found it out yet. How does she bear?' he shouted, and, not waiting for an answer, both he and his brother shinned aloft to the lookout.

"'That's her!' he shouted again, as soon as he laid eyes on her. 'I'd know the scoundrel among a thousand. Hard up and steer for him.'

"Off went the gallant Ichabod, obedient to her helm, and as she got before the wind the men from aloft cried out 'Steady,' that we were running right for her.

"In a few minutes she was plainly visible from the deck, and in an hour we were within long range. A few men only could be seen moving about the decks, and our approach was evidently unnoticed. They no doubt took us for some small island toward which they were fast driving, and were getting the square-sail and fore-topsail set to run before the wind.

"Old Captain Brownrig could not resist his desire to let fly a shot at her. 'Come here, Longjaw,' he said, 'and see if you can't bring that feller's square-sail down. It is time to let him see who's in the bushes.'

"Longjaw cast loose the gun, which was already loaded, and, depositing a large quid of tobacco (he took from his mouth) on the muzzle as a sight, and squaring himself, he pointed deliberately and fired; the shot fell about ten yards behind her, and, skipping along the water, went right through her stern-frame, knocking the splinters right and left, and creating terrible confusion among the pirates, who were not prepared for so singular an attack.

"'Well behaved, Longjaw!' shouted old Brownrig. 'Now, boys, give 'em every gun that will bear, and when we kin git alongside I reckon we'll give 'em the darndest broadside they ever hearn tell on.'

"Shot after shot now struck the schooner from the Ichabod's two bow-guns, and one lucky ball brought the foresail on deck; next down came the foremast with all its gear, and the pirates were in our power.

"Ranging up alongside of her, we poured in broadside after broadside, until not a soul could be seen above the rail. They asked no quarter and we gave none. At length she began to settle, and two or three pirates jumped into the boats preparatory to lowering, and two persons, whom I recognized as Parricidio and Falsario, were lifted carefully into the stern-sheets. They were either wounded or suffering yet from their last debauch.

"Atherton laughed when he saw them get into the boat. 'The first oar they pull will snap in two,' he cried. 'For I sawed them all half through before I left the schooner, and the boat will sink as soon as she touches the water.' And indeed that brave fellow had left nothing undone to prevent them from following us.

"'Clear away two boats!' shouted old Brownrig. 'Eight men,

THE PIRATE STORY CONTINUED. 357

each well armed.' As our boats touched the sea two boats were lowered from the schooner, and had no sooner left their tackles than they sunk nearly to their gunwales, half full of water. The pirates tried to get the oars out to endeavor to reach the schooner again, but as fast as they put them in the rowlocks they snapped off, as Atherton foretold they would, and they were left completely at our mercy.

"'Now, boys,' said the captain, 'let us stand by to pick 'em up. We only want that feller's figure-head to make our voyage complete.'

"'And, daddy,' says Sal, 'let me go with the harpoon, and take Patience with me to haul in the line when I strike.'

"'That you shall, gal,' said the old fellow. And, not wishing to be outdone by a woman, I jumped into the boat with them.

"By this time the pirates were in the water, holding on to the gunwale of the boat, and as we pulled up they cried most piteously for quarter. The only answer they got was a volley from the men's pistols, and five of them sank to rise no more.

"The crew were pulling with all their might, and the boat went with such force that she struck the pirate's pinnace amidships and shivered her nearly to pieces. Falsario jumped at the bow of our boat, and, holding a knife between his teeth, while his eyes flashed with rage, he succeeded in getting hold of the gunwale, and had clutched the knife in his right hand ready to strike, when Atherton, who was in the bow, drove the boat-hook into his brain, and with a yell of anguish he sank under the waters. The other wretches were soon disposed of, but Parricidio, who seemed determined to struggle to the last, swam off as fast as his strength would let him.

"'Now's your time, Sal,' said old Brownrig. 'Stand by to harpoon him.'

"With that Sal jumped into the bow, handling the harpoon with the dexterity of an old whaler, while Patience stood by to haul in the line. 'Pull easy, boys, and stand by to starn all when I strike,' she coolly said. 'There now, oars.' And, as the boat came within twenty feet of the pirate, the harpoon flew from her hand as unerring as a ball from a rifle, and pierced the villain Parricidio right through the heart. 'Stern all, men,' she ordered, 'and haul in the line, Patience. He won't want no line, daddy,' she said, patting the old man on the head. 'He's done for, and the lady is avenged.'

"We all took a look at the form and face of this once dreaded monster, and almost every one shuddered as they beheld him.

His lips were swollen, and his eyes blood-red from the effects of his last drinking bout. But at last there was an end to his crimes. And so perished the dreaded Parricidio. Cutting the harpoon from his body, we left him as food for those same sharks which he had so often fed with the bodies of his numerous victims. There was no chance of saving the schooner. She was so riddled with shot that she sank before anything could be taken out of her, and with her perished every record of the numerous crimes committed by those who were in her. How many hapless cries went up for succor from those hounds of hell no one knows, but, from what Atherton learned while he was on board, their atrocities must have beaten anything hitherto heard of.

"Well, Mr. Marline," said old Ben, wiping the perspiration from his brow, "your dog-watch is just out, and all that remains to be told is that the Ichabod arrived safe in Boston, where thousands from all parts of the country flocked to see her.

"Mrs. Laroche took a house a short distance from Boston, where she devoted her life to the education of little Antoinette, and performed many noble acts of charity. When there was an end of the French revolution, and her brother-in-law was killed, she recovered part of her husband's estate, but preferred living in America to going back to France, where everything reminded her of her departed happiness.

"Antoinette grew up a beautiful young woman, and married a man every way worthy of her. She always cherished a kindness for me, and as my only parent died a short time after the occurrence of these events, I lived with them until my roving disposition induced me to go to sea, and I have been in the American navy ever since, and, God willing, intend to die in it."

Thus ended Ben's yarn, and I only regret that I can not do full justice to it. I have sometimes thought that Ben drew upon his imagination for the guano-ship. I have looked over the papers of that time, but though I saw the name of Captain Brownrig commanding the Ichabod, I saw no mention of the curious events related to me by the old quartermaster. Others may, however, have better sources of information than I had, and I only give it as I heard it.

CHAPTER XXVII,

AND LAST.

ORDERS had been given to prepare the ship for sea, in consequence of instructions from the Navy Department to proceed to the coast of Syria and look after our missionaries in that quarter.

The Turks at Jerusalem had been interfering with the American missionaries and the Greek Catholics for indulging in a free fight—a very common event in that quarter, for it is frequently the case that the different denominations of Christians clapper-claw each other over the tomb of the Saviour, while the Turks, though Mohammedans, treat the tomb with more veneration than some of the so-called Christian sects.

On an occasion of a quarrel over the tomb the Turks thought it necessary to apply the bastinado to both parties, which effectually settled all difficulties. It is a universal panacea among the Turks for the adjustment of disputes, and might possibly be adopted elsewhere with advantage.

The mail had arrived from the United States, bringing us all tidings from sweet home, and also important political intelligence. Martin Van Buren had been elected President. "Who is he?" was the anxious inquiry, for hardly any one on board remembered hearing of him. We also learned that the Honorable Whalebone Broadbrim, of Duluth, had been appointed Secretary of the Navy.

We were much more intimately interested in the latter personage than in the new President, and everybody was wondering who Broadbrim was and what sort of a Secretary he would make; but we could only learn that the Honorable Secretary was from the desert regions of Duluth, had been largely engaged in the leather business, and was also an extensive dealer in rope, which latter circumstance, no doubt, drew attention to his naval abilities, and pointed him out as a person particularly qualified for the position of head of the Navy Department.

We were not at all surprised at having a man of whom we had never before heard appointed as head of a service which European nations think of sufficient importance to place under the direction of professional men. It only shows how effete these old worn-out despotisms have become, and how much wiser are we republicans, although we have not yet reached our centennial.

Instead of intrusting the appropriations for the navy to the hands of experts, who would probably expend them in building and equipping ships, we wisely put such matters in the hands of a civilian, who, although he probably knows nothing at all about naval matters, understands where to put the money "so that it will do the most good."

Mr. Whalebone Broadbrim was evidently the right man in the right place, and we soon learned that he had gone to work energetically to reform the navy. The first order he gave was to place every officer who was not at sea on furlough pay. He reduced the navy ration from twenty-five to twelve and a half cents, and expended what was thus saved in other directions. He gave the purchasing of all supplies to his grandmother, old Mrs. Bumble, an energetic lady, who kept a little shop somewhere in the wilds of Duluth, and it was not uncommon to see this venerable female purchasing anchors for a line-of-battle ship, a pair of oxen, or a dozen sail-needles at the same moment.

Under such a system the navy could not do otherwise than prosper, and as time wore on and the Honorable Whalebone Broadbrim became more familiar with the duties of his office, he launched out into various plans for the future benefit of the service.

Perhaps the most judicious order ever given by this distinguished man was that every ship in the navy, before sailing on a cruise, should proceed to Duluth, or as close thereto as the depth of water would permit! and lay in a supply of sand and holy-stones to last for three years, the price of the sand in no case to exceed fifty cents a bushel, and that of holy-stones not to be more than the contract price for live-oak.

The Honorable Whalebone Broadbrim very soon comprehended the wants of the service as regards building-places, and accordingly procured an act of Congress establishing two additional navy-yards, one at Duluth and the other four miles off, so that, being only four miles apart, they could be a mutual support to each other, and in case one yard wanted anything the other would be able to supply the deficiency.

All ships of the navy were ordered to be built and repaired in these yards, and, notwithstanding the factious opposition made by the old navy commissioners, the Secretary directed the keel of a five-decker, to be called the Duluth, to be laid forthwith.

This vessel was completed about the time the Honorable Whalebone Broadbrim went out of office; but in launching her she stuck on the ways, and, there not being water enough to float her, she lay on her side, and was finally "wrecked," as they call it, by the Duluth pirates. To this day fragments of the hull may be seen in the huts along that shore.

I do not hesitate to say that the navy had never before received such an impetus as was produced by the appointment of the Honorable Whalebone Broadbrim. The night we heard the news we went to sleep with the satisfaction of knowing that a man had at last taken the helm who would steer the department through "contract shoals" and "claim reefs," and that as long as he could keep his "tricks" at the wheel the navy and the country were safe.

As we became more familiar with the history of the Honorable Whalebone Broadbrim we learned to love and honor him, and hardly a night passed over our heads that fervent prayers did not ascend that the shadow of the Honorable Secretary "might never grow less"; that he might "live a thousand years"; that "a thousand tom-cats might defile the graves of his enemies," etc.

We have had many secretaries since the days of Broadbrim, but none who ever quite came up to the Honorable Whalebone. When that distinguished statesman left the department, the entire service bore it with Christian resignation, in the hope that the new chief might be as good a man as his predecessor.

I will give a little sketch, in this connection, of one or two others of our secretaries, although it would take up too much space to enumerate all their virtues.

The immediate successor of the Honorable Whalebone Broadbrim was the Honorable Ebenezer Pinebur, and he hailed from the tar, pitch, and turpentine regions of North Carolina. Like his predecessor, he showed from the beginning an intimate knowledge of naval affairs, although some people thought he rather overdid the tar, pitch, and turpentine business.

The Honorable Secretary was no sooner installed than he issued an order that in future all ships should be built of North Carolina pine, and was very much surprised when a venerable old commodore rolled into his office and informed him that there was a board of navy commissioners appointed by law to supervise such matters, and that large supplies of live-oak had been collected with which to build vessels of war, that North Carolina pine was only used for the decks and planking, and for that reason comparatively little of it was required.

"We must reverse all that," said the Secretary. "We will build all the hulls, masts, etc., of North Carolina pine, and I will compromise so far as to build the decks of live-oak." The same Secretary proposed to Congress to establish a navy-yard in Albemarle Sound, and met the objections of the navy commissioners, who told him there was not water enough in the place to float a schooner, much less a ship of the line, by saying, "Well, then, we will abolish ships of the line and build schooners."

Now this was a style of argument for which these stupid old navy officers were not prepared, so they met in council to consider what was best to be done. They agreed to build a very large class of schooners, of little draught of water, and without any timbers whatever, constructed entirely of North Carolina pine. A vessel of this description was accordingly built and named the Pawnee, which was for many years the delight of the navy and the admiration of the civilized world. We should have had a navy composed entirely of these beautiful vessels had not the Honorable Ebenezer Pinebur, broken down in health, been sent by the President as Minister to the Court of St. James's.

Then came in an Honorable Secretary from Pennsylvania, and he, in the interest of all the coal and iron mines, directed that the ships of the navy should be constructed of iron, and that no fuel but coal should anywhere be consumed. This made a new set of galleys, or cook-stoves, necessary for all ships, and gave the iron trade of the Keystone State an impetus it had never known before.

The venerable Mrs. Bumble again came to the surface during this administration, for, although not the grandmother of the Honorable Secretary from Pennsylvania, she was nearly related, being second cousin to his wife's aunt, and she continued during his administration to supply oxen, anchors, galleys, hemp, sail-needles, etc., as of old. We should in time have had the largest iron navy in the world, but, unfortunately, this Secretary accepted a mission to the King of Dahomey, and was killed and eaten at a feast given in honor of his Majesty's birthday.

Then the navy was delighted with the appointment of a very clever gentleman from Delaware, who did much for the advancement of the service. His first act was to abolish the use of the "cat" and to establish the whipping-post in accordance with the time-honored custom of his little State. He also established a navy-

THE NAVAL BUREAU. 363

yard at Lewes and another at the Delaware Breakwater, and had these two places made ports of entry. There is no knowing how much benefit this gentleman would have conferred upon the navy had he stayed in the department, but he was appointed Minister to the Feejee Islands, and lived there for many years, beloved and esteemed by all who knew him.

Then we were favored with a Secretary from Maine. The first thing he did was to establish the Maine liquor law in the navy. This, although by no means a popular move, was one in the right direction. The Honorable Secretary substituted molasses and water in lieu of grog, and, in default of whisky, this beverage became very popular. He also established codfish as part of the naval ration, which had several advantages : it induced the men to drink great quantities of water to quench their thirst, thereby familiarizing them with temperance drink, and in a fog the ships of war were enabled to tell each other's position by the smell of the codfish which was stowed in boxes under the tops.

These successive encroachments upon the duties of the old commissioners had a visible effect upon them ; they gradually declined in health and finally died. The navy list decreased so rapidly that at length no more burly old commodores could be found of whom to make commissioners. So the useless office was abolished and the naval bureau system was adopted, under which the service has flourished so greatly since that time. Younger men were appointed to take charge of the bureaus, and the secretaries took care to appoint officers who were not so opinionated and cared less what the head of the department did with the appropriations. Some of these chiefs of bureaus remained in office for more than thirty years, and I remember one who stayed there so long that he thought the navy belonged to him. So when he died he bequeathed all the navy-yards to his eldest daughter, who had considerable architectural talent, and designed several of the ship-houses which adorn those establishments.

Strange to say, some of these distinguished secretaries had their detractors among the few old commodores who were still in existence, and some of these ancient mariners are supposed to have started the following story.

It seems in fitting out the great naval armament, consisting of two sloops and a schooner, sent to wage war against the Qualla Battooans, it was found, after the fleet had been twenty days at sea, there were only two weeks' provisions left, and, consequently, the crews had to be put on one-quarter allowance. One of the vessels got separated from the rest, and, being a dull sailer, expended all her provisions, and the ship's company, after terrible suffering, were compelled to cast lots to see who should help to prolong the existence of the others. The result was that finally the captain and an old quarter-gunner were the only persons left alive, they being too tough to be eaten. The fleet was also short of powder, and what they had, being made in Delaware, was of inferior quality, so that when the bombardment of Qualla Battoo commenced the shot only reached half-way to the shore. So the commodore was compelled to land his men and capture the place at the point of the bayonet, for the cartridges were so worthless that the musket-balls, striking the natives in the stomach, only doubled them up and enabled the sailors to take them alive, which circumstance will account for the small list of killed and wounded among the enemy.

These, however, were only trifling accidents, liable to happen in the best-regulated navy; we conquered in every instance where we attempted to make war, although I do not remember any great battle except that at Qualla Battoo; all I know is that great rejoicing took place on board the Thunderbum at Naples when we heard of the appointment of the Honorable Whalebone Broadbrim, and we anticipated a brilliant future for our navy.

We were all sorry when it came time for us to leave Naples. The commodore considered that no officers had ever benefited so much by a sojourn in that quarter as his own, for, in his opinion, we had all learned to speak Italian fluently, and Shy had (as he informed an English captain) mastered two more languages in addition to the great number he already knew. The commodore often reminded us how much we owed to him by having the opportunity to revel in the study of beautiful art at Pompeii and Herculaneum, and promised us a visit to Pæstum, where we should see the temple of Jupiter Toenails and the celebrated Laycoon which had destroyed Hercules and swept out the Augean stables.

I bade adieu to Naples with a sigh. To me it was the most interesting city in the Mediterranean; with all its poverty and all its tyranny, it should be equally so to the philosopher, the antiquary, the poet, and the lover. Its glories are fast departing, though the numerous monuments of art will ever bear witness to the fact that here once rocked the cradle of science and of liberty. Poor, downtrodden Naples, who can help but feel sympathy for thy suffering people, ground down and groaning under a despotism too terrible to bear? Well may we say, in the language of the poet,

> "Italia, Italia, thou art but the grave,
> Where flowers luxuriate over the brave."

Adieu to thee and thy departed glories, thy classic groves and sculptured monuments. Nature never intended that such despotism should rule over scenes so fair and beautiful, trampling into dust every germ of liberty and knowledge, and filling the prisons with the groans of those who dare not attempt to rise above this miserable thralldom.

The land-breeze was just beginning to fan our cheeks when we lifted our anchor to depart. The splash of the distant oar came faintly o'er the water as with the first breath of morning air the hardy fishermen put to sea intent upon their daily toil, and the faint hum of the moving city fell softly on the ear. Dawn had already yoked her dappled grays for the first slow stage, and jocund morn, leaping from her bed, took the ribbons in her rosy fingers, and, after a dram of dew, blew her bugle and drove like blazes right on toward the gates of day. The top-sails bellied to the breeze, while sail after sail was spread like magic aloft on the towering masts, and we glided quickly out of the bay. In plain English, reader, we got under way about daylight, with a fair wind, and on as lovely a morning as my eyes ever beheld. Whether I shall have an opportunity of telling where we went, or what happened to me in the course of my sailings, remains to be seen. If these "Notes from a Lucky Bag" do not have the misfortune to be bought up by the trunk-makers, more of the same kind may find their way into the world hereafter.

Nineteen months had passed away since I first entered the navy, and I was rapidly growing into the clothes my disinterested friend Reckless had taken so much pains to see me measured for; at the same time I was reaping a harvest of knowledge well calculated to benefit me in the career I had chosen. I could cut down a hammock without being discovered with as much adroitness as any oldster on board; I could shy a boot from one steerage to the other with the precision of a Kentucky rifleman, and I could elude the vigilance of the officer of the deck as well as some who had been to sea over three years. Had I displayed half the industry in any other profession that I exhibited in learning the pranks of midshipmen, I might at this time have been at the top of the ladder, and in very comfortable if not affluent circumstances. And I have lived to see pig-headed fellows (who were my inferiors and fags at school) ride by me in their carriages, while the extent of my driving is a sixpence-worth in an omnibus; they are living in Omnium Gatherum Square, perhaps in a neat brownstone front, every stone of which is their own, while I don't own a brick in the world, and have not laid by enough to buy the ground to bury me in. I plod along in the dull routine of naval duty, with the hope of commanding a ship some of these days at the advanced age of one hundred and twenty years, when my great-grandson will likely be the respected head of a respectable insurance company, or be sending his dozen ships to China to bring home teas and fire-crackers.

You may laugh at the idea, "Young America," as much as you please, but it is no laughing matter I assure you; you may sit back on your high stool with that cigar in your mouth (which you are vainly endeavoring to smoke without being sick) and your morning paper before you, and chuckle to yourself at your luck in not having to serve your country, but you must not laugh at an old fellow who does part of your duty when he is one hundred and twenty years old: Respect his gray hairs, sir, if you don't respect his feelings.

Perhaps, had I felt so inclined, "Young America," I might have been as well off as you are, enjoying myself in the pork business, or head of a respectable bone-boiling establishment on the great road to Boneville. An old friend of my grandfather, after I had been fifteen years in the service, offered me a share in the profits of his bone-boiling concern, provided I would become a sleeping partner and advance him the modest sum of five thousand dollars (only think how cheap!); but as I had been so long in the habit of keeping watches, I came to the conclusion that I was too wide awake an individual to be a sleeping partner in any scheme unless it was in the scheme of matrimony, when wife and I would be "bone of one flesh." So the bone-boiling business was rejected; "that cock would not fight."

Again, I ran a chance of making my fortune by going into a speculation for hatching chickens by steam, as they do in Egypt in ovens; but before I had compromised myself so far as to put my name to paper, the boiler of the steam-engine burst, and nearly twenty thousand eggs (Law, how eggs riz about that time!) were

SOME OF MY SPECULATIONS.

scattered to the winds of heaven, leaving in the county an odor of polecat which it has not got rid of to this day.

I once went so far as to commit myself seriously in a scheme for making molasses-candy on a large scale, and likely, if the first attempt had succeeded, the country would have lost the services of a very valuable officer. I should now without doubt be calmly contemplating that staid and venerable matron, Mrs. Marline, as she industriously wiped off the mahogany and made the fire comfortable for the morning; and my eldest son, Tom (I know I should have called him Tom), would likely now be about taking my place in the business, considering me entirely too old to attend to it properly. I should then be enjoying my *otium cum*, etc., behind a respectable newspaper, in a snug little study of my own, and with a fragrant Havana in my mouth (I have a great weakness for Havanas), while the aforesaid Mrs. M. would be kindly preparing something over the dining-room fire to relieve this infernal rheumatism which almost sets me crazy.

But that speculation was the deadest kind of failure; my kind friends Skinflint and Grinder, who invited me to go in with them, were unfortunate in losing the first cargo of molasses they shipped from the West Indies. The vessel was wrecked on the Florida Reefs, and, not being insured, was a loss to the whole concern; and as the original capital of one thousand dollars was all laid out in that unfortunate adventure, the molasses-candy scheme turned out a smash.

My next attempt at speculating drained my pockets of a few hundreds, but, as I gained some experience in the matter, I did not regret it, and, as the loss was trifling, I soon recovered from it by going a three-years' cruise around Cape Horn in a four-gun schooner. I lived economically on codfish and potatoes, had all my clothes washed on board, gave up cigars and brandy-punches, and returned home a free man. It is true I might have gone to jail and worked the "dead horse" out there more to my comfort and satisfaction, but then that was not so respectable as taking a cruise 'round the Horn, and one has sometimes to consult appearances and the opinion of the world. The speculation I allude to was a good one, and would have succeeded but for the elements. There are accidents over which the keenest foresight can exercise no control, and this was one of them: A cousin of mine (Bob Limberjaw) had invented a machine for catching and skinning eels to supply the New York market, and after a few trials he succeeded, with my assistance, in putting it into successful operation. One hundred thousand eels were caught in one day, were neatly skinned for market, and were on the point of being shipped, when in the year 18— (in that terrible hurricane which swept our coast) the patent self-regulating eel-skinner was driven to sea and across the ocean, up the St. George's Channel, and was finally picked up off Holyhead by some of the pilots. Not knowing what it was, it was subjected to the inspection of the government authorities, who at once pronounced it to be an infernal machine left in the channel by the Americans in the war of 1812, and it is preserved to this day in Somerset House as a specimen of our blood-thirstiness.

My last speculation made me resolve to stick to the service of my country; for though (I said to myself) republics are ungrateful, is not the navy the right arm of national defense? and what right have I to cripple the country's right arm by withdrawing myself from her service? Is it not bad enough (I asked myself) to have your own right arm crippled with rheumatism, and knowing how worthless you are without the use of it, without going to work to cripple your country's right arm when she most needs your services? Of course it is. At that time we were about to war with Qualla Battoo, and as two extra sloops were fitting out for the occasion and one schooner (the first lieutenancy of the schooner being offered to me), I declined the hand of one of the handsomest women in Buttermilk County, worth two hundred thousand dollars in her own right, and no kit or kin to trouble her. That was a great mistake in me, as I have since learned, but there is no use crying over spilt milk. Poor girl! she married a stone-quarry, who ran through her money in about six years; she took to drink in consequence, and was finally immured in a private mad-house, where, I am told, she raves me incessantly, and bitterly curses the battle of Qualla Battoo for tearing me away from her arms.

There is no use in philosophizing over the past, or calculating what we might have been had Providence so ordained it. What matters it a thousand years hence whether I was a bone-boiler or an admiral of the blue? (we have admirals of the blue—the blue noses) for there will be quite as much uncertainty about the spot where my bones lie as there now exists with regard to the mortal remains of Cheops, or those of Antony and Cleopatra.

The greatest disappointment I ever met with in the navy was in the occasion of inventing a cannon, a patent-leather, back-action, breech-loading, water-piercing, air-shaking piece of ordnance in-

I INVENT A WONDERFUL GUN.

tended for shooting around a corner, over the top of a house or under it, above water or below water—in fact, anyhow and anywhere.

I did not care which way you wanted to fire with this gun, I stood ready with a supply of algebraic formulæ to prove that it could be done. I had spent six years in perfecting my invention, which was not entirely original, as the chase, breech, and muzzle were taken from the French, while the breech-pin was Irish, and the carriage and implements were a mixture of the army and navy ordnance. The shell was the idea of a clever Yankee, though patented by Grouse, of the ordnance office, but the touch-hole was entirely mine, which I could swear to on a stack of shells twenty feet high.

I first presented my patent gun to the naval ordnance department, accompanied by a written communication, and by return mail received orders to proceed without delay to the coast of Africa in the brig Swampus, that was to sail the next day for that pleasant station. I found when I got on board the brig that I was a supernumerary, and that the captain had been notified that I was demented on the subject of guns, and that he was under no circumstances to forward any letters to the ordnance bureau relating to my double-patent-back-action-shoot-round-the-corner gun.

I was kept on the coast of Africa three years, and, notwithstanding all the care of the department, succeeded in perfecting my invention so as to shoot up under a vessel's bottom instead of through her sides, and the day I returned to the United States I forwarded a communication to the Honorable Secretary of the Navy, which was immediately referred to the bureau of ordnance. By return mail I received preparatory orders back to the coast of Africa, but, as the sloop of war Damper would not be ready to sail for some days, I got hold of the member of Congress from my district; for it was just then becoming the custom for every officer to adopt a member of Congress, and a most agreeable set of fellows they were, always ready to do a friend a good turn.

We called together on the Honorable Secretary, who had just been appointed from Texas on account of the vast amount of copper and live-oak that was supposed to exist in that quarter. Unfortunately, all the live-oak had been cut off before the Secretary assumed control of affairs, and what little copper was visible was at a place called Wolf Mountain, some two thousand miles from the coast, and under the immediate charge of a Comanche chief, who swore that he would scalp any pale-face Secretary of the Navy who dared to interfere with that property.

When my member entered the presence of the Secretary and told him he wanted me to stay on shore for a time, the Secretary remarked, "I am sorry to say that Mr. Marline has been guilty of a flagrant breach of discipline and violation of the articles of war, which particularly say, 'No one shall draw, or offer to draw,' etc. Now this officer has been drawing a patent back-action, self-loading, water-overcoming, leather-piercing gun, which invention interferes materially with the bureau of ordnance, which claims the exclusive right to invent everything of that kind, and to make use of the inventions of others as it may suit their purposes, and, though this officer has not received any formal rebuke from the department, it was thought that he would take the hint by sending him to the coast of Africa; but, instead of appreciating the forbearance of the department, Mr. Marline no sooner arrived in the waters of the United States than he again wrote to the bureau in relation to certain improvements in his gun, and it therefore became necessary to order him immediately back to the coast of Africa. I can only do one thing," continued the Honorable Secretary, "and this I do only to oblige you, Mr. Bacon, member from Hominy district. If Mr. Marline will abstain from all further meddling in ordnance inventions I will revoke his orders, and give him permission to stay on shore for three months. He ought to know better than to interfere with the distinguished officer at the head of the bureau, who has taken out patents for every kind of gun that has ever been thought of, and he proposes that after his death his family shall be reimbursed for the sacrifices he has made and the genius he has manifested in the cause of his country."

I told the Honorable Secretary that I would willingly refrain from further troubling the bureau, but would not pledge myself not to apply to Congress to have my invention tested, as I considered that an inherent right of every American citizen, and my adopted member agreeing with me, the Secretary made no objection.

"I am satisfied," said the Honorable Secretary, "that you will get very sick of applying to Congress. I had a claim before them once for twenty years, during which time every member had been changed, and I grew to be the gray-headed old man you now see me, and finally had to give the matter up and run for Secretary of the Navy. I am convinced you will have no better success."

MY GUN IN CONGRESS. 371

I thanked the venerable statesman and bade him good-by. As I opened the door I nearly knocked down Mr. Grouse, the chief clerk of the ordnance bureau, who was listening at the key-hole, and who scowled malignantly at me as I left the department.

As it was now the long session, I made preparations to go before Congress with my gun and get my adopted member to introduce me to the chairman of the House Naval Committee, Mr. Wary, of Ironworks, Pa., and to the chairman of the Senate Committee, Mr. Spitsbergen, and was informed that I must prepare a metallic model of my gun to lay before the committees. The honorable gentlemen seemed to be somewhat surprised when I explained to them that mine was a leather gun for shooting around corners, but they agreed that I should prepare a model for the use of the committee, and the day was appointed for me to appear before them.

I at once went to work, and prepared two models at a cost of fifty dollars each, or a whole month's pay. On the appointed day I appeared at the House committee-room with my model under my arm. The committee were very busily discussing the merits of a fifteen-inch glass gun, the invention of an ingenious Yankee, one Denmark Wart, who also claimed to be the originator of the auger for boring square holes. As I entered the room I heard Mr. Wart say that he only wanted a million dollars to enable him to place one of his guns in complete order on board ship. The most original feature of Mr. Wart's gun seemed to be that it would burst just as a party of the enemy were attempting to board, the fragments of the gun acting as shrapnel against the attacking force. This idea struck the committee as being a decided novelty, and they began to look on Mr. Wart's invention with favor.

One of the members, however, asked a very foolish question as to whether the gun had ever been examined by any competent officers of the navy, such as would be called upon to use it in service; but he was promptly silenced by General Pogram, another member, who said, "What have the navy or navy officers got to do with ordnance?" which convincing argument effectually silenced all opposition, and Mr. Denmark Wart not only received a million dollars to experiment with his gun, but also an additional five hundred thousand to perfect a shell which he had no doubt could be sent a distance of twelve miles.

After Mr. Wart had bowed himself out I approached the committee, and, smiling complacently, laid the beautiful leather model of my gun on the table, saying to myself, "If that idiot with his glass gun gets along so well, what may I not expect with a leather one that will shoot around the corner?" but it appears the committee saw the matter in a different light.

One of the gentlemen said, "Commodore, you will please answer the questions asked, which answers will be taken down by a stenographer."

"I am not a commodore," I responded, "but only a lieutenant."

"All the same," said the gentleman. "Please answer the questions."

I complied with the request, and here give questions and answers for the benefit of future inventors:

Q. "How old are you?"
A. "Fifty-one years."
Q. "How long have you been in the navy?"
A. "Thirty-six years; entered at fifteen."
Q. "How long have you been at sea?"
A. "Thirty-three years."
Q. "Have you ever been in the bureau of ordnance?"
A. "No, sir."
Q. "If you have never been in the bureau, how can you know anything about guns?"

That was certainly a stumper, and I hesitated for some time, asking myself, "Well, how could I?" but on consideration I finally answered,

"Well, sir, I learned it by the force of circumstances."

This seemed satisfactory, and the questioning continued.

Q. "Can you tell me the number of guns in the Chinese fleet?"
A. "I can not."
Q. "Can you inform me whether the Chinese use leather guns?'
A. "I can not."
Q. "Are you acquainted with the present emperor of China?"
A. "Yes, sir; Chang Fung."
Q. "Do you know the name of the empress?"
A. "Yes, sir; Yung Fung."
Q. "Do you know the population of Timbuctoo?"
A. "Yes, sir; nine millions."
Q. "What kind of guns do they use?"
A. "Leather, sir, if they use any."
Q. "Can you tell me the names of all the islands in the Pacific Ocean, their population, chief towns, and names of their chiefs?"

I UNDERGO AN EXAMINATION.

A. "Yes, sir; I know them all, and have dined on missionary's leg with every one of them."

The gentleman announced that he had no further questions to ask; my testimony was read over to me, and then another member took me up and propounded the following questions:

Q. "How many touch-holes has your gun?"

A. "Only one, sir."

"I wish the committee particularly to notice that the commodore says *only one touch-hole*," said the examiner.

Q. "Suppose, sir, that you were called upon to make a gun of nine feet diameter of shot and six feet thickness of leather, what would be the difference of weight between that and a cast-iron gun of the same size?"

A. "The iron gun will weigh 68·040 tons, and the difference of weight will be that between iron and leather."

Q. "What would be the cost of the iron gun?"

A. "Four millions of dollars."

Q. "What would be the cost of the leather gun?"

A. "Merely the price of the leather and the expense of sewing the same and boring out the touch-hole."

I could see that my answers rather bothered the committee, and I was much pleased at the favorable turn my affairs were taking, when another gentleman of the committee took up the examination.

Q. "Let us suppose that the enemy were to attempt to board a vessel armed with your gun, what would you do?"

A. "I would hang a sign over the quarter, 'No boarders taken here,' and notify those anxious to board that we had nothing to eat but grape-shot soup and shell sass."

Q. "Don't you think the Denmark Wart glass gun would do more damage to the enemy by bursting in their faces than your leather gun would?"

A. "That depends on circumstances; if the glass gun were to burst inboard it might be unpleasant for our own men."

"Ah, yes," said the gentleman; "I believe I have no more questions to ask."

I was told to call next day, which I did, and kept calling every day for nine months, but somehow or other the committee never found any money which could be appropriated for my gun. My stay in Washington caused an attack of fever and ague, which took a month's pay for doctors' bills.

I didn't think it worth while to go near the Senate Committee, for everybody told me that all wisdom on the subject of ordnance resided in the House Committee, whose chairman was a man of judicial mind with a head like a bombshell, and when he opened on any subject it was like firing grape and canister.

I was advised to patent my invention, and at my death my wife could apply to Congress for remuneration. So with a sad heart I bade farewell to the metropolis, as it is called, though I can not tell for what reason, for, instead of its being the chief city of the nation, it is the smallest-potato concern I ever lived in, and I hoped never to see it again.

That night, in company with nine other passengers, I took the stage for Baltimore, so sick that I could hardly hold my head up. I tossed around on the back seat to the infinite annoyance of the other passengers, one of whom finally broke out, "Sir, you act as if this stage belonged to you; you are inconveniencing everybody, and if you carry on in this way we shall have to put you out."

"My good sir," said I, faintly, "have patience with me for a little while; you see before you a dying man, for I can not last much longer. I had a claim before Congress, and besieged the naval committee for nine months without avail. I took the chills and fever, paid the doctors one hundred dollars, and here I am, the most miserable wretch on earth."

"Good God, sir!" replied my fellow-passenger, with horror depicted on his countenance, "if you lived nine months in Washington trying to get a claim through Congress, and took the fever 'n ager, and had them doctors working on you and paid a hundred dollars, I pity you from the bottom of my soul. You may wallop about in this here stage just as much as you please, for you've earned the right to do so." And thus did I encounter a liberal Christian, although I must confess he swore a little oftener than was absolutely necessary.

Since that eventful session of Congress I have never visited Washington nor written to the bureau of ordnance, notwithstanding I have made many valuable improvements in guns, besides devising an ingenious plan for getting in a ship's masts by heaving a vessel down and floating them on board, a method which I do not believe any other person every thought of.

Some "Young America" may say as he reads these pages,

"Thunder! governor, why didn't you get us a midshipman's appointment when you were member of Congress from Woodchuck County? What deuced fine fun those devils must have in the steerage, and what a jolly thing it is to be a commodore of the blue, leading your country's ships to glory and renown!" The governor will likely ask "Young America" what the price of pork is that morning in market, and tell him to thank his stars that he was not in the battle of Graytown and limping about with a wooden leg. To be sure they do make those things so beautifully nowadays, with such harmonious musical-boxes on the inside, that it would be rather a pleasure to wear one, and a man advanced in life with a growing family around him (especially if they are musical) could not do better, in case of losing a leg, than to invest his money in one of the self-acting, heat-radiating, gum-elastic, calf-displaying, boot-saving, music-making wooden legs; they are guaranteed to last until they wear out, and calculated to play twenty of the most popular tunes, including the air of that old ballad, "The Ups and Downs of Life." On the whole, though, "Young America," I don't know but that it was wise in your governor not to have filled your noddle with martial notions; your life, it is true, has been one unvaried round of tameness from the time you swept out the country house until the present moment, when you are head clerk to "Dripping & Fat" in the pork business, with a yearly percentage on the profits, or third partner of "Beam, Scantling & Co.," with the privilege of shipping on your own account one load of timber yearly.

No doubt as a single man in the navy you would have been smiled on by Miss Araminta Taroil, daughter of the old and respected gentleman of the firm of Taroil & Junk in Grub Alley, and your imperial and moustache would have been thought perfection by Miss Crankum; but, Lord help you, young fellow, old Crankum would in his soul have cursed all young men who wore "Napoleons," and, in kindness to his daughter, would have exerted his very best interest with Senator Sly, or the member from Bowling Green, to have you ordered to sea in the first ship that was fitting out; and if you were not sent to the West Indies in the fever season, you would likely have gone to the coast of Africa. The result, a bald head after a three-years' cruise and large increase of crow's-feet, moustachios very wiry, and "Napoleon" shaved off.

I have not as yet amassed any amount of wealth (during my

naval career), that talisman to which all doors fly open, and which insures you a bow and a smile at almost every corner; indeed, I have often wondered where those little ravens came from that supplied my necessities in this wilderness of life. I have, however, in the hardest times carried with me an easy conscience, and that we are told is better by far than gold or diamonds.

At times, it is true, I have thought I did not act exactly right in that affair of Biddy Growler; at least I ought to have sent her "King Charles" back to her before it became all filled with tar and pitch; but then she was a very strong-minded person and with severe principles, and, Lord bless your soul! she did not feel it any more than she would crossing the Thames in a wherry. I have often pictured her to myself, sobbing and sighing at nights on her little white pillow, with her dumpling of a hand pressed to her throbbing brow, and her long eyelashes glistening with a tear, while she thought of the heartlessness of one Harry Marline; but, pshaw; what nonsense in me to talk so! Didn't I see her with Meekly, two days after the affair at her house, quietly eating all kinds of good things near the Villa Reale? Didn't she laugh at me as I walked past her, and put Meekly's glass to her eye, and say she wondered how midshipmen could be such spooneys? and didn't she?— But never mind what; my conscience is quiet on that business, and I can calmly say there is nothing on it that can give me a moment's uneasiness. Had I been a merchant, I might now have had cause to reproach myself for cutting the friend who had started me in life, because he had been unfortunate in business, and his account in bank not with so large a balance as mine. Had I been a lawyer of repute, I might in the course of my pleadings have talked away the life of a fellow-creature, or consigned him for ten years to a dark and dismal dungeon; or had I been a doctor— but then doctors are not supposed to have conscience, and see so much of human misery that they become indifferent to it, as confectioners are to the sweetmeats and other good things which only tempt their customers—if I slipped some old fellow off before his time, why it would all have been in the way of business, and nothing would be thought of so common an event.

What faults I have committed in the exercise of my duty I won't pretend to say. I have always endeavored to uphold the honor of the flag, and the most I can accuse myself of is coming on board ship now and then with a brick in my hat, my mind no doubt wandering to the subject of architecture, and being desirous of accumulating materials for a house when I should finally settle upon the future Mrs. Marline.

"Grim-visaged war" has called me to the ocean, but I can truly say, on the honor of a gentleman, that even in the heat of battle at Qualla Battoo (the only engagement I have ever been in) I never killed an innocent child or helpless woman, though the latter fought like tigers, and scratched our men's faces with their nails like cats (there were no men in the town); and I don't blush to mention now that it was through my philanthropic feelings that the leaden covers to the shell fuses were not taken off, thereby preventing the shell from exploding and killing hundreds, an idea of my own entirely. It is true that a valuable invention for killing men was picked up by a British officer and sent home to the Admiralty, whereby they became possessed of our secret; but as they will likely use it against the French and never against us, why there is no harm done, and we will see how they work before we have cause to use it ourselves.

I may in these "Notes from a Lucky Bag" have been a little hard on some of my imaginary characters, if you may so please to call them, but then in a lucky bag one can not very well discriminate in the articles, and the first thing that comes handy is tossed out without respect of persons. I might have smoothed over some little matters, but then what was to become of truth? Is that sacred principle to be tampered with out of a feeling of compassion? Truth has been the object I have aimed at throughout this journal, and if I have not hit it in the estimation of my readers, all I can say is that they are dull of comprehending me. I feel the importance of truth as much as Captain Marvellous ever did, and if I have said anything at all bearing the character of levity, I must throw myself on the charity of my readers and promise to do so no more.

And now, good friends, I must say good-night. I have no time at present to give you any more of my stray notes if I had the will —I have this moment received orders to go round the Horn in command of the four-gun schooner Pitchaway, having been executive officer in the same vessel in the above-mentioned battle of Qualla Battoo.

She is a wretched little affair, and the cabin is not big enough "to sling a cat around by the tail," but as I have no necessity or desire to sling a cat around by the tail in the above-mentioned cabin, no doubt I shall find it quite large enough for all practical purposes. There are shelves and lockers enough to put my papers in, and the country (with a liberality that does it credit) has supplied me with half a ream of foolscap, a bottle of ink, and a bunch of quills. What better use can I make of them than to jot down the tough yarns I hear in the Pacific? It shall be done, and, good reader, you and I may yet meet again.

AU REVOIR.

NEW FICTION.

Allan Dare and Robert Le Diable.

A ROMANCE. By ADMIRAL PORTER. Illustrated by Alfred Fredericks. 8vo, 2 vols., paper, $2.00.

Admiral Porter has shown in this work a striking natural talent for romance-writing, and the world will wonder how it is that he did not give his attention to it years ago. His invention is remarkable and apparently exhaustless, his discernment of character is good, his power of picture-making noteworthy, his dramatic perceptions vivid, and his sense of humor excellent. . . . The large body of readers will be delighted to find in it a greater store of mystery, intrigues, contentions, dangers, escapes, and all the marvels of romantic adventure, than probably the whole body of fiction of the present day can furnish them.

"Admiral Porter is the latest distinguished accession to the list of authors. He produces not a work on navigation but—a novel. Men of all professions are trying their hands at romancing nowadays. Admiral Porter need not be afraid of comparing his work with that of some professional novelists. The admiral excites the curiosity of the reader with a great deal of artfulness. The story has a mystery to which the author is leading up with much skill; he displays humor, touches of pathos, and a knack of sketching characters."—*New York Journal of Commerce.*

"All the well-known qualities of the successful romance are present in this one, and contribute to make it the great and most popular work of fiction of the year."—*Boston Sunday Globe.*

"It promises to be one of the best works of the kind."—*Boston Times.*

"The narrative is crowded with stirring episodes, and the plot is developed with consummate art."—*Albany Argus.*

"A plain, robust tale of the older type, full of life and action, bustling with movement, and fairly brimming with mystery, intrigue, and romantic adventure."—*Syracuse Herald.*

"All wonderfully vivid, exciting, and picturesque, with enough plot and incident already to furnish out some half-dozen ordinary novels. Admiral Porter has surprising vigor and freshness of style in narration, of picturesqueness in description of scenes and incidents, and of vividness in character-sketching. His story is wildly improbable, but it rivets the attention, nevertheless, and holds it steadily by its force, originality, and daring."—*Boston Gazette.*

"Since the Earl of Beaconsfield's time, no famous man in public affairs has written a novel that could excite public interest more than this one."—*Philadelphia Bulletin.*

"One of the most remarkable romances of the time, full of a great variety of incident and adventure."—*New York Christian at Work.*

New York: D. APPLETON & CO., 1, 3, & 5 Bond Street.

NEW FICTION.

Colonel Enderby's Wife.

A NOVEL. By LUCAS MALET, author of "Mrs. Lorimer: A Sketch." 12mo, paper, 50 cents. Authorized edition.

As in the case of "Mrs. Lorimer," the author's former novel, the authorship of this book is veiled under the pseudonym of "Lucas Malet," but it is now generally known that the writer is Mrs. Harrison, daughter of Charles Kingsley.

"There is another novelist coming forward who, if we do not misread 'Colonel Enderby's Wife,' will speedily be recognized as belonging to the front rank in literature."—*The Spectator.*

The Tinted Venus.

A FARCICAL ROMANCE. By F. ANSTEY, author of "Vice Versâ," "The Giant's Robe," etc. 12mo, paper, 25 cents. Authorized edition.

"The Tinted Venus," by the author of "Vice Versâ," which appears here at the same time of its publication in London, is designated by the author "a farcical romance" rightly enough, for in strange and grotesque invention it equals, if it does not outdo, his "Vice Versâ."

The Giant's Robe.

A NOVEL. By F. ANSTEY, author of "Vice Versâ." From advance sheets, by arrangement with the author. With numerous Illustrations. 16mo, cloth, $1.25.

"For ingenuity of construction, sustained interest, and finished workmanship, there has been nothing in serial fiction for many a long day equal to 'The Giant's Robe.'"—*Pall Mall Gazette.*

"This novel is as interesting in its style as its plot is original, and this is saying much, because the story is quite unlike anything hitherto seen in books. It is a story of modern life in which its ambitions, not always noble, its hopes, not always worthy, its aspirations, not always lofty, and its perpetual struggle for recognized place, power, and fortune, are most clearly, even vividly portrayed."
—*Home Journal.*

Vice Versa; or, a Lesson to Fathers.

By F. ANSTEY. 16mo, cloth, $1.00.

"'Vice Versâ' is one of the most diverting books that we have read for many a day. It is equally calculated to amuse the August idler and to keep up the spirits of those who stay in town and work while others are holiday-making. . . . The book is singularly well written, graphic, terse, and full of *verve.* The school-boy conversations are to the life, and every scene is brisk and well considered."—*Pall Mall Gazette.*

The Black Poodle, and other Stories.

By F. ANSTEY, author of "Vice Versâ." Illustrated. 16mo, paper, 50 cents.

New York: D. APPLETON & CO., 1, 3, & 5 Bond Street.

NEW FICTION.

A Fresh, Charming, Unconventional Novel.

The Adventures of Timias Terrystone.

A NOVEL. By OLIVER B. BUNCE, author of "Bachelor Bluff," "My House," etc. 16mo, paper, 50 cents.

"A particularly good story; well conceived, well told, well ended; . . . full of fresh air, pleasant comments on men and things and art, and altogether delightful reading."—*Boston Beacon.*

"The action proceeds in a course of never-failing interest. In conception, treatment, and tone, it is very pleasing."—*Boston Globe.*

"A book that sets the reader's attention on edge. . . . Will be read with eager interest by the thoughtful, and not without pleasure by those who read only for amusement."—*Commercial Advertiser.*

"Fresh, natural, and unaffected. . . . The whole book seems like a chapter out of real life."—*Boston Gazette.*

"Containing at least one of the most charming figures of recent fiction—Alice Grace; . . . so quaint a bit of Quaker purity, so rich a piece of modern freshness, it would be difficult to find. There is the smell of new-mown hay about her, and the rich red strawberries with which she regales her lover still stain her taper fingers."—*Hartford Post.*

The Money-Makers; A Social Parable.

A NOVEL. 16mo, $1.00.

"A brilliant and in many respects a remarkable book. . . . Sure of a wide circle of readers. It is by no means a faultless work of fiction, but it may be confidently asserted that its 300 and odd pages contain more strength and material than go to the making of three ordinary novels."—*Chicago Tribune.*

"'The Money-Makers' is not that anticipated coming American novel, nor is it a novel, in the sense of being a work of art, at all, but there is in it so much of truth, of earnestness, and of conviction, that the work inspires respect."—*Boston Traveller.*

"It is often brilliant, often vigorously picturesque, and never dull. . . . This virile novel may justly take rank with the very best of our later native fiction."—*Boston Gazette.*

"Undoubtedly the most effective novel written for many a day—virile, vigorous, full of broad and quick movement, rich in surprises, and actuated with a high purpose."—*Chicago Herald.*

"Well constructed, well written, economically supplied with adjectives and epithets that have a cut-glass clearness and cleverness, and thoroughly readable as a whole."—*The Telegram.*

For sale by all booksellers; or will be sent by mail, post-paid, on receipt of price.

New York: D. APPLETON & CO., 1, 3, & 5 Bond Street.

NEW FICTION.

DR. HAMMOND'S NOVELS.

I.—Mr. Oldmixon.

A NOVEL. By WILLIAM A. HAMMOND, M. D., author of "Lal" and "Doctor Grattan." 12mo, cloth, $1.50.

In "Mr. Oldmixon" Dr. Hammond considers several phases of New York life from new points of view, and presents pictures the truth of which will be readily recognized, but which it is believed have not hitherto been drawn by the novelist. "Mr. Oldmixon" is dramatic from first to last, and the climax arouses the emotions of the reader to a high pitch.

II.—Doctor Grattan.

A NOVEL. By WILLIAM A. HAMMOND, M. D. 12mo, cloth, $1.50.

"'Doctor Grattan' is really a capital book. . . . Dr. Grattan himself is a pleasant, practical man, who makes an excellent and original hero. But Mr. Hammond must be congratulated on his women."—*London Saturday Review.*

III.—Lal.

A NOVEL. By WILLIAM A. HAMMOND, M. D. 12mo, cloth, $1.50.

"It possesses the great merit of being interesting from beginning to end. The characters are striking, and several of them have an element of originality; the incidents are abundant and effective; the situations are well devised, and if there is not much intricacy in the plot there is a certain bustle and rapidity of movement which answers instead of more complicated machinery."—*New York Tribune.*

New York: D. APPLETON & CO., 1, 3, & 5 Bond Street.

NEW FICTION.

THREE WIDELY-READ NOVELS.

Deldee; or, The Iron Hand.

A NOVEL. By the author of "The House on the Marsh" and "At the World's Mercy." 12mo, paper, 25 cents.

"Now we have a third book by the author of 'At the World's Mercy,' a book of nearly 400 pages of fine type. It is a good story, with a knotty plot, which unravels at the end happily."—*Brooklyn Union.*

The House on the Marsh.

A ROMANCE. 12mo, paper, 25 cents.

"The story is told with dramatic power, is absorbing in its interest, and will be read with sustained attention to the end. It is evidently the work of an experienced writer, though published anonymously. Those who wish a well-woven chain of mystery and romance will find it in this work."—*Boston Commonwealth.*

At the World's Mercy.

A NOVEL. By the author of "The House on the Marsh." 12mo, paper, 25 cents.

"'At the World's Mercy' is the telling title chosen by the ingenious author of 'The House on the Marsh' for her new story, which we have read with pleasure, and can heartily commend as a good specimen of its class. . . . Here are all the elements of a delightful complication, and the author is not unequal to the situation. The catastrophe has the merit of originality."—*Saturday Review.*

New York: D. APPLETON & CO., 1, 3, & 5 Bond Street.

CHRISTIAN REID'S NOVELS.

"The author has wrought with care and with a good ethical and artistic purpose; and these are the essential needs in the building up of an American literature."

Valerie Aylmer.
1 vol., 8vo. Paper, 75 cents; cloth, $1.25.
Morton House.
1 vol., 8vo. Paper, 75 cents; cloth, $1.25.
Mabel Lee.
1 vol., 8vo. Paper, 75 cents; cloth, $1.25.
Ebb-Tide.
1 vol., 8vo. Paper, 75 cents; cloth, $1.25.
Nina's Atonement, and other Stories.
1 vol., 8vo. Paper, 75 cents; cloth, $1.25.
A Daughter of Bohemia.
1 vol., 8vo. Paper, 75 cents; cloth, $1.25.
Bonny Kate.
1 vol., 8vo. Paper, 75 cents; cloth, $1.25.
The Land of the Sky.
Illustrated. 8vo. Paper, 75 cents; cloth, $1.25.
After Many Days.
1 vol., 8vo. Paper, 75 cents; cloth, $1.25.
Hearts and Hands.
8vo. Paper, 50 cents.
A Gentle Belle.
8vo. Paper, 50 cents.
A Question of Honor.
12mo. Cloth, $1.25.
A Summer Idyl.
Forming No. XII in Appletons' "New Handy-Volume Series." 18mo. Paper, 30 cents; cloth, 60 cents.
Heart of Steel.
16mo. Cloth, $1.25.

For sale by all booksellers; or sent by mail, post-paid, on receipt of price.

New York: D. APPLETON & CO., 1, 3, & 5 Bond Street.